# WHEN WE WERE Young

# WHEN WE WERE Young

ANTONY SMITH

PRIMIX
PUBLISHING
THE WRITE CHOICE

Primix Publishing
11620 Wilshire Blvd
Suite 900, West Wilshire Center, Los Angeles, CA, 90025
www.primixpublishing.com
Phone: 1-800-538-5788



Published by Primix Publishing    04/18/2022

ISBN: 978-1-957676-05-0(sc)
ISBN: 978-1-957676-06-7(e)

Library of Congress Control Number: 2022904499

# Contents

# Prologue

Nowadays he was an early riser. His eyelids flickered in the eerie light of dawn that heralded the beginning of a new day. The silence of the room was broken only by the sound of shallow breathing. The familiar musky smell of her skin perfumed the air as he slowly withdrew his arm from around her shoulders, moving his long, lean body to the edge of the four-poster bed. He paused, rubbing his arm and admiring the naked silhouette of her body—the perfectly rounded breasts high on her chest, the narrow waist, slender hips, the long elegant legs, and her jet-black hair spilling across the pillow. He smiled. She was as beautiful as she had been so many years ago when she had told him for the first time, "I think I like you."

He threw on his red dressing gown and walked bare-footed over the thick, cushioned Axminster carpet, entering the kitchen, he brewed a pot of English breakfast tea. Then he walked slowly to the veranda and settled in the rocking chair while scanning the beauty of the scene below. The early-morning mist was blanketing the summer flora and fauna and the numerous stands of oak trees. In the distance, above the mist, he could see the peaks of the Welsh mountains. This was a magic time of day—the early mystical time before the rising of the sun, before the shrill sound of the cuckoo leading the dawn chorus. It was a time to think clearly, to remember the past and to contemplate the future.

His mind wandered back to the early days—the days of innocence.

The long, hot summer days before the war that were spent with his father and mother were the halcyon days of his childhood. They were the early days of Maggie, walking hand in hand down to the lake from their cottage on the hill. Then the war began and everything changed.

# Chapter 1

"In the Name of the Father, and of the Son, and of the Holy Ghost, Amen," so ended the Reverend James' morning sermon on this, the first Sunday of September 1939.

The sermon was as usual, boring stuff to the young choirboys of Saint Paul's parish church who, on the occasion, irreverently manufactured airplanes out of the hymn sheets to pass the time. Somehow, this Sunday service was different from normal. His favorite hymn, "All Things Bright and Beautiful," was sung without the usual vigor. The Reverend James was somewhat hesitant to leave his pulpit. Then Jim heard the west church door open and close with its usual thud. The congregation turned to watch as the tall, grey haired, military figure of Major Smith, the churchwarden, soberly walk down the aisle with measured footsteps, bow to the altar, and hand the Reverend James a note. At first, he appeared to freeze in disbelief. His normally ruddy colored face turned ashen grey as he, in an emotional voice, read the contents. "Dear Parishioners, it is my sad duty to inform you that the Prime Minister, Neville Chamberlain, has not received the assurances on the Poland situation that he had requested from the German Chancellor, Adolf Hitler. Consequently, we are now in a state of war with Germany. God save the King!"

The congregation knelt. Jim looked at his friend Derek. There were tears in his eyes. Yesterday Derek's father, a reserve naval officer, joined his ship in Portsmouth.

Jim's thoughts were broken by the Vicar's voice as he blessed the congregation. His final words, "Go in peace," were omitted. The morning service was over. Jim walked to the altar, slowly bowing to his Maker, and received the ceremonial cross of St. Peter from the vicar. Then, turning slowly, he walked down the aisle, leading the choir to the ceremonial strains of Elgar's "Pomp and Circumstance," biting his lower lip to quell the emotions of the hour.

The sun was shining as the St. Paul parishioners left the church that Sunday morning. The male congregation headed for the Horse and Jockey Pub for the traditional pint of beer and their usual discussion on the world in general, in particular, Adolf Hitler and the German war machine. By now the whole of the United Kingdom were aware that the country was at war. Once again, they would be fighting the Germans in another bloody encounter. The village had lost many good men in the last war.

How many more would be lost this time? Jim wondered.

"Let's take the hill path home," said Richard as he joined Jim and his friends Derek and Brian.

"Okay," they replied.

The gang of four had been friends for many years, since that memorable day, Jim's first day at the village junior school, the day that he bloodied the school bully's nose, and they had rescued him from the ensuing melee.

The path up the hill was narrow at this time of the year. The Australian ferns and rhododendrons had grown tremendously during the spring and a mostly wet summer. Eventually, they reached the red rock summit, a favorite meeting place, a place where you could see for miles. To the north were the city of Liverpool and the shipyards of Birkenhead that had built the Cunard Shipping Company's passenger liner, *Mauritania*. Looking westward, he saw the Snowdonia Mountain Range, to the east South Lancashire, and to the south, the Cheshire Plains and his Granddad's farm. They sat for a while in silence. The Vicar's announcement had brought little cheer to their hearts. There was not a lot to say. The die was cast. Once again, England was at war with Germany. The baton had passed to another generation. One by one, they left, leaving Jim alone with his thoughts.

Suddenly, he found himself on his knees, his hands clasped together looking into the sky. "Oh God," he prayed. "Take care of my family: Granddad, Grandma, Aunty Lucy and Uncle Mac, Sheila, Rosemarie, Aunty Ethel and Uncle Will, Mum and Dad, and my dearest cousin Maggie. Please keep them safe, out of harm's way." His last thought was for his Dad. He was the only member of the family serving in this bloody fight against the onslaught of Adolf Hitler's German war machine.

Jim sat for a while regarding the vista before him lost in thought, his village, his England, with its rows of houses, small shops, the church school, the village hall, and the church built of Redstone Rock carved from the village quarry. The quarry in the past had supplied stone for the construction of homes and the Liverpool dockland in the nineteenth century. There was a sense of pride within him as he remembered the history. There were the Roman fortifications at the nearby county seat of Chester; the Manchester Ship Canal, constructed in the late nineteenth century to allow the Manchester merchants access to the sea; and the gallant men of the village who had given their lives to defend their freedom in the past.

Suddenly, gripped with an emotion that welled deep inside his body, Jim silently said to himself, "Now, now we will face the German war machine yet again, and we will fight as we have never fought before to defend this, our fair and pleasant land."

His thoughts turned to his father, his hero, the man who always seemed to do the right thing. The goals that he scored for the village soccer team, the way he wielded his bat on the cricket field. He recalled the day he tied their mascot to the back of the opposing team's mascot, a goat; then slapped his rump, causing him to run amok around the field. He recollected stories his father told him before he went to sleep at night, and the art of boxing.

It had now been two months since he had last seen him and two weeks since his last letter, most of which had been censored. He knew that he must have been abroad or else he would have come home. He tried in his schoolchild mind to fathom out where he was. It was then that he remembered him talking about parachute training that he had received on his annual two-week training in the Territorial Reserves. He remembered his dad saying how exhilarating his first jump was and how much he had enjoyed it. It was then that a tear welled in his eye. "Come home soon, Dad," he said to himself silently. "Stay safe. We need you, come home soon," he cried aloud.

Then, he remembered how brave his dad looked in his uniform, his Sam Brown belt and his light blueberry. He looked as though he could win the war single-handed. Jim thought about his dad's smile as he returned the gangs final salute, his last lingering kiss with Mum and his last words before he left to join his regiment, The Royal Engineers. "Don't worry. It will all be over by Christmas."

Jim arose from his rocky seat and moved slowly down the hill. There was a tear in his eye as he remembered his Granddad's words, "Man's inhumanity to man."

It's been a good academic year for Jim and his friends. There was Richard, who had physical strength, a rare sense of humor, and above all, his kindness; they had dubbed him the gentle giant. He was the leader of the gang. Brian, on the other hand, was a prankster, full of fun, never taking anything seriously. On occasion, he could charm the birds out of the trees with a smile. A tall boy, brilliant at sports, Mum always said with a fond smile that he would be a ladies' man when he grew to his majority. Derek, small and skinny, whose sport was track and field, ran 100 yards in 10.1 seconds and had ambitions of becoming an Olympian. His nickname was 'Brains', the homework guru.

They had passed the Eleven Plus examinations with excellence, thanks to their hard work, and a hell of a lot of support from the schools head mistress, Miss Kinrade. Now, Brian was leaving to attend his father's old school, Shrewsbury. Richard, Derek, and Jim would be attending the grammar school. They had some good to times together. Jim smiled as he recalled the battles they had won in junior football, cricket, and rugby. It had not been smooth sailing. Despite their different characters and stations in life, they remained the best of friends, each contributing to the friendship in their own way.

# Chapter 2

It was a cold winter's night in the middle of November, when the Member of Parliament, Henry Kite, summoned the residents of the village to a meeting. He had represented the parliamentary constituency for a number of years. Jim's mother admired him for his political persuasion. He had an excellent reputation in the constituency for his fairness in dealing with constituent's problems. Mum, who was a member of the Labor Party, was known for her views on political matters. Jim smiled at the memory of his Mum and his Granddad, debating political matters on many occasions. The stage was set with long banquet tables. Sitting behind were a number of important men, some dressed in uniform, others in civilian clothes.

"Good evening, Ladies and Gentlemen," said the first speaker, a small rotund man. "Good evening, my name is Henry Kite. I represent you in the Parliament." He paused for a moment surveying his audience. "On behalf of our government and our local county officials that you see in front of you, I would like to welcome you to the first of many meetings that we will have in the future, to keep you apprised of the war effort and our plans to defend our village." The remark was greeted with loud cheers. "First, let me introduce the members of our Homeland Defense Force. On the far right is Jack Welsh. Jack, as you know, heads up our fire brigade. Second is Bill Willard, he will serve as liaison officer to the county. Next to him is Major Jack Smith, who as many of you know is your churchwarden. He will command the Home Guard. On my left are Jack Nicholson who will be your Chief Air Raid Warden, and finally, Ron Charles who will be in charge of our new 'Dig for Victory' campaign." He paused for a moment before each of these fine man dwelled on their individual subjects. "I would like to clear out a couple of questions that have been asked of me with reference to our homeland defense. Firstly, the barriers that have been set up in to the roads leading into your village will be in position for the duration. They are put there meet the needs of our defenses. Secondly, you all noticed by now, that there is a lot of noise emanating from the top of the hill. The army is installing anti-aircraft guns and searchlights, and they will be cordoned off with a barb wire fence to protect this installation, and I would ask you on behalf of our government to stay away from this area for the duration." He paused. "I know many of you lads that are here tonight like to play on the hill. In the future, I would ask you to keep away from the upper part. Thank you. Now, I will sit down and let these good people tell you how they propose to defend our village should the Nazis be foolish enough to attempt an attack on this our fair and pleasant land."

One by one, the leaders of the Civil Defense Force gave their presentations. Upon completion, the vicar asked for prayers and a round of applause for, as he put it, "these fine Gentlemen," and concluded with an announcement "that the Women's Institute is providing tea and cakes in the Village Hall Annex."

Jim and his Mum walked home, hand in hand. "What did you think of the meeting?" Jim asked her.

"I don't really know," she said to him in reply. "I am confused and it worries me."

"Why Mum?" he asked.

She paused for a moment before replying, "Well, it sounds to me as though we were expecting Adolf Hitler to come knocking at our door at any moment."

"I don't think so, Mum. But don't you think it's better to be prepared to defend this village of ours?"

"Yes, you're right," then added, "I do wish that your Dad was here with us."

"What did Dad say in his letter?"

"Not a lot," she replied, "more than half of the letter was blacked out. It's getting worse and worse all the time." She was quiet for a moment.

"Are you okay, Mum?" Jim asked her.

"Not really, my love," she replied. "There is a lot to talk about. I have asked Granddad and Grandma to have tea with us tomorrow afternoon. Granddad said he would come over early, so that he could watch you play in the rugby match."

Jim smiled as he greeted his grandparents and mother after a hard game.

"You played well, Jim," said Granddad.

"Thanks," replied Jim, "we could have done better."

Grandma smiled as her thoughts went back a few years when she watched her son play the game. She murmured to herself as she looked at her grandson, "Two peas in a pod."

"Would you like some more tea, Mum?" she said addressing Jim's Grandma.

"Yes, please, Edith."

"Granddad?"

I'm fine love," he replied, "but I would like another piece of that excellent chocolate cake."

"But of course, Granddad," she replied with a smile knowing damned well that he preferred her chocolate cake to Grandma's.

"Well, Edith what do you want to talk about?" Granddad asked.

"Well," she replied somewhat hesitantly. "I'd had some thoughts about how Jim and I are going to manage during the war, and I want to get your opinion."

"Fire away, love," he said.

"Well, I'm a bit worried about the food rationing. I think we have enough acreage to support a couple of sheep, maybe a pig, possibly a few more hens, a few ducks in the pond and enlarging our vegetable patch. I was wondering if you would help us?"

"Yes of course, my dear" he replied. "But I would be wary about having pigs. They can cause a lot of trouble. I'm sure that we can do some trading when it comes to pig meat. Let me know what you decide, and I'll give you all the help I can."

"The other thing that I need to talk to you about is the mortgage on our home. It's becoming increasingly difficult to keep up with the payments since Jim has been away."

"I'm sorry, love. Let me have a word with Joe Abrams at the bank. Don't worry your little head. I will sort it out."

Mum smiled and walked across the room and gave him a kiss and murmured, "Thanks, Dad."

"Anything else Edith?" he asked.

"Yes, I have been asked by a number of my friends in the Women's Institute to do some repairs and alterations for them. As you know, I trained as a seamstress before I met Jim. Is there anything I need to do?"

"Not really, love," he replied. "You don't need a license," then added with a laugh, "Make sure you charge them well, and that they pay you on time."

"There is one other thing," she said. "We have a meeting next week with the gang. From what I understand they have some ideas on a market garden project."

"Let me know what happens," he said with a smile.

"Thanks, Granddad," she said. "I don't know what I would do without you!"

The following week Mum, Jim, Derek and Richard sat around the kitchen table to discuss the 'Dig for Victory' campaign.

"Mrs. Mitchell," said Derek, "Richard and I have been thinking." He hesitated for a moment then asked, "Do you think it is possible that we could use your upper field?"

"All of it?" interjected Mum, somewhat surprised by the size of the scheme they had in mind.

"Yes," replied Derek, "then we could all work together growing stuff." He was struggling for words. "It would be like running a business."

Mum looked at Derek somewhat bemused, then said, "Sounds like a good idea to me."

There was a pause then Derek added, "There's a bit more to it than that." Mum looked at him and smiled. She was acutely aware of the reasons that the gang called him brains. He paused after a moment then continued, "We could all put in money to buy seeds and plants then we could split the profits four ways."

"Don't go too fast young man, we will split it five ways remember. I own the land," she said with a smile. It was a sort of smile that she gave when she trumped your best card in a close card game. It was eventually agreed, and they shook hands on the deal.

One evening Jim stepped off the school bus to see his mother in the distance running down the lane, wearing shorts and a shirt and her running shoes. He smiled to himself. "What was she up to now?" he asked himself. He had known for some time, well, most of his life really, that Mum was not a typical mother. Somehow, she was much different, independent, non–conformist, an athlete. She was also temperamental. There were times that she had her highs and lows. When she was up, she was marvelous. When she was down, he supported her. She wore her heart on her sleeve. She was the epitome of a woman that he hoped he would marry one day.

"What are you doing now?" He shouted, as she neared him.

"Running, don't you see? I just want to be fit for when your dad comes home. Why don't you join me?"

"Oh Mum," he protested. "I play football on Sunday, rugby on Saturday, and I walk a mile each day to the bus stop." She looked somewhat crestfallen. Jim could tell from her demeanor that she was disappointed. He loved her dearly, and as usual, he relented. "Okay", he said as he put his arms around her shoulder, "two mornings a week."

"That's my boy," she said, running off in the distance yelling, "I'll put the kettle on for a cup of tea."

He smiled as she disappeared around the first bend of the lane. She was in many ways, like his cousin Maggie, gentle in persuasion, and an extrovert, yet graceful. She was a redhead. Both wore their hearts on their sleeve, both Irish. "You just got to love them," he said to himself with a fond a smile.

Derek John Watson, nicknamed brains, walked slowly down the

lane leading to his home. For once, he did not admire the shrubbery, which was kept in first class condition by his Mum who devoted much of her free time to her pride and joy. There was much on his mind. Today had not been the best day in his life. His recent form in the 100 yards, 500 yards and in the 1,000-yard races had been poor, and he found it very difficult to understand. "Why? I am fit," he said to himself. "I trained well. Yes, I did have a cold a few weeks ago which somewhat upset my system, and resulted in my exclusion from the upcoming county championship." There was a wry smile on his face. "Cheer up," he said to himself. "There is always next year, and you never know. One member of the team may drop out before the finals next Saturday. Then you will get the reserve place."

Derek reminisced on the gang. None of them was what you could call field track experts and, whilst they were sympathetic to his demise, there was little that any of them could do. Mitchell had suggested that maybe his Mum could help. After all, she had won the county championship for Lancashire a few years ago. She appeared, to him, to be a possible lifeline to regain his former glory. He had always been very proud of his achievements and was fully aware that his small frame was an asset in sport. He smiled. It did little in the past to attract the opposite sex.

Richard and Brian had little trouble in that department, and Mitchell showed little interest, apart from his friendship with his cousin Maggie, a young lady he had always admired. There was a hope in his breast, that one day, Mitchell might find another, then he could pursue Maggie Bernadette O'Toole. To do that, he needed to become famous in his field and track. There was a light in the end of the tunnel. The solution, training with Jim Mitchell's Mum. She was also a good dancer. Maybe she could teach him to dance.

It was a dull, wet winter's morning as Jim stood in the old historic school assembly hall. The service, as usual, concluded with the national anthem. The headmaster smiled benevolently from his podium. "Happy Christmas to all," he said, sounding somewhat relieved. It was the last day of Jim's first term at high school. He was looking forward to the holidays with great anticipation. Dad had written that he would be home for Christmas. Mum was beside herself in anticipation of his homecoming. There would be long walks with the gang, football, a movie starring his favorite Actress Barbara Stanwyck, horse riding with Maggie, Grandma's Christmas party with all his relations, and his last solo at midnight Mass on Christmas Eve. "Life, despite the war, was good," he said to himself silently.

Jim stood in the well of the church flanked afoot by Richard and Brian as the church bell rang eleven times. It was Christmas Eve. The church was finely decorated, lit only by candles. There was an eerie silence of anticipation, awaiting the service celebrating the birth of our Lord and Master, Jesus Christ.

Jim took a deep breath then sang the opening verse:

> Once in Royal David's city
> In a lowly cattle shed
> Where a mother laid her baby
> In a manger for his bed

The organ joined with the choir in the remaining hymn. "He came down to earth from heaven…"

Slowly, Jim led the choir procession to the glittering Christmas tree, then turned east at the font, facing the magnificent stained-glass window depicting the, Virgin Mary holding her child. It was then that he saw the tall, slim figure of his Dad, resplendent in his dress uniform. As he passed his pew, there was a smile, a nod to acknowledge him. The years of training in the choir had taught him how to control his emotions. They did little to control his tears of joy. Dad was home for Christmas.

# Chapter 3

"Hurry along, Ladies, we are going to be late for Grandma Mitchell's Christmas party," Lucy added ruefully, "again..." The vision of last year's tardiness and her mother's somewhat icy reception lingered in her mind as the girls climbed onto the rear seats of her husband's latest car, an Austin 7. "He," she said to herself, "should never have bought this car; its' not big enough. "Are you alright, Maggie?"

She turned to look at her youngest daughter realizing as she spoke that it was a foolish remark. Her younger daughter had been sitting in the car for at least ten minutes, awaiting the arrival of the rest of her family, her arms folded and a look on her face that would have startled a lion at hundred yards should she chose to do so. Maggie Bernadette O'Toole was indignant. They were keeping her away from the two things she loved in life, her Cousin Jim and Grandma's horse, Betty.

Lucy sat in the front passenger seat considering her lot in life. Her mind wandered back to the day she had met Mac whilst on holiday at his sister Susan's home in County Clare. She had spent her childhood, and growing years, helping her mother and father on the farm. She was adept at most farm duties from scrubbing the kitchen floor to milking the cows. The arrival of Matthew Hennessey O'Toole into her life added a new and exciting dimension. He was more exciting than the other boys she had known. A glorious and somewhat ardent suitor, it took him a long time to ask her to marry him. When he did, she accepted, much against the will of her parents. He was a Roman Catholic. She and her family were Methodists. Eventually they relented, fully aware that she was not the beauty of the county, and possible spinsterhood loomed heavily on the horizon. Over the years, Mac had been a kind and loving husband in his own way. The three girls gave her solace. Life had become a sort of routine; one week's holiday in the seaside town of Blackpool with Mac and her children, the Horse of the Year show with her mother in November, and Christmas with her the family on her parent's farm.

Lucy's thoughts turned to the girls. The elder twins Sheila and Rosemary were kind, sensitive and good-looking; however, they were not academically minded. Their main interests in their lives were boys. She smiled. She would have no problems marrying them off when the time came. Her youngest Maggie was the total opposite of the twins. She was by all school reports, academically brilliant. In the words of her Headmistress, "If she liked the subject, she would get straight 'A's; if, she didn't, then maybe she would get a passing grade C." She was without doubt, her Dad's favorite, a position she accepted with grace. She had never encouraged boyfriends, and was known for her reputation to totally discourage them. The tall, curly haired cousin Jim was the exception. They had been close friends for years, ever since the night, several years ago, when Jim had suffered a nightmare. Maggie had stayed with him. The next morning, Lucy found her daughter lying on the bed with her arm around Jim. Lucy had bathed them together in the same bath many times in the past. Both were academically minded and shared many of the same interests; both were loners joined together by a strong bond of friendship since they were babies many years ago. She paused. Her body went stiff for a moment. Her mind, flashing back to her child-hood days, Cousin Edward, was it love? "Oh, not again!" she cried silently. The thoughts flooded back "Eddy, my love, where are you?"

# Chapter 4

Grandma Mitchell stepped out of her fluted Victorian enamel bath, steadying herself on the newly installed handrail. "Yes," she thought to herself silently. "Her husband Jim has done a fine job on the recent renovations."

"Not bad for an old lady," she said admiring the reflection of the body in the gold framed mirror. Time had been kind to her body. The three pregnancies had taken the little toll on this feisty Lady from Yorkshire. She slowly toweled herself off with a luxurious white cotton towel, recently purchased from 'Browns of Chester,' musing to herself about the family Christmas party. "Take your time, Mary," she said to herself as she turned her attention to her once raven black hair, now steel grey. She wasn't surprised by the change of color. Life had not been easy for her and her man, since they had eloped from Yorkshire as youngsters, with enough money to purchase a small holding in the county of Cheshire. Now, they were the proud owners of one of the most successful farms in the County. Slowly, she brushed her locks. "Two hundred and fifty strokes a day," she said remembering her Mum's advice to her as a girl. She stood for moment, admiring herself in the mirror. She smiled, mother of three, grandmother of four. "Not bad," she said with a smile. "Jenny, where is my dress?" she yelled.

"Coming, Mrs. Mitchell. I've just finished pressing it."

The sound of her footsteps on the creaky staircase, announced the arrival of Jenny and her dress in her dressing room.

"Thank you, Jenny." She was a good girl, the daughter of Jim's cowman, a girl that cooked and cleaned for her. During the last few years, she had suffered arthritis in her knees, which the doctor blamed on her style of riding to the hounds.

Mary glanced at the gold Mondovi wristwatch. It was time to inspect the preparations for the Christmas party. Slowly, she climbed down the creaky staircase to the main entrance of their home, muttering to herself, "How many times must I ask him to attend to these blasted stairs?"

Over the last few years, they had paid off the last of the mortgage on the Bottom fifty acres. Following much conniving and perseverance, she had persuaded her husband to make some additions and renovations to their home, including the construction of a "Tea Room" which would serve meals to visitors to the local hospital, and passers-by. She smiled with satisfaction. "This will be a very profitable venture."

She stood at the entrance of her living room surveying the decorations and the splendid Christmas tree. Suddenly, she felt his presence. A chill ran down her spine as his arms encircled her slender waist. She smiled. The feeling hadn't changed since the first day she saw him walking off the cricket pitch with a broad smile on his face. He had just completed a century for his cricket team.

"It looks lovely, Mary. It really does." Then he turned her around to see the smile on her face.

"Give me a kiss, love," she smiled looking into his eyes. As their lips parted, she said, "Was it worth it, Jim Mitchell?"

"Yes," he replied. "It was, my love."

"Hold me close, Jim," she whispered. There was a tear in her eye.

"What's the matter, my love?"

"You have given me everything that I have ever wanted, my son, my daughters. You have made me so bloody happy, Jim Mitchell, it hurts."

It was a beautiful, crisp Christmas Day as Edith walked hand-in-hand with her husband and her blonde curly haired son along the red and gold leafed trees of the Ridgeway, overlooking the wooden encampment of Fox-hill. She smiled to herself reminiscing. It had been sixteen years since she had first met this tall blond haired man at a dancehall in the town of Blackpoll. He had swept her off her feet and married her within the year this, was a journey that they had made together many times in the past to his Mum and Dad's. They had adopted her following the tragic death of her parents in a car crash years ago. At first, it had not been easy for her living in a small village, her being a town girl by birth and nature. She had left school at an early age to support her family, a seamstress by trade, a field and track athlete by choice. She had inherited her mother's genes, auburn hair, slim body, and long slim legs. As they crossed the four lane end crossroads, she could hear the sound of the Christmas music coming from Granddad's farm at the top of the hill. The party had started. She was excited. She felt inner warmth, a feeling of happiness, beyond her wildest dreams.

Margaret Bernadette O Toole breathed a sigh. "Huh," she said to herself. "At last the family is on the way to Grandma Mitchell's Christmas party." She was excited at the prospect of seeing her relatives again. She smiled, closing her long black eye lashes, hoping that the time would pass quickly. There was more than that, she admitted to herself. She was overcome by a sense of anticipation at seeing her tall, slim, blonde curly haired blue-eyed cousin, Jim Mitchell. It seemed like years, yet it was only months, since he had kissed her on the lips. She could still hear his parting words, "See you at Christmas Maggie," then added, "Behave you." She smiled fondly remembering the times that they had spent together. She, a couple of years older, had nursed him carefully on her lap and listened to his first words. Now, he had become her friend, someone that really did understand her. He made her laugh, when she felt low, shared her joy when she was high. There was a mischievous twinkle in his eyes when he told her silly jokes. She smiled again, remembering their last holiday , when they had laid together on the banks of the Manchester Ship Canal following a long and hard swim, listening to her reading from William Shakespeare's sonnets.

As the car wound its way along the tree-lined Ridgeway, she recalled her embarrassing attempt to make an "entrance" into the party the previous year; it was a failure. So much so, that even Jim didn't comment on it. Aided by twelve months of acting lessons, the success of which were warmly greeted by her dramatic art tutor, who, on occasion had been known to use suitable adjectives, caused Maggie to review her career opportunities. She was excited, at the prospect of impressing the family, but more to the point, the prospect of impressing him. "This year would be different," she said to herself.

As the Austin car entered the farmyard, she immediately opened the rear door of the car, determined to be the first to enter. Then with a confident smile knocked and opened the front door slowly. "Hello everyone, we have arrived." There was a moment's silence as her family and guests gazed upon her. "Yes," she said to herself silently, "I did it." Then with a radiant smile approached her grandma, "Happy Christmas, Grandma," kissing her on the cheek. "My!" she exclaimed. "The Christmas tree looks wonderful!"

One by one, she circled the living room, smiling radiantly, wishing and kissing her family and their guests "Happy Christmas." Jim stood in the background, watching her performance. He smiled noting that she dallied with the men of the family.

"That's my Maggie," he said to himself. This untamed moody, temperamental shaggy girl had grown into a radiant beauty with sparkling blue eyes, long raven black hair, a slim body, and vivacious personality.

"Mitchell, last but not least!" said Maggie as she approached her cousin. "Do I get a kiss?" she asked.

"Where," he asked.

There was a mischievous twinkle in her eyes as she threw her arms around his neck. "On the lips of course, my darling, it's Christmas, don't you know."

"Everybody is watching," he protested.

"I don't give a damn," she replied adamantly. "Kiss me, my darling, I've missed you like hell."

Grandma Mitchell smiled as she saw her youngest grandchildren embrace. Musing to herself, "How the hell did we manage to spawn them?" her thoughts were broken by her housekeeper "Dinner is served, Marm,"

Grandma Mitchell smiled. She loved to surround herself with family and close friends to celebrate the birth of Jesus Christ. It was time for the Gentlemen to escort their Ladies into the dining room. Granddad and Grandma led the procession with the young ones bringing up the rear.

"Will you take me in Jim?" murmured Maggie.

"Don't I always?" he replied, teasing her.

"Thank you," she said softly. Her mood changed as he held her arm. Gone was the glorious young Lady that had entered the house with a flourish, barely an hour ago. She was now a kind, submissive, soft tender loving girl. The girl he had fallen in love with so many years ago. She held his hand firmly as they walked into the dining room together.

"I like your dress, Maggie," he said.

She smiled, "Well thank you sir. You clean up nicely."

"How many times have you made that remark?" asked Jim laughing at her remark.

"I don't know," she replied with an impish smile. "But it's true."

The dining room was superbly dressed for the festivities red tablecloth with white linen napkins, the best silver, illuminated with red candles in gold candlesticks. It was tradition that they sat next to their Granddad, at the head of the table. Jim on his right-hand, Maggie on his left hand. Jim admired the tall elegant figure of his granddad, the jet-black hair, the ready smile. He loved him for his kindness, admired him for his strength, and his success as a farmer and preacher in the Methodist Chapel. They stood in silence, hands clasped, awaiting the blessing.

"Dear Lord," Granddad began in a fine tenor voice. "We thank you for your blessings, the air we breathe, the food and wine that you place on our table to celebrate your Son's birthday, your kindness, and the love that you have shown us throughout the year. We pray that you take care of our loved ones that are now serving our country in the war against Nazi Germany. Bring them home safely, dear Lord, to the love of their family, through Jesus Christ, our Lord, Amen."

Jim observed his Dad and Mum sitting across the table from him as he finished the remains of the second course of this year's Christmas feast. They were holding hands, looking into each other's eyes oblivious to the scene around them. He smiled as he kissed her on her sweet lips. They were in love. Twas always the same, he recollected.

He remembered his Dad's tales of Christmas in his younger days, when children stood at the table, and were only allowed to speak when spoken to. Times have changed. He smiled. Maggie must have changed the rules. There she was as usual, monopolizing her Granddad in conversation.

"How's school?" asked Granddad.

She considered the question for a moment. "Fine, thanks," she replied. "My teachers tell me that I could do better."

"Any thoughts on what you want to do?"

"I don't really know Granddad, maybe become a doctor, or maybe an actress. I've been taking acting lessons. That may help me to start a career on the stage or films.

Jim smiled, "That was some entrance that she made to the party," he said to himself. He smiled in admiration. There was something special about this young lady. She seemed sort of different than her two sisters.

"What do you think Jim?" he said turning to face his Grandson.

"Don't really know, Granddad. Much depends on the day and the way she feels."

Maggie laughed. "That's not very kind, Mitchell," she said mockingly, rebuking him, then with a smile, added, "I will be famous, just like Barbara Stanwyck. Then, dear cousin, you will have to pay to see me on the stage."

Granddad laughed. "You certainly have this young lady summed up, don't you, Jim?"

"Yes, I think so, Granddad. But then again, you never know with Maggie, do you?"

Granddad regarded Jim "Your dad and mum are very pleased with your exams report. Well done, my boy"

"Thanks, Granddad. It was pretty hard going. I guess I had a modicum of luck with the questions."

The dining room buzzed with conversation throughout the meal. Grandma, sitting at the other end of the table, was as usual, monopolizing the conversation. "The matriarch of our family had mellowed over the years," he said to himself silently.

"Jim" said Maggie, as they were leaving the dining room. "Will you take me to see Betty?"

"Yes," he replied quickly, realizing an opportunity to be alone with her. They walked slowly along the path leading to the stables in the paddock. She felt the warmth of his arm around her waist.

"I've missed you," she murmured.

"I know, Maggie," he said in a solemn voice.

"I know, love" she replied, "but I've got some good news. Your Mum said I can stay over for a couple of days."

"That means that we could go riding!" he cried jubilantly.

"I know," she replied. "Isn't that marvelous? That's the best Christmas present I have ever had."

# Chapter 5

The following morning, Maggie rose early from her bed excited for the day. She loved Aunty Edith's Cottage, tucked in the hillside overlooking their four acres of land and the distant lake. This was her favorite place to live. She busied herself making tea and biscuits for her cousin. She smiled as Jim entered the kitchen somewhat bleary eyed, his long blonde hair bedraggled, and still wearing his dressing gown.

"Morning, cousin," she said, offering him his favorite Garibaldi biscuits and hot tea.

"Morning Maggie," he replied. "Did you sleep well?" then added, "You're up early. It's only five-thirty."

"I know," she replied. "I thought that we would make an early start. The horses enjoy the early morning run over the hills and for that matter, so do I."

"Okay," he said kissing on her forehead. "Make me bacon butty; we can leave in thirty minutes." He then added, "I don't think Mum and Dad will be riding this morning." She smiled inwardly. One day, it would be her time.

They arrived at the stable at first light, both anxious to ride. Jim quickly saddled old Nellie then turned to watch his cousin. She was gently stroking Grandma's big gelding on his neck, whispering sweet nothings into his ear. His head slowly lowered, inviting her to ride him. Jim smiled, recognizing the bond of friendship between the fourteen hand horse and his five-foot nothing cousin, Maggie. They rode side-by-side through the lower fifties fields cantering to a Gallup. The horses enjoyed the early morning run. Over the years, Grandma taught them well.

She could feel the fresh early morning breeze in her hair as they galloped side-by-side across the fields. Then she pulled away yelling, "Let's go to Pinewood."

Jim's smile broadened as he watched her gallop into the distance, all the while thinking, "Maggie was a 'Natural. She was a winner, she was his girl."

"See you," she yelled as she jumped the first hedge, knowing full well that Jim would have to take the longer route on Nellie. She dismounted at the entrance to the stand of trees watching old Nellie and her cousin approach at a canter. "How's Nellie?"

"She's getting older, but she's not ready to pasture yet," he said stroking her mane.

They sat in silence on an old tree trunk for a while, recovering from the hard ride.

"It's beautiful," said Maggie, as they watched the early morning sunrise slowly over the frost covered valley below. "Jim," she said, her small hand gripping his hand tightly. "Can we live here one day?"

"Maggie," he cried in anguish! "Don't spoil it, Love"

"I'm not," she retorted, "I realize that one day we will have to part. They will never let us be together." She was silent for a moment, then turned, clasping his head with her tiny hands, "Kiss me, Jim." As their lips parted, there were tears in her eyes. "I love you Jim Mitchell," she sobbed. "I always have and I always will."

"I know Maggie, I know, and there's not a bloody thing that we can do about it."

"I can dream, can't I?"

"Yes, you can, my darling cousin," he said to himself silently.

# *Chapter 6*

During the three months following Christmas, there was little activity in the war in Europe. The Daily Express newspaper described the period, as a 'Phony War.' The battle of the Atlantic between the German U boats and the convoy of ships bringing much needed war supplies and food from America, was beginning to take its toll; rationed food supplies declined. The market garden was coming into its own. Root vegetables, cabbage and Brussels sprouts were in great demand. The nation's inhabitants were slimming, incidents of flu, and other diseases were on the increase. School meals, which were once really scrumptious, were gradually declining in quality and quantity. In a lighter moment, the school joke, "If its cheese soup for lunch, it must be Friday." We were slowly building a nation of slim inhabitants.

The war had some affect on education. The younger teachers were called up for service in military, being replaced by retired teachers.

The gang swapped their knowledge of subjects and combined their homework. Luckily, they were able to continue with sporting activities. Somehow they bonded together closer than they had ever done in the past.

In April of that year, the war activity in Europe began to unfold. The BBC News reported heavy fighting in the lowlands, Belgium and Holland. The French defensive positions, known as the Maginot line, designed after World War I to withstand any German invasion, had been breached by a superior German force, now sweeping onwards to

Paris and the Channel ports, leaving some two hundred thousand British and Allied troops surrounded at the port and beaches of Dunkirk. The only possible retreat was The English Channel, some twenty miles from the coastal town of Dover.

What followed was the historical miracle of Dunkirk. In May, and early June, of that year hundreds of thousands of Allied troops were evacuated by a huge Armada of the small ships, ranging from small yachts to sailing dinghies supported by the Royal Navy warships. Within days, the French government had surrendered to the Germans England was left to fight alone, with only twenty miles of water separating their homeland from the mighty force of the German war machine. It was a disaster of huge proportion, as this island faced the German onslaught alone.

There were lighter moments in life. One night the gang watched the local defense volunteer parade through the village. They were mostly young boys of sixteen years of age and older men would who had fought in the First World War, armed with garden forks or spades.

"Where are your guns?" shouted one joker.

"They're coming next week," said the sergeant leading the parade somewhat irritably.

Finally, they reached their destination, the car park at the Robin Hood pub. "Attention!" yelled the sergeant. "Left turn, stand at ease," he paused "dismiss!"

The forks and spades were hastily abandoned as they rushed into the pub for a couple of pints of Greenall Whitley's beer.

Richard laughed.

"It's not funny", said Derek rebuking him. "If the war continues much longer, we will be doing the same."

## Chapter 7

It was a warm humid night in June as Jim and his mother Edith sat listening to the nine o'clock BBC News. Jim heard a knock on the front door of his home. On opening the door, Jim saw a small elderly army officer standing with a piece of paper in his hand.

"Is your mother in, young man?" He asked.

"Mum!" he shouted. "There's someone to see you."

"Oh my God!" she yelled as she saw the visitor. "Please don't tell me they have got my Jim," she said expecting the worst.

The major stiffened. "Oh good god, when will this ever end!" he prayed silently. "I'm sorry to tell you, Mrs. Mitchell that your husband died of his wounds early this morning. We will bring him home tomorrow."

Edith collapsed onto the floor. The love of her life, her man had given his life, defending his country.

"Bring Mrs. Smith!" ordered Jim to the Officer. "She lives in the next house down the lane. Ask her to telephone the doctor!" Slowly, with tears blinding his eyes, Jim lifted his Mum into his arms, climbed the stairs and laid her on her bed.

The day of his father's funeral was bright and sunny for most people, dark and dismal for Jim's family. Today they were burying his Dad, the man who had taken care of him over the years, his rock, his foundation, and his hero.

The funeral procession to the church was led by the village Brass

Band, followed by members of his regiment and the Home Guard. The hearse was pulled by two black horses regailed with cheviots. Granddad and Uncle Mac supported his Mum on the long walk to the church. The tall erect figure of young Jim, his head held high, marched behind with measured footsteps, his final salute to the man he admired and loved for so many years, suppressing tears of emotion.

Maggie, knowing he needed her, broke with tradition, rushed to him, and walked at his side. Aunty Lucy, Aunt Ethel and Grandma, followed closely behind with friends and relatives. The A.R.P. and the Fire Brigade brought up the rear. The village brass band played Dad's favorite marches as the procession made its way slowly to Saint Paul's church. The villagers, heads bowed, lined the route. The old soldiers saluted as the coffin passed. They had seen this ceremony many times in the past. The Reverend James conducted the service and the choir sang his favorite hymns. Granddad in an emotional voice read the eulogy. The choir sang a hymn a single 'Kettle Drummer,' who in tradition 'Beat the Retreat,' led the final hymn, "Abide with Me," Then the procession to the cemetery. The bugler played "The Last Post," as they lowered him into his grave, his members of his regiment fired their last salute. His mother Edith stepped forward, slowly lowering her hand to mother earth, and cast a handful onto his coffin her final salute to the man she had loved.

In the emotional days that followed his father's passing, Maggie and her mother stayed with their loved ones to support them in their hour of need. Aunty Lucy was his mother's rock and link to the sanity of the outside world, while Maggie cared for Jim, the love of her life. They walked for hours in silence over the hills and the valleys as he slowly recovered from the devastating loss of his father. One evening, they sat on the bench watching the sunshine over the Lake as they had done many times in the past. It was the right time and the right moment. She clasped her hands on his cheek asking, "Do you feel like talking, Jim?"

"I think so Maggie" slowly, he began to talk about the old days when they were kids together, remembering the good times that they had together, the summer barbecues in the garden, swimming in the lake, fishing with Granddad, Uncle Will and Uncle Mac, the Christmas parties, Granddad's farm, and the long ride on their horses.

"Is that all?" she asked with a smile. "Don't you remember the day I told you I liked you?"

He smiled for first time as he exclaimed. "Maggie Bernadette O'Toole, you were a very forward young Lady."

She laughed. "Yes I was, don't you love it?"

Suddenly, the pent up emotions of the loss of his dad were more than he could bear. "Oh Maggie," he cried shaking violently. "I miss him so much," he cried as the tears of the anguish ran down his cheeks.

"Let me hold you my love," she murmured. Suddenly he felt the strength of her love flowing into his body. There was a sense of relief as she held him. "Jim, my love, I will always be here for you." She paused looking into his eyes. "I love you, my sweet Jim. I guess I always will."

In the days and weeks that followed, Jim and his mum slowly recovered from the tragedy that had beset their family. Somehow, the grass in the fields seems to be greener; the birds chirping seemed clearer. Edith no longer cried herself to sleep at night. The days of mourning were coming towards the inevitable end. They would miss him in their lives forever.

Jim and his mum devoted their time to running along the country lanes together, reading and listening to the BBC Radio programs.

One evening after supper, they sat together on the settee, listening to one of Chopin's nocturnes on the radio. "That was so beautiful Jim," she exclaimed as she rose, turning off the radio. "Can we talk for a while?" she asked.

"Oh dear," he said to himself, recalling Richards recent experience with his parents discussion with him on the subject of sex. "Is it about sex, Mum?" he asked somewhat defensively.

"Well, not really," replied his mum. She smiled, "but as you mentioned the subject, I guess it's about time we did." She stood, walked over to the small library and selected a book. "Let's look at this together, shall we."

Page by page they reviewed the words and the pictures. "Do you have any questions, my love?" she asked.

"Yes," Jim replied. "Maggie and I have talked about the subject. Mum, I guess there's only one question I need to ask you."

"And what's that my son?" she asked.

"Can Maggie and I be married one day?"

Edith had feared this moment in her life, she being aware of their young love for each other. She hesitated, "No my love, you and Maggie are blood cousins and you have the same genes. Your children may be deformed, or mentally handicapped, and you would not like that to happen, would you my love?"

"No, Mum, that wouldn't be fair. Oh Mum," he cried in anguish, "we love each other, Mum, and it's not bloody fair."

"I know my love, oh how I know," Edith cried. "I know it's not fair, but those are the cards that we have been dealt in this life."

"Can we go out together?"

"Of course, you can," she replied, holding his face in the palms of her hands. There were tears in her eyes as she murmured softly. "Promise me you will never have babies with Maggie. It will ruin both of your lives and shame the family. Are you okay, my love?" she asked holding him close.

"Yes, I suppose so Mum," he cried, "Has anyone talk to Maggie."

"Yes, Aunty Lucy has. Now, young man," she said with a smile, "now that we have gotten that out of the way, let me tell you what I was going to talk to you about. I am thinking about starting a business. As you know, I have been doing some repairs on people's clothing, and it's gotten to the stage, where I cannot handle it all by myself. I need help; so, I am going to get some help. Yesterday I spoke to Granddad when he called. He reckons that he could renovate one of the outhouses, which will enable me to train a couple of girls from the village to help me."

"That sounds good to me, Mum," he said enthusiastically. "Will you make lots of money?"

Edith laughed. "According to Granddad's inspection of my accounts, he reckons that I could make a small fortune."

Jim was quiet for a while then asked, "What about our market garden business?"

"Well, I have spoken to Derek's mother and she's prepared to do my job, which to be honest, is not a lot of work. All I have to do is a walk down the garden occasionally and do the books."

"Okay," he replied. "That sounds good to me. What was the other thing you wanted to talk about, Mum?" asked Jim.

She smiled. "How would you like to go and stay with Aunty Lucy for a couple of weeks? It would do us both good, don't you think?"

Jim jumped from his seat and embraced his mother. "Thanks Mum, when can we go?" he asked.

Edith smiled, "Would Tuesday morning be okay?"

Jim put his arm around her and kissed her on her forehead exclaiming, "You're the best mother in the world, and I love you."

# Chapter 8

Maggie Bernadette O'Toole lay in her bed attempting to read her latest novel. She was unable to concentrate. "Today," she said to herself, "had not been the best day of your young life." Earlier that evening, she had sat on her favorite chair in the living room pretending to read her novel. Her Dad was as usual reading the evening paper, her Mum fussing around making the final touches in preparation for the visit of Aunty Edith and her cousin Jim. She was excited. The anticipation of seeing Jim again was overwhelming. Her feelings were somewhat dampened by a sense of foreboding that had lingered with her since the previous Christmas when she had foolishly shown her true feelings for her cousin in front of the family. She had half expected to receive some words of disapproval from her parents. However, none had come. She was aware that she had purposely set out to make an 'entrance' at Grandma's Christmas party. There was also her sense of elation in seeing Jim again. She knew she was, by nature, a "show off." An extrovert, she had been aware of this trait, from an early age when she had experienced the highs and lows of her young life much to the consternation of her parents. The highs came mostly from her studies, and when she was with her cousin Jim, her lows, born out of frustration.

"Maggie, Me Darling, we need to talk," said her father as he placed his newspaper aside on the coffee table, removing his glasses in the process.

"Is it about Jim's visit?" she asked hoping for some advantage in what she knew was to come.

"Yes," replied her father. Somehow, she sensed that he was having some difficulty in starting the conversation. He knew that she was a determined young lady, independently minded, and that she loved them both with all her heart. However, there were times when they did not really understand her.

"What about him?" she asked.

It was then that her Mother joined in the conversation. "Are you in love with him?"

"Yes, I am, Mum," Maggie replied. "I've been in love with him since we were kids together. You, above all, should know that."

"Yes", she replied. "I do. It was okay when you were children," her Mum retorted. "Now you're growing up. Things are different."

"What do you mean, things are different?" said Maggie angrily. "They're not!" she argued emphatically. "I have loved him since we were babies, and I still do," she said defiantly. "Jim and I don't do anything wrong, Mum!" she shouted. "We don't have real sex dammit," she cried angrily! "Do you think I am stupid?" she exclaimed. "We have too much to lose. We have our whole lives ahead of us," she said emphatically. "We have never had sex and we never will. I love him just the same, Mum," she cried. "When I am with him, life is so bloody wonderful. Oh Mum, it's so good," she exclaimed. "I know there will be a time when Jim and I will go our separate ways. Until that happens, I just want to be with him. Don't you see how much this means to me?" Her temper slowly subsided. She stood from her chair and walked slowly towards her parents. "Mum, Dad, I love you so much, and I owe you so much. Please, please," she cried the tears running down her face. "Don't part us. He makes me so bloody happy."

*Chapter 9*

"We've got lots to talk about," said Maggie as they walked hand in hand to her secret place.

"What do you want to talk about?" Jim asked.

"Well, there's a dance at school on Saturday night. I want you to take me there."

Jim looked at her. "Maggie," he muttered, "you know I don't dance, don't you?"

"That's not the point," she retorted. "Most of the girls don't think I have a boy friend. I want to show you off."

"Why?"

She looked at him before she answered. "Mitchell, there are times when you just don't understand a girl's needs. I just want to. Isn't that enough?" she said in a stern voice.

"Yes, I suppose so. I am sorry," he said relenting. "What else would you like to do?"

"I would like to go and see the film, *Gone with the Wind*, then go to Old Trafford to watch a cricket match. The Halle Orchestra is giving a concert on Sunday afternoon. Will you take me please?"

"Okay," he said. "Anything else?" he said in a conciliatory tone.

"Yes, I want to swim every day. Is there anything you want to do?"

Jim thought for a moment, replying, "No, I think you've covered it all Maggie."

She smiled, tenderly. "Thank you, Jim."

After a long swim in the warm water of the canal, they lay on their towels soaking up the warmth of a hot summer day. "You look a bit tired this morning, Maggie," said Jim.

"Yes," she replied. "I suppose I am. I didn't sleep well last night."

"Why?" He felt her hand touching his.

"We need to talk, Jim." She paused. "I had a bloody awful experience last night. Dad and Mum wanted to talk about us."

"What about us?" Jim exclaimed.

"Well, they reckon I'm showing you too much affection when we are together. I think Grandma must have said something to her," said Maggie.

Jim laughed. "Why?"

"Do you remember at the Christmas party when I put my arms around your neck and kissed you on the lips?"

"Yes, I do," he said with a smile. "That felt good, Maggie."

She smiled. "It was meant to be, silly. Apparently, everybody in the room was watching. They no doubt talked about us. And you know Grandma doesn't like that sort of thing."

Jim laughed. "She sort of rules the roost, doesn't she?"

"Yes, I suppose so," said Maggie.

"Is that all?" asked Jim.

"No, not really, it gets worse;" said Maggie quietly "They are concerned that we were having sex together." Jim blushed, his face turning a color of beetroot red.

She laughed, "Mitchell, you're blushing."

He felt embarrassed and turned his head away.

"I'm sorry, Love," she said putting her arm around him. "We've got to talk about that, you know."

"Yes," he replied. "I know. Mum talked about it the other day. You know, Maggie, I didn't feel at all embarrassed."

She smiled as he turned back over to face her. "You have a great Mum Jim. I know that she understands you. I wish my parents did." She paused. "Are you okay, now?" she said tussling his hair.

"Yes, I think so, Maggie," he replied

"I love you, Jim Mitchell, and I always will; however, I know what

I am going to do in my life, and I don't want to get 'knocked up' like some of the other girls in the village. One day," she said sounding much older than her years, "I'm going to "That's enough of that," she said.

"No, it's not," said Jim assertively. Maggie looked surprised. "We are avoiding the real issue."

A faint smile appeared on her face. "Yes, I know, Jim. I didn't think you were ready for that yet."

"I am," said Jim boldly. "Mum and I had a long talk two weeks ago."

"About sex?" she injected.

"Yes," he continued, "and about you and me. She said we could never have babies together."

"Yes, I know that. My mother told me. I also talked to the Biology teacher about it. And they're right, Jim. We have never talked about making love, have we?"

He felt her hand touching his cheek. "No we haven't," he replied. "The sad thing is that it's a natural thing for you and me to do."

"I know, Jim. Oh how I know, my love."

"It's so bloody frustrating," he said as she looked into his eyes and saw the tears slowly running down his cheek. "Jim Mitchell," she murmured. "You will always be my number one. You're mine forever, my love, no matter what we do with our lives." They lay together until the sun crossed the horizon. Maggie broke the silence.

"Are you all right, Jim?" she asked.

"No I am not!" he cried, "It's just not fair, you see," he said gently. "I love you, Maggie O'Toole. And I want you."

She clasped her hands on his face and looked deeply into his eyes. "Jim Mitchell," she cried. "There is no end to you and me. There never will be my love."

It was then he remembered her reading Thomas Gray's elegy in a country courtyard.

> The curfew tolls the knell of parting day,
> The lowing heard winds slowly o'er the lea
> The Ploughman homeward plods his weary way.
> And leaves the world of darkness, and to me

He rests his head upon the lap of the Earth.
A youth of fortune, and to fame unknown
Fair science frowns upon his humble birth.
And melancholy marked him for her own.
Large was his bounty, and his soul sincere.
Heav'n did recompense as largely send.
He gave to mis'ry all he had, a tear.
He gained from heav'n
T'was all he wished, a Friend.

# *Chapter 10*

Edith sat on the top deck of the old double-decker bus as it wound its way along the lanes, and roads, of the Cheshire countryside, returning her to her home. It had been a lovely holiday. It was good to see her old friend, Lucy, again. They had reminisced over the past years, about the holidays at the seaside town of Rhyl that they and their families had spent together with Jim, her husband, and the love that he had given them. There were tears in her eyes, many tears. She knew it was part of the healing process of her tragic loss. They had bonded together to resolve openly the close love and friendship of their two kids, Maggie and Jim. Over the last two weeks, she had seen the sadness in their bodies. Both of them had accepted the inevitable, that they would never marry. She knew that they would always remain friends, with a special love, which would last to eternity. She had cried the night that they had left together for Maggie's school dance. Jim dressed in his best Sunday suit. She smiled. He looked so handsome, just like his Dad: tall, slim, with blonde curly hair. He had a way with him, which reminded her of her Jim, a gentleman. He was wearing a rose in his buttonhole that Maggie had given him. Maggie, dear Maggie, small and slender, was blossoming into a radiant beauty. Yes, black-and-white were her colors, the white blouse, long black skirt her shimmering black hair falling over her shoulders; however, it was the radiant smile that masked her fiery spirit, told her story. This night, she was taking her man to the dance. "It was sad," she said to herself silently, "her radiant smile for the evening would mask her sadness."

Edith's thoughts turned to her home. She was excited at the prospect of starting her own business. "Jim," she said silently to herself, "would be pleased with her, dear man." He had left her a wonderful legacy. Love, oh so much love, her son, a home, and now her own business. Suddenly, she felt a tear running down her cheek.

"Are you okay, Mum?"

"Yes," she replied, "Just memories, my love."

That night Jim lay in his bed. His mind turned back to his holiday. Part of it was fun; The Halle Orchestra's performance of Dvorak's, "New World Symphony," the music told of the story of a voyage to the new world; the Cricket match at Old Trafford, the school dance. He smiled. Maggie looked so beautiful, as she paraded him around the room. He closed his eyes and recalled her laughter, her smile, a sort of presence about her, bewitching him; the way she curtsied to him when he asked her to dance, her polite, "No," when some of the boys asked her to dance. It was her evening, but he knew beneath the radiant smile bespoke a broken heart. "Maggie, Maggie," he cried as he drifted into a restless sleep. "I love you, dearest cousin."

# *Chapter 11*

"Morning gang," said Edith. "Yes, he's up," she said referring to her son. "He's ready for work. Would you like a cup of tea," she paused, "and a bacon sandwich?"

"Oh, yes please, Mrs. Mitchell," they replied.

They sat around the kitchen table devouring their second breakfast of the day as Jim joined them. "How's it going?" he asked.

"Not bad," said Derek. "Old Horton's bought a lot of the potatoes and lettuce and my Mum has opened a stall in Chester market. She," he said proudly, "has sold a lot of stuff. We're out of potatoes, lettuce and carrots, and it's time to plant some more."

"Have we made a profit?" asked Jim.

"Yes," Derek replied, "A bloody good one."

Edith laughed. "That's the first time I've heard you swear, Derek."

"Sorry, Mrs. Mitchell, we have done so well!"

Granddad Mitchell replaced the black telephone earpiece into its cradle. There was a smile of satisfaction on his ruddy face. His plan had worked. His daughter-in-law, and daughter, had "nipped" this in the bud' using kind words and compassion. Edith's sensitivity, and Lucy's determination, had resolved the situation and, hopefully, won the day. "Or had they," he wondered, knowing both of them were strong willed."

"Who was that on the telephone, Jim?" she inquired.

"Edith, my love, she and Lucy have talked to the kids."

"Thank God for that," she replied. "I am going to have a long soak in the bath."

Jim smiled. He looked at his old Singer pocket watch. It was four thirty in the afternoon. "She is taking longer to prepare herself these days," he said to himself. Tonight was her night, the night she would hold court at the social highlight of the year: The Cheshire Hunt Ball.

He regarded the antique Chippendale drinks cabinet. "It's a bit early," he said to himself, then smiled as he opened the cabinet door and reached for the Gilbey's gin bottle. "Why not," he said expunging his conscious. "Why not," he repeated. "You've had a good day, and you deserve it." Then a further sop to his conscience as he reminded himself of a bottle of sherry that she had concealed in the towel cupboard near her bath.

He sat on his old leather, Italian chair listening to his favorite composer, Tchaikovsky, and lit a cigar, settling himself in for a 'Jim time', an occasion in time when he could relax and contemplate. His mind wandered back to his conversation with Edith. She was pleased and grateful that he had been able to finish the renovation of her workshop. "This would help the healing process following his son's passing. Dear Jim," he said to himself silently, "I miss you."

His mind wandered back to his two young ones. Jim would be okay. He was strong and kind, just like his Dad. Maggie, dearest Maggie, his favorite, she was the Temptress. He remembered the Christmas party when young Jim and Maggie kissed under the tree. He smiled. They looked so good together.

His mind wandered back to his own early days, when he listened for hours to Granddad Mitchell, his tales of his life in the old days. They had sat together for many hours on the old bench outside of their stone Cottage, overlooking Whitby Bay and the North Sea, listening to the tales of the sea. His grandfather had told him about of the voyages around the world by his great, great grandfather. He was a young midshipman on Captain Cook's H.M.S. Endeavor. On one voyage, they had, for the first time, watched the transit of Venus over the Sun, as they anchored off the island of Tahiti. He had watched the scantily dressed, dark skinned natives in their longboats, sweet, tempting and alluring. He described the feel of the soft white sand on his feet as he stepped ashore onto the tropical beaches of that beautiful, sunny, green foliage island. His first step on a foreign soil was a lot different to the sands of the cold beaches of his hometown, Whitby in Yorkshire.

After provisioning, the ship had sailed on calmer seas to discover the twin islands of New Zealand. The North Island, a paradise with beautiful beaches and lush green rolling hills, was in stark contrast to the mountains and snow covered terrain of the South Island. On glistening clear nights, there was a mass of twinkling stars visible in the heavens. Then, they sailed westward to a continent known as Australia, where they spent many weeks charting the east coast. Eventually, they sailed into Sydney Harbor with its huge profusion of plants and flowers; then onward to the northwest, to the tropical islands of New Guinea and Java. He told of their homeward voyage across the Indian Ocean, the huge rolling waves of The Cape of Good Hope, a place where the Indian Ocean meets the vast rolling seas of the Atlantic Ocean, the southern tip of Africa, then homeward bound to England.

As he regarded the gin and tonic, he gazed through the window overlooking the bottom fifty. He felt a chill reminding him of the cold nights as a young man in the North Riding of Yorkshire. Not always a pleasant memory, reminding him of years gone by, when as a boy, he had worked on his father's farm. It was hard work on the lean terrain of the North Yorkshire moors, far from the fertile lands of Cheshire. It was mostly sheep country, the spring wool their main cash crop. He remembered his father's passing, his derisory will, leaving a third of the land to him and each of his two brothers. Wanting no part of the bitter family feud that followed, he decided to sell his share and move from this beautiful part of Yorkshire, for the rolling hills of Cheshire with his love, Mary. He smiled remembering their first meeting at the Methodist Chapel when he, as a boy, gave his first sermon. He was aware that Mary was looking at him intensely. She had watched him play cricket in the summer months and rugby the winter. She was the Squire's only daughter. He remembered the day he asked her to marry him, her answer, "Yes, please." When her parents objected, she packed a bag and together they caught the train to Crewe, Jim with a hundred pounds Sterling in his pocket, and Mary with a smile on her face. "Nothing much had changed over the years," he said to himself as he felt her long fingers run through his dark black hair whispering, "It's time to get ready, my love."

# *Chapter 12*

During the middle of May 1940, Winston Spencer Churchill was appointed Britain's Prime Minister and Minister of Defense. The war was not going well on the European front. In the middle of May that year, Holland and Belgium surrendered to the might of the German army. At the beginning of June, Italy declared war on France and Great Britain. In late June, France capitulated and signed an armistice with Germany, leaving Great Britain to stand alone against the mighty force of the German war machine. The German army amassed on the French coast for a planned invasion of the British Isles. An island that had been blessed in the past with twenty miles of the English Channel, their traditional first line of Defense, a determined and brave British people, a somewhat bruised army following their defeat at Dunkirk, and an Air Force that was growing stronger with each day.

The German high command had realized that they would need supremacy in the air to be successful, and in the middle of July, German air force, mounted an air assault on Britain. Their objective was supremacy in the skies in southern England, and the destruction of Britain's fighting resources.

It was a warm night in July. Jim lay on his bed, exhausted by the day, hoping and praying that the German bombing would stop. The experience had been horrendous, along with the incessant droning sound of the bombers as they flew over his home. The flashing of the searchlight batteries and the noise of the anti aircraft fire hoping against hope to destroy some of the aircraft before the German bombers could unload their deadly cargo on the city and port of Liverpool. There was fear and apprehension in his soul waiting for what could be his last night on God's earth. That night Jim prayed with his mother that the bombs would drop on someone else's backyard. The following morning, there were reports of aircraft being shot down near the village. Later that day, after the Saturday morning soccer game, Jim and the gang walked down to the canal looking for the German aircraft. In the distance, they saw two aircraft, both guarded by Major Smith and the Home Guard. As they approached, they could see the pilot and some of the crew were still within the aircraft. The onlookers were cheering.

"Bastards!" exclaimed Jim quietly to himself. His thoughts were for the poor dead German Air Force crew who probably had children of their own at home, just like him. "What," he exclaimed, "is the world coming to." Later that night, Jim was awakened by the sound of the air raid warning. "Mum!" He yelled, "under the stairs quickly."

In the distance, he could hear the drones of the German bombers making their way over the village to their targets, Liverpool Docks. The sound of the bombs exploding as the planes came nearer and nearer to his home was incessant. He clung desperately to his Mum as they prayed together for deliverance. Then they heard a huge blast.

"Oh my God!" his mother yelled as their home shook on its foundations.

There were sounds of breaking glass, and things falling all over the place. The sound of whistling bombs diminished as the planes flew further and further away.

After a while, Jim attempted to leave their refuge. The door was jammed. They were trapped in their shelter. Jim made further efforts to release the door to no avail.

"What can we do?" his mum yelled. "Oh, Jim," she cried, "what can we do?"

He looked at her in that the dim light of the single candle. "Nothing, Mum" he cried. "Don't worry," he cried in an attempt to console her. "Someone will come to release us. Then I will make you a cup of tea." Later, which seemed like hours, they heard voices.

"Are you alright?" yelled a voice.

"Yes," yelled Jim. "The cupboard door under the stairs is jammed."

"Do not worry," they yelled, "we will get you out in no time."

Jim surveyed the scene as he and his Mum crawled out of their shelter.

"Oh my God!" exclaimed Mum. "It's a bloody mess."

"You are lucky to be alive," said Constable Onions. "The village has taken a battering. There are direct hits on houses along Chester Road, and there is a huge fire at the factory."

Later that morning, Granddad Mitchell arrived with his tractor-trailer and two of his farm laborers. Mum rushed to greet him "Granddad!" she cried as his arms encircled her tired and shaking body. "Thank God, you are here!"

In the distance, they saw the local Home Guard Sergeant pedaling his bike furiously towards them. "You will have to leave this area. There are unexploded bombs near your lake. The Army Corps will be along later today to deal with them. In the meantime Mr. Mitchell, get your family away from here."

That night, Edith lay in her bed at Granddad's farm. It had been a horrible day. She had lost many of her valued possessions: her husband's Westminster chime clock, their Sunday best dinner service a present from her mother and father, and a Singer sewing machine which was her prized position. The sleepless nights and the fear of further bombing had drained her energy. Her morale had sunk to new depths. "This bloody war," she cursed to herself, sobbing violently. "They have taken my man and they have nearly destroyed my home. Oh, Jim," she cried praying to her husband, "I need you my love, so much."

It was also a sleepless night for young Jim. He could hear his Mum sobbing in the next room. She was, by nature, a highly-strung person. The wrecking of the house had been the final straw in her struggle to maintain her sanity. He threw the cloths off his bed and slowly entered her room, "Are you okay, Mum?"

"No, Love, I feel as though I am going out of my mind."

"Shush, Mum" he murmured. "Let me make you a cup of tea. It will help you sleep."

The next morning, Edith awoke from a sound sleep. She smiled. Her head was lying on his chest, his arms encircling her, his long blond hair cascading over her face. Somehow, she felt refreshed. She smiled as she felt the strength of her son, comforting her. "Oh Jim" she cried to her husband. "When I look at him, I know, you have left me a good son. Thank you, my love."

By the end of the month, Granddad had organized the repairs on the cottage and outbuildings. "We were lucky," reflected Jim as he entered the cottage. The village had been hit badly by the bombings. A major part of the factory was destroyed, together with numerous houses. The death toll was high and the village mourned their losses.

The British Broadcasting Corporation (BBC) reported heavy damage and casualties to the cities of Liverpool, Manchester, Coventry, and Plymouth. In the following weeks, the air raids gradually reduced in frequency, and, by the middle of September, the bombing had stopped altogether.

The Germans had postponed their planned invasion of England. They had lost their bid for supremacy in the battle of the air. Thanks to be brave men and women of the Royal Air Force, who had won victory in the skies. Later that week, Winston Churchill spoke to the nation over the radio, announcing that the Battle of Britain was over. The nation had saved the day and he declared, "Never in the field of human conflict was so much owed by so many to so few."

The following month, a young pilot officer from the next village, 'an old boy' from Jim's school, had given a lecture at the school. The boys stood in awe as he described the history of flying. He talked about this famous fighter plane, the Spitfire, which together with the Hawker-Siddeley Hurricane Fighter Aircraft, had won the Battle of Britain and saved our country from the threat of German invasion. He spoke in a soft, cultured voice, portraying a deep sense of pride as he described the history of the Spitfire. "The fighter aircraft was designed originally as a seaplane, by the Super Marine Aircraft Company Chief designer, R. J. Mitchell, who had previously won three trophies for seaplane races in the early 1930s. The prototype conversion of the seaplane had been constructed in 1936, when it was fitted with armaments, machine guns and cannons, and was capable of speeds in excess of 350 mph.

"The class applauded as he finished his narration. Many of the boys at school had ambitions to join the Royal Air Force as pilots and were enthralled to listen to a real pilot speaking with such authority. He then asked the boys for questions.

Richard stood. "Sir," he asked, "why is the aircraft called the Spitfire?"

The young pilot smiled. "The word 'Spitfire,'" he replied, "date's back to Elizabethan times. It refers to a particularly fiery ferocious type of person." He paused for a moment surveying the class then added, "usually a woman." The all male assembly laughed.

The headmaster approached the podium, thanked the young Pilot Officer, wished him success in his future career then asked for three cheers from the boys. "Hip, Hip, Hooray! Hip, Hip, Hooray! Hip, Hip, Hooray!" They applauded.

# Chapter 13

It was a warm sunny morning in September 1943. The early morning sun shone through Edith Mitchell's bedroom window. She placed her hands over her head as she lay on her bed welcoming the day. She smiled. Today was a village holiday to celebrate the third anniversary of the Battle of Britain, a day of rest from her daily chores in her workshop, a fun day, a day to rebuild the morale of the village. The day started with a twenty over cricket match between the village and a Cheshire County 11. At Noon, the Women's Institute food stalls would open to feed the villagers. Aromas filled the air from a pig roast, numerous chickens on the bone, freshly baked bread, various puddings and Coca-Cola. The juices were all supplied from the American Air Force Base just outside of Warrington in Lancashire. After everyone ate, the carnival would begin with a fashion show on the lawn adjacent to the village hall. There were various stalls where one could win prizes, a rag doll game, role a penny, mini golf, and a host of other entertaining side stalls. Then, at five o'clock, the parade of our fighting forces would begin from the village hall to the sports ground. At eight o'clock, a dance was held in the village hall with glorious melodies provided by a Big Band Orchestra from the Air Force base near Warrington.

"Yes, it would be a fun day," said Edith to herself as she placed her hands underneath her head and stretched her lithe body for the last time. "Mitchell!" she yelled to her son, "time to get up. Your cricket match starts at ten o'clock." There was no reply. "Mitchell!" she yelled again. "Time to get up, my son. You, my son, have got a busy day ahead of you."

"Yes, Mum." He replied, "I know. What's for breakfast?" he asked.

"I do not know," she replied. "Ethel and Uncle Will are here in the next half hour and they're bringing goodies."

"I hope there are some sausages!" he exclaimed then added, somewhat selfishly, "I'm hungry."

Jim and the gang stood with their families awaiting the highlight of the day, the arrival of the military parade marking the anniversary of the Battle of Britain. The featured highlight of the afternoon was a fly-past of a single Spitfire fighter aircraft from the Royal Air Force Base near to the city of Liverpool. The village was proud of their recent effort to support the war against Nazi Germany, the purchase of their own Spitfire aircraft through the purchase of defense bonds supporting the Wings for Victory campaign.

In the distance, they could hear the sound of a Spitfire aircraft approaching. As it flew over the Village Green, "looped the loop," then circled over the parade and disappeared into the distance. The villagers applauded and a final salute was given by the Royal Air Force Squadron leader as he marched through the entrance gates of the sports ground.

"He has not changed much from last year," Jim observed. "Still the same nonchalant strut, his hair plastered down with Brylcreem hair lotion, and the top button of his uniform jacket open, a distinction usually reserved for experienced top fighter pilots."

"He looks like Clark Gable," said Mum. The memories of the film *Gone with the Wind* still lingered in her mind.

He was followed closely by the village brass band then by a contingent of the Women's Royal Air Force, led by a tall, slim, attractive, young female Air Force officer. "Wow!" he said to himself. "She is beautiful."

"Not bad," observed Brian recognizing Jim's attraction to her.

There was a contingent of nurses from the local hospital, followed by the Fire Brigade riding astride their engine, a detachment of Air Raid Wardens then a contingent of smartly dressed soldiers in Brown uniforms wearing what appeared to be Officers caps.

"They're Americans," said Richard knowledgeably.

"They don't appear to be much older than you boys," said Mum.

"Thank God, they have arrived", said Granddad referring to the American contingent in the parade. "Now, perhaps, we might win this bloody war. They helped us the last time," he cried, "and they will this time."

"One of them tried to date my sister," said Richard.

"Did she accept?" asked Derek.

"I don't think so. All he wanted was to get into her pants."

An armored car brought up the rear of the procession, a gift to the Home Guard from the local factory, an old truck that had been modified by the factory engineers. It looked very impressive as it moved down the road leading to the cricket pitch.

"If it doesn't stop now, they will mark the bloody cricket pitch," said Derek alarmed at on the possible damage to their hallowed ground.

"That's a bloody bit of cheek," said Brian as the vehicle proceeded to the center of the pitch.

The Captain of the home guard had a serious look on his face as he alighted from the contraption with a flourish, carrying with him a shiny new rifle. The spectators stood in awe as he marched ten paces from the vehicle, saluted, raised his rifle, took aim at the vehicle then fired a shot, presumably to prove the armored plating would stand up to enemy fire. This was the decisive moment. Richard laughed as the bullet entered one side of the vehicle and exited through the other.

"It's nothing to laugh at," said Granddad in a half-hearted attempt to rebuke Richard.

That evening the village social committee organized a dance in village hall to celebrate the anniversary, and to thank the members of the procession. Jim, as usual, had the first dance with his Mum. There was a sense of satisfaction within her as she looked at him.

"Jim Mitchell," she said. "You're getting taller and more handsome each day."

Jim looked at her and smiled, "Thanks Mum, but I'm also getting older."

"Yes, I know," she replied. "It's about time, that you danced with some of the local girls."

"Oh not again," he said to himself, Mum harping on about the local girls again. "Oh Mum!" he cried. "Leave it please!"

"I'm sorry, Love. Damn, Damn, Damn", she swore underneath her breath, "He is still missing Maggie." She had set a standard for future girlfriends and she was aware that few if any would attain that position.

Jim sat alone next to the bar sipping a half pint of Newcastle Brown Ale. His Mum's words had upset him. "God damn it!" he said to himself, swearing inwardly. "There are times when I wish she would keep her thoughts on my relationships to herself." It had been months since he had last seen Maggie and he missed her terribly. Jim remembered his mother's remark again. "Why don't you dance with some of the local girls? Because there isn't any girl remotely like Maggie here," he answered inwardly. *"God damn it!"* he swore aloud as he finished the last sips of the Newcastle Brown. He was angry and frustrated. His thoughts were for home. "It had been a good sports day, the team had won the cricket match," he said to himself. Suddenly his mood changed as he saw the Royal Air Force officer sitting by herself across the hall.

"Ask her to dance," said the confident side of his brain. You are just a boy, with little, or no, experience of the opposite sex. She will turn you down, you're just a boy," said the other side? Jim smiled remembering an old Proverb that Granddad had taught him a few years ago. "If at first you don't succeed, try and try again."

"Why not?" He said himself. "You're sitting here by yourself feeling bloody miserable, missing Maggie, and you are having a bloody awful time. Snap out of it," he said to himself, "ask her to dance."

Slowly, with a determination to succeed, Jim walked across the dance floor. He paused for a moment, and looked into her eyes. "Hello" holding out his hand to greet her, "My name is Jim Mitchell."

She smiled, her lips parting to reveal beautiful white teeth. "Hello, Jim Mitchell, my name is Lydia Henning."

He felt nervous and unsure of himself. He stuttered then muttered, "Oh hell, I've made a mess of it."

She laughed. "No you haven't, Jim Mitchell. Would you like to dance, or shall we just talk?"

"Can we talk, please? I am not much of dancer."

She smiled, "Ok."

Jim's confidence grew as they talked for a while. She was not only beautiful, but also intelligent. He mused to himself.

"Feeling better now?" she asked.

"Yes, thank you. You have been very kind. Would you like to dance? I won't tread on your toes."

She laughed, lifting up her legs and pointing to her feet. "Do not worry," she said, "these are regulation issue," pointing to her shoes, "they, Jim Mitchell, have strong toe caps."

Lydia Louise Henning smiled as his arm encircled her slim waist as they danced the last waltz. "Jim Mitchell", she said, "It has been fun, thank you."

"May I see you home?" he asked.

"I appreciate your offer but I have to travel to my base tonight. Maybe sometime in the future?" She smiled to herself as she entered her jeep. That was the boy that she had had a crush on when she was a girl. My, he has grown into a handsome young man.

"The summer holidays had passed remarkably quickly," said Brian to himself as he made the final survey of his gear, ready for the next term. He loved his village and the gang. They had spent many long hours on the kitchen garden project, making, as Derek would say, "a fair and reasonable profit." The work was hard, but it did afford the camping holidays. The first one to Snowdonia, he recalled, was a disaster. Derek broke the chain on his bike, the gang pitched their tent in the usual field, unfortunately, and the Farmer had forgotten to tell them that there was a bull in the field. Derek slipped and cut himself as they climbed the stony path to the top of Mt. Snowdon. Richard declared the camp a disaster zone. The decision to leave was hastened by thunder, lightning and heavy rain. A few days later, they made their way to a campsite on the bank of the Manchester Ship Canal. By then, the weather was perfect. They spent long summer evenings cooking and talking, visits from their parents and a regular visit from Richards's new girl friend. Jim had foreseen her visits and packed some additional plates and eating tools. The days were spent mostly swimming, watching the birds on the Mersey - flats, reading, much talking, and watching the merchant ships pass in their transitional journey to Liverpool from the Manchester docks. As they slowly past, led by a single tugboat. Brian would ask their destination. The answer was always the same, "Sorry lads, we can't tell you. It's classified."

Brian could see that Jim and Richard were very interested in joining the Merchant Marine. Jim had told them the stories that his grandfather had told him about a distant relative sailing to foreign parts.

Brian laid on his camp bed thinking about Jim's granddads, grandfathers, and father and their travels to foreign parts. One day, as they were talking, Jim announced his intention to travel around the world.

"That would be a good thing to do," said Richard. "Maybe I will join you."

That night, there last night together, Brian considered the future. He had spent a considerable amount of time talking to his father during the holiday, and it was with some reluctance that he agreed to seriously think about joining his father in the banking business after his 'A' levels. "This," he said to himself many times, "is not what I really want to do." His ideal dream would be to have lots of money, play cricket for his county side, and maybe the Marylebone Cricket Club. However, there was much at stake; the old man has the money and he enjoyed a good lifestyle. He remembered the parties that the Bank had given at his home before the war, mostly for the businessmen of the northwest of England. "Maybe he would give it a go!" he said to himself with a smile. "Maybe a position in the international branch, if you're lucky."

His thoughts turned to his life at home. He had known at an early age that he was lonely. It had been a number of years since he had felt love and affection from his parents. His father was consumed by the business of banking; his mother, the Chair of the Women's Institute, and several other committees was far too busy. At times, they didn't even talk to him. His old nanny, who had shown him love and affection, was now retired. His older sister, with whom he had never really bonded, had married at an early age, and had not been seen for some considerable amount of time. However, there was some solace in his life. He was really good at sports, and popular with the young ladies.

Above all, he enjoyed the company of the gang. They had readily accepted him as a member without question despite an apparent difference in class, an asset which he had done his best to conceal. Yes, they had come from a working-class background, but they were happy. They were all loved by their parents. "Mitchell, in particular, was adored by his mum," he reflected with a smile. "That was a loving relationship," he had observed. They were more like good friends, than mother and son. It was sad Jim's dad dying. He was a very kind man that had showed him affection and had willingly taught him some of the finer points of cricket and soccer. "Now," he said himself, "the dreaded moment has arrived. He must leave the village for his 'seat of learning,' leaving behind him the working-class village, and his friends that he loved, until the Christmas break."

The first year had been tough. He had to deal with the sixth form bullies. After many bruises he had gained there grudging respect, only to lose the few friends that he had. "Yes," he admitted to himself, he was lonely now and he must face another term. "Not again", he cried as the tears ran down his cheeks.

# *Chapter 14*

Jim stood in front of the solid oak door, guarding the entrance to his Master's study. He took a deep breath, and knocked on the solid brass knocker three times.

"Come," said a voice from the inside."

He opened the door slowly, within was the gaze of the horned rimed bespectacled figure immersed behind a mountain of paperwork that lay on the oak desk. "Mitchell Sir," muttered Jim.

"Yes, yes, I know who you are Mitchell." He said in a somewhat irritable voice. "What can I do for you?"

"I wish to be excused, Sir."

"Excused!" he yelled, "What do you mean, excused?" He said, as his attention moved from the pile of paperwork to focus on the youth standing in front of him.

This normally charismatic, tall youth, who always impressed him with his sporting ability. He was a brilliant midfield soccer player, Captain of the school cricket was physically hurting and he could feel the pain a "May I ask why?"

"My mother needs me."

A slow smile appeared on his face. In the thirty years of the ruling of the third form at this seat of learning, "This was a first", he said to himself silently.

"Is everything all right Mitchell?" He asked somewhat apologetically.

Jim paused, "Not really, Sir," he replied. "You see, today is the anniversary of my dad's death, and I know Mum needs me at home."

"Then you'd better run along Mitchell, hadn't you?"

Jim sat on the top deck of the double-decker bus, knowing it would be quiet. At this time of day, most of the passengers were old, and did not care to climb the steep metal steps of the stairway leading to the top seats. He closed his eyes and focused his thoughts on his Dad. Life without him had been tough. He missed the things that they used to do together, whilst it wasn't a lot. He knew Dad had other things to do, his band concerts, practice at sports, and the darts night at the Robin Hood pub.

The one thing he missed most, his dad was always there when he needed him. He remembered his Dad's words as he left their home that snowy morning in January to join his regiment, "You're the man of the house. Take care of your Mum." He had done so and he was proud. Jim loved his Mum with a passion. She was all he had and he was so dammed proud of her.

There was a hate inside his body, a deep hate. He hated war and all it stood for. He remembered listening to his Granddad as he talked about the First World War, of how the troops fought the trench warfare. When they were told to advance, any one that refused the order to go 'Over the top,' as they say, was shot by a line officer.

There were stories about Gallipoli, the landing, the futile climb. To climb the rugged cliffs was, by all accounts, a catastrophe of huge dimensions. Thousands upon thousands of New Zealand, Australian and British soldiers were killed in the operation. What he had seen and heard of this bloody war had fashioned his thinking. He was not pacifist, but he would never "turn his cheek." One thing he was sure off, he loved his England and he would give his life to defend this fair and pleasant land.

"Mum, I'm home!" he shouted as he opened the front gate to the path that led to their cottage.

She smiled when he she saw him, "You're home early, Jim," She replied as she opened the rear door of the cottage.

"Are you okay?" He asked as he saw her tear stained face.

"Yes, I think so", she said as he held her close.

"I just wanted to be with you," he replied as he kissed her forehead.

They sat for a while on the old wooden bench that Dad had made when they first moved into the cottage. He felt her hand clasp his. "Thank you, my son." She paused. "Would you mind if I went and had a lie down for a while?"

"That's okay, Mum," he replied. "Would you like me to wake you in a little while?"

"No, Love," she smiled, "it's been a hard day."

Jim walked down to the lake and sat awhile, thinking about Edith. He loved her dearly. Over the years, he had learned to respect her words of wisdom, her judgment, and above all her kindness and understanding for her fellow human being. He recalled his Dad's passing. During the weeks that followed, she had wandered around without purpose. The doctor had prescribed sleeping drafts, which was not acceptable to her. Slowly, with determination, she found the road to recovery. A couple of weeks later, Granddad gave her a box of annual plants and a new trowel. Jim arrived home from school one evening to find her on her hands and knees planting them.

"Don't they look lovely, Jim?"

"Yes they do, Mum," Jim smiled recognizing the first signs of her recovery.

One evening in the beginning of June the following year, Edith sat in her chair sipping her bedtime drink of 'ovaltine' awaiting The British Broadcasting Corporation evening news bulletin. She reflected on her day in the workshop, contemplating the future for the business, distinctly aware that one woman's effort to supplement her widow's pension had quickly grown into a small profitable business. The demand for her services now exceeded the capacity of her small workshop. "What to do?" She asked herself silently, contemplating the future. "Should she expand the business, or stay owning a small workshop in her garden, employing three young girls from the village?"

She looked across the room observing her son busying himself with his school homework. She felt the pang of conscience, aware that she was beginning to neglect him. Their early morning runs had become less frequent, and she missed a number of his soccer games. Somehow, she was losing touch with him. Her eyes closed; it had been a long day. In the distance, she heard his voice, "Mum it's time for the news!"

"This is the BBC evening News, read by Alva Liddell. The Supreme Allied Command announced, "That during the night and the early hours of this morning, the first of the series of landings on the European continent had taken place."

Edith jumped from her chair excited by the news. She threw her arms around him and yelled, "Hold me tight, Love, he didn't die in vain! We are going to win this bloody war!"

The following week, Edith received a letter from her friend Lucy, bringing her up to date on all the recent happenings in her family. Sheila, her eldest girl had a new boyfriend. His name was Cecil, a Flight Lieutenant in the American Army Air Force; apparently, they had been seeing a lot of each other during the last three months. He had now proposed marriage to her. A few days later Jim received a letter from his cousin, Maggie, telling him that she had passed the entrance exam for the London School of Dramatic Arts and would like to spend a few days with him, and his Mum, before she left to take up her scholarship in London.

Edith agreed immediately, knowing that it would please Jim. She was still painfully aware that the action she and Lucy had taken on their relationship sometime ago had not sat well with them. Their initial resentment was slowly passing, and she was aware that both of them had suffered badly, Jim hiding the matter deep inside, Maggie openly angry and rebellious as ever, depending on her mood. Edith had never been completely happy with the action she and Lucy had taken at the time, consoling herself at times that it was for the best. There were times when she fretted for Jim. He had worked so hard on the garden project slowly recovering from a blow that had affected his young life. She had encouraged him to attend the weekly dances at the village hall hoping that he would show some interest in one of the local girls, however, to no avail, refusing when asked to dance by his most ardent female admirers. She smiled. There was one exception, the young female Royal Air Force Officer.

# Chapter 15

I t was a glorious midsummer evening, as Jim sat on the old weathered-beaten wooden bench that his dad had constructed many years ago. The sun was slowly setting over the valley below. He smiled with satisfaction. This is his favorite time of day. There was a moment in time, when the sun directly hit the middle of the lake below, then spread endlessly towards the banks, illuminating the valley in the glow of red light that gathered with intensity until it climaxed, holding for a moment in time then slowly turning into the twilight of the day. He recalled the first time he had seen this glorious sight while sitting on his Dad's knee. At first, he was frightened, then, he felt the strength of his Dad's arm tighten around him. The memory of his Dad still languished in his mind. The pain of his death was slowly passing, the tears of sadness slowly turning into sweet memories of yesterday.

The sun was sinking slowly over the distant hills to the west as Jim considered the imminent arrival of his cousin Margaret Bernadette O'Toole. She was the key that opened the door to the memories of their last meeting, a meeting that had brought sadness into their lives. Their parent's edict on their future relationship had destroyed their childhood dreams, their hopes and aspirations for the future, and realization that the hope they had shared since they were kids together had come to its inevitable conclusion. Now, with her visit, the wound was opening again, revealing the hurt that he had suffered during the months of separation. He had worked hard to the exclusion of all things, hoping that time would pass quickly and with time, the wounds would heal. During this time, he had learned the wisdom of maturity. The innocence of their childhood was slowly passing and replaced by another feeling, a feeling of warmth.

# Chapter 16

T he O'Toole family's Westminster chime struck six o'clock on what
promised to be a hot summers day in July 1944 Maggie had beaten
the usual rush to the bathroom and stood putting the finishing touches
to her hair, the length of which now extended to her waist line. "One
day," she vowed to herself, "I would wear it short." She smiled. The
decision on her hair length and been made many years ago, just days
after she had told Jim for the first time, that she loved him. In turn, he
had told her that he liked her hair long. She still did not know to this
day, what prompted her cousin Jim to make that remark, but he did
and she had kept it that way. She dressed slowly with attention to every
detail. Suddenly, she felt an air of anticipation overwhelm her. She was
nervous. "This was not unusual," she said to herself, in a vain attempt
to control herself. The last days had been filled with anticipation of
seeing him again. Now, she would be with him by noon today. "Is it
real?" she said looking into the mirror. The reflection replied, "You bet
your sweet arse it is girl!"

"The plan was working," she said to herself. If he had visited her,
they would have been followed throughout his stay. Now they were in
charge of Aunt Edith. She felt comfortable with that situation. During
the months since she had last seen Jim, she had plenty of time to consider
the problem she and Jim had set for their parents. Their relationship
was born out of love, the love of two kids, brought together by a family
relationship. Their friendship built on the respect for each other's

abilities. There was a tenderness in their relationship, an understanding there for all to see. They had done everything together. They studied together, walked together, swam together, listened to music together and danced together; they were above all, friends. "This," she said adamantly, "would never change."

"Shadwell Lane", shouted the bus conductor, "Your stop, young Lady." He said addressing Maggie.

"Thank you kindly, Sir," she said as he placed her suitcase on the rear, lower level of the red bus. Her heart was beating strongly as the bus slowly came to a stop. As Jim approached, their eyes met with intensity that only they knew. She felt his strong hands cup her face, a touch that felt so tender to her soul. They stood, oblivious to the world.

"Welcome home, Maggie," he murmured as his arms encircled her tiny waist.

She smiled. "Thank you, Jim," she replied looking into his deep blue eyes. "It's so bloody good to be with you, my love."

Later that day they walked to the lake. "Who's a clever young Lady?" said Jim.

She smiled, "Thank you, Jim that sounds good coming from you."

He could tell from the smile on her face that she was looking forward to joining the Academy and becoming an actress one day. "Tell me more," said Jim.

"There is not a lot to tell really. It's a two-year training program which includes scene study, voice, movement, auditioning skills, cold reading techniques, monologue presentation, and acting on stage."

"Are you looking forward to it?" he asked.

"You know me, Jim. One day I am full of it, the next I am as scared as hell, frightened out of my pants. The thing that really scares me, Jim, is that this is the first time in my life I am leaving home, and leaving you. At the moment I am a big fish in a small bowl; however, when

I get to the Academy, I will be a little fish in a very big bowl, and it scares the hell out of me."

"You will be okay, Maggie," replied Jim confidently. "You are a survivor. You always have been and always will be. Maggie Bernadette O'Toole," Jim said emphatically, "you will do well."

Jim felt her grip on his hand tighten. Suddenly, there were tears in her eyes. "What happens if I fail?"

"Don't cry Love. If that happens at least you will have tried, and you have got the idea out of your system. Then you can come home and go to medical school and become a doctor."

She smiled. "Mitchell, what would life be without you? You have always guided me haven't you?"

"Yes, I always have and I always will," he said affectionately.

"That's the one thing that they can't take away from us," she cried. "Jim, Jim, it hurts, my love, it really hurts. Hold me for a minute, if you would."

"Shush Maggie," he cried as he wiped the tears from her face. There was a smile on her face as he gently asked, "What have you planned for the rest of the week?"

"I would like to see a couple of days of cricket. Yorkshire is playing Lancashire at Old Trafford. The Halle Orchestra is performing at the Gaumont Cinema in Chester. It's a good program, including Dvorjak's, "New World Symphony." I would like to do some swimming. Granddad has invited us to stay for couple of days. Then we must go home for my graduation. Oh God," she exclaimed, "I hope that I have passed with a decent score."

Jim smiled, "You really are becoming a worry guts Maggie, aren't you?"

"Yes, I suppose I am. Jim, I have worked hard to be the best student in my year. Anything less than first is not good enough for me. Can you understand that?"

"Yes, I can Maggie. You have always been that way, since the first day that you and I met," he paused, "We are just a pair of egotistical kids trying to reach our ambitions in life."

"Mitchell, I would give it all up just to be with you," she replied looking deep into his eyes. "What we are doing, the pair of us, is not our choice is it?"

"No it's not, Maggie," Jim said holding her close looking deep into her eyes. "It's not, Maggie, my love. Please do not let us go there. Let's have some fun together while we may."

The following morning Maggie rose early from her bed and made tea and biscuits for her Aunt Edith and Jim. She was excited for the day. "This," she said to herself, "will be Jim's day. Time to get up, Mitchell, tea and biscuits in your Mum's room." There was no reply. "Shake a leg, Mitchell!" she shouted. "It's a glorious day and your Mum would like you to read to her before we go to Old Trafford."

They sat on his mother's bed as they had done many times in the past enjoying the refreshing Darjeeling tea and Garibaldi biscuits. Jim selected one of his mother's favorite yarns, *Lorna Doone*. She smiled as he began. "Chapter one, Elements of Education." Over the years, she had enjoyed his readings. His elocution had improved tremendously, and she was pleased.

"If anybody cares to read a simple tale, told simply, I, John Rudd of the parish of Oar in the County of Somerset, your man and churchwarden, have seen and had a share in some of the doings of this neighborhood which I will try set down in order. God sparing my life and memory and many who light upon this book should bear in mind that only I write for the clearing of our parish from some ill fame, and calamity but also a thing, which will like Schroeder, will appear too often in it. To wit, that I am nothing more than a plain and lettered man, not read in foreign languages as a gentleman might be nor gifted with any long words. Even in mine own tongue save what I have one from the Bible or Master Sir William Shakespeare, who in the face of common opinion I value highly, in short, I am an ignoramus, but pretty well for a yeoman."

Maggie smiled as Jim finished the reading of the second chapter. His mum, as usual, had work to do.

"Time to go Mitchell," said Maggie.

"Give me thirty minutes, I will be ready."

"My, you look pretty," said Jim as she walked into the living room wearing a black and white polka dot dress. A black hat trimmed in white accentuated her beautiful long neck- line.

As they entered the main pavilion stands, Maggie was greeted by an older gentleman with long grey hair. "Alec, how nice to see you," she said as she extended her hand towards him. He smiled. He was gallant and a gentleman of the old school with an air of grace. He kissed her hand. Jim smiled to himself. These were some of the old customs, which had somehow sadly disappeared with the advent of the war. "Alec, I would like you to meet my cousin, Jim. I have spoken about him many times. He plays the game in Cheshire."

"Nice to meet you, young Sir, he said, "Welcome."

"Thank you kindly, Sir," Jim said in reply.

"Shall we take our seats?" said Maggie anxious to see the game.

Cricket is a team sport, which involves two teams of eleven players on each side. Similar in many respects to the American baseball game, it is played all over the world: India, Australia, New Zealand, South Africa, Canada, the Netherlands and in some parts of the United States. During the match, the team that wins the toss elects either to bowl or to bat. The batsmen, eleven in number, attempt to score runs from the opposing team's bowling; once either team are bowled out, they retire and their opposition would come in to bat, and they in turn could bowl. Jim smiled remembering a cartoon in one of the newspapers, the Daily Express, illustrating a young boy sitting in the stands watching a game of cricket and trying to explain to an American Sergeant the intricacies of the game. The American Sergeant, resplendent his uniform, seemed somewhat perplexed at the explanation as indeed was the usual case.

Lancashire won the toss and decided to bat. The opening batsmen were Cyril Washbrook and Jack Price, both of whom had played for Lancashire for a number of years. There was an air of great expectancy as they walked out to the pitch to the spectator's applause. The decision to bat was well founded by lunchtime. They had scored 120 runs and the loss of Price's wicket. The spectators rose to applaud the batsmen as they left the field of play. "Will you join us at the lunch, Maggie?" asked Alec as they made their way to the Members dining room.

"Yes, please, Alec. Perhaps I could buy you a glass of wine?"

"No, young Lady, lunch will be on me. Your membership has come through and we must celebrate." He smiled. "Are you aware Maggie O'Toole, that you are only the third lady member in the club?"

Maggie beamed. "Thanks to your sponsorship, Alec, I will always be grateful to you."

"My pleasure ma'am," he said gallantly bowing toward her.

In recent years under the direction of the club secretary, the ground had made some considerable improvements and was now regarded as one of the finest in county cricket grounds in the land. Jim admired Alec for his British ways, and in particular, his kindness.

Alec looked at the menu, "Oh good, Lancashire hot pot. You must try this Maggie, I am sure you will enjoy it."

During her formative years, Maggie had enjoyed the game of cricket, both at Old Trafford, where she was now a member, and also watching Jim and his dad play for village club. She was well versed in the art of this famous game, and she was well at home with the members who listened to her every word. As she answered questions from knowledgeable guests around the lunch table, she spoke with an air of confidence as to the outcome of the match in the game that she loved with a passion. Jim watched her face as she smiled. She was truly a Lady for all seasons.

During the next two days, the ebb and flow of the match fell into Lancashire's favor. Despite gallant innings by Yorkshire, there was much celebration in the Pavilion that late afternoon, and the young Lancashire players had matched the might of Yorkshire in a memorable game.

It was time to leave. "Goodbye Alec, thank you for your kindness."

"My pleasure," said Alec as he gallantly bowed to her. He regarded Jim. "Goodbye James. It was nice to meet you, please come again now that Maggie is a member. I am sure it will be easier for you. Goodbye Maggie," he smiled again and kissed her on the cheek.

"They are such sweet darlings are they not, Jim?"

The concert hall the following afternoon was crowded as Jim and Maggie made their way to the balcony, front row seats. Over the years, as kids and young adults, they had learned to appreciate classical music. Under the tutelage of Aunt Lucy and Grandma, the appreciation had turned into a great love, which had strengthened the bond between them. "This is a special occasion, Jim," said Maggie as she enthusiastically turned the pages of the program notes. She smiled as she watched her cousin and murmured to herself, "Jim Mitchell I am going to miss you so much."

Jim Mitchell regarded his cousin. This was a special occasion. It was moments like this when he would miss her, the way she held his hand throughout the concert, the animated applause, and her enthusiastic love of music.

"You look good, Maggie," Jim whispered.

"Well thank you kindly," she replied. Then with a quizzical look on her face she declared, "Young Sir, you clean up very nicely."

The lights dimmed as the slight figure of Sir Malcolm Sergeant stepped to the podium and the applause of the audience assembled in at the Gaumont Theatre. The program that Sunday afternoon was particularly splendid: Rachmaninoff's, "Piano Concerto Number Two in C minor," followed by the "Rhapsody on a Theme from Paganini, Opus 43."

"This will please you," said Maggie as she read the final piece of the comps concert, "The 1812 Overture."

"Oh it was good for the soul," said Jim referring to the final strains of "The 1812 Overture." The audience applauded rapturously and raised the orchestra to their feet three times.

"It was beautiful, Jimmy. It really was beautiful," she said as she flung her arms around his neck. "Oh darling man," she said, "Life is so good when you are around." Then with a vivacious smile said, "Let us go eat, Jim, I am starving."

"Good evening Sir, good evening Madam," welcomed the maitre d' as they entered Grandma's favorite restaurant. "Will you be dining with us this evening?" he asked.

"Yes," replied Maggie. "My grandmother, Mrs. Mary Mitchell, recommended that we have one of the booths on the right-hand side."

"Oh yes, I remember her, good choice Madam," he said as he led the way to the table for the evening.

Maggie was in the one of her flamboyant moods having just enjoyed one of her favorite concerts. "Mitchell," she said, "Shall we splash out and have a half bottle of wine?"

"Yes, Maggie, that would be nice, but it's a bit expensive, isn't it?"

"Huh," she replied, "I am paying for it."

"Would you like to order, Sir?" asked the waiter, as he approached the table. "Yes, we will have a rack of lamb for two and a bottle of the Beaujolais," said Jim assertively.

"Good choice, if I may say so, Sir. I will bring the wine and your food should be ready in about twenty minutes."

"A rare feast, Jim," observed Maggie.

The conversation over the meal covered the full spectrum of education, politics, their pasts and their future.

When the waiter approached, Maggie complimented him on the meal, and in particular, on the bottle of Beaujolais.

"Thank you Ma'am," he replied.

Jim looked a little perturbed. She smiled graciously, "Don't argue, Mitchell," she said. "Granddad sent me a check. Aren't they just so bloody wonderful," she said as they lingered over the last sips of their wine. They had shared the joys of just being with each other. The touch of a hand, a smile, there was tenderness about them, a feeling that only they knew. There was a twinkle in her eyes. "Do you think that they would put us up for the night?"

Jim, in the process of drinking his wine, swallowed the wrong way.

"Are you okay, Jim?" she asked. She said concerned, "I was only joking!" She smiled, as he recovered, "Maybe not, it has been a wonderful day." As their eyes met, she murmured, "Are you sure my love?"

His hand touched hers. "Yes Maggie," he said with feeling. "Yes, I am sure. Don't spoil it. Maggie, it would change the whole of our lives. You know it, I know it."

The bus slowly made its way to the village as she held Jim's hand.

Then with a wry smile she murmured, "Oh hell, and its graduation day tomorrow."

Jim entered the assembly Hall, and sat with the family. "This," he said to himself, "was her day. The day when she had earned her degree; the day she had worked so hard for over the years." There was a time when Jim thought that studying had come easily to her. The last two years of her education had been tough on her, and they had talked about it many times.

One by one, the students rose to receive their graduation certificates and Jim saw Maggie sitting with the remaining student. The final prize, her hour of anticipation was upon her. Her adversary for the ultimate prize was the tall blond haired young man that he had met at the dance.

"Robert Mills," called the Usher.

"She's got it," yelled Jim in delight. Maggie was the top of her class for her year.

"Maggie Bernadette O'Toole," called the Usher.

Maggie stood and regarded the audience then slowly walked to the podium to the applause of her fellow students and the audience. Slowly she retrieved a note from her pocket and held it in her hand, then tore the pages apart. She turned to the Proctor and bowed. "Sir, this is not a day for speeches. It is a day when I, Maggie O'Toole, thank you for all the hard work, kindness and understanding over the years. You have seen my lows, and I stand before you on a high today." Slowly she turned to the audience. "Ladies and Gentlemen, this is a day to thank my family. They have seen my agony and my frustrations over the years. To the head of my family, my Granddad, thank you for being here. I love you my sweet, kind man." Slowly the emotions of the day were taking over. "To my Dad, the best in the world, thank you for your guidance, your compassion, and your tolerance over the years. I will never be able to thank you enough. To my uncles and aunts, thank you for your kindness and your love, and my sisters Prudi and Kerry, thank you, dear sisters, for always being there for me; it hasn't been easy. Finally, my sweet cousin, Jim, thank you for your encouragement, your understanding, and your support. Over the years, you have seen my lows and my highs." Her hand touched her lips. "I love you, Jim

Mitchell," she said with emotion. The faculty smiled. The audience applauded. She threw her hat into the air, jumped off the stage ran to her father and flung her arms around him. "This is a good day for the Irish! And good day for our family," she yelled.

Jim smiled, "A good day for Maggie Bernadette O' Toole!"

That evening the family celebrated Maggie's graduation in the private dining room of the local pub; a hostelry that had become famous in 1850's having housed the roundhead, Oliver Cromwell, on his way to yet, another battle with the royalists.

All eyes focused on Granddad as he rose to toast his favorite grandchild. He was in fine form. "Maggie Bernadette O'Toole, this is a proud day for you and for this, our family. Over the years we have watched you grow with pride," he smiled, "through your good days, and indeed we were there for you on your bad days. You have charmed us with your winning ways and tonight we are here as your family on your graduation from the college," he paused, "and also sadly to say goodbye, Maggie, for a while, and wish you good fortune in your chosen profession. Godspeed and keep you safe. To Maggie Bernadette O'Toole, may your success in the world continue, my little Irish rose." He paused. "The toast is, Maggie Bernadette O'Toole, we wish you joy and success in the life before you."

The family rose from their seats. "To Maggie," they replied.

Maggie rose slowly from her seat. There was an air of confidence about this young lady Jim had not seen in many a day. "Today," she said, "has been a good day." She smiled, "I think that I deserve one." The audience laughed. "Over the years, you my family have sustained and nourished me with your kindness and your understanding. Mum, Dad, I am proud to be your daughter, as I am indeed proud to to be part of this loving family. Thank you, generous family, for your support over the years. I love you." She paused, "I have been fortunate to have this wonderful opportunity placed before me. This is a challenge, which I savor with all my body and readily accept. There will be good times, and there will be bad times," she smiled, "but that's the story of my life, isn't it? Thank you for being with me this day to share in my success." There was a tear in her eye as she murmured, "You ain't got rid of me yet!"

Later that evening, Jim and Maggie strolled hand in hand in the moonlight to her secret place on the banks of the canal.

"How did I do, Jim?" she asked referring to the speeches of the day.

Jim looked deep into her eyes, "You did well, Maggie, I am so bloody proud of you."

"Oh, Jim," she said flinging her arms around his neck. "Don't you see that's all that matters to me? You have sustained me over the years. You have always been there for me. Hold me tight, Jim, hold me tight." Her hands clasped his cheeks. "You and me together would have been glorious. Hold me tight, Jim, hold me tight. Kiss me hard, sweet man. It's going to be a long time before we see each other again. Oh God I am going to miss you like hell."

Maggie Bernadette O'Toole sat alone in the first-class compartment of the noon train to Waterloo Station, London, reflecting on the happenings of the last few days with her family. It had been perfect, the happy days with Jim and her family, her success with her A-levels and now she said to herself, "You are all alone in a new world. Yes," she admitted to herself, "it is frightening; it's going to be hell." Throughout her life she had strived be the 'best of the best' and now, she would start a new career and face the challenge that she knew was upon her. Yes, there had been disappointments in the past and she had overcome them. The hurt that she and Jim had suffered were now behind her. She was starting a new life. Hopefully, she would meet new friends, knowing there would be times when she would miss her family, the very heart of things that had buoyed her up over the years. Throughout that time, she could always call on the love of her Mum and Dad; but most of all, she would miss the strength of her cousin Jim. Slowly, the tears fell down her cheeks. Yes, she was frightened and then she remembered some of Jim's words as they parted. "You are made of tough stuff, Maggie and you will succeed, of that you can be assured." She smiled remembering his words then murmured to herself, "You will be a little thing in a very large pond and you will get used to it one day. Maggie Bernadette O'Toole you will be successful; you will be a star." She cried through the tears. Then she smiled remembering the Christmas of years ago at the Christmas table, when she said, to Jim, "One day, I will be a star, then you and Granddad will have to pay to come and see me." She smiled remembering those happy days, glorious days, a wonderful life. The tears dried as she reminisced over the past. There were times when Jim had told her that she was a pain in the arse. He was right of course. He was the only one that could tell her that. He was the only one that really enjoyed her high days and supported her low days. "Dear Jim," she cried, "I love you, I guess I always will."

# Chapter 17

"This is the BBC home service. Yesterday morning, at 2:41 a.m., at the headquarters of General Jodl, the representative of the German high command, and Grand Admiral Doenitz, the designated head of the German State, signed the act of unconditional surrender of all German land, sea, and air forces in Europe to the Allied Expeditionary Force and simultaneously to the Soviet High Command," so spoke Winston Spencer Churchill announcing victory in Europe.

"The lights went out, and the bombs came down," Winston Churchill's words as he spoke on the evening of our victory in Europe May 1945, so ended the Second World War in Europe. The nation had stood alone against Germany and the axis forces. In the words of Winston Churchill, "My dear friends, this is your hour. This is not a victory of any party or any class. It's a victory of the great British nation as a whole. These ancient islands were the first to draw the sword against tyranny. After a while we were left all alone against the most tremendous military power the world had ever seen, and we were alone in this struggle for a whole year."

Jim looked at his Mum; her expression was one of disbelief. We had been at war with Nazi Germany, since that memorable Sunday in September 1939. That was truly the time when the lights went out and the bombs began to fall.

They had suffered through the long years: the loss of his Dad, the threat of the German invasion, food rationing, the loss of friends and family in the air raids. The uncertain stress of never knowing what would be happening in the next day, the fall of Europe. They had stood alone against a mighty enemy the likes of which, the world had never known, in the history of man.

The village had lost ten of their best men during the fighting against this merciless opponent. Jim knew that life would never be the same again. England had suffered, and he had grown much older than his years.

Now was the time for the villagers to celebrate, each in their own way. They were battered and bruised. There was a smile on his lips. The nation with its "John Bull attitude" had borne of the thrust of the war, and the country had survived, and was victorious. Jim looked into his mother's eyes as she held him close.

"Tonight my love," she murmured, "we will celebrate and give thanks. Tomorrow will count the cost."

Jim and his Mum walked to the village hall together, hand in hand. In the glow of the village streetlights the Union Jack flags were flying. The patriotic bunting Red White and Blue was strewn across the streets. Street parties were in full swing to celebrate the victory over Nazi Germany. The villagers were dancing in the streets. The dark clouds of war had been lifted from the nation. Jim remembered Churchill's words, "The lights went out, and the bombs dropped." It was then that he felt for the first time in many years, as though a burden had been lifted from his shoulders. The load felt lighter, and he mused, "The lights were on again."

Lydia Louise Henning sat at her dressing room table, preparing herself for the evening celebration at the village hall. She was nervous, unsure of herself. Suddenly her body began to shake uncontrollably. The memories of her interrogation by the Gestapo flooded back. They had tortured and savaged her body, a horrific experience. She had survived, the cost, the latent fear of men. The decision to attend the dance tonight had not come easy for her. She had been isolated from the world at her parents home for several months recovering from her ordeal, her only visitors, apart from the medical staff, were her close friends June and her husband John.

"Are you okay, Love?" exclaimed June as she entered Lydia's bedroom.

"I don't really know," she replied. "Oh June, I am scared," she cried. "Would you mind if I didn't come with you?"

"Yes, I would," she replied emphatically. "It's going to be a fun night; and God knows you need one, Lydia Henning. We are celebrating the end of this bloody war. Remember girl, you played an important part in the victory. Don't you forget it? Now, snap out of it, and get ready!"

Lydia was somewhat shocked by her friend's remarks. They had jolted her mind back to reality. She smiled through her tears, "Thank you my friend." Her mind wandered back to the last village hall function that she had attended to celebrate the Wings for Victory parade. She smiled. That was the night that she had met young Jim Mitchell again. She had been the young Royal Air Force officer leading her team in the parade through the attending the village dance, and Jim, the village boy, had walked across the dance floor, in obvious fear and trepidation, to ask her for a dance? She smiled as she remembered his words "Oh hell! Sorry, I made a bloody mess of it." Now, apart from her father and John, he was the only man that she felt comfortable with, "Would he be there? Would he remember her? Did she care?" She thought as looked into the mirror. "That was a bloody stupid remark, Henning." The memories of her ordeal were slowly receding into the background. Of course she cared. She had enjoyed herself that evening. Little did he know that she had a crush on him since the first time they had met at a football match before the war. His Granddad had introduced her family to Jim.

"Nice to meet you, Miss," he said politely, then winked at her with an audacious smile.

Much to her surprise, she winked back at him and blushed. There was something about this boy that she liked. Suddenly, she felt pangs of anticipation. Somehow she knew that they would meet again. The sense was overwhelming. Her face brightened.

"Are you ready, Lydia?"

"Yes June" she replied. Then under her breath she murmured, 'Too bloody right I am ready." She was on a high.

There were smiles of recognition as she strode purposefully across the floor of the village Hall. Two weeks ago, the local newspaper, the Chronicle had published an article, its headline: "Local Girl Decorated for Gallantry," giving an account of her wartime experiences. She entered the Hall with her head high, to the applause returning their smiles of recognition, all the while scanning the room for Jim. "Where are you?" she asked herself as she sat at the table.

"Drinks ladies?" asked John.

"Small gin and tonic," replied June.

He looked at Lydia. She looked radiant. There was a smile of anticipation on her face. "Lydia?"

"A pint of Newcastle Brown ale and a Hennessy brandy chaser, if you please, Sir." Her sense of anticipation to see Jim slowly diminished. There was no sign of him. Suddenly she felt disappointed. "Oh well, that's life," she said as she drank a mouthful of beer. Then with one gulp, she swallowed the brandy. "Oh what the hell!" she cried to herself.

The American Army Air Force Band was playing the Big Band music of the Glenn Miller Orchestra as Jim the entered the village Hall. The party was in full swing. During the last two years, the village had adopted the band, many of whom were romancing the village girls. They were lonely, miles from home, fighting a war. Many of them were killed in daylight raids over Germany. There were good times. Jim smiled remembering the previous summer and the occasion when the village cricket team had attempted to teach them the game of cricket. Somehow, they could never get the hang of it. The following week they turned up with baseball bats. It had been a fun time: the Yanks batting with their beloved baseball bats, the Brits batting with their cricket bats. Yes, it had been a fiasco, but it had been fun. God only knows they needed some fun. The war had taken a heavy toll on both men and aircraft from their base.

"Do you think your Mum will buy us a beer?" Said Richard as he joined Jim, Brian, and Derek at the bar the Village Hall.

"I would hope so," said Jim. "Four half pints of Newcastle Brown ale, please landlord," then added, "Mum will pay for it."

Henry Gibbons, the barman smiled as he poured four half pints of Newcastle Brown Ale. He admired the young men standing before him. They were the backbone of the village sports. They had flair. Yes, they were cocky at times and occasionally a pain in the backside. 'The gang' as they were known, was led by Richard Stevens, the young man who had encouraged his youngest son Alan to play cricket a couple of years ago. Now he held a regular place in the Junior 11.

"Watch out," said Derek, "Your Mum is approaching, nine o'clock, Mitchell."

"Good evening gentlemen," said Edith as she approached. "Rumor has it that I am buying the beer tonight?"

"Thank you Mrs. Mitchell," replied the gang. "Would you like a drink?"

"Not at the moment thank you, Derek, but I would like a dance," She replied focusing her attention on her son.

Jim smiled, "I guess I am the lucky one."

She curtsied deeply. "Thank you, my son." Edith broke the silence as she danced with the second love of her life. "Are you enjoying yourself?"

"Yes," he replied. "Tonight Mum, we are going to have a ball."

"Good, you deserve to," she said. "You, my boy, have worked dammed hard. It's over! It's over!" she cried. "Jim, the bloody war is over. Let's go to the bar and have a drink together, just you and me, my love."

"Cheers, Mum!" exclaimed Jim. "Cheers, my son," she replied. "Here's to us," as they raised their glasses, "and the memories of the passing years." It was a poignant moment for Edith. She had lost her man; yet she had gained a son, a chip off the old block. Their moments together were brief, their thoughts profound.

Derek approached. "Hello, Mrs. Mitchell, may I have this dance?"

"Well thank you, young Sir."

Richard laughed as he watched them on a dance floor. "Mitchell" he said, "I think Derek is 'chatting up your Mum.'"

"You are joking, of course," he replied somewhat amused. "Mum is the only partner that he has that doesn't complain when he treads on her feet."

Jim and the gang, sat around their usual table discussing the soccer, which, by all accounts, had been a disaster for the village team. There was no optimistic outlook for the upcoming cricket season. "She's coming back again," said Richard.

"Who?" asked Jim.

"You're Mum of course"

"Jim Mitchell, I have just met an old friend of your dad's, John Bromley, and he would like to meet you."

"Hello, young Jim," he smiled as they shook hands in greeting. "I understand from Edith that you play football?"

Jim laughed. "She is my only supporter, and she has a great capacity for exaggerating what little talent I have."

"If you're half as good as your dad, I would like you on my team next year."

"Thank you, Sir," said Jim. "I won't let you down," replied Jim while glancing several time at the ladies standing next to John Bromley.

"I am so sorry, where are my manners! Let me introduce you. This is my wife, June."

"Nice to meet you, Jim Mitchell. This is my friend, Lydia." Jim turned to regard an immaculately dressed, auburn haired lady standing in front of him.

"Remember me?" asked Lydia.

"Yes-yes," he replied excitedly, "I do." His smile broadened. "Nice to see you again, Lydia," he mumbled. "Didn't we meet at the Wings for Victory dance a couple of years ago?"

"Yes we did." They stood from moment, smiling in remembrance.

"Jim Mitchell, are you going to ask me for a dance? Or, are we going to stand around grinning like Cheshire cats all night?"

There was a silence. Heads turned, one could hear a pin drop. For once in her life his Mum stood, her mouth ajar unable to speak.

"Oh good heavens," she said to herself. "He's found another." Her smile broadened as she declared, "Oh My."

Jim broke the silence, "Lydia may I have this dance?"

"Well thank you, Sir, "she said, "I would love to dance with you, James Mitchell," surrendering to him with a deep curtsy.

They danced to a slow waltz looking into each other's eyes, enjoying the moment. Slowly Jim's confidence returned and he smiled, "It's good to see you again Lydia."

"Well thank you, Sir; it's good to see you. It's been a long time." She paused. "Sorry about my invitation," she said with a slightly embarrassing laugh. "I tend to do that at times."

Jim looked at her and laughed. "That, Lady, is the understatement of the year. I have never seen my Mum look so dumbfounded in her life. The only one that was not shocked was June."

"I am not surprised," she said with a laugh, "She is my best friend and understands my moods."

There was an air of confidence about Jim now. Gone was the shy, young man who had nervously approached her at their last meeting, celebrating the Battle of Britain. She smiled to herself. He had matured. There was something about this tall blond haired young man that intrigued her.

"When do you leave the village again?"

"I don't, "she replied. "I am staying for a while. At the moment I am living with John and June until my home is redecorated."

"Where?"

"Rose cottage."

"Wow," replied Jim, "that's a beautiful house, way off the beaten path."

She smiled, "Peace and solitude, Jim."

The music stopped. Jim bowed and led her back to her table. "Thank you Lydia, I really did enjoy the dance. It's so nice to see you again."

She smiled, "Yes, it is, come join us."

Yes-yes, she said to herself with a broad smile. There was an inward glow of warmth in her body and she felt good.

The celebrations were coming to an end, and the orchestra leader announced "the last dance" of the evening. It had been a fun evening. Their first together

Suddenly, he held her hand and looked deep into her eyes, "May I have the last waltz ma'am?"

She curtsied low, her eyes smiling as she regarded him. There was empathy between them. As they danced, she looked into Jim's eyes; then, in a low voice whispered, "Jim, thank you. I have enjoyed this evening. It's been a while since I have enjoyed myself as much as this."

"Me too," he replied enthusiastically.

"Your Mum is going to John and June's home for coffee. Would you like to join us?"

"I would love to, Lydia, but I can't," he faltered. "I promised Mum to escort one of her girl's home."

"Maybe another time, we don't seem to have much luck do we?" she murmured. "Good night Jim, sleep-tight."

What are you laughing about?" Jim asked as they walked along the moonlit country lane to Joyce's home.

"You," he replied. "You're walking like a drunken sailor."

"No I am not!" she replied defensively. Then after consideration replied "Yes I suppose I am. It was a good night."

"Did you enjoy yourself?" Jim asked.

"Yes, Jim, it was wonderful, thanks for bringing me home. Would you like some coffee before you go?" she asked.

"That would be nice, thank you," Jim replied.

"Sit ya down," said Joyce as they entered the living room. "Over there, by the fire place on the settee. Jim looked a little apprehensive. She laughed, "Don't worry, Jim Mitchell I ain't going to eat ya."

"Do you like working for my Mum?" said Jim attempting to start a conversation.

"Yes," she replied. "She is a very nice lady and we love working for her." She paused for a moment, "What makes you tick, Jim Mitchell?"

"I don't know really know," he replied. "I suppose being who I am."

"Who are you?" she inquired.

"Jim Mitchell. I like doing what I do. I enjoy college, sports, love my family and my mates and I know what I'm going to do with my life."

She considered his reply for a moment, "You haven't mentioned girlfriends!"

Jim's discussion on the opposite sex, made him feel uncomfortable. He still hasn't gotten over Maggie and was in no mood to discuss it with anybody, particularly the girls of the village. All in all, he felt a little embarrassed. "What about girls?" he said somewhat defensively.

"Well," she replied, "you never seemed to take any notice of the girls in the village. The words got 'round that you're a snob."

"That's not fair," said Jim angrily. "Anyway, that's my business." He paused then added, "I think I should go home. Thanks for the coffee."

"I am sorry, Jim," she said knowing that her last remark had hurt his feelings. "Don't go yet. I was only trying to get to know ya."

Jim looked at her face. There was a tear in her eye.

"I am sorry," she repeated. "I just wanted you and me to be friends."

The air was cool and fresh as Jim walked along the lane to his home reflecting on the conversation. He realized what Joyce had said bore an essence of truth. "Yes," he said to himself. "There was a lot of truth in her remarks." He didn't socialize with the villagers, especially with the girls. The fact that his mum had a successful business, he went to the best college in the area, and his Granddad owned a big farm, had nothing to do with it. Maybe he was a snob. He had not recognized it in the past. It's a mixed up world that we live in," he said to himself. He was in love and still absorbed with Maggie and didn't have time to consider other people's needs. Maybe he needed to change his attitude.

It was then that he realized that Joyce had also suffered. Her dad had been killed in the war; her boy friend was in the army, somewhere overseas. Suddenly, he felt the urge to console her, he turned and ran back to her home and knocked on the door. As it opened, Jim saw the outline of her naked figure silhouetted against the fire in the background, there were tears running down her cheeks. "I am so sorry, Joyce," he said. "That was so damned inconsiderate of me."

There was an essence of a smile on her tear stained face as her arms encircled his waist. She murmured, "Come in, Jim. I guess I'm feeling sorry for myself."

"That's okay, girl. I guess we've all got our problems."

She smiled thru the tears, "Stay for a while please."

# *Chapter 18*

Lydia Louise Henning, her body-dripping wet, stepped out of her warm shower and surveyed her tall slim, body in the full length the mirror. "Bastards," said she cried as she saw the reflection. "Bastards!" She shouted again, as she examined the nipples of her breasts and marks around her sex. They were healing fast. She slowly dried herself with a warm towel. "Oh God!" she cried, "Will this never end?"

It had been at fifteen months since she had been rescued from the Gestapo by the French resistance fighters who had carried her to safety, her body bent and broken. During the months that followed, she had taken the long torturous journey over the Pyrenees Mountains into Spain. From there she had taken a slow foreign cargo ship bound for England, where, after a long medical and physiological hospitalization, she returned to the sanctuary of her parents and their home in North Wales. The experience had changed her life. She was proud of what she had done for her country; she hated men for what they had done to her. At first, she would shake in fear when a man approached her. Then slowly, with the help of a wonderful Lady psychiatrist, she had learned to mask her fear knowing that she would never conquer it completely. She smiled as she remembered the Psychiatrist's parting words, "Have faith my dear, one day you will meet a man who will conquer all your fears."

Lydia lay on the white cotton sheets of her bed reflecting on the celebrations. This had been her first journey into the world following a long recuperation. She had spent many hours contemplating her future life with her friends John and June, whom she had served with during the war. They had suggested that she should live near them. She was excited with the prospect. She knew the village well, having spent some time there as a child and a young woman before the war.

Her mind turned to the evening. She had met old, and new, friends. It had been her first evening out in a long time. She had always enjoyed being with the people of the village, particularly John and June and an old school chum, Elizabeth Harden. During coffee that night, Lydia recounted how she had met Edith's husband in the halcyon days before the war, when she, as a girl, had supported her local village football team, which was captained by her brother. There was a grin on her face as she retold the story of the Cheshire Cup Final match in the 1937. When prior to the start of the match the home captain, a man called Mitchell, had tied the home team's dummy, which was dressed in football kit, on the back of her team mascot, a Welsh goat, then proceeded to slap his rump as he raced around the football pitch. Later, they were introduced by Jim Mitchell's father, who was a friend of her father. The young boy, Mitchell, shook her hand, bowed, and said politely, "Nice to meet you Miss," then with a huge audacious smile, he winked his left eye at her. At first, she felt somewhat embarrassed then she realized that there was something special about him that attracted her. So she returned his smile and winked back at him.

He was the same boy that had walked across the floor of the village hall, shaking in his boots, to ask her to dance. She laughed, remembering his words. "Oh hell, I have made a bloody mess of it."

It had been two years since they had last met. "My, oh my," she mused, he had grown into a very fine young man, tall and handsome. "Was he the one?" she asked herself. When she saw him, there was a feeling of excitement in her body. She had curtsied low when he asked her to dance. It had been years since she had felt that way and it felt so bloody good. There was warmth in her body. Lydia Louise Henning was smiling as she fell into a deep satisfying sleep.

Jim Mitchell lay in his bed. His thoughts turned to his first conversation of any meaning with Joyce, or for that matter with any of the village girls. She was a nice girl, and he was surprised when she called him a snob. The statement had really hurt him. He had always considered himself to be a kind and loving boy. Maybe a little naive at times, yet he had never intentionally hurt anyone. Maybe he was a little cocky at times, self assured in his sporting activities, proud of his school and proud of belonging to the gang. Her words had really upset him. He would talk the matter over with Richard. Maybe she felt the same way about the gang. He wasn't sure, but he did know he cared. "Yes," he said to himself. "She may well have a point."

Jim's thoughts turned to his meeting with Lydia. It had been a fun evening and he had enjoyed meeting her again. She had complimented him on his dancing, and he had enjoyed talking with her. He smiled. There was another side to this lady, a side that he had never seen before. He was impressed by her intellect, and he felt comfortable in her presence. "Oh well," he said to himself, "she would probably find a boyfriend and that will be the end of that."

Jim's thoughts turned to Maggie. He was missing her. What was she doing? How was she? She was slow at answering his letters and he didn't understand why. "Maybe she's got herself a boyfriend?" Was he jealous? "Yes," he admitted to himself. His love for her was still there, and he knew that it always would be. He also knew that it was going to be one of those restless nights, a night when he would explore the whole of his world in his mind before falling into a deep sleep.

The sun shone brightly as he rose from his bed the following morning to be greeted by his Mum carrying a huge mug of tea. He smiled at her opening remarks, "You look tired love. Did you sleep well?"

His smile turned into a laugh. "No," he replied. "I just tore my world apart, and, hopefully, it will fall into place soon."

She smiled. "One of those nights, eh Jim," she said then added, "breakfast in ten minutes. I need to talk to you before I start work."

"What do you want to talk about?" asked Jim as he joined her at the breakfast table.

"There is going to be a general election before too long. I have been asked to join the election committee for our Labor candidate." She paused, "You know Mr. Jenkins, don't you?"

"Yes," Jim replied. "He is a very nice fellow. Why do you support the Labor Party?"

"Because they are going to do the things that I believe in, the nationalization of all major industry, the freedom of every worker to belong to a union, and a good national health program, similar to 'Beverage Report' recommendations."

Jim smiled to himself. She would be a good advocate for the cause. "What does Granddad think?"

She laughed. "The mountain to Mohammed, seriously Jim, he knows that I respect his point of view as a Conservative party member, and he respects my views as a Labor party member. He also reckons that I'm batting on a sticky wicket. After all, Churchill did win the war and now leads the Conservative party."

"Good for you," said Jim. "The only thing I ask from you is that you don't overdo it. You are very special to me."

"Stop worrying about me." She paused, ruffling his hair, "Seriously, Jim, I need your support, my love. Now I'm off to work, you have a nice day."

"What would you have done if I said no?" Jim asked as she was leaving.

"I don't know." she replied. There was a curious grin on her face as she added, "What do you think Mitchell?"

Jim smiled at his mother's "Have a nice day" greeting. "She was getting really hip with her conversation," Jim mused. She had made no comment about Lydia.

# Chapter 19

It was a damp, seasonable, Monday morning in January when the Form Master announced that the mock examination results were complete, and that he would review them with the candidates. The times and dates were to be posted on the school notice board. Jim looked at the tall, gray haired man, the man who had guided him through the vagaries of his disciplines during last five years. He remembered his dedication and kindness. He had the ability to bring the best out of him in class and on the sports field. He had a wonderful gift of making things appear to be easy. Jim smiled as he remembered the struggle he had with his French and English lit lessons. At first, his objective view on the subjects was obscure. Slowly, with patience, he unraveled the mystery. He was a very experienced tutor, who had come out of retirement during the war to help in the education of England's future engineers and scientists, subjects he had taught for so many years. Now that the war was over, he would retire again to the peace and tranquility of his native Anglesey. Jim smiled to himself thinking about his odd ways and habits. "Thank you Sir," he said a silently. "Thank you for all you have given me."

The notice board read Mr. Stevens nine thirty a.m., Mr. Mitchell ten o'clock a.m. Jim looked at Richard as he came out of Mr. Griffin's office looking terribly glum.

"How was it?"

"Bloody awful," Richard replied.

"Mitchell, where are you?" rang the voice of his Form Master, "Your next."

Jim sat on the seat opposite his desk. Mr. Griffith had a habit of looking over the top of his glasses, particularly when he was upset with you. Today was no exception. "Mitchell I thought you would have done better than this," he said as he glanced at my report.

"*Oh God*" Jim said to himself. He thought that he was into the wrath of 'His Nibs', a nickname that we gave him in our first year. He could be testy at times, particularly when his pupils had not performed to his expectation. Suddenly, his Form Master smiled: 'A reprieve,' thought Jim grabbing for straws.

"Huh, not as bad as it looks. Your mathematics, chemistry, physics, English language, geography, and history are good. Your English lit and French language needs a fair amount of the work. You know the syllabus?"

Jim nodded. "Yes Sir, *The Tale of Two Cities;* Wuthering *Heights;* and *All's Well That Ends Well.*"

"Your French," he paused for a moment then threw his hands up in horror and despair. "You might just make it given a fair wind and a modicum of luck.

Do you have anyone at home who can help you?"

"I think so, Sir."

"Good, you need it."

As he left Mr. Griffith's office, he met Derek.

"How did you get on?" inquired Derek.

"Not too bad," replied Jim, "although English lit and French languages are not up to scratch. What about you, Derek?"

He smiled, "The usual, bloody awful."

That evening after dinner, Jim sought his mother's advice.

"Why don't you ask John Evans, your new coach? He used to be a schoolteacher before the war."

"I don't know him," replied Jim.

Mum laughed. "I think he knows you, and I'm sure that's all that matters. They also have a friend, Lydia, and I understand she is quite a clever young lady. Do you remember her?"

Jim smiled, a blush on his cheek, "Of course I do, Mum."

The following night Jim walked to the home of John Evans. June his wife opened the door

"Hello Jim, your mum said that you might be calling. I saw her in the village today. Come on in. What can we do to help you?" Her remarks made him feel comfortable. "Sit you down," she said as they entered the living room. "Would you like a cup of tea? John will be back in about ten minutes, he just popped down to the pub."

"Yes please, Mrs. Evans." He looked around the room admiring the photographs of the football team that won the cup in '37 including his dad, people in RAF uniforms, and wedding pictures of June and John. In the corner were some photographs of a young girl in a wedding picture.

"Hello Jim," said John as he walked into the living room. "How are you?"

"Fine thank you, Sir" he replied. "I need some advice."

"What's the problem?"

"My Matric examinations," replied Jim. "There are a couple of subjects on which I need some help, English lit and French language."

John smiled, "The two subjects which I've never taught. Come to think of it, I wasn't much good at them subject at College." He paused, "Sorry Jim, I can't help you. Not to worry, I think I have the answer."

"Who?" inquired Jim.

"Lydia. She is fluent in French and has a good grasp of the English Literature. She's away at the moment with her mother and father." He paused, "She will be back mid –day on Saturday. Why don't you come and have dinner with us on Saturday night? I want to talk to you about the next season anyway, and we could kill two birds with one stone."

The football match the following Saturday, the first of the year, promised to be competitive. Before the match, couch Evans came into the changing rooms to wish the team luck. His only advice was simple, "Go and enjoy yourselves."

The game, our local derby, was tough and competitive. The team moved the ball around the pitch from left to right to center. There were shots on the goal that we would never have attempted the previous season. The team had trained hard. The coach's strategy gave the team a new perspective of the game, a different way of playing, and it was fun. They walked off the pitch, their heads high and they knew that they had played well. Their supporters applauded; they had won the game by three goals to two.

"We played a 'blinder', Jim Mitchell," Richard cried enthusiastically. "We are a team again!"

"It was time to celebrate. Their reward: a pint of beer at the Robin Hood Pub. They were excited for the game and their prospects under their new leadership.

"Why did we win?" asked Richard.

"You played football for the first time in ages" said Derek "and what's more, you enjoyed it. Anybody could see that," he said with a laugh. "Even me, and as of you know, I don't play the stupid game."

# Chapter 20

It was a cold winter night as Jim walked along the road leading to John Evans home. He was excited. There was hope for a successful end to the season, something that they hadn't enjoyed for some time. He loved the game and enjoyed it tremendously, giving his all to the glory of the team. "Team spirit," he muttered to himself, "team spirit." They were on a 'high'.

June greeted him as he walked up the long drive to their home. "How do you feel Jim?" she asked. "You got a few knocks and bruises today, young man."

"I guess so," he answered. "Somehow when you're winning, they don't hurt."

She laughed. "Yes, I know the feeling. I used to do field and track a few years ago."

"Hello James," said Lydia as she entered the room. "You had a good game. Congratulations."

"Thank you, did you watch the game?" asked Jim.

"Yes I did; the village should be proud of you."

"Thanks Lydia, I appreciate it. It was bloody hard work today."

She raised an eyebrow at his remark, and then smiled inwardly saying to herself. "This is one tough young man, dedicated to his team." It was more than that. There was a determination about him that she had never seen before, a trait that she liked.

The conversation around the dinner table rested mostly on John's favorite sport, football, specifically the prewar team. "Didn't you used to watch the game, Lydia?" asked John. "Isn't that where we first met?"

"I thought that you had forgotten!" exclaimed Lydia.

"No, not really. I didn't want to tell everyone that you blushed," replied John teasingly.

"Well thank you, that was very gallant of you. I feel like a turn round the garden before coffee," said Lydia. "Will you join me, James?"

As they walked, she pointed at the outline of the Welsh mountains in the distance. She smiled, "It's been a while since we met Jim, how are you?"

"I'm fine," he replied, "a little concerned about my matriculation examination."

"Yes, John mentioned it earlier." She smiled, "Don't worry, Jim, I will help you."

"How are you, Lydia?" inquired Jim.

"Busy," she replied. "I have started my legal articles and I'm having fun."

Later that evening they strolled along Pit Lane in the moonlight. Lydia looked at him and smiled. "I'm looking forward to helping you." She paused, "When would you like to start?"

"Would yesterday be okay?" he said jokingly.

Lydia laughed, "Sure what are you doing on Tuesday evening?"

"Coming to see you I hope?"

She laughed, "I'm looking forward to it. Goodnight James thanks for bringing me home."

"Goodnight, Lydia," he replied.

It was five minutes to six o'clock, when Jim approached Lydia's home, which was somewhat isolated and set in a stand of woods. The house had character, a clay tile roof, old English rough brickwork and small pane windows set in an old English garden.

"Hello Jim," she smiled. "Welcome to my home. I've just finished my evening meal, would you like some coffee?"

"Thank you, that would be fine," replied Jim nervously.

"Did you bring your exam results papers?"

"Yes," he replied rummaging in his duffel bag.

Lydia sat for a while examining the paperwork. She smiled "Not too bad, Jim; however, I agree with your Form Master."

"When can we start?" asked Jim anxiously.

She looked a little perturbed. "Let's talk, shall we? During the next few weeks you and I will be spending a lot of time together."

"Is it that bad thing Lydia?" said Jim with a nervous laugh.

"No, not really, it's a fact. We have a lot of work to do, and there's no doubt about it. The rumor mongers in the village will have a 'Hay Day' when they learn that you're coming to see me on a regular basis." She laughed. "June told me that after the dance, that the rumors have started about you and me. To be honest with you Jim, I don't give two hoots."

Jim laughed. "Yes, I talked it over with my mother and she expressed the same feelings. She doesn't give two hoots either. She trusts me, and she trusts you, and that's really all that counts, isn't it?"

"Even so," said Lydia, "I feel that we should make some rules. I am a great believer in rules. I suppose that comes from my training in the Air Force. How's this for starters? Firstly, I think it is important that we should be honest with one another and express our feelings fully without reservation. Secondly, let's not take the tuition too seriously, otherwise, it will overcome us and take away the enjoyment, and last but not least, let's have some fun. Let's enjoy ourselves, Okay?""

"That's fine by me," replied Jim. "I'm looking forward to it."

"Now, I think I should tell you a little about me. Yes, the Mrs. is accurate. When I was young, I didn't have boyfriends, and as I grew I had all the men I needed in my life, my brother and my dad, and they were marvelous to me. Yes, I had a couple of dates when I was eighteen." She laughed, "top half only,' so I guess I was naive. Shortly after I joined the Air Force, I met Rupert and we married. That was a mistake as we were incompatible so I sued for divorce. Shortly afterward,

I volunteered for the Special Forces unit. The training was arduous, but I just wanted to get away from the base. Don't get me wrong, I enjoyed it. I learned a lot of how to parachute, and hand-to-hand fighting. Eventually, I went on missions into France to support the French resistance. In addition to my fluency in the French language, I also became an explosives expert. After a few jumps, I tended to get a little blasé. Unfortunately, on my last jump, I broke my leg and was captured by the Germans, who turned me over to the Gestapo. When I was interrogated, I refused to answer their questions. I was tortured and eventually they savaged my body. I was found, dumped in a field outside the town by the French resistance and they transported me over the Pyrenees Mountains into Spain, where I shipped back to England. After a lengthy stay in the surgical and psychological hospital, I was discharged and sent home to recover. You see, Jim; I have a deep-seated fear of men and sex following that experience. Sure, it's getting better, but I still avoid men." She smiled, "My first night out was the night of the VE dance when I thanked you for entertaining me. I really did mean it." She smiled, "I had a great time, thank you again, Jim."

"Are you okay with me around?"

She smiled. "I have thought about that, Jim. To be honest, it's fine. As a matter of fact, Mitchell, you're helping me to return to normal," she laughed, "whatever that is."

"Shall we start?" asked Jim.

"Do you really want to, Jim? I think it's going to take me time to compose myself after baring my 'breast' to you. Would you like a beer?"

Jim smiled. "I agree, Lydia. Yes, I would like a beer. I would still like to talk if that's okay?"

"Yes, sure, what would you like to talk about?"

"You," replied Jim as he gently gazed at her.

Lydia laughed, "Me! I don't think you will find that interesting."

"What do you do in your spare time?" asked Jim.

Lydia contemplated the question. "Well, I enjoy classical music. I like watching football, I run quite a bit, lift weights, dressmaking and above all, I like going to the cinema. I enjoy the Rita Haworth and Cary Grant films."

Jim smiled, "We have a lot in common."

She laughed, "Do you like dressmaking?"

"Not really, my claim to fame in that department is the ability to sew on the odd button," confessed Jim.

"Thank God for that!" Lydia exclaimed while laughing.

"You mentioned that you would like to be a lawyer one day."

"Yes," she replied, "my ambition in life is to become a lawyer dealing with international affairs. Improving the lives of under- privileged peoples in the nations of this world. I know it sounds highfaluting, but I really want to do it, particularly in Africa. What about you?" she asked.

"There's not a hell of a lot to know. When I was a kid, I got into a fight at school. Richard, Bryan, and Derek came to my rescue. Since then, we have been firm friends." He laughed, "We seem to do everything together, and I guess we are a 'club.' We're all in the same academic level, and we enjoy the same sports. Unfortunately, we have found ourselves the subject of jealousy. You see, none of us have girlfriends from the village, and I guess we have the reputation of being somewhat snobbish. To be honest, I don't know why, but that is the way it is in this village, probably because we're successful in what we do, mostly in sports. I suppose we are the only boys from the village that go to the College. To be honest Lydia, we have tried to be friendly, but I guess the resentment is deep seated. Oh hell, it will sort itself out, I hope. In the meantime, life goes on."

"What about girls?" she asked with a smile.

Jim laughed, "There's not much to say. Derek, Brian, and Richard's girlfriends come from Chester, and I have my cousin Maggie."

"Do you want to talk about her?"

"There's not a lot to talk about really. We had been friends since we were babies. We grew up together. We studied together. I guess we did everything together. Then we grew up and started taking our relationship seriously. We had our rules, 'Top Half Only.'" The family thought that we may go further than that in our relationship, so they read us the riot act." Jim recanted. "I don't really know why. We knew we were cousins; we also knew that we could never marry and have kids. We're still friends, and we always will be, we have reconciled ourselves to the situation. She is a very beautiful young lady, and when she comes to the village, she tends to aggravate the local girls with her attitude: 'Hands off girls, he's mine!'"

"I am looking forward to meeting her," Lydia said warmly.

"One day I hope you will," said Jim to himself envisaging the conversation.

"What of your future, Jim Mitchell?"

"Once I have graduated, I am going to train as an electrical engineer, then I am going to sea as a marine engineer. My objective is to get my degree in electrical engineering and my Chief Engineer's certificate before I am twenty-five. It's doable, and it's going to be damned hard work. My Granddad wants me to take over the farm when he retires. I like farming, Lydia. It's a very honest profession." Jim looked at his watch. "I guess I'm keeping you up," he murmured. "When can we meet again?"

"Tomorrow night, six o'clock, is that okay?"

"Yes Lydia. Thank you, Good night."

She smiled as he left her home "I have a poor boy in my hands and I am going to turn him into a genius in English lit and French language."

Jim ran to Pit Lane. He was late. "Sorry, Lydia," he exclaimed. "Minor problem, Mum burnt the mince pie."

"Have you eaten?"

"Not really."

"I've got some cottage pie left over from my meal, would you like it?"

"Thank you, I appreciate that. I met your dad and my granddad in Chester today. Apparently they are very good friends. They just finished lunch at the Grosvenor Hotel. Your dad looks like an interesting man. Tell me about him."

"There's not a lot to tell really. He is an American by birth, came over to this country as a pilot in the First World War. He met mom and settled here. He joined an old firm of solicitors in Chester. That is how he got to know your granddad many years ago. He supported our football team. They used to play against your granddad's team about four times a year. They were tough matches. My dad and your granddad always sat together in the stands. They still see each other occasionally for lunch. My dad takes care of your granddad's affairs."

"So that's how you know so much about me," replied Jim.

"Let's get down to work shall we, what do you want to start with?"

"English literature" he replied, "Will Shakespeare's, *Alls Well That Ends Well.*"

Jim read a while with little interruption She had an aptitude for teaching and one could feel her kindness, the odd smile of encouragement. It was fun. After couple of hours of deep concentration Jim realized, that an acting career would not be his forte in life.

"Are you tired?"

Jim grimaced. "I am whacked."

"Can you quote?" she asked.

"You mean the King?"

She nodded. "Yes, I will give it a try."

> The King's a beggar now the play is done
> All is well-ended if this suit is won
> That you express content, which we'll pay
> With strife to please you day exceeding day
> Hours to be your patients then, and yours our parts
> Your gentle hands lend us, and take our hearts.

"Well done, Jim," she said with a warm smile, "is that enough for tonight?"

"Yes I think so, Lydia."

"It's going to be hard work, but between us, we can do it," she said with a confident smile.

"Yes, we will," Jim replied.

"Would you like a drink before you go?"

"A cup of tea, please."

Lydia relaxed. The session was over. She sat on the floor with her legs crossed looking like a rag-a- muffin, her long Auburn hair sweeping over her shoulders, her hazel eyes smiling enjoying the experience.

"Did you ever think of teaching as a career?" asked Jim

She laughed, "No, not really, the thought of teaching a bunch of the snotty nosed kids has never appealed to me somehow."

"You taught me well tonight Lydia, what's the difference?"

"Well thank you, Sir, I appreciate the compliment. The difference?" she repeated. "I guess you're eager to learn. You have goals to complete. And anyway, I just like teaching you, is that okay?"

"I will see you on Tuesday, thanks, Lydia," he replied looking forward to it. "Do I need to research anything?"

"No, you're fine," she replied.

The following weeks passed quickly. It had been hard work with the intensity that she prescribed. There were times when he was aggravated, and times when she threw up hands in desperation, particularly when it came to the French language. There were evenings when they just sat around and talked. Jim was impressed with her knowledge of world affairs. She had the ability to make him feel good about himself. He was gaining in confidence, and starting to express his feeling about life and his studies. His grasp of grammar and elocution improved tremendously. She was a strong advocate of self-expression and occasionally swore at him. It was obvious to Jim that she was an intelligent lady, and that learning had never been a problem for her.

During the past few weeks, the nearness of him was beginning to excite her; there was something about him that was slowly nurturing her back to health. She smiled thinking about her words at the dance when she had curtsied low to him accepting his invitation to dance. "Do you want to dance, or shall we stand here all night like Cheshire cats grinning?" She was aware that her remark had surprised the onlookers. Jim had thought that they were hilarious. She smiled, then he would, wouldn't he? He was kind and his sense of humor supported her misgivings over her mischievous remarks.

Her life had been one misery until that night. She smiled, fondly remembering, her heart missed a beat. She was shaking with excitement when she saw him. He had grown into a man, a handsome man. During the following weeks, the memories, the bad memories of her life were less frequent. She knew that she was on the road to recovery and a degree of happiness. "Oh God!" she cried, "Please make it so!" She was recovering from a hell, and in desperate need of friendship. There was something about him. Yes, there was his thoughtfulness, gentleness and understanding. His friendship was making her stronger each day and each passing week

# Chapter 21

It was several weeks since Jim had visited his grandparents. He felt guilty that he had neglected them. The following Sunday Jim rose early and rode through the familiar landscape on his bicycle to see them, arriving hopefully in time to share the morning meal.

As he walked into the kitchen, his grandmother greeted him, "hullo stranger" mockingly admonishing him for his tardiness. "Do I get a kiss?" During the last couple of years, their relationship had grown into one of a deep friendship. He felt more like a son than a Grandchild. "You're just in time for breakfast."

The meal, as usual, was sumptuous, and he devoured his serving as though he had not eaten for several days. "Your Mum tells me that you have been extremely busy swatting for your 'A' levels."

"That," he thought to himself, "is grandma's understatement of the year."

"Yes I have," said Jim. "It's been hard work, but I feel confident now, more than I ever have in the past."

"Your Mum tells me that you have been tutored by Lydia Henning."

"Yes, she's great!" he replied. "She is teaching me well. Then, changing the subject, he asked, "How's the farm coming along, Granddad?"

"Best darned year we have ever had," he replied. "The early cut of silage was excellent, and the new potato crop was as good as I have ever seen. My Friesian cows seem to be happy. They are producing milk on average of nine hundred and fifty gallons a year. Life is good."

"How's the café, Grandma?" Jim inquired.

"Not quite as good as last year," she replied. "The catering side is down a little. Now that the war is over, I am expecting that there will be lots of weddings and my girls and I will be busy."

"I am pleased, Grandma," replied Jim. "You have worked dammed hard."

"Thank you, Jim, I appreciate that. Yes I have, and we have made a handsome profit," she said with a huge smile.

Jim smiled inwardly, the words Grandma and profits were synonymous.

"Have you heard from Maggie lately?" asked Grandma

"Yes," replied Jim "I had a letter a couple of weeks ago. She thinks that she may be free," he laughed, "or out of a job in November. She also said that she has a part in a pantomime at Christmas as Maid Marian."

Granddad laughed, "Isn't that the part where they wear net stockings right up to their backsides?"

"Yes," replied Jim with a laugh.

"Anyone for more coffee?" asked Grandma hopefully to get her men off the subject of net stockings.

"I have got an idea," said Granddad. "If Maggie's home in November, that will coincide with the annual Hunt Ball. It would be rather nice for you and Maggie to attend with us."

"Thanks, Granddad," replied Jim. The prospect of attending the premium ball of the year, the Cheshire Hunt with Maggie excited him. "I am sure Maggie will want to go. Anyway, I will write to her."

"Thanks," replied granddad. "Grandma and I are getting a little upset with her. She is not very good at replying to our letters." He smiled, "If she does not want to go, we could always ask one of your girlfriends?"

"Your joking Granddad, I haven't got one," Jim retorted.

Later they sat in the garden, enjoying their last cup of coffee for the day, admiring the roses.

"Your dad planted those about fifteen years ago," said Grandma. "Why not take some to your Mum? I am sure she will enjoy them, and some for Ms Henning."

Jim looked at his watch. "Time to go!" He exclaimed, "The cricket match starts at midday. Will you be their Granddad?" he asked.

"Of course, I will, I haven't missed a game for years. Your team has got their work cut out today. You're facing tough opposition."

"Yes," replied Jim "It's going to be a tough game, but we are up for it."

Jim walked to the crease with Richard to open the inning and asked the umpire for "middle and off" bat position. The game he knew would be hard going. "Nothing given, nothing asked," said Jim to himself as he received the first ball of the first over. "Play yourself in boy." He said you are due for a good inning. Suddenly there was an air of confidence in his play, willed on by his overwhelming personal need to win the match, which reflected in Richard's performance. By lunchtime, they had scored a hundred and ten runs between them.

"We should declare at 250 to 280," advised Richard as they made their way to the crease after lunch.

"Okay," said Jim. "Let's knock the hell out of them." By two thirty in the afternoon, they had scored 250 runs. Jim knew that the wicket was wearing. The last thing that he wanted to do was play against spin bowlers at this time. Richard asked the umpire to remove the bails. The inning declared.

Jim's reading of the wicket proved to be correct. It was turning. Now was the time to use his skill as spin bowler and, by six o'clock p.m., the opposing team was all out for 210 runs. The village team had won the day.

Later Jim walked across the fields to Rose Cottage carrying a bunch of flowers for Lydia.

She smiled as she opened the door. "Are those for me?" she asked excitedly.

"Yes", he replied, "they are for you, Ms. Henning, from my granddad's garden."

"Well thank you kindly, Sir," she said. "I don't get flowers any more.

They are lovely," she exclaimed excited by the gift. "Come in, sit down and stay for awhile. Let me put them in some water. Jim, they are so beautiful," she said as she returned to the room carrying her roses in a crystal vase.

"There' a story behind them, Lydia."

"Do tell," she exclaimed.

"My dad was a bit of a gardener in his younger years. Apparently, he planted the rose bushes before the war. They are, by all accounts, Grandma's pride and joy."

"Do you think I should write her a thank-you note?"

"Yes," Jim replied. "I am sure she would appreciate the thought."

There was tenderness in Lydia's voice as she murmured, "You are very kind to me, Jim Mitchell. Why?"

"Oh, I don't know," he replied with a nervous laugh. "I guess you make me happy. I just like being with you." Jim felt a blush in the cheeks. "I'm sorry, Lydia, I shouldn't have said that should I?"

Lydia Louise Hemming smiled, "Why not, if it's true?"

Her answer encouraged him, giving him confidence to ask his next question.

"Would you be my guest at the annual cricket dinner?"

Her green eyes sparkled with pleasure as she replied, "Yes I would be honored, Sir, thank you."

The Sun was shining brightly that morning, as Jim rose from his bed, anticipating the day. The traditional opening game against their old foe from the next village, the first game in the prized Cheshire cup competition opening, followed the cricket clubs annual dinner and dance. He smiled. The swashbuckling Brian had returned from his school, the team was at full strength. It would be a tough game and he was looking forward to captaining this team for the season.

Jim won the toss and decided to bowl on a good wicket, electing to bowl at the Pavilion end, with Brian bowling from the Factory end.

By lunchtime, they had dismissed the old foe for a hundred and two runs much to the chagrin of the opposing team.

It was two thirty p.m., when Brian and he walked out to the wicket. Their strategy, Jim would play the game safely as he usually did, Brian would go for the runs. By five o'clock p.m., they had scored a hundred and three runs.

This was an unprecedented victory in the history of our small cricket club. Brian and Jim walked off the field to the cheers of our jubilant supporters. In the distance, Jim caught a glimpse of Mum and Granddad and Lydia waving madly, greeting the heroes of the game. Edith smiled as she threw her arms around her son "You were magnificent Mitchell."

Jim looked deep into her eyes as he murmured. "Thanks Mum, I hope Dad was watching."

The annual cricket dinner and dance was underway as Jim walked confidently, escorting his date of the night, to their table to be greeted by his Mum and the local member of Parliament, Coach, June, his Granddad, and his Grandma. Lydia looked ravishingly beautiful, dressed in a long black skirt slit to thigh and an off the shoulder, chiffon deep plunge blouse, her long Auburn hair over her broad athletic shoulders.

His mother gasped. "Oh my, this will give the villagers something to talk about," she breathed as Lydia greeted them.

Granddad rose to shake her hand. "Hello Lydia, nice to see you again, my dear." There was a twinkle in his eye as he murmured, "You look gorgeous, young Lady."

"Thank you, Sir," Lydia said graciously.

Grandma smiled, "Nice to see you again, my dear."

Coach and June waved at her in salutation. Then looking at Jim, Coach breathed "Cocky bugger, just like his dad."

Jim looked at Lydia. "Would you mind if I join the team at the bar. I won't be long."

She smiled touching his hand. "No it's your night Jim."

Jim raised his pint of Newcastle Brown Ale, "A toast gentlemen, to a good football season and a better cricket season. Let the celebrations begin. Now, if you will excuse me. There's a Lady waiting for me."

Jim's first dance of the evening was with his Grandma. She looked at him and murmured softly. "You had a good day today, my son; the cricket gods looked on you favorably and that pleases me." She smiled as she looked into his eyes.

Holding his hand firmly, "You make me so pleased, and so happy, young Jim."

As the evening wore on he danced with his Mum, June and Lydia, fulfilling his obligations on the dance floor.

Edith, now the Chairwomen of the local Labor party, introduced the local Member of Parliament, who had just been reelected to the government, and he proposed a toast to the team.

"And the village," Jim Mitchell replied eloquently thanking the village for the support, referring to the successful teams of days gone by, and their hopes and ambitions for the future.

"It's been a wonderful day, Jim," Lydia said. "Would you care for a night-cap?" Jim hesitated. "I think you deserve one after your hard slog at the wicket today." Occasionally their fingers touched tantalizing him, arousing his senses, as she laid the two drinks on the low table kneeling before him showing the fullness of her breasts. She smiled somewhat embarrassed, feeling his eyes admiring her body. "Mitchell I am so bloody proud of you," she murmured softly. "Thank you for inviting me tonight. I really did enjoy myself!"

Jim smiled as she sat beside him. "You, Lady, looked beautiful tonight, your dress," he paused, unsure of how he described his feelings.

"Yes?" Lydia asked, encouraging him to finish his sentence.

Jim felt the warmth in the cheeks as he replied, "Sexy."

"Did I please you?" she asked in a tantalizing manor.

"Yes, you did, Lydia, it was a beautiful exciting evening and I enjoyed being with you," he said softly.

"Thank you," she murmured, "Can we talk?"

"Sure," he replied.

Pausing momentarily, Lydia said, "During the last few weeks, I have enjoyed tutoring you. I really have!" she exclaimed. "It's been fun" she laughed, "well not all fun. We have had our problems and some disagreements, particularly when you 'pissed me off" and I adopted an attitude. Now you are primed and ready for the fray ahead. Your tuition is complete." She hesitated. "Jim we didn't break the rules, and we both agreed that we would be honest with each other and express our feelings freely. Hold me for a moment."

He placed the palms of his hand on to her cheeks looked into her eyes. There was a tear glistening. "Shush," he said tenderly as he kissed her forehead. "Are you okay?"

"Yes," she said softly "I'm okay. I guess it's over!" She sobbed, "The last few weeks you have changed my life," she paused. "I guess what I'm trying to say is, where do we go from here?"

Jim looked at her in the twilight of the burning fire as their eyes met he murmured softly, "It's been fun, Lydia, I admire for your intellect. You are truly beautiful and I want to be with you. You are exciting, you are sexy, and you are magnificent. Oh hell" he cried, "can we date when this is over?"

"Yes," she murmured softly, "I don't want to talk about love. I don't want to talk about marriage. I just want to be your girl for a while, you have made me feel so good tonight!" she exclaimed. "Good luck next week."

Lydia Louise Henning lay in the bed reliving the day. Her long fingers slowly caressed her body. She was excited as she recalled the last dance. Jim had held her close as they danced to the last haunting, sensual music. She had moved her head back slightly thrusting her hips against him, unashamedly feeling the hardness of his erection against her. She had smiled seductively, audaciously winking an eye. He had smiled in recognition holding her close knowing that she wanted him. "Oh,-oh, ----Ah" she cried as she raised her hips thrusting them hard against her long fingers. Her body shuddered as she slowly brought herself to a climax.

Next Friday would be the last day of his examinations. Saturday would be his eighteenth birthday. He was a young man who excited every part of her body. The long months dreaming about him, fantasizing about him in every detail, were over. Her time was nigh. "Yes," she said excitedly. "I am a woman again, a horny, sexy Bitch." She smiled as she closed her eyes murmuring "Happy birthday, Jim."

# Chapter 22

The witching hours had passed that were full of apprehension for the 'morrow, slowly the first light of day shone through his bedroom window, the apprehension of the night gave way to a feeling of confidence. This was the day he would pit his mind and body against reality of life, facing the board of examiners in a battle for success.

The glow of determination had taken hold. He smiled as he stretched his tall, lean body, taking a deep breath. The air of confidence had returned. This would be his day. The game was on and failure was not an option.

"How did you do, Mitchell?" asked Richard as he joined his friends for the homeward journey to the village.

"Bloody marvelous!" he replied. "What say you to a couple, or three, pints of the good ale tonight?"

"That," said Derek "has got my name written all over it, Mitchell."

"It wasn't fun," interjected Richard.

"No," replied Jim. "It was more like a bloody war, but we won, boyo. We won," he cried triumphantly.

Jim alighted from the bus and ran to Lydia's home. He had promised that she would be the first to know, of his success, or failure.

"How did you get on Mitchell?" she asked somewhat nervously.

"I passed!" he shouted. "I bloody well passed, Lydia!"

"Oh," she cried excitedly. "Thank goodness for that. I've been worried all week."

"Ye of little faith," he quoted.

She laughed. "To the victor come spoils. Get in here Mitchell!"

There was a deep sense of emotion in her body as she placed her hands on his cheeks. "Oh Jim Mitchell," she cried. "I am so dammed proud of you." Then with a coquettish smile she murmured, "May I kiss you?"

"I thought you would never ask."

She smiled as their lips parted. "What's your position on lamb chops?"

"I adore lamb chops."

"Then, Sir, I will cook you dinner tomorrow night. Let us celebrate shall we, I feel like dressing up for the occasion. Will you wear a suit?"

There was an impish grin on his face as he replied, "Yes ma'am."

The early morning sun was shining as Jim Mitchell stirred from his bed feeling the effects of the celebration the night before. "Happy Birthday, shake a leg, Mitchell!" Edith cried as she entered the room with a mug of hot tea. "How do you feel?"

"Fine thanks, Mum," he cried. "If you really must know, I feel bloody marvelous. It's going to be a good day."

She kissed him on his forehead. "I am so bloody proud of you my son," she cried emotionally. "You have worked so hard, Jim Mitchell, you deserve your success," she murmured as she kissed him on his forehead, "breakfast in fifteen minutes."

It was Saturday, a day to visit his friends and relations who had supported him over the years through his trials and tribulations at his seat of learning. His first call was to his Uncle Will and his Aunty Ethel who had been deeply kind to him, she a close friend and sister of his dad.

Jim smiled as he entered their backyard. Uncle Will, as usual was tinkering with his car, his pride and joy, a Riley RMC. "How did you get on?" he yelled referring to his examinations.

"I passed!" Jim cried jubilantly.

"Jim's here Ethel, he's passed!" Will yelled.

Ethel walked slowly towards him throwing her arms around his neck, holding him tight as is she kissed him on his lip. They sat for a while talking about his success in the examinations, his plans and reminiscing of days gone-by. They had been kind and generous to him over the years since his dad passed, and he loved them dearly.

The scenic route from his Aunty Ethel's home to his Granddad's farm was one of Jim's favorite trips. Descending to the Ridgeway, he saw a merchant ship in the distance moving along the Manchester ship Canal heading towards the River Mersey. He stopped for a while to enjoy the scene, absorbing the atmosphere, admiring a fine stand of oak trees, fascinated by their strength, a scene that typified the beauty of the English countryside.

It was 'coffee time,' an old English tradition. As Jim arrived at his Grandparents farm, they were sitting in the south garden. Granddad was reading his copy of the *Times* newspaper, Grandma knitting, as was her custom on Saturday morning. Jim lingered for a moment to admire the beauty of their well-kept garden overlooking the lower ten fields. That was the first piece of land that they had bought when they had migrated to Cheshire so many years ago. His Grandma smiled as she greeted him warmly. Kissing him on his forehead, "Well, how did you get on my son?"

"I passed, Grandma," replied Jim gleefully.

"Oh well done my boy," said Granddad. "Mary this calls for a celebration. Bring the sherry bottle."

"It's been a long time, no see!" said Granddad.

"Yes Granddad, it has. I have been swatting hard. What's been happening?"

Granddad raised his eyebrows in astonishment, "You haven't heard? While you were away, old man Mason's farm came on the market and I bought it."

"That's great news!" exclaimed Jim. "Congratulations, Granddad. It will add two hundred acres to your farm."

"Yes you're right, my boy," he said with a smile. "Your Grandma and I have achieved another milestone in our lives."

"Take a look in the lower barn, Jim," said Grandma with a smile. "Better still, I will come with you."

Jim opened the door of the old barn. "Oh my!" he exclaimed admiring the Riley R M C car. "It's a beauty, Grandma!" he cried ecstatically. "Who does it belong to?"

There was a tear in her eyes as she murmured softly. "You, my Boy. It's our present to you for your birthday and graduation."

"Oh, Grandma!" he cried ecstatically hugging her. "Thank you, my dear."

She smiled, "Give your old Grandma a kiss. I am so bloody proud of you, Jim Mitchell," she said as the tears of joy welled in her eyes.

"Thank you, Grandma," said Jim. "I've always wanted one."

She smiled, "Yes I know my lovely your Uncle Will found it at the auction. It was going for a 'song,' so I bid for it. He tells me that we have a bargain," she cried triumphantly. "You should have seen it at auction, Jim! It looked a right mess. Your granddad's men cleaned it, and he went to Chester in it yesterday."

"What do you think, Jim?" asked Granddad as they returned to the garden.

"It looks good, Granddad. It's a car that I've always wanted," he replied, hugging him. "Thank you."

"Drive it home; I will drop your bike off next week." He paused. "Now tell me about your exams."

"There is not a lot to tell really, Granddad. I guess that I was lucky with the questions." He mused, "It was hard work. Ms Henning was a great help to me, and I will always be grateful to her."

"I guess you will be celebrating tonight."

"I am going to have a dinner with, Lydia."

"A date?" she inquired.

Jim felt his face blushing as he replied defensively. "No, I don't think so," somewhat intrigued by her question. "Well sort of, Grandma," he replied somewhat hesitantly. "She's older than me and she's been married before," he replied.

"What the hell has that got to do with it?" Granddad replied emphatically. "Her father Jack and I have been friends the years, and she is a nice young lady," he smiled. "She's a 'looker' to boot. You two look good together, and from what Jack tells me, you are friends. Don't you think so, Mary?" he asked.

"Yes, dear," she replied looking up from her knitting. "Bring her to dinner sometime. She has been very kind to you and I wish to thank her personally. I agree with your Granddad, I don't give two hoots about the gossip in the village. Believe you me, Jim Mitchell, if she makes you happy, run with it. Happiness doesn't come easy in this life, does it, Love?"

"No, it doesn't, my love," agreed his Granddad.

Jim drove the Riley to his last visit of the day, his dad's grave. The surrounding grass was dry and he sat looking at the head stone. "I passed, Dad," he said quietly. "I hope you're pleased. I will be joining your old company as an apprentice electrical engineer and I'm looking forward to walking in your footsteps." Jim said his usual prayer. There was, as usual, a tear in his eye as he stood and slowly walked away. "Miss you, Dad," he cried.

Jim arrived at the cricket ground just before noon. The sky was covered by dark rain clouds, a typical spring day 'cloudy with intermittent rain.' "Today," he said to himself "will be one of those days; the chances of playing the cricket match was in the lap of the gods. What are our chances, Richard?" inquired Jim referring to the possibility of play that day.

"Fifty, fifty," Richard replied.

By early afternoon, the rain stopped, and the grey clouds disappeared to the west as the sun began to shine, a typical English summer afternoon. "The cricket gods were on their side," thought Jim.

Richard, the captain for the day, won the toss and elected to bat. The weather had restricted the game to 20 'over's' a side. Jim opened the batting with young Albert, 'mine host's son' from the Robin Hood, and together they scored a hundred and twenty runs. Richard and Brian were in fine form, bowling well and dismissing the opposing side for ninety runs. The village team had won the match by thirty runs.

Granddad looked on from his seat in the stand. His grandson appeared to be on a high. "I wonder," he mused.

Lydia walked down the garden path to greet her date for the night, dressed in a tight fitting body suit and running shoes. "Happy birthday, Jim, welcome," she cried as she regarded the tall blond haired athletic figure of Jim Mitchell, carrying a dozen red roses. She curtsied low as she received the gift from "Thank you kindly, Sir," she murmured softly. "Wow," she cried in surprise as she saw the Riley Automobile. "Nice wheels, Mitchell!"

"Thanks," he replied. "My birthday and graduation present from Granddad and Grandma."

"It looks gorgeous," she exclaimed, "When do I get a ride?"

"Now, if you wish!"

"Sorry, I'm running late, I went for a run across the fields thinking that I had plenty

of time before you arrived. Then daddy rang, which takes time. Take your jacket off, make a couple of gin and tonics and bring mine to the bathroom, please. I'm going to take a shower. Dinner will be ready in about an hour."

Jim regarded her as she walked to the stairs. "Nice legs," he quipped. She turned, raising her eyebrows in mock astonishment. Then with a broad smile she replied, "Thank you kindly, Sir."

Jim sat in a lounge chair in the living room. Slowly sipping a gin and tonic, smoking his first Dunhill of the day and listening to slow sensual music of Edmondo Ross in the background. The sight of Lydia's body behind the shower door excited him. She was so beautiful, all that he had imagined on the long nights as he lay on his bed fantasizing, and that wonderful feeling stirring in his loins. He smiled as his thoughts turned to the night of the Cricket Club Annual Dinner and Dance, especially the last dance. There had been a coquettish smile on her lips as she felt his hand caressing her shoulder blades, the tender exciting touch sending a shiver down her spine. She had smiled. "Yes, they would date. Was he teasing her? Would her fantasies be realized?" He was unsure. "Oh what the hell," he murmured softly.

Lydia Louise Henning smiled with satisfaction as the warm water cascaded over her as she massaged the length of her tall, lithe body with a louver, anticipating a night of sexual pleasure with the man of her dreams. She stepped out of the shower admiring her well-tanned body in the full-length mirror, the result of hours spent lying naked on the banks of the canal in the warm sunshine of an English spring. She reached for the bath towel, vigorously drying her body, gently patting the wetness of the folds of her sex, her full breasts, and the roundness of her firm buttocks. Then moving the towel to her back, she dried her muscular shoulders; moving her hips from side to side, her breasts move seductively to the beat of the music. "You look good girl," she murmured softly to herself as she massaged the body lotion into her skin. The long hours of cross-country running, the hours of exercise and press-ups had toned her body to perfection. She reached for her hairbrush applying the final touches to her straight, long hair auburn hair. "Huh!" she exclaimed as her hair tantalized the dark nipples of her breasts. She slipped into her high heels and evening gown, and regarded herself in the full-length mirror, admiring her sculptured high cheekbones, full lips, long eyelashes, and manicured eyebrows. She blushed slightly as she saw the reflection of her dress. "Is it too sexy?" she asked herself. "Oh, what the hell," she murmured nervously. "You're up for it tonight." The dark memories of the past had hopefully passed. She was a sensual rampant woman again.

She walked nervously down the stairs like a panther stalking its prey, with her wide, full red lips slightly parted, smiling seductively, her long auburn hair cascading over her shoulders, the deep plunging V- neck, white, silk dress, barely concealing the hard nipples of her breasts.

Jim's heart missed a beat as she slowly descended the stairs His body quavering with excitement as their eyes met. The white silk skirt parted as she turned her hips showing the length of her shapely legs. She stood momentarily, placing her long fingers seductively on her hips striking a pose.

Jim gulped excitedly, mesmerized by the sheer beauty of the woman standing before him. She turned, smiling seductively, revealing her muscular back, the taut skin covering the outline of her fine shoulder blades, her dress, scalloped below her hip line, outlining her buttocks.

"You like?" she murmured seductively.

Jim breathed silently, as he met her on the stairway. "You- you, you look absolutely gorgeous, Lydia," he murmured

There was a twinkle in her eyes as she murmured, "Well, thank you, Sir. Light me one of your Dunhill cigarettes." She paused, then with a nervous smile murmured, "Let's have another cocktail. Dinner will be ready in thirty minutes."

Jim walked over to the drinks cabinet. His hands were shaking as he refreshed the cocktails. Suddenly, inexplicably, the nervous tension in his body faded as he turned and walked toward her, "Your drink, Madam."

"Thank you kindly, Sir," she said while smiling seductively. "Happy birthday."

The haunting strings of Mozart's violin concerto heightened their senses as they slowly ate their meal, both eagerly anticipating the night before them. Finally, Lydia asked, breaking the silence, "How was your Grandma and Granddad?"

"There having fun. Granddad has just bought another farm. Grandma's business is doing well, and we talked about you for a while."

"Really," she exclaimed raising an eyebrow. "I hope it was all good?"

"Of course they think very highly of you. Grandma asked if you would have dinner with them."

"That would be wonderful," she said somewhat nervously. "I don't know her very well, but your granddad is a poppet, thank you."

"Apparently, your dad and my granddad met for lunch in Chester last week. He told Granddad that he was considering going back to the United States for an extended tour."

"Yes I know," she replied. "They have asked me to join them," she paused. I would like to see my Uncle Henry, again. He is my Dad's only relation, and I love him dearly, Jim. He's a poppet."

"When will you leave?"

"Don't really know," she replied. "I hope it is not for a while. She paused, "I would like to be around for your graduation. After all," she murmured softly, "I was part of the team."

"That you were, Lydia. Without your help I would have never passed."

She arose from the table with a smile, "Thank you kindly, Sir."

"That was a superb meal, Lydia," exclaimed Jim as he joined her. "The Merlot was excellent, the lamb chops were absolutely perfect and the crepes were out of this world."

She smiled, preening with pleasure. "Thank you, Jim." She paused, "I'm not a very good cook, somehow the gods were kind to me tonight. Would you like a coffee and Bailey's?"

"Yes please, shall I pour?"

"Thank you," she murmured softly. "Light me a cigar." She patted a place on the settee. "Come sit with me, let's relax for a moment." She smiled as their eyes met.

The soft sensual music, the scent of her perfume, the intoxication of the Merlot wine, the warmth of the log fire, the occasional touch enhanced the rich ambience in this beautiful room, the nearness of her excited him. She looked sexy, desirable, her sensual smile inviting him into another world, a world that he had fantasized of since the night of the Cricket Club Dinner and Dance. Emboldened by his feelings, he moved her dress, exposing the beauty of her breasts. Her body quivered with excitement as he dipped his thumb and forefinger into her glass, spreading the liquid over her breasts, slowly shaping them with the palm of his hand, holding her taut nipple between his thumb and forefinger, raising it hard. She whimpered, softly, as she pulled his head onto her heaving breast. Her body writhed with erotic pleasure as his lips sucked deeply against her hard nipple, drawing her breast, into his mouth, teasing the nipple with his tongue. Her body writhed in ecstasy as he drew her breast deeper into his mouth, suckling it harder. She screamed with pleasure, not knowing whether she was in heaven, or hell. "You are driving me wild! Hold me for a minute, Jim. I don't want this night to end."

"Shush, my beauty," he murmured softly as they sat engulfed in the flickering light of the log fire, sipping their drinks, as Samba music softly played in the background. The incessant beat of the drums, raised their senses higher and higher until they were nigh on to oblivion. His heart throbbing wildly, he saw the dim outline of her pursed lips. Teasing his mind, his body, she whimpered softly as he moved her dress to one side revealing her long muscular legs.

She felt the soft touch of his fingers, parting her thighs, feeling as wild as a tigress bucking against him as he gently massaged her sex. "Oh Jim!" she cried. "Let me love you," she murmured softly as she moved to kneel before him. Her lips parted seductively, as she slowly removed his clothing, piece by piece, casting them to one side until he was naked. "Oh Jim, you have a beautiful body, " she cried ecstatically as her long fingers gently fondled his sack, raising his cock, stroking its length with her tongue until she had raised him full.

"Oh my God, Lydia!" he yelled as she gently positioned his buttocks on the edge of the couch, lifting his legs over her shoulders. He gasped, with excitement as he felt the silken warmth of her lips devouring him, inch by inch, one hand on the base of his cock, the other fondling his sack. "Oh Lydia-- Oh my God," he cried as she stroked him faster and faster until his body writhed in agony, crying aloud, "I'm--I'm coming my beauty!" She smiled seductively withdrawing her lips teasing his tip gently with her tongue bringing him to a slow excruciating climax spilling him onto the nipples of her naked breasts.

"Oh Lydia!" he cried ecstatically, his body shaking, "that was so beautiful."

There was a coquettish smile on her face as she held his limp cock in one hand, holding his sac with the other as she slowly raised him again with her lips. "Now my beauty," she cried as she moved to stand before him while releasing the halter of her dress. Lowering it inch by inch, until it fell on the floor, she stepped out of the dress holding her breasts, molding them together with the palms of her hands pinching the nipples as she walked naked to the middle of the room, turning her head, then with a coquettish smile she shimmied her buttocks murmuring, "Dance with me."

The music was hot, and so was she. She danced, seductively, around the floor, raising her hands, placing them atop her head, wiggling her buttocks, teasing him, wanting him. She moaned softly as she felt his hands on her hips, instinctively reached for the nearest chair, bending her knees parting her thighs to receive him.

Suddenly, her world turned upside down as the darkness of her past invaded her body. "Oh, not again," she cried. "Not again, please God, not again," she cried as she fell into another world, the world of her horrific wartime experience at the hands of the bloody Gestapo. Suddenly, her body shook violently, her eyes glazed in fear as the memories of her ordeal flashed before her. Visions of the Nazi bastards standing watching, cheering, as they watched their comrades rape her incessantly, one after the other until they had had their fill. "You bastards, you bastards," she cried, her body convulsing at the memory, beads of sweat pouring off her body. Her breasts heaving as she sobbed violently, her face contorted in anger. Suddenly she felt relief as tender arms carried her away from her nightmare laying her on the softness of a cloud.

Jim lifted her tear stained, sweat covered body onto the couch unsure of how to deal with the situation. This was his friend. The Lady that had taught him, his mentor and she needed his help. He raced upstairs, soaking a bath towel in cold water to wipe the sweat from her distraught body "You are safe; you are safe, Lydia." he whispered.

Slowly her breathing eased; she began the recovery from a nightmare.

"What had happened?" he asked himself. "Had he hurt her? No, it must be something from her past." Remembering her story of the war when the Nazis had captured and tortured her. "You bastards," he cried. The effects of the bloody war were still with him, his grandfather's words, "Man's inhumanity to man." He had lost his father, and he had lost friends and now they were hurting his girl. "Will this bloody war ever end?" he yelled. He felt her pulse again. This time it was slower.

Suddenly, her eyes blinked and opened. "Where am I?" she asked, softly.

"You're home, you're safe, Lydia," he replied.

"Oh, my God," she cried in anguish as the harsh memories of her circumstance slowly returned to her. "Oh, what have I done to you, Jim? What have I done to you? I should have told you," she cried in anguish. "It's not you, sweet man.," she sobbed. "It's not you, dear Jim." the tears of remorse welled in her eyes "Hold me for a moment please, I feel so bloody ashamed of myself. Please forgive me. I am so sorry," she sobbed.

"Shush Lydia" he murmured. "Are you okay now?"

"Yes, I think so," she replied softly, looking at him through a hazy tear stained eyes. "I think so," she repeated. "What did I say, what did I do? Tell me! I want to know!" she demanded sobbing, her body shaking with fear.

"Shush, Lydia," he murmured softly. "Whatever it was, it's gone. It was a nasty dream."

"No, Jim!" she cried. "It was a nasty memory from my past. I should have told you," she cried her body shaking apprehensively, knowing that she would now have to reveal the secrets that would drive him away from her "I didn't want to tell you, Jim. Oh God, I thought that you wouldn't want me. I'm second-hand goods. I feel dirty, I feel ashamed, please forgive me. I need to talk to you. Oh God," she cried, "I hope it's not too late. I need to talk. Pour me a whiskey," she demanded her mind and body traumatized by her circumstance.

"Are you sure Lydia?" exclaimed Jim.

"Yes Damm-it! Yes, I need a drink. I should have told you before," she cried angrily. Sitting in front of the fire on the sheepskin rug, a sheet wrapped around her body, she spoke softly.

"When I was a young girl, I dreamt of fighting for my country, so I joined the Royal Air Force to follow in the footsteps of my brother. It was then I met Joe. A few weeks later, we were married. He was one of the gallant Air Force fighter pilots who fought the war in their 'Spitfires.' It was tough for them. They never knew what day they were going to die. He drank heavily, and beat me occasionally. I forgave him. Then, he started to mistreat me in harsher ways until, finally, it became intolerable, so I sued him for divorce. Following that bloody awful experience, I wanted to get away from the whole bloody mess, so I volunteered for the special operations unit, first as a linguist, then, later I was trained as a saboteur, parachuting into France many times to do the job that I was trained for. On my last drop, I fell awkwardly, injuring my leg and, unable to walk. The unit left me behind to fend for myself; those were the rules. Eventually, I was captured by the Germans. In the beginning, they were kind to me, particularly the young lieutenant. I knew that he wanted my body and he promised that he would free me if I had sex with him and his sergeant. I knew what they wanted, and I was prepared to do anything to gain my freedom. Oh, Jim." she cried, "It was no big deal. I guess I had a reputation for being a good fuck. Life was cheap in those days. There were times when we didn't know from day-to-day how long we would live. Yes, we partied a lot and I wasn't averse to sexual orgies, so I agreed. Anything to get me out my predicament. Then the Gestapo arrived. At first, they treated me well until I claimed my rights under the Geneva Convention. They laughed. I was wearing civilian clothes, and they started to interrogate me. At first, I refused to answer their questions. Therefore, they resorted to torture, beating me hard until I was bleeding. It was not too bad to start with. I was trained to withstand this type of infliction. Then, when I refused to answer their questions, they stripped me naked, and left me in a dark cellar without light, food or water. A few days later they returned, and began further interrogating me again. When I still refused to answer their questions, they gave me an electric shock treatment. The bastards! Oh God, it hurt, Jim, it hurt. I have never known such pain. I knew what they wanted, but I was no traitor to the cause. I still refuse knowing as I did the names of members of the French resistance movement."

"Oh Jim," she cried, "I couldn't give them that information. I would never have lived with myself. Finally, when I refused the last time, they strapped me onto a low bench and raped me day after day, until I prayed that I might die. Finally, when they had, had their fill of me, they dumped my naked, battered and bruised body into a field outside of the town and left me for dead.

Eventually, I was rescued by the French resistance, who also attended to my leg. When I recovered, they escorted me over the Pyrenees to Spain and I was shipped back to England. I spent several months in the hospital receiving psychological treatment. They were kind to me, Jim. The parting words of my female Doctor were, "One day, you will find a man who will take care of you."

"Oh, Jim," she sobbed. "I have had no luck with men in my life, first Joe, and then those German bastards." She sobbed. "I had hated men until you came into my life."

"Shush, Lydia," Jim whispered. "You don't have to go on. The past is the past," he cried.

She looked at him through her eyes glazed in tears. "I must, Jim. I must, you need to know the truth about me."

"These last few weeks that we have spent together have been wonderful. You made me feel alive, wanted. I should have told about my past, but I didn't want you to feel that I was second-hand goods. I had hoped that your gentle and caring ways had driven those memories away. All I wanted Jim," she said touching his hand, "was to be your woman. You have made me so happy and I have repaid you by bringing my baggage to you. Please forgive me." She sobbed, "You don't deserve this, Jim Mitchell." She looked at him, "Jim what happened tonight is not your fault. It was the bloody war. They decorated me for my service. I didn't want their bloody medal; I want my mind back." The tear-stained lids of her eyes closed. She was exhausted from her ordeal and fell into a deep sleep.

Jim carried her to her bed, resting her head on the pillow, then he lay beside her, holding her tenderly. "Sleep tight Lydia, I will guard you. Oh, God," he cried, "Will this never end? I have lost my dad, I have lost my friends from the village, and I don't want to lose her."

He awoke as the sun shone on the eastern horizon shedding its glimmering light on the room. He smiled tenderly. She was sound asleep. He rose from the bedside, leaving her a note.

"Meet me at the Robin Hood at lunchtime. If you don't come, I will understand."

Lydia Louise Henning stood for a moment at the outer door of the Robin Hood pub gathering her nerve. "Oh what the hell, you're a tough girl, Lydia," she said as she slowly opened the door.

Jim looked at her as he saw her approaching. She was walking with an attitude, like a tiger seeking its prey. Her full red lips pursed, dressed in a tight fitting, white shirt, slim blue jeans, high- heeled boots, an American cowboy hat, and her hair in a ponytail. Lydia Louise Henning looked determined. She had made at mess of her life once, and was unsure of her future.

"Good morning gentlemen," she murmured her hands on her hips adopting a defensive attitude.

"Good morning, Lydia," they replied.

"My you look good, if I may say so," said Derek.

She smiled. "You may, Sir, and I thank you."

"Hello you." Jim cried affectionately. "How are you feeling?"

She ignored the question. "I would like a pint of Newcastle Brown ale with two raw eggs and the biggest pork pie they've got, I'm starving, Mitchell."

Derek surveyed the scene, looking at Lydia. She was the most beautiful woman on two legs that he had ever seen. She also had a temper. "Oh my," he murmured to himself. "What's Mitchell done now?" He smiled, "This will cost him dearly."

"Last orders please," yelled mine host.

"Another one, Lydia?" asked Richard. "It's my turn."

"No thank you, my friend," replied Lydia politely. "I'm taking Jim for a walk,"

*"Oh,"* said Derek to himself. *"I don't think I would like to be in Mitchell's boots today."*

"How are you feeling?" Jim asked as they walked slowly hand in hand to the top of the hill.

"Okay, I've had better days and better nights. Sorry, about last night. I really am, Jim. I completely ruined the whole bloody evening, didn't I? Will you forgive me?"

"There's nothing to forgive Lydia, it was bloody war; the bloody fucking war."

She regarded him. "Jim, I can understand how you feel. You're looking at a woman, a used woman that is trying desperately hard to get rid of her past." The tears welled in her eyes as she spoke. "Over the last weeks, you and I have become friends, and we both wanted to take our friendship to a new level." There was an ironic smile on her face as she spoke. "I was up for it last night, and my bloody past got in the way."

"That's not your fault," interrupted Jim.

"Yes it is, Jim," she protested. "I should have told you; I should have been honest with you. Foolishly, I thought the memories were in the past, and that it didn't matter if I told you. You may not have wanted me. Oh Jim, my life is a bloody mess again," she sobbed violently. "I know that one day I can put the past behind me. I now know that it will take time and I'm bloody sure neither of us will want my past to get in the way every time we make love. Jim, I am a good person. Can we be friends?"

He placed the palms of his hands on the cheeks of her tired face and looked deep into her eyes. "Lydia Louise Henning, I owe you so much. You have done so much for me and I'm so grateful. I guess that I always be. Yes, we will always be friends."

She smiled. "Thank you, Jim. I guess this is goodbye. We leave next Tuesday."

Jim looked into her eyes again, "You are Lydia Louise Henning, and you have so much to give to this world that we live in. Take care. Think of me sometime, as I will think of you."

She smiled. "Yes, I will Jim," hopefully there will be a space in your life for me."

## *Chapter 23*

The first summer leaves were changing from a deep green to a light brown. The first signs of autumn were upon them. It was time for the Annual Hunt Ball, a time for Grandma to celebrate her year in office. It was also a time for Maggie Bernadette O'Toole to return to her roots.

Today, he would travel through the rolling hills of Cheshire, passing the beautiful manicured hedgerows crisscrossing the fields, the farmers harvesting the last of the autumn barley. The brightly colored barges lined the shore at the village of Sutton on the Cheshire-Stafford Canal. The swing bridge was open to allow a small coastal vessel to join the Manchester Ship Canal. Jim parked his car to watch the proceedings, which happened several times a day. The ship's whistle blew at the stern of the boat as it passed the bridge in greeting. Then the bridge opened to allow vehicular traffic to pass since time immemorial. The coastal vessel heading to the Manchester Ship Canal and, onward to the ocean, reminded Jim of the poem that he had recited many years ago, "Down to the Sea:"

> Down to the sea my boy
> Down to the sea in your ship
> To the Spanish Main, My boys
> To fight the Spanish foe
> There plunder do we seek
> We'll fly the flag of England
> For the glory, and of their plunder

James 'Mac' O'Toole slowly turned in his head to face his wife Lucy. He smiled, as he looked at her blonde hair covering most of her face. He loved this woman with all his being. She had given him daughters, and their life together was good.

"What time is it Mac?" said a voice from under the bedclothes.

"Its eight o'clock, my darling. Would you like some tea?"

"Yes please," said Lucy with a broad smile "and a kiss, please."

He arose from his bed saying to himself. "This will be a good day," his first day off work in two months. The war had lain heavily on this Irishman. The bombing of the factories had given him rapid promotion to head up the production lines. The job had lain heavily on his shoulders, giving him a little time to spend with his family.

Lucy snuggled underneath the bedclothes. This was a rarity. He was at home for the day, a little loving, just like the old days. Slowly her mind was reviewing her plans for the day, a lazy breakfast, pottering in the garden, tending to the roses then a long walk with her man. Last, but not least, the arrival of young Jim. This, his first visit to her home since Maggie had departed for London.

Mac placed a tray on the bed and gently climbed beneath the blankets.

"What time does he arrive?" asked Lucy.

"I am not sure," he replied. "All I know is that Maggie O'Toole is sitting on the bench in the front garden with her bags packed."

"Oh dear," said Lucy.

"Shush, my love," said Mac. "Don't get yourself into a state. We have been over this many times and it is not going to spoil our day, Lucy. You know, and I know, that it's over between them."

"I know, Mac," she cried. "I know," she paused. "But we both know that Maggie is a rebel at heart."

"Yes, I know my love, but we must learn to trust them. Jim is a sensible lad. From what I hear, he's met a nice young Lady. Maggie won't be short of boyfriends either."

"I know," she replied, "They have always been so happy together." She paused looking into his eyes, "I have this feeling Mac, and it scares me," she cried.

# Chapter 24

In the distance, Maggie could see Jim's car approaching. She rose from her bench to **meet** him. Nothing had changed. She felt the same flutter in her heart, the tingling feeling of expectation in her body as he stepped from his car.

"Maggie O Toole, how are you doing, my darling?"

She smiled through her tears of joy. "Better, for seeing you, cousin," she mumbled as his arms encircled her slim waist. She looked into his deep blue eyes and murmured, "Hold me, Jim, it's so bloody good to see you again."

They stood for a moment, oblivious to all, as their bodies fused in a warm embrace. Maggie smiled as she stroked his long blonde hair and murmured. "I have missed you, Jim Mitchell. Oh, Jim, life is hell without you my love."

"I know my sweet," he cried. "It's good to have you home again. Are you okay?"

"Yes," she replied. "We can talk later. Let's go and see Mum and Dad before we leave. The twins are away." She laughed, "They need to be on their own for a while. What a super car, Jim!" exclaimed Maggie as the Riley sped along the country lanes to their Grandma's home.

"Thanks," he replied. "I am enjoying it tremendously. Uncle Will has done wonders with it. It took ages to clean it up. It needs work, new carpets and a bit of interior work. One day, when I can afford it, a new paint job. The engine and the transmission are all in really good condition."

"Good, I'm pleased for you. Can we stop for a while? I'm hungry, Mitchell."

"Okay," replied Jim. "There is a transport cafe about two miles along the A 50. We can stop there. I am told that the food is excellent."

"Thank you, that is decent of you, cousin," she paused looking directly at him. "There's' a small matter which we should discuss," she murmured somewhat reluctantly.

"What's that?" he replied.

"I don't have money."

Jim roared with laughter. The thought of Maggie Bernadette O Toole superbly dressed in jeans, white shirt, high-heeled shoes, and her hair in a ponytail and wearing a black cloth cap, looking like a million dollars, without a cent to her name was hilarious.

"What are you laughing at Mitchell?" she cried.

"You, you look like one million dollars and you ain't got a cent to your name."

She laughed, posing with a coquettish smile. "Am I worth it, Mitchell?"

"You had better believe it, baby," Jim cried.

The transport cafes, one of the highlights of the British Road transport system used by truck drivers and the odd tourist, provide great food for a low cost. "It is not the Grosvenor," observed Maggie as they walked through the door. She was attracting lots of attention as she strutted with an attitude past the bar to a table at the far end of the restaurant. Jim watched in amusement. There was no doubt Maggie Bernadette O'Toole was a sharp dresser. A habit she had learned since she had joined the ranks of the Theatrical Society.

"Lucky bugger," said one who was sitting at the bar.

Jim regarded him. "Thank you, Sir," he replied. "What would you like, Maggie?"

"Fish, chips, hot tea and buttered bread."

"I will have the same," said Jim with a smile

"You're really broke, Maggie?" asked Jim.

"Yes, I am. I don't want to talk about it," she said dismissing the subject. "How long a does it takes to get to Granddad's farm?" she asked as they finished their meal.

"About thirty minutes," replied Jim.

"Can I drive?"

"Sure," he replied handing her keys to the car.

"It is a beauty!" exclaimed Maggie as she drove at speed along the A 50. "Huh!" she mused, "I think that I will get one of these one day when I am rich and famous."

"I thought you were rich," said Jim.

"You must be joking. On my pittance!" she exclaimed. "My career so far, dear cousin, consists of several walk on parts, and assistant to the director of my last play; a job that consisted mostly of sweeping floors for nineteen shillings per week. I posed nude on the stage at the Windmill Theatre for a while. Oh, Jim, it was so bloody boring. I had to shave my crotch and stand naked on stage. One night a fly landed on my arse, so I swatted it with my hand and they fired me." She laughed. "You see we were not allowed to move."

Oh, Jim," she cried, "I really do not know what I should do. If it was not for the help of my Mum and Dad, and an occasional check from Grandma, I would probably become a stripper. They make good money." She added with a laugh, "Now, Mitchell, you can see why I am always hungry. I have lost weight. It ain't easy for a girl, but there is a light at the end of the tunnel, dear boy. The Maid Marian part over the Christmas holidays should net me a minimum of five pounds per week. Then, dear boy, I shall be rich. By the way, Mitchell, thank you for the meal. If it's okay with you, I will be relying on you for my expenses during this holiday." She laughed, "I have often wondered what a kept woman feels, now I know."

"That's okay, Maggie," said Jim seriously. "I still have a fair amount of money from the rent of our market garden."

"Hello, anyone at home?" yelled Maggie as she waltzed into the kitchen throwing her arms around Grandma, kissing her lips. "How are you Grandma?"

"I am fine Maggie," she said. "My, you have lost weight, my love."

"Yes I know," she replied. "Hopefully, you will fatten me up a bit while I'm here."

Grandma laughed admiring her granddaughter. "You haven't changed much, Maggie," she said. "Somehow you are talking 'posher.'" She smiled holding her hand, "I like it. Well done. Now, let us go and try your Ball dress on to make sure that it fits. Where's Jim?" asked Grandma.

"He is outside talking to Granddad."

The dinner that evening was memorable, both for the food and for Maggie's funny remarks describing the work that she had done, imitating some of the well-known actors and actresses. "It's been great fun, Granddad, they have all got there 'airs and graces.'" She paused looking at her Grandma. "Most of them think they are God's gift to the opposite sex. My friend, who has been at the Academy for eighteen months, swears that she could have completed the course in a shorter time if she had dropped her knickers."

"Maggie!" yelled Jim in astonishment.

Grandma smiled.

"That's not for me." Then she recited a line from a famous play. "No bloody way darling, I am a good girl."

"So that's what is taking you a long time, Maggie?" kidded Granddad.

"I'm a good girl, Granddad," she retorted winking her eye.

Maggie rose early the following morning. Today was to be the highlight of her holiday, a day in the saddle riding with Jim. The early morning mist cloaked the farm as she regarded Grandma's new stallion. "This is not going to be easy," she said as she surveyed her new mount. Then with a degree of self-assurance, she whispered sweet nothings into Jack's ear. Slowly, the fifteen hand stallion bonded with her. Maggie grimaced. "If Grandma can ride him, so can I."

Jim, as usual, had mounted his horse and was watching the proceeding with interest. Eventually she mounted him and they cantered across the lower 10 to survey Granddad's new acquisition. Maggie, for some unknown reason, began to sing, "The cows in the meadow, the sheep in the corn."

"She's going off her rocker," he said to himself, "something to do with this acting thing," he mused. Her general demeanor had changed. She was less inclined to be agitated. The Maggie of old was changing. She had become more "laid back" in her approach to life, "or was she?" Jim asked himself. Whatever it was, he liked it.

Following a hard ride, they sat on the old fallen tree trunk as they had done so many times in the past to watch the early morning sun rising over the valley. The mist was eerie, reminding Jim of a scene from the film *King Arthur and the Knights of the Round Table.*

"This is fun!" she exclaimed as Jim slipped his arm around her shoulders to hold her close.

"I have missed you, Jim, can we talk."

"Yes we can, Maggie" Jim replied.

"I am getting fed up with this acting business," she exclaimed. "We do not seem to be learning a lot, and it upsets me. It is not what I thought it would be," she exclaimed. "Maybe I was carried away with the idea that I would be famous overnight. You know how I get at times. I am either up on top of the world, or down in despair. These last months have not been my best. Somehow, for some unknown reason, they have closed part of the Academy without notice. They don't seem to give a damn as to what happens to the poor students! Now we have to travel three miles on foot to an old theatre for the next couple of months or maybe more." She paused holding Jim's hand tightly. "There are rumors that they are going to increase the tuition fees, Jim," she cried. "I am going through one of my down periods. That, my love, is why I wanted to be near you. What do you think I should do?" she asked.

Jim held her face in the palms of his hands. "Maggie, you are a very talented young lady, and I am sure that you have a future ahead of you."

"Am I really, Jim?" she murmured the tears welling in her eyes.

"Yes you are, Maggie. The family is with you and we will support you in the good days, and the bad days. You see, Maggie O Toole, everybody loves you, and we will support you through thick and thin."

"Will they really, Jim?" she murmured as her tears abated. "I have always thought that most of them didn't care too much for me."

"What makes you think that?" Jim asked.

"Well, I'm moody, I have a temper at times, I am so full of my own bloody importance and now my sisters tell me that I am a temptress."

Jim laughed "So? It could be worse."

"Damn you, Mitchell!" she retorted. "Do you agree?"

"Well, yes to be honest, Maggie. You are all of those things, and maybe more, you lady, are Maggie Bernadette O Toole. You are special, oh so dammed special!" Jim cried. "Life is not going to be easy for you my love."

"Oh Jim," she cried. "I can't change, can I?"

"No, my love, you can't do that. No one would want you to. You see Maggie, you give so much pleasure to me, to the family and to everyone you meet."

"Oh Jim," she cried kissing him passionately. "You are magic to me. You are always there for me, Jim Mitchell."

"My advice," said Jim, "for what it's worth, is to stick with it. Maybe it will be hard for a while. You are a fighter, and I am here for you."

Maggie placed her hands on his cheeks and kissed him on his lips. "Thank you, my love. I owe you one."

"Yes you do, Maggie!" he exclaimed. "The only thing that I ask from you, is when you become a star, I would like free tickets for the show, and a pass to your dressing room."

"That's a deal, Mitchell. Oh, Jim," she murmured softly, "I feel much better now that we have talked. It was always this way, wasn't it?"

"Yes, it was, Maggie," he replied. "We will always be there for each other."

The following morning, the rattle of a teacup, and a familiar voice, awakened Jim. "I brought you some tea, my dear," Maggie said softly, kissing him on his lips.

"What are we doing today?" Jim asked.

"Will you take me to Blackpool?"

Jim smiled to himself. "She's back" he breathed. "That would be fun."

"Oh good," she exclaimed, "breakfast in thirty minutes."

Blackpool is the working man's North Lancashire seaside resort, known for its fine beaches and long wooden piers jutting out to the sea. The piers house musical revue theatres, starring such comedians as Tommy Handley and a host of showgirls; some of the famous ones were the 'Blue Bell Girls.'

The town boasts the biggest fairgrounds in the world, offering exciting rides on roller coasters, role a penny stalls with odds of fifty to one, rifle shooting stalls, and bumper car rides. "Roll up! Roll up!" shouted the buskers inviting the holiday makers to their stalls. If you were lucky, you could win a stuffed doll for your girl friend. Along the promenade, there were endless miles of amusement stalls, where one can buy candy floss, and have your fortune told. The city is a real fun place for the working class people of northern England and Scotland. You can stay cheaply in Mrs. Block's boardinghouse for a week, for less than two pounds. Fish and chips are the staple diet for the young visitors, costing three pennies.

The famous landmark is Blackpool Tower, a remarkable steel structure similar in design to the French Eiffel tower, is the inspiration of one of England's most famous comedian's, Stanley Holloway, who, composed, and recited, verses and the monologue, "Our Albert in the Lions Den." There were elevator rides to the top of the tower to view the surrounding picturesque landscape of Liverpool, Southport and the nearby holiday town, Morecambe Bay. One of the other highlights of the tower is the magnificent ballroom featuring the best in the Big Band music, featuring bandleaders like Joe Loss and Stan Kenton, a place where boy meets girl. He smiled. This was where Mum met Dad many years ago.

Maggie and Jim walked along the seafront. The fresh morning breeze was playing havoc with the young girl's skirts. Jim smiled with amusement as the wind tossed Maggie's skirt into the air, showing the length of her shapely legs. She laughed with some embarrassment. The young boys on holiday were having fun watching the scene. After a while, as the novelty had passed, the boys from Lancashire turned to watch the sea.

"What would you like to do now, Maggie?"

She paused a moment to consider her options. "Jim, will you win me a stuffed doll?"

"Sure," he replied. "Is that all?"

"No, I would like my fortune told, then we could go to the top of the tower, then," with an impish smile she murmured softly, "I would like to go dancing."

Jim held her tenderly and whispered, "I will do anything for you. Maggie."

"Isn't life wonderful, Jim?" asked Maggie tenderly gazing at him.

It had been an exhausting day. She slept with her head resting on Jim's lap during the journey back to the farm. Jim occasionally glanced, stroking her long black hair. This was his Irish Colleen, the first love of his life. Maggie O'Toole was a girl of moods who could excite him with a glance, then frustrate him with a word. She was a girl that wore her heart on her sleeve. Her mood would change quickly from despair to elation. "She was all of those things," he said to himself. She was his girl for so many years. It was sad. Soon they would part, each going their way to lead a separate life that was their fate. Those were the cards that were dealt. Moments like this were always precious in their lives.

Slowly she emerged from her sleep. "Are we there yet, Jim?" she murmured.

There was a knock on his bedroom door, "Shake a leg Mitchell. It is a beautiful day, tea and biscuits," Maggie said placing the tray on the side table of the bed.

"Thank you, Jim for a lovely day, my darling," she said, stroking his long blond hair. "Grandma says the breakfast will be ready in thirty minutes and Granddad is 'chaffing at the bit'. We," she announced with a smile, "are potato picking today."

Granddad Mitchell smiled as he regarded his crew for the day: Brian, Richard, Derek, Jim, and Maggie, together with two women from the village, as they boarded the tractor-trailer. It was seven o'clock a.m. "Maggie your driving," ordered Granddad.

"Who me?" she exclaimed.

"Yes you, girl. Put a move on."

"Okay, Granddad," she replied excited for the day. She started the Fordson tractor. The motley crew was on their way for a hard days work in the lower 10 potato field.

"Hitch the potato digger, Jim," yelled Granddad. "Maggie you're driving again, my dear."

"Okay, Granddad." she replied with a broad smile.

Row, after row, the potatoes were lifted by the machine as the remainder of the crew loaded them into hundred pound bags for the wholesale merchant to transport away.

"The work continued until the last bag was filled. It was four thirty p.m. as the crew gathered round Granddad to receive their pay for the day.

"You have done well," he said somewhat gratified that he had the last of his potatoes harvested. "Come up to the house and join me in a beer."

"How are you feeling, Love?" asked Jim.

She gave Jim a wry smile. "Bloody tired, Jim, I think I have an ache in every bone of my body."

"Cheer up. Grandma will run a hot bath for you. Have a good soak, then, if you're lucky, I will give you one of my famous massages, or wash your back, whichever you choose."

"Huh" she replied, "A girl should be so lucky."

Jim concluded from her words that Maggie's sense of humor had gone out of the door.

Maggie, slowly walked up the stairs, stripping the clothing off her back as she went, then stepped gingerly into Grandma's oversize bath, slowly recovering from the hardest working day of her life, vowing that she would never, never marry a farmer. "That is better," she said as she eased herself into the bath, soaked herself for a while, then slowly dried herself with one of Grandma's best towels. There was a quizzical look on her face as she looked into the mirror, "What was Grandma's news about? Huh, that can wait. I need a drink." She tied the towel around her body and walked into the living room.

Granddad smiled as he saw her and murmured to himself. "That's my girl." He paused, admiring her. "What would you like to drink, Maggie?"

"A stiff gin and tonic please, Granddad."

"Cheers," she murmured having drunk two thirds of the glass.

"I have some news," said Grandma as they sat outside in the garden drinking their after dinner coffee. "Do you remember Sam Waterston's daughter, Mary Jane Henderson?"

"Yes, she's my Godmother," replied Maggie.

"Yes, she is" said Grandma. "Her mother and I used to ride in the hunt before she had that terrible fall around five years ago. Do you remember her, Jim?"

"Yes," replied Jim. "Didn't she have a daughter?"

"Yes, Mary Lou. I met her last week when I was shopping in Chester. She asked how you were, and I told her that you would be starting your apprenticeship soon, and that Maggie was attending the Academy. Apparently, she runs a theatrical agency from the Manchester office, which I believe is very successful. She would like you to go and see her sometime. She also added that she thought that you, Maggie, would make a very fine photographic and fashion model. Anyway, she asked if she could meet you both at the Hunt Ball next Saturday. Apparently, they are sitting at the next table to us."

"It's getting a bit chilly, Mary," said Granddad. "Let's go inside, I want to talk to the children. Would you like another beer, Jim? Maggie, how's your drink?"

"I will have another, Granddad. This gin and tonic of yours is absolutely splendid."

"Well thank you, Maggie. I am glad that that you're enjoying it."

"Cheers, Grandma! Cheers, Granddad! Cheers, Mitchell!" exclaimed Maggie."

"Salute," they replied.

Granddad Mitchell regarded his two favorite grandchildren "Your Grandma and I have recently revised our wills, and I would like to discuss them with you since you are the main beneficiaries." He paused. "I have talked to your parents, Uncle Will and Aunty Ethel. As you know they are pretty well off, and I've left annuities for your two sisters. What would you like, Maggie?"

She smiled, "Granddad, would you build me a house in Pinewood, overlooking the valley?"

"Consider it done, young lady." She jumped from her seat and flung her arms around him, tears welling in her eyes. "Oh thank you, thank you, thank you, thank you, Granddad. I love you." She walked slowly across the room to her Grandma, and knelt beside her, holding her face in her hands, then with a gesture looked into her eyes, "Grandma you have put up with a lot from me over the years. I know that I have been a pain in the arse. Thank you, my darling," she cried as she held her closely.

Jim sat quietly in his chair, sipping his beer observing the family. This was a moment in time, when he realized that one day he would take over the farm from his Granddad.

"Last, but not least, young Jim, it is my intention to leave the farm in your hands. I know that you will regard my wishes. The first is to carry on with the family name and its traditions. The second is to maintain the farm, and when the time comes, I would wish you to expand it." Jim stood and walked across to his Granddad and hugged him closely. "Thank you, Sir; you leave it in good hands."

Maggie Bernadette O Toole, her body still recovering from the hard work of potato picking, lay in her bed. Her thoughts were on the previous evening. The opportunity of furthering her career was exciting. She had met Mary Lou on a number of occasions, remembering her as a tall, immaculately dressed lady, kind and very considerate, who had always remembered her birthday with a card and a modest check; a gift which Maggie always acknowledged by sending a thank you note and a card each and every Christmas. Now, she was presenting her with an opportunity that could further her career.

"I have a lot to offer," she said to herself confidentially. "My facial features are classic. I have a beautiful body, my elocution is by all standards, extremely good. I have an elegant posture and I am photogenic." There was a confident smile on her face as she murmured, "And I have talent."

"Yes, I am confident in my manner, I'm enthusiastic for things that I like. My expectations are high. Yes," she said to herself, "I have my faults and I have a temper that needs to be controlled. I expect people to wait on me hand and foot. There are days when I am down and miserable and days when life is just wonderful. Maggie Bernadette O Toole," she said to herself, "you are a spoiled brat at times. Jim tells me that I am unique. Oh well, you will have to work on those things, my dear," she said to herself as she slowly fell asleep.

The Westminster clock in the living room struck four o'clock. Maggie was awake and restless. She could not wait until the early morn, a time when she and Jim would go to Pinewood, and 'peg out' the site of her new home. "Oh hell," she murmured, "I cannot sleep. Please make the morning come quickly."

Jim was awakened by the rustle of a nightgown as his bedroom door opened, then closed. "Shush, move over, Jim. I can't sleep, I am too excited," she said pulling the sheets over their heads. "Just hold me love!" she said tenderly. "Last night, news was too much for me, I can't wait until we go to Pinewood."

"What time is it?"

"It's nearly five o'clock. The sun will be up in half an hour."

"Okay," he replied.

The sun was breaking over the eastern valley as they saddled their horses and rode swiftly over the fields to Pinewood where they sat on an old tree trunk surveying the scene.

"Hold me for a minute please, Jim," she cried excitedly. "I have dreamed of this moment for so many years. Oh, Jim, this is so wonderful!" she cried as the tears of joy welled in her eyes.

"Shush, my love," he murmured holding her close. "Let's have some fun shall we?"

"Oh Mitchell" she cried. "I just can't believe it! This had always been my dearest wish that one day I would build a house here." Her face brightened, the tears dried. "Shall we start?" she exclaimed. "The living room," she said confidently, "should face south, that way," she said pointing into the distance. "I want my bedroom to face east, so that I can see the early morning mist and the sun rise. There are some stones over there," she pointed, "Can we mark it out?"

"Sure," said Jim eager to share her enthusiasm.

"And we will have three bedrooms over there," she said with a smile.

Jim laughed, "I think you will have three trees in your living room, and two in your bedroom."

"Don't be silly, Jim," she said reprimanding him. "They will take those away before they start building. I just wanted to see a rough outline."

"Will that do you?" Jim asked after he had labored for a couple of hours moving stones until the basic layout was to her satisfaction.

"Yes", she replied, "Thank you. You have done a good job, my love. Now, can you imagine living here?"

"Yes, I can, Maggie, I am sure that your home will be very elegant." He laughed, "Suitable for a lady of the theatre."

She curtsied low with a smile looking into his eyes. "Thank you kindly, Sir."

They sat for a while holding hands absorbing the view of the extraordinary beauty of the Cheshire countryside. "It's beautiful, Maggie."

"Oh God," she cried. "There is one thing missing, Mitchell."

"What's that Maggie?"

"Damn it! You don't see you. It's nothing without you!" exclaimed Maggie "Can we go now, please?"

"How do I look?" said Maggie as she strutted along the dining room floor wearing her jeans, and carrying a book on her head.

"Don't the models wiggle their hips like Rita Hayworth?"

"I don't know," she replied, "I am trying to walk elegantly, Mitchell. I am sure that Mary Lou will be watching me tomorrow night."

"I think you look fine Maggie, don't panic," Jim replied. "Your smile, your figure, and your photographs, will please her. Seriously, Love, she would be daft if she didn't hire you."

"You really think so?" Maggie asked with a quizzical look on her face...

"Of course I do, silly. I wouldn't tell you if it wasn't true."

"Oh, there you are," said Grandma as she entered the room. "Oh my!" she exclaimed. "Maggie you look beautiful, my dear."

"Thank you Grandma, I'm trying. Will she ask me questions?"

"Yes, I suppose so," replied Grandma. "Do you want me to interview you?"

"Yes, if you would, I want to be at my best Grandma," she said assertively.

Jim sat at the end of the dining room listening to his Grandma conducting a mock interview with Maggie. There was an aura of confidence about his cousin as she answered her questions.

"What do you see yourself doing in five years time, Maggie?"

"I want to be happy," she said with a smile. "Secondly, I want be at the top of my profession as a model."

"Is that all Maggie?" asked Grandma.

"Yes," she replied. "Short, sweet and to the point."

"What do you think, Jim?" said Grandma as she exited the room.

"I thought you were both very good, Grandma," he said tenderly. "I am sure that

Maggie will do well."

"Well thank you, Mitchell," said Maggie with a deep curtsy.

# Chapter 25

"Today," Maggie said to herself, "is a good day as she rode Jack, Grandma's stallion, at a gallop. Her long black hair trailed in the wind as she rode through the lower 10, then gradually climbing to the top of the hill, to revisit the site of her future home, 'Pinewood.' The night before, she had made rough pencil stretches of the house. The thought that one day, her Granddad would build her dream home overlooking the Cheshire plains excited her body and soul. She somehow wished that it would happen quickly. Sadly, that would mean the demise of her Granddad and Grandma. "That", she said emphatically to herself, "is not acceptable." With a twinkle in her eye, she thought, "Maybe, Granddad would build it sooner. I will need to work on that over the next few years."

"Mitchell", she said as her cousin approached. "This is the layout of my new home," she said proudly. "What do you think?"

"Huh, it looks good, Maggie. How many levels are there?" he inquired.

"I don't know," she admitted. "I had only thought of one at the moment."

"Maybe," he said, "it should be two levels! That would give you a better view from the top floor." He paused looking at her, "Why don't you climb the tree and take a look?"

"Typical, Mitchell," she muttered, "detail oriented. Oh God," she muttered as she climbed higher and higher, "he's right, as usual." The additional height gave her spectacular views of the valley. "How do I get down from here?" she yelled to Jim standing below.

Jim laughed, "Slowly, with feeling, Maggie."

"A fine help you are, Mitchell," she exclaimed as she slowly climbed down the tree.

"Well, what you think?" he asked.

"Your right as usual, Mitchell, it's a good idea. Can we sit for a while and talk about the plans?"

"Sure, lend me your pad and pencil!" Jim sketched for a while using copious amount of paper until he was satisfied with his plan. "What do think of this? We could move the living room to the second floor and include a balcony so you can see the setting sun."

"How do we get up there?"

"Construct an ornate wrought iron, winding staircase?"

"Brilliant, Mitchell!" she exclaimed. "I love it, thank you," her eyes misted as she murmured softly, "Hold me close for a minute please, Jim. My dream is coming true."

Maggie sat in the passenger seat of the Riley, her legs tucked underneath her backside. "Oh Jim, this has been a marvelous day, my love. I feel so excited about my new home."

"It's not over yet, Maggie," he cried over the noise of the Riley engine. "We, my girl, have the whole night together: Grandma's cocktail party, the Hunt Ball, and staying at the luxurious Grosvenor Hotel. You and I will have a ball tonight!"

"Hum," she smiled in anticipation.

"Good afternoon, Sir; Good afternoon, Madam. Welcome to the Grosvenor." The desk clerk paused, "Will you be staying with us, Sir?" he asked.

"Yes," replied Jim. "My grandmother, Ms Mary Mitchell has booked two rooms. One for Maggie Bernadette O'Toole, and one for myself, Jim Mitchell."

"Yes Sir, I have your reservations, checking out at noon tomorrow. Here are your room keys. The bellman will deliver your luggage in a few minutes."

"Wow!" cried Maggie as they rode the elevator to the fourth floor. "This is really posh, Mitchell!" she exclaimed. "Better than I'm used to, my dear Mitchell!" she cried as they entered into her suite. "We have inter-communicating doors. Oh my!" she cried excitedly as she entered the bathroom. "The bath is so much bigger than Grandma's. This is a posh hotel, Jim; I love it. A girl could get carried away with this." There was a coquettish smile on her face as she murmured. "I'm going to have a bath. Stay and wash my back from me, please!"

"Maggie you're a temptress, my dear."

She laughed, "Yes I know. Isn't it fun?"

Jim regarded his suite as he prepared himself for the evening, and Grandma Mitchell's cocktail party - the meal, followed by the ball, and just being with Granddad and Grandma again. His thoughts turned to Maggie. They had spent a wonderful holiday together. Maggie was constantly on his mind. "Oh, Maggie," he cried. "What the hell am I going to do about you?" A perplexed Jim questioned as he realized that their relationship was changing. They were no longer just friends, or kids, together. She was now a beautiful, sensuous woman. Yes, a temptress, that part of her makeup hadn't changed. Last night, when she had climbed into his bed, she had held him close, rousing him with her tender touches, tempting him, teasing him, inviting him to love her. He paused examining his thoughts. Last night was different, much different than he had ever known before. "Oh God," he cried. He had wanted her as a woman without fear or reservation. His body had yearned for her, yet he had drawn back from the finale "Oh, Maggie," he cried, "what the hell am I going and to do with you my darling?"

There was a sense of relief from his dilemma as the cold water from the shower cascaded over his taut muscular body. Slowly, his thoughts turned to his Grandma and Granddad. During the past few months, he had grown closer to them. His Granddad had talked to him about his intention to hand over the farm to him one day in the future. They had quite intimately talked about him getting married in the future, producing a son, an heir to the estate.

"There was plenty of time for that," he said to himself. Granddad was still in rude health. He could fulfill his dream to become a chief engineer in the mercantile marine before assuming the responsibilities of running the farm. His thoughts had gone further. Should anything unforeseen happen, he would promote one of Granddad's men as foreman, using the services of a land agent to take overall responsibility until such times as he had fulfilled his dream to travel the world. His thoughts turned again to his relationship with Maggie Bernadette O'Toole. He was aware that his Granddad adored her from when she was a small child.

Remembering his words many years ago, "You look good together my children," never realizing how deep their love was for one another. When they had parted on her mother's edict years ago, Jim's mother had told him that she was sad. Now Grandma and Granddad had brought them together into an intimate surrounding. It seems strange in a way, just as though he and Maggie had their blessing. "Oh Dad," he cried, "I wish you were here to help me."

Jim dismissed the subject as he stepped out of the shower. He was looking forward to the evening, the cocktail party, the meal, and dancing with Maggie. His face brightened, "Maggie Bernadette O'Toole, you and I, my darling, are going to have a ball tonight."

There was a knock on the inter-communicating door. "Are you decent?" she inquired as she walked into the room wearing a garter belt, silk stockings and high heels shoes. "Are my seams straight, Mitchell?"

"No they're not Maggie, come here! Oh, Maggie," he laughed in amazement, "You've forgotten your knickers!"

"Oh don't be such a bloody prude. Mitchell. Straighten my stockings for me, please. That's a good fellow."

"Okay, stand on the dressing stool." His hands moved up her legs slowly manipulating the seams of her stockings. "That will do," he said.

"Thank you, dear boy," she murmured with a coquettish smile on her face. "One has to look one's best tonight, doesn't one?" She laughed as he lightly spanked her buttocks. "Kinky, Mitchell, I like it." Her arms encircled his shoulders as he lifted her from the stool. She looked into his eyes, "Do you remember the time when you promised me *one wish*?"

"Yes I do, Maggie," whispered Jim looking directly in her eyes.

She smiled, seductively, "Can I sleep with you tonight?"

"Oh hell, Maggie," he murmured. "We promised our parents years ago that we would never do that."

"I know, my Love," she murmured softly. "The only bloody reason was that they didn't want you and me to bring a child into this world. That's the only bloody reason," she cried emphatically, tears welling in her eyes. "Oh, Jim, my Love, it's safe, I know my body." Suddenly her tears turned to a coquettish smile, "Anyway I have three of those things! From the chemist!"

"Oh Maggie what am I to do with you?"

She looked into his eyes. "Mitchell, don't tell me that you don't want me!" she exclaimed.

"I do, Maggie," he cried. "You know damn well I do!" he exclaimed passionately.

"Oh good," she murmured as she left the room. "Now get your sweet arse into your pants and take me to the ball."

"Time to go Mitchell," she cried as she opened the door to his bedroom. "How do I look?" she said striking a seductive pose. Jim stood momentarily absorbing the sheer beauty of his cousin, dressed in a fashionable red empire evening gown the deep plunging neckline emphasizing her breasts, her slim waist, rounded hips and her shapely long legs.

"Lost your voice, Mitchell?" she asked.

"No Maggie," he said nervously. "You look, you look so incredibly beautiful," he said regaining his composure. "I have never seen you look so damned beautiful as you do tonight. Your hair looks absolutely gorgeous. You know I love it atop. You look radiant my dear." He paused in admiration. "Your gown fits beautifully, Maggie."

"In and out in the right places, would you say, Mitchell?"

"Yes, I would," he replied as he slipped his arms around her waist holding her close. "Maggie Bernadette O Toole, you are a truly beautiful lady."

She was quiet for a moment. Her eyes moistened as she murmured softly "It's for you, Jim, it' all for you, my Love."

"Shush-shush," he murmured softly kissing her sweet lips.

She smiled looking through the mist into his eyes. "A girl could get carried away by a guy like you, Mitchell. You look so bloody good." There was a coquettish smile on her face willing him, loving him, teasing him. She murmured softly "What are my chances for tonight, Sir?"

Jim looked into her eyes. "Maggie Bernadette O'Toole, tonight, you and I, will have a ball, Lady."

The cocktail party was in full swing as Jim and Maggie entered their Grandparent's suite. Grandma, as usual, was greeting her friends, while Granddad, as usual, was busy entertaining the Ladies with his charismatic charm.

"Maggie, my darling," Grandma said as she embraced her. "You look so beautiful tonight."

Jim smiled as she regarded him. "Hello, Love, sorry were late, I been making some sketches for Maggie's new home. How are you?"

She smiled, "Better for seeing you, my grandson. You, young sir, look absolutely gorgeous."

"Thank you ma'am," he smiled. "You look beautiful as usual."

"Mitchell, you're getting more like your Granddad every day." She winked, "I like it."

"How nice to see you, my dear," said Mary Lou addressing Maggie.

"You, my dear, look absolutely stunning. The latest fashion!" She laughed, "My memories of you are that you were a skinny lass." She paused, "Now, my dear, you have grown into a beautiful woman. I just love your gown."

"Thank you," replied Maggie, "you're most kind."

Eyeing Jim, Mary Lou said, "You must be Jim Mitchell?"

"That I am, Ma'am. I am pleased to meet you."

"It's been a long time, Jim Mitchell. You look handsome, Sir, just like your dad."

"Well thank you ma'am, I appreciate the complement."

"Would you mind if I stole Maggie for a moment?" Jim nodded in agreement.

"Let's talk for a moment Maggie, shall we? Over there," she said pointing to a quiet corner of the room. "Your Grandma Mary tells me that you have aspirations to become an actress. How is it going?" she inquired.

"I am learning," replied Maggie. "I have served my time as the sweeper upper and polisher of sets, and I make an excellent cup of tea."

Mary Lou laughed. "That's show business, my dear," she said. "That's show business," she repeated. "Do you have an agent?"

"No," Maggie replied. "There's no one interested in me, as far as I can see."

Mary Lou smiled "That's not quite true, Maggie. I would like to represent you; not just on the stage, but there are some opportunities in film, and modeling. Why don't' you come and see me one day next week, say Wednesday. Then we can do some tests and all that stuff. If all goes well, I will introduce you around, and, hopefully, I can get you a few auditions."

"Thank you," said Maggie, "I am so grateful to you!"

"One has to take care of one's goddaughter, doesn't one," Mary Lou said with a smile.

The annual Cheshire Hunt Ball was a lavish affair, according to Grandma, a sort of who's who in the Cheshire Society. The meal was rich and splendid consisting of split bean soup, roast leg of lamb, sorbet of strawberries and washed down with a fine Chardonnay.

Jim felt proud as his Grandma stood to propose the toast of the evening. He smiled, the Yorkshire accent was still with her, after some thirty odd years of living in Cheshire. "My Lords, Ladies and Gentlemen," she began. "It is my proud honor to propose the toast of the evening. Alas, it is also my job, as the outgoing ladies president, to add a few comments on the year. They will be brief as anyone who knows me will tell you," she paused, "it's been an outstanding year, and I would like to thank everyone one of you, for assistance in making it so. It has also been a tough year in many respects. Now we look forward to more peaceful times in this fair and pleasant county of ours." She smiled. "I have two stories to tell…" The assembly laughed at her jokes. She finished on a high. Then, she stood smiling, looking around the floor, and added, "The toast is to our new president."

"The new president!" they replied. There was an unprecedented applause as she sat murmuring softly to herself, "Thank God that is over. Now I can dance the night away with my man."

The famous Scottish song, "Auld Lang Sine," drew the gathering to a close. Granddad smiled. "Let's have a nightcap at the bar to crown the evening."

"You were wonderful tonight, Grandma," said Maggie. "One day, my Love, I will lead the hunt."

"Cheers, my dear. I will drink to that," smiled Grandma.

"It's been a great evening," said Granddad. He paused, "Unfortunately, I have an early start in the morning. Take your time coming home. We will see you when you arrive. Goodnight, my Love," he said holding Maggie in his arms. "Good night, my son."

"Thank you, Sir," Jim replied shaking his hand. "Last, but not least" Jim murmured softly as he hugged his Grandma. "You were wonderful tonight, Grandma. I am proud to be your grandson."

"Well thank you, Jim," she murmured softly. "You make me proud, my son." she paused, looking into his eyes, then whispered, "Take good care of our Maggie—*she's special.*"

"That was a damn good night, Maggie," he said as they walked along the corridor to their rooms. "Did you hear Grandma's remark?"

"No, what was that?" she inquired.

"Take care of Maggie; she's special."

"Oh hell," she murmured silently to herself. "She knows! Oh what the hell. I love him and I want him," she cried.

A nervous apprehension swept through Jim's body as he entered the key into the lock, opening the door to his suite. Maggie entered the suite kissing him lightly, bringing her forefinger to her lips as she walked to the four-poster bed. She stood for a moment releasing the halter of her dress. She turned slowly. Smiling seductively, she lowered her dress inch by inch to the floor, then, with a deft move, raised her slim arms to her head, releasing the gold clasp, unfurling her hair.

"Oh, Maggie," Jim breathed as memories raced through his mind as he stood admiring the girl he had loved as a child, and as a young girl; sweet poignant memories of yesteryear and her words "I think I like you," uttered when they were children. He was remembering the Christmas party when she murmured softly to him, "on the lips Darling, it's Christmas don't you know;" and the long summer days, lying naked on the grass in her secret place. Memories. This was a girl who had entertained the party that evening with her winning ways. "Oh my God," he breathed, this was the girl that he had fallen in love with so many years ago, now a magnificent rare beauty. "Maggie, my Darling," he murmured. "You are truly beautiful."

She smiled tenderly. "For you, my Love," she murmured softly as he gathered her in his arms laying her head gently on the bed pillow.

The autumn sun was shining through the bedroom as she looked at him lying on his belly, fast asleep. "I love you Jim Mitchell," she murmured "with all my heart, with all my body, with all my soul. The memories of tonight I will cherish forever my darling Jim. It was beautiful; so unbelievable. Oh my God," she murmured softly. The tenderness of his touch as he caressed her, overwhelmed her, taking her body and, her mind, into a world of love and deep sexual satisfaction. Her body shuddered with emotion as she murmured softly, "Jim my Love, when you stroked me, we looked into each other's eyes with an unbelievable intensity. Oh Jim, it was so beautiful my darling," she cried. The tears of happiness welled in her eyes falling over her high cheek- bones onto the pillow. Her body shuddered remembering the deep emotion she had felt as he lovingly brought her to a slow unbelievable climax. Then tenderly again, and again until her body entered into a blue haze of deep sexual satisfaction. Then, slowly, with a deep sense of emotion, she had thrust her hips hard against him, crying, "Let it come, my Love, I want to feel it inside me," as she brought him into a slow lingering climax, holding his face between her hands as his body shuddered in ecstasy. He smiled, as only her man could smile, murmuring, "I love you, Maggie, with all my heart, with all my body, with all my soul, my darling."

That night, his tenderness, had exposed her deep feelings for the man that she had loved for so many years, as a baby in her arms, as a boy, and now as a man. The tears welled in her eyes again as she sobbed, "It doesn't change our lives, my Love. It brings us closer." She paused. "I know that we will never marry. I know that I will never have your children. Isn't life so bloody ironic?" she cried. "That's the cards that you and I have been dealt, my Love," she had murmured passionately. "Promise me a one thing, my Love, let's meet whenever we can, until such times as we marry and go our separate ways."

"Well, how did you get on?" Jim inquired as she stepped into the Riley parked outside the offices of Henderson & Co. She laughed excitedly, her body shaking with elation, tears of joy running down her beautiful cheeks.

"Bloody marvelous, Jim," she muttered emotionally, "bloody marvelous. Jim, it was wonderful. Just hold me for a moment. Kiss me, I can't believe it!" she cried. As their lips parted, she opened the brown manila envelope. "These are my pictures," she cried triumphantly.

"Wow! These are good, Maggie," said Jim admiring her photographs. There were a couple of photographs of her in bathing suits, others showing her wearing different types of apparel, different shoes, and different hairstyles. "You look like a million dollars, Maggie."

"Thank you, Jim. Mary Lou tells me that I am very photogenic."

"How was the rest of the meeting?"

They were impressed with my stage presence. I read for her, and she complimented me on my elocution. I strutted on the catwalk, and wiggled my backside. It felt good. "Oh Jim, it was so wonderful. I feel really good about it."

"There's more," she said triumphantly. "Guess what?" she cried excitedly. "I have two auditions and one photographic session in London next week. You're not going to believe this. Mary Lou has been kind enough to pay my expenses. Oh Jim," she cried. "Isn't it bloody marvelous? I have funds!" she yelled. "Mitchell, tonight I am taking you to dinner, at our hotel," she murmured with a coquettish smile. "It is already paid for. Oh, Jim!" she cried. "Isn't life wonderful? I have a career!" She touched his hand looking lovingly into his eyes, "and I've been laid beautifully by the kindest, loving man in this bloody world."

# Chapter 26

"Welcome back, Jim," said Richard as he walked into the Robin Hood pub.

"Thanks guys," he replied. "It's good to be back. What's happening?"

"Not a lot" said Derek, "Apart from the local derby football match next week."

"What sort of shape are you in?" asked Richard.

Derek laughed. "Just look at him, he looks knackered."

"Leave it off," Jim cried irritably. "Okay, I have missed a couple of matches and put on a couple of pounds, which I can lose before Saturday's game."

The following morning, Jim awoke at six thirty a.m., dressed into his running gear, and sprinted to Richard's house. "Rise and shine, big boy. Rise and shine," he shouted.

"You're bloody early," Richard cried as he saw him.

"You told me to get into shape. Here I am, ready to go. We can pick up Brian and Derek on the way."

"What's the plan?" asked Richard.

"Granddad's farm, then back again over the hill to Mum's cottage; let's go, big boy!" he yelled.

The first three miles was fairly easy going, and then Jim felt a cramp in his leg.

"Oh hell!" he cried.

"What's up?" asked Derek.

"Cramps in my right leg!" he shouted.

"Sit you down," he ordered. "Let's see if we can work it out." Slowly, with feeling, Derek's expertise relieved his malady, and they continued. Jim was determined to be in good shape for the game.

During the following days, Jim worked out with an intensity that his teammates had never seen before. They knew that he was determined to be included in the side. In form, he was a terrific asset to any team.

"Welcome back," said coach as he entered the dressing room prior to the game.

"Why the hell did you drop me?" inquired Jim angrily.

"I haven't dropped you, Mitchell, you are the first reserve. My plan is to put you on in the second half. Okay?"

"Cheer up," said Brian as the team walked down the pitch. "Someone is bound to get injured. It's going to be a bloody rough game."

Jim watched his team from the dugout. The opposing team was a formable size. Mostly farm workers from the next village, they had started the game well, pressuring the home team in the first fifteen minutes. Slowly, the home team gained the supremacy of the mid field game and the tempo changed. Richard, as usual, was firm in defense. Brian was fetching and carrying from the midfield, but somehow, the strikers were not finishing, missing a couple of good opportunities to score goals, much to the consternation of the supporters.

The half-time whistle blew, and he could see relief on coach's face. The first half had not gone well for the home team. Jim overheard Richard mumbling that the team had not taken advantage of the two opportunities to score. However, coach was not panicking, and made no changes in the team. With fifteen minutes to go, the game was evenly matched. Coach ordered Jim to ready himself to enter the fray. "Here's the plan, you play up front. Tell Brian, Richard and Noby Jones to get the ball high in the air in the penalty box. That will give you an opportunity to score."

"Yes, sure coach," he said. "I will have a go."

There was five minutes to go when young Noby placed a beautiful high pass into the penalty area. Jim brushed aside a defender, then glanced the ball inside the far post, "Goal" yelled the crowd. "Goal," yelled Jim as he picked himself up from the grass. Only to be knocked down again by his teammates celebrating the goal, "Noby!" Jim yelled as he picked himself up from the ground, "that was a pass of a lifetime, my friend, thanks."

The game was over. They had beaten the team that had led the league for last two years. "You played well, lads," said coach. "The first pint is on me."

"Why did you drop me?" asked Jim as he talked to coach after the game.

"Two reasons, he replied. The first is that I didn't think you could play ninety minutes, and I knew that the game would be tight." He smiled. "I needed you in good shape for the last fifteen minutes. The second reason! No, I do not think I will tell you."

"Please do," begged Jim, "I would like to know."

"You are just like your dad used to be. There are times when you can be so dammed cocky, and I just wanted to pull you down a peg."

"Thanks for the word." He paused. "Don't try it again. There are plenty of other teams that I can play for!"

The coach smiled to himself at the memory, *A chip off the old block.*

Later, Jim and the gang had a pint and a couple of meat pies at the Robin Hood pub.

"There's a party at the canal tonight. Do you want to come?" inquired Richard.

"I don't think so," Jim replied.

"Oh come on, Mitchell, it will cheer you up, you look as miserable as hell. What's up? Missing your girl?"

"Yes, I suppose, I am," he replied.

"Leave him alone, Richard!" exclaimed Derek "Let him be miserable if he wants to. We are going to have a good time. There are a couple of new girls coming. I am told that they're fun."

"Okay," said Jim intrigued by Derek's statement, "I will meet you down there."

It was a clear moonlit night as Jim walked to the banks of the canal. In the distance, he could hear the beat of samba music bringing back the memories of the wartime parties when life was cheap, and they drowned their sorrows seeking relief from the bloody war. The tales of suffering and death told by the young evacuees from Liverpool, following the German bombing raids, were horrific. Yes, life had been cheap in those days. The parties had brought some relief. Lots of beer, and dress optional, he smiled. Life hadn't changed much in post-war England. Food and clothing was still rationed. The Labor Party, now in office, was committed to nationalizing industry. The wartime debt still outstanding, made it hard for the gallant people of England who defeated the might of Nazi Germany. He smiled, he was lucky. The Mitchell family had survived the war. Granddad had increased the size of his farm. His Mum's clothing repair business flourished, his aunts and uncles, and the gang's parents, had prospered; yes, he had lost his dad. It was tragic. Yet, in a way, he was lucky. He was receiving a first-class education, and his prospects in life were good. "Life was good, or was it?" he asked himself as he sat on the bank of the canal. Thinking about the girls in his life he smiled, the beautiful sensual temptress, Maggie, they had succumbed to the inevitable force of nature, breaking their vows to their parents. Lost in a night of tender love, the night when they vowed to meet again and again until the day they would marry another and lead separate lives, knowing that their love for each other would last an eternity.

Jim's thoughts turned to Lydia, the kind and generous, beautiful, elegant Lady, who had helped him in his hour of need. It had been many months since that fatal night, when she had suffered a horrific nightmare from her past life, leaving her distraught. It had also been several months since she had joined her parents on a visit to United States. The parting words still rang in his mind. He had written to her several times, without reply. Maybe, she had found another. He didn't know. Yes, he cared; the memories of their night together were slowly fading.

The beat of samba music was reeling in his ears. Suddenly he had the urge to swim to remove the thoughts from his mind. "Women" he cried, as he undressed and plunged into the water, hoping against hope to rid his thoughts of the girls he loved. He swam back and forth across the canal, then lay exhausted in the warm evening sunshine.

"Hullo" said a voice. He looked up and smiled. " Betty" he replied looking at her smiling face.

"Can I sit with you for awhile?"

"Yes. What's up?"

"Can we talk?" she asked.

"Sure," he replied.

"Gerald, my boyfriend, told me before he left that it was all over between him and me," she cried emotionally.

"I am so sorry," said Jim, "You two really looked good together."

"Yes, I know", she said. "I really do miss him, Jim."

"It's better to find out now than later," said Jim.

"Yes, I suppose your right," she replied. "It still hurts like hell. Will you get me a drink? I feel like drowning my sorrows."

Jim laughed. "Join the club, so do I."

"What is up with you?" she asked.

"Maggie's gone to London and I am missing her; apart from that, I had a good game this afternoon."

"Yes, I watched you Jim. You were brilliant," she replied. "It has been a long time since I saw a goal like that. It was bloody wonderful." She paused "Whoops, sorry, I do not normally swear. I guess this drink is going to my head."

"Yes, it is going to mine," replied Jim. "Do you want to go home?"

"Yes, please," she replied.

They walked together along the country lanes leading to her home in the woods. "You have been kind to me; I really do appreciate it," she turned and looked into Jim's eyes. "Ask me out sometime, Jim."

"Thanks Betty, I will," Jim replied. "Goodnight."

# Chapter 27

The following week Jim received a letter from the examination board; a letter that he was dreading. The final results of his the examinations.

"What's that?" inquired his Mum as he held the letter in his hand.

"The results of my A-levels examination, Mum."

"Well aren't you going to open it?"

Full of apprehension, he slowly opened the letter, his heart pounding as he read the contents, then came the sense of elation. "Mum! I passed, Love. I'm in the top grade."

"Oh, Jim!" she cried. "Oh, my Jim, I am so bloody pleased for you."

They stood for a while holding each other close as they felt the warmth of their bodies flowing to each other. Jim smiled as he looked at her. This was the lady who had nurtured him over the years.

"When is the graduation day?" she asked.

"Two weeks next Friday," Jim replied, "ten o'clock a.m. in the Assembly Hall."

"What grade did you get?" asked Richard, as they met in the changing room.

"Honors, of course," Jim replied. "And you?"

"But of course, so did I. Derek rang me before I left home, so did he!"

"Well done you two," said Brian.

"When do you expect to know your results, Brian?" asked Jim.

"Sometime later this month and I know that I, too, will be in the top tier," he said triumphantly in his usual cocky way.

"Pub crawl tonight," said Derek as he arrived. "Horse and Jockey seven o'clock."

The gang celebrated with beer and meat pies at each of the four village pubs returning home singing the old songs.

> O, we ain't got a barrel of money.
> Maybe it's raining or sunny.
> But we travel a long, singing a song,
> Side by side

"What's next?" said Derek slurring his words.
"The Jolly Miller," said Jim.
"That's a good idea," said Richard giggling.

> There was a jolly Miller once
> Lived on the River Dee
> He worked from a mourn til night
> And not a friend had he
> I care for no one, no not I
> And that no one cares for me…"

"Goodnight, Richard."
"Goodnight, Brian."
"Goodnight, Derek."
"Goodnight, lads," said Constable Onions, "Sleep well."

The graduation class assembled in the school hall, the tutors lined the stage, which was decorated with flowers of the season. The headmaster swept into the hallway with his usual flourish. The 'passing out ceremony' began, school prayers were said, following the Lord's Prayer.

One, by one, the students proceeded to receive their diplomas leaving the last three: Richard, Derek, and Jim. "Mr. Kitchener, 87%."

Jim smiled. "Well done, Richard," he said offering his hand to congratulate him as he proceeded to the podium.

"Mr. Stevens, 89%."

Jim stood to embrace his diminutive childhood friend. "Well done, Derek. Oh my God, I did it," exclaimed Jim, silently.

"Mr. Mitchell 89.3%." Jim walked slowly with measured steps. The outward calm appearance hid a feeling of triumph within his body. "Well done, my boy," said the headmaster as he shook Jim's hand.

"Thank you, Sir." He stepped on to the podium in a haze and bowed to the headmaster and his staff. "Sir, today is a landmark day in the life of your humble student, a day when I thank you and your staff for your kindness, your tolerance and, above all, your wisdom. You have prepared me well for the future, and I thank each and every one of you from the bottom of my heart." Jim turned to receive the applause of the audience. There was a lump in his throat as he saw Maggie walking down the center aisle, the nervous tension left his body. He smiled. His girl had arrived.

"Ladies and gentlemen, friends and family," he paused. "This is a wonderful day for me, a day when I, Jim Mitchell, thank my family, who over the years have sustained and nourished me through the good days, and the bad days. Yes, there has been few bad days recently. Mum thank you for your loving kindness, for all you have done for me over the years, my lovely Lady. My Dad," Jim looked high, "Thank you, Dad. To the head of our family, my mentor over the years my Granddad and my dearest Grandma, thank you for your wisdom. Aunt Ethel, Uncle Will, Uncle Mac, Aunty Lucy who have loved me and nurtured me through difficult times, you have my ever dying gratitude. Ms Henning, wherever you are, thanks you. You guided me through the vagaries of the French language and English Lit. To my friends over the years, Richard, Brian, Derek, the class of '35, and The Club, you will always remain a part of my heart," Jim smiled as he gazed out over the crowd. "Miss Kinraid, I wish that you could be here today. Last, but never least, my dearest friend, my cousin Maggie. I love you girl."

Jim bowed to the audience, "Thank you for being here today to share my good fortune. I love you." Jim threw his cap into the air and ran into the waiting arms of his Mum. The ceremony was over, *Let the celebrations begin*," he said to himself.

"This is a proud day for the family," said Granddad as he stood to toast his grandson at the family reception. "Let us remember."

Jim stood alone silently, remembering his father, the happy, full of fun, loving man who had left this earth so early in his life.

There was a deep emotion in his Granddad's voice. "This is a proud and happy day for our family. It is a day to give thanks to the good Lord, a day to celebrate Jim's success. Over the years, we have seen him grow, work, play, laugh, and we have shared both his good days and his bad days. Now he has grown into a man, a man much older than his years. A tall, handsome man, just like his grandfather," he quipped. The audience laughed. "Now, we wish him well, as he enters into the wonderful world of technology, a world free from the bloody wars that have cursed our country over the years. Jim, as my boy, on behalf of your loving family, we wish you good fortune in your endeavors. To Jim!" he said raising his glass.

"To Jim," replied the family, the love shining through there tears of happiness.

Jim rose to reply to his granddad's eloquent speech. "Thank you, Granddad, today is a day that I will always remember, a day of success in the arms of my loving family. Over the years, you have nourished me with your love, your kindness, and your generosity. You have taught me a sense of family values; to love, to be kind, and to cherish the ones you love. You have taught me to respect my fellow men, a teaching which will guide me through the years to come." He paused. "This is a time to give thanks for the blessings of my life. It is also a time when we…," Jim looked Maggie. She knew what he was going to say and rose to stand beside him. He felt a deep sense of emotion in his body as he regarded each member of the family. "This is also a time," he paused looking at Maggie through his tear-blurred eyes, "we thank you, for your understanding of our young love. We have reached our majority, and we are going our separate ways into this world knowing, hoping that our paths will cross again. Each knowing that we will cherish the love that we have for each other forever. Thank you."

Later that afternoon, they sat on the bench at his home, a seat that they knew well over the years in the good times and the bad times, when she had comforted him in his hour of need. He looked into her eyes. "Thank you for being with me today," he murmured softly holding her close.

She smiled, "Do you remember the first time that we sat on this bench together." She stood placing her hands around his shoulders looking into his eyes as she exclaimed, "Jim, that was the day, I told you that I would always be there for you." Her eyes misted as she murmured, "Nothing has changed, my Love. Nothing will ever change, my Love."

Jim lay in bed that evening reliving the memories of the day. A glorious day to remember, a bittersweet day in his life; he was entering into a tough new world, and a world of opportunity. What could be the crossroad in his young life, a world without Maggie? "Oh God," he cried as he fell asleep. "Take care of her."

# Chapter 28

"Good morning gentlemen. Welcome to the world of electrical technology. My name is a Watson, Derek Watson. For my sins, I am the Director of Personnel and your mentor for the next two years. Our goal within that time, both for you and for the company, is to educate you to become degreed electrical engineers. You, Gentlemen, are the best of the best. You are the first entry into this fast track technology course. You have joined us at an exciting time. The world is changing, Gentlemen, and we, as a company, and you, as individuals, will train to meet the demands in the latter half of the Twentieth Century. I know, and you know, that the recent war has generated many new facets and opportunities in the world of technology presenting new opportunities for advancement, not just in the field of Electrical Engineering, but also in science generally. This is the time, when the political, mechanical, and human technology, will advance at an unbelievable pace, which we have never seen before. We, as a company, need to be abreast of the enormous changes necessary to maintain our role as leaders in the manufacture of the tools for future technology."

"Gentlemen, you are our engineers of the future. Through you, and with you, our joint dedication will lead this company on an exciting journey, a journey that will take us into a new world, a world of automation, a world of travel on this our Mother Earth, and indeed the Galaxy. The road in front of us creates opportunities for both you and the company. Through your efforts, and our commitment to your future, we will succeed in meeting the challenges of the global future." He surveyed the class of 1948. "Gentlemen, we are going to have fun and it is my job to ensure that you enjoy this experience. Should you, at any time, need to talk to me, my door is always open to you. Thank you, now let's go and grab some coffee shall we?"

During the following days, their orientation was exciting, totally different from anything that Richard and Jim had ever imagined, or seen, before. The opportunities presented to their young minds were exciting and fascinating. There was something about this company of electrical engineers, which fascinated Jim. In the days that followed, they met with the senior management, the chief research engineers and introduced to many opportunities for the future in technology, including new power plants. The class of '50 was on a journey, which would take them into a new world, a world of excitement, a world of opportunity to learn and open the path to the future and the future of the peoples of the world.

# Chapter 29

"Hello Mum!" cried Jim as he walked through the door of the cottage.

"Did you have a good day?" she asked.

"Yes, thank you, ma'am," he replied.

"There is a letter for you, from America, on the mantelpiece. It looks like Lydia's writing."

"Huh, at long last!" he exclaimed as he read the letter.

"Well, what did she say?"

"She's sailing home on the Queen Elizabeth at the end of the month, and she wants to know if I'll take a couple of weeks off," Jim replied.

"That would be nice," replied Edith. "You haven't had a holiday since you started work. It will do you good!"

"Yes, I suppose so," he replied. "It will be a couple of weeks after I graduate, and a few months before I join Blue Star Shipping Company. Yes," he said to himself. He needed a holiday. Over the last two years, Jim had found his college studies, and hands-on training, exciting, but exhausting. During that time, Richard and he had made a decision. They would decline Her Majesty's invitation for the mandatory national service in the armed services, electing instead to spend four years in the Mercantile-Marine.

The graduate training that he was receiving was challenging. "Not too challenging," he told himself. There had been plenty of opportunity to play sports, particularly, cricket and football, and a new game that had come into his life, tennis. During the previous year, Richard and Jim had taken the top two prizes in their class as "students of the year." Their prize: A couple of weeks at the Outward Bound Sea School in Aberdovey, with their fellow students from industry all over the United Kingdom. During that time, they had learned to sail on an old onion ship called the *Garibaldi*. It had been a fun time and a great experience. The football and cricket teams had done well. Life was good. "Bloody good," as Richard had commented on many occasions.

It was a warm summer night as Jim lay in his bed, his body tired and yearning for sleep. His mind wrestled as how he should react to Lydia's letter. It had been two years since he had last seen her. How did it all begin? The memories came flooding back to him. Something about her had attracted him. There always had been since he first saw her leading the contingent of young Royal Air Force cadets in the 'Wings for Victory' parade back in '43. Later that evening, he had walked across the dance floor, to ask her for a dance. He smiled at the memory. He was nervous, and made a real ass of himself fumbling for the words to introduce him. She had been kind and gentle, understanding his plight. The smile broadened as he recalled their second meeting. The night of the Victory in Europe dance, her words, "Are you going to ask me to dance? Or should we just stand here grinning like two Cheshire cats?" She had come to his rescue when he needed help with his French language and English Literature in his upcoming matriculation examination. During the months that followed, she had taught him well. They had become friends. Slowly, the friendship had turned into one of affection, talking intimately about their past life.

Towards the end of his tuition, he had asked her to be his guest at the annual Cricket Club dance. It was a romantic evening and they had agreed to date, after he had completed his examinations. What followed was still a haze in his mind: a night of ecstasy, followed by her nightmare and her revelations on her past life. He had been kind to her, but the experience frightened, and scared the hell out of him.

Jim awoke early the following morning after a fitful night's sleep. His mind wandered again to his problem. He smiled, the decision had been made. She was Lydia Louise Henning, a heroine of the last world war, a beautiful kind lady. He would be her friend and help her, should she need him. Yes, he cared for her and yes, he would be her friend. He picked up paper and pen and wrote, "Lydia, it will be good to see you again."

He enjoyed reading her somewhat graphic descriptions of the places that she visited, such as, her travels on the West Coast, Washington State, Sierra Nevada Mountains, San Francisco, Los Angeles, Lake Tahoe, Mammoth Lakes, Death Valley, and Colorado. She told him about the beauty of the east coast, of Boston and Philadelphia, of New York, particularly the theatres, the shopping, Washington D. C., the Carolinas, New Orleans, and Palm Beach, Florida, where her uncle lived over the years. She had sent many postcards to his Grandma and his Mum.

"Had things changed in the village since she had left?" she had asked.

"Yes, in a way," Jim reflected. The gang had matured, the teams had added three more trophies to coach's collection, and Brian and Derek would be off to the university this summer. Yes, things had changed. The boys that she had left behind were now men. "Well almost," he said with a laugh. Their careers had been cast in stone. Brian would join his father's bank after graduation; Derek had decided on a career as a public accountant; and Richard and Jim would soon graduate as electrical engineers joining the Blue Star Shipping Company. Yes, Lydia things had changed. "Had they changed between her and him?" he asked himself. "Only time would tell."

# Chapter 30

Lydia Louise Henning lay in her bed tossing and turning, feeling apprehensive about her homecoming, knowing that she would meet him Jim again. How would he feel, how would he react? How would she react to the situation?

She smiled, parting her thighs slowly fingering her sex, exciting her body, reliving her affair with the suave, outrageous Peter Finch. Where, how did it begin? "Way back," she recalled to the night when she had a wantonly began her seduction of Jim, broken by the memory of her horrific, vivid nightmare in the hands of the German Gestapo leaving her desolate, broken, ruining their fledgling relationship. Ashamed of her past, she had fled with her parents to America hoping and praying that one day, when they met again, time would have healed the traumatic episode in her life.

During the months she spent in United States, her mind was consumed by her need to finally put the nightmare of her past behind her. She had sought advice from a number of the world's leading psychiatrists to no avail except for one, who suggested that she might possibly recreate an opportunity to revisit the experience on her terms. The thought had intrigued her. Yes, there were risks involved. She was willing to pay any price to achieve her objective, the love of the only man she wanted, Jim Mitchell. Could she play the part? "Yes." she assured herself. "Would she give herself wholeheartedly? Yes. Would she be safe?" she pondered nervously. "Yes!" she said emphatically. Her wartime training in hand-to-hand combat would help her to survive any physical encounters. She had played the seductress many times in her wartime escapades. Was she willing? "Yes, damn right I am," she replied, knowing that she was she would go to any length to secure the ultimate prize, the love of the man she adored. Slowly, over the months, she formulated a scheme. She knew men. She knew their needs, and she knew their weaknesses. Would she enjoy the experience? She smiled, hopefully!

One evening during the absence of her parents, she had hosted her ailing uncle's cocktail party, an enjoyable experience, giving her the opportunity of renewing friendships and meeting new people. There was lull in the room, giving her an opportunity to walk onto the patio to observe the setting sun. That's where she met Peter Finch.

"Hello," said a voice in the background. She turned to see a tall, middle aged, grey haired, handsome man, standing alone, slowly sipping on a cocktail.

Intrigued by his presence, she walked to greet him. "Hello," she murmured softly. "I'm Lydia, are you enjoying yourself?"

"Yes, I am," he had replied with a roguish grin. "Actually, I have been admiring your body. You look absolutely delicious, my dear."

Somewhat taken aback by his forthright manner, she replied somewhat nervously. "Thank you kindly, Sir, may I offer you another drink?"

"No thank you," he had replied in a soft southern drawl, "not at the moment. Will you have dinner with me later this evening?"

She smiled inwardly thinking, "This could be the man. I would be delighted, Sir," she murmured softly.

"Shall we say nine o'clock?" He suggested while touching her hand. "I suppose I had better introduce myself, Peter Finch at your service. It's nice to meet you, Lydia Louise Henning."

She smiled somewhat intrigued, "How did you know my name?"

"That's for me to know and you to find out," he said with a roguish laugh. "Oh I'm sorry, that was so rude of me, forgive me. Actually, I am the son of one of your uncle's friends." He paused. "It's nice to meet you Lydia. Now, if you would excuse me, I have a couple of things to attend to." He smiled, again touching her hand, "I am looking forward to this evening."

She regarded her watch. Bidding the last of her guests farewell, she escorted her beloved uncle to the care of his nurse and kissed him goodnight. Then, racing too her bungalow, she quickly discarding her cocktail dress, stepping into the mirrored shower to prepare her toilette, Lydia Louise Henning smiled with satisfaction as the warm water cascaded over her head. She massaged her tall lithe body while anticipating the night with the tall, grey haired stranger. She dressed slowly, paying attention to every detail. Selecting a full-length white silk dress with a deep plunging neckline, she regarded the reflection in the full-length mirror. "Yes, Lydia Louise Henning, you my girl are up for it tonight." Then she added, "On my terms!"

Peter greeted her at the entrance to her uncle's mansion, looking handsome, dressed in a loose silk shirt and a pair of tight fitting trousers emphasizing his firm body.

He smiled. "Young Lady, you look devastating."

She returned his smile murmuring, "Well thank you, Sir," and curtsying seductively, revealing a glimpse of her hard full breasts.

"Thank you ma'am," he said softly, as he escorted her to the waiting limousine.

As Lydia was entering the limo, she seductively replied, "Thank you kindly, Sir."

The maitre d' rushed to greet them this as they entered the restaurant. "Monsieur Finch," he cried bowing his head to greet them, "how nice to see you again. I have reserved your usual table for the evening. Mademoiselle, you look absolutely beautiful if I may say so."

"You may, and I thank you," Lydia replied.

The Sommelier greeted them as they sat in the secluded booth. "You're usual, Sir?"

"Yes," Peter replied, "a bottle of Tattinger thirty nine." The lights were seductively low, enhancing the rich ambiance of the restaurant.

"Hmm," she murmured as she glanced at the menu. "What would you recommend, Peter?" she inquired.

"The Dover sole and the west coast oysters." Peter replied

"Thank you," she replied with a coquettish smile. "I just love the taste of oysters," she murmured as the split shelled oysters arrived on the silver platter.

"Allow me," he said with a roguish smile as he selected her first oyster, pouring it onto her waiting tongue. She drew it slowly between her lips, seductively sucking hard, tasting its juices then swallowing it with a gulp.

"Oh, my," she cried as she tasted the delicacy. "I just love the salty taste. May I have another one?" she asked softly.

The dinner conversation intrigued her as he talked about the love of his life, sailing. She was further intrigued as she inquired as to his profession.

He smiled, pondering for a moment, "Well I suppose you could say that I am in show business. Actually, I have some interests in night clubs."

Fascinated by his reply, she murmured "May I have an opportunity to see what you do?"

He smiled, "Later, yes you will enjoy!"

They finished their meal with coffee and a fine Hennessy brandy. Lydia noted that there was no charge and no tips. He was obviously a man of importance. She smiled, he was fun, he was sexy, and she was looking forward to the night with him.

"What would you like to do now? The night is still young!" he inquired

"You choose," she replied.

He raised his hand, summoning the waiting limousine his hand guiding her into the rear seats. "Oh my," she cried some-what embarrassed as she regarded her dress. The skirt was askew exposing her small g-string. "Ex-ex," she faltered. "Excuse me," she murmured attempting to adjust her dress.

Peter smiled. "You have a beautiful body, my dear. Don't move!" he commanded. "I am enjoying the experience. You look truly delicious."

She regarded him with a saucy smile, "Thank you, Sir."

Yes murmured to herself, her body quivering with excitement. She was up for it tonight.

The moment had passed as the limousine came to a stop. "We have arrived, my dear." A tall, elegant man guided them through a maze of tables to a reserved booth overlooking the dance floor. The deep red hue of the lighting created a seductive atmosphere, exciting her body.

She had entered into another world, a world of lust. She was craving for sexual gratification. "Will you dance with me?"

He smiled, "Would you mind if I watched you, my dear?"

"Not at all, Peter," she murmured somewhat disappointed, "I am going to enjoy myself."

"Oh my," she cried ecstatically as she entered the small stage. She danced wildly around the floor parting the slit in her skirt, exposing her buttocks caressing her inner thighs, bearing her breasts, molding them with the palms of her hands pinching the nipples. She was wild. She was free. Yes, this was the night when she, Lydia Louise Henning, would banish her fear of men. Suddenly the red hue of the dance floor entered into darkness. Oh my" she cried as she felt the thrust of strong hips against her buttocks hands molding her exposed breasts. Fingers, roughly pinching her hard taught nipples. "Oh, yes!" Instinctively, she placed her hands high on a dance floor pillar, spreading her thighs in expectation. "Yes," she yelled, "Oh yes," she yelled again as she felt the tip of a hard cock teasing her sex, caressing her inner thighs. Feeling its length between her thighs, she cried loudly, "Oh yes, oh yes!" Feeling its length sliding into her cunt inch by inch. Her words were lost to the sound of the music, "Yes, yes," she cried her body shuddering in ecstasy as she felt a hot penis driving deep into her. She pushed hard against him feeling her buttocks against his groin, meeting him stroke for stroke, her whole body throbbing in sublime ecstasy. His hands moved to her hips, fingers dug deep. "Bastard!" she cried not knowing whether she was in heaven or hell, her body shuddered overcoming the pain. He stroked her harder and harder until she climaxed feeling the warmth of his manhood spread over her buttocks. Then the light returned. She laughed somewhat ironically, as she looked at the face. It was not him.

"Thank you ma'am, you have a beautiful body," he knelt to the ground retrieving her G-string. He smiled. "Yours, I believe young, Lady?"

"Thank you kindly, Sir," Lydia replied somewhat dazed.

"Did you enjoy that my dear?" Peter asked as she entered the waiting limousine paying attention to her dress, her sexual gratification fulfilled. She leaned back, thinking about the young man, who laid her royally. He was no older than Jim. "Oh, my love," she cried. "What the hell am I doing? It's for you, my love, it's for you. This was the night when I put those bloody demons to bed. Hopefully, for good, my love, hopefully, for good," she repeated.

Lydia's thoughts were interrupted by the sound of waves hitting the seashore. The limousine slowly entered through the gates of one of the compounds. In the distance, she saw the dim outline of one of the sea front mansions. Peter smiled, "Welcome to my home," as he led her through the heavy doors to a large vaulted-ceiling reception area, leading her through an art gallery to his den. She admired the collection of nude art some of couples in erotic poses, stone statues of naked male and females. The huge leather couches, beautiful Moroccan drapes and a huge lamb-wool carpet in front of the burning fireplace. She smiled as she looked at her reflection in one of the many mirrors. This was a room, where one could live out one's sexual fantasies. This was the room, where she would relive her ordeal and finally vanquish her nightmare.

She smiled as Peter approached her. He was now but a pawn for her seduction. Smiling seductively, she slowly removed his clothing piece by piece, until he was naked.

"Oh my God!" he cried as he looked at her. She was young, she was beautiful the most beautiful woman he had ever seen. His body shuddered with delight. She was seducing him and he wanted her more than he had ever wanted a woman in his life.

"Oh my!" cried Lydia, somewhat taken aback by the sheer size of his sack. "You really are magnificent, Peter," she exclaimed stroking the full length of his throbbing cock.

"Dance for me, beautiful Lady," he murmured softly as he reclined on the leather couch in front of the fire.

She smiled as she began an erotic dance, remembering a striptease dancer that had entertained her during the evening. Extending her arms so that her hands balanced on her head, she then, seductively molding her breasts with the palms of her hands, turned caressing her buttocks. She parted her skirt, fingering her sex, smoothing her hands back over her breasts. There was a coquettish smile on her face, teasing him as she released the clasp holding her halter neck, lowering her dress inch by inch over her breasts, down her thighs until it cascaded onto the floor. She moved near to him slowly, removing her G-string, and bending forward exposing her sex, wetting her finger suggestively, teasing him as her hands moved from her thighs tracing a path with her fingers, until she touched her shoes.

"Oh my God!" he cried. "I want you. I want you beautiful creature!" he cried, hoping, praying that she would grant him the ultimate sexual satisfaction and, knowing that he was no longer in charge of the situation, a feeling that disturbed him.

She knelt before him removing the long white feather from her hair, gently stroking the length of his cock until it was throbbing in her hand. Then she placed her legs astride his on the couch.

She smiled. "How would you like me, Sir?"

"As you are, madam," he pleaded. Holding the weight of her breasts in each hand, Lydia felt his lips suckling her breasts hard, sucking them deep between his lips until she moaned in ecstasy. She took him in hand, raising her hips as she guided his length into her hot, waiting sex.

"Oh, my beauty!" he cried. "It feels good, it feels good, so good!" he cried as she slowly began to stroke him lifting her buttocks, stroking him harder and harder into a flowing rhythm as she held his face in her hands murmuring, softly, "Tell me when."

"Slowly, my beauty," he cried then he gasped, crying "Ah oh ahhhhhhhhh," as she felt his throbbing cock releasing the warmth of his manhood inside her.

In the background, she could hear the sound of tinkling glasses on a tray. Tilting her head to one side, she saw a huge, heavy framed man entering the room. She went to move, but Peter he held her firm.

"Oh my God," Lydia yelled, her body shivering with delight as she felt warm fingers gently caressing her shoulder blades, tracing a path between her raised arms. "Oh my God!" she cried as the huge hands held the weight of her breasts, holding her nipples between his finger and thumb, squeezing them hard until she cried aloud in ecstasy from the touch. Leaning back against his body she felt his hands tracing a path to her belly then to her hips instinctively. She raised her buttocks as she felt the hand stroking her, feeling her sex. "Oh my God," she cried, as the erotic touch of his finger teased her.

Peter released her and she stood shortly, unsteady. The stranger standing beside her held her steady. She smiled somewhat sheepishly, embarrassed. He had watched her fucking Peter. Somehow, she didn't care. Her sexual gratification had overcome whatever modesty she may have held during the evening.

Peter smiled. Standing naked, next to the table pouring champagne, "Lydia, I would like you to meet my friend, Fritz. He would like to join us! Would you like that?" he said in a rakish smile.

Lydia's body shuddered. The memories of her experience at the hands of the German Gestapo had vanished. There were no more voices, no more laughing. She had overcome her fear of men. She laughed. This was the last hurrah before she returned to the man she loved. "Tonight" she murmured softly to herself, "she would celebrate her victory. They could have her anyway, they chose. She was willing, eager to bring this chapter of her life to a close."

"Would you like, my dear?" he asked again with a rakish smile.

Lydia smiled. "Gentleman, I would be delighted. Would you mind if I finish my drink and smoked a cigar!" She smiled, "after all, Peter, you have just had me, and a girl needs the occasional respite. Besides," she said with a seductive smile, "The night is still young."

# Chapter 31

The sun was rising over the horizon as she awoke. She smiled. Peter's hand was on her breast, Fritz's hand between her thighs. She slowly extracted herself from the two men that had pleasured her, vanquishing her fear she was ready for her man. This had been an experience of a lifetime. Her smile broadened. "How many times?" she wondered. "How many ways?" Her smile turned into a grin of satisfaction. She hadn't counted.

She quietly opened the door of the bedroom, throwing her stained dress over her shoulders, leaving a note on the top of her G-string. "Thank you, gentlemen, goodbye!" She closed the door, closing forever an episode of her life. She walked into the warmth of the Atlantic Ocean, soothing her tired, aching, bloody body. "Yes," she smiled. She had enjoyed the experience, every precious moment! The thoughts of the German Gestapo raping her had gone forever, replaced by fond memories of two men who had laid her beautifully.

"I'm coming home, my Love!" she cried. There were no tears of remorse just a feeling of elation.

# Chapter 32

The sun was setting as he left the canal. His mind warmed at the prospect of a pint of the good Newcastle Brown Ale at the Robin Hood, his favorite pub, where he had hosted many celebrations over the years and was now part of their life, part of the village life, an institution beyond compare.

"Hello," said coach as he entered the bar. "What will you have, Jim?"

"A pint of Newcastle please, John," Jim replied.

"Are you excited?"

"Yes, I am," Jim replied. "I'm looking forward to the game tomorrow."

"Is that all?" asked John with a laugh.

"No," he said with a wry smile. "I'm looking forward to seeing Lydia again."

"So are we. June is cooking a dinner for us tomorrow night."

"Another one?" asked Jim, offering his friend another beer.

"No thanks, June's up to her eyes in it. I had better go and give her hand. You know what women are like you, don't you?"

There was an ironic smile on Jim's face as he exclaimed. "No, not really, John, but I guess I am learning!"

During the last couple of years, Jim had been good friends with coach and his wife June. The birth of their son had changed their lives. Sunday he would be the Godfather of John Junior, and Lydia his Godmother. He was a happy, little lad and they idolized him. Jim had spent time reading stories to him; his favorite was *Rupert Bear.* "One day," he said to himself. "I will have a son of my own to play with and love as much as John and June."

"Hello Love, did you have a good day?" inquired Edith as he arrived home.

"Yes," thanks Mum. "I walked down to the canal and had a pint of Newcastle with Coach."

"There's a letter from Maggie. I will make you a cup of tea while you read it."

"What did she have to say for herself?" said Edith as she poured the tea.

"Not a lot really. Her play closes down in mid-December so she will be home at Christmas." He laughed. "Apparently she split from her husband, and she's got another boyfriend."

"That should be interesting," replied Edith. "I am looking forward to seeing her."

# Chapter 33

Lydia Louise Henning lay on her bed, the sun shining through the stateroom window. She regarded the clock. It had been a restless night. The *Queen Elizabeth* would be docking in Southampton at six o'clock a.m., and she and her parents would soon be home again in their native North Wales.

She had been away from her homeland nigh over two years. "Too long," she said to herself as she stood in the warm shower preparing her for the journey home. The last twelve months she had spent with her uncle in Palm Beach, Florida. He had been ill for some time, and she had nursed him until his passing. Dear Uncle Albert, she had loved this man since the first day she had met him many years ago. "Farewell my friend," she murmured, "One day I will join you."

She dressed slowly. Today's forecast indicated that it would be warm in the North West of England, and she had decided to wear a white linen suit, a black wide brimmed hat, stockings and black patent leather shoes. She was excited for the day. In a few hours, she would be reunited with the love of her life. The *Queen Elizabeth* was passing the Cowes Yacht Club, on the Isle of Wight, when she stepped onto the deck. There was always something special about returning to one's homeland, a lump in one's throat and extra beat in one's heart. Her excitement, her nervous tension, was heightened. In eight hours, she would see Jim again. How would he feel? Would he still want her? She was scared remembering their last night together. "Oh, Jim, my darling, I need you so much," she cried.

In a few hours, they would be reunited at June's 'welcome home dinner.' Sunday was John Junior's christening. That night they would go to her parent's home, and Monday, to the cottage in Portmeirion. The thought of kissing Jim, the thought of holding him, made her legs feel wobbly with excitement. "Oh God," she cried, "Please let him want me."

"You look as nervous as hell," said Richard as Jim and he walked to the batting crease to open the innings of this, the most difficult cricket match of the year.

"I will be okay," said Jim.

"Are you sure?"

"Dammed right, I'm sure," said Jim somewhat irritably. "Richard," he exclaimed, I am going to make a bundle. All we need is one hundred fifty three runs to win."

Jim stood at the wicket fascinated by Richards stroke play. He was a natural batsman. The opening partnership moved along at a quick pace, towards the end, they met at the middle of the pitch to confer. "We need twenty runs from the next two overs," said Richard. "Hold your end, and I'll go for the runs okay?" The tall, broad figure of Richard hit the first ball over the boundary line for six runs then proceeded to hit two more. Jim hit the next ball for two runs. They ran to greet each other. "We did it, Jim, we did it!" yelled Richard elated for their victory. They had won the match. They had beaten their old adversary for the first time in many years.

"Thank God for that!" exclaimed a happy Jim. The two batsmen walked from the pitch to a generous applause from their supporters.

In the distance, he saw his Granddad standing next to a tall, slim, longhaired beauty. "It's her!" he yelled throwing his bat in the air as he ran to meet her.

They stood looking into each other's eyes oblivious to all, absorbing the pleasure of their reunion. Her heart was beating wildly with deep emotion as they embraced.

She looked deep into his eyes, "Am I forgiven?" she cried.

"For what?" he asked.

She looked at him somewhat astounded by his question. "Our last night together," she stuttered.

He smiled. "Lydia Louise Henning, I have missed you, girl. Are we still friends?"

"Oh, yes we are, Jim. Do I get a kiss?" she asked.

"Bloody right you do girl. Welcome home," he murmured softly as their lips parted.

She smiled as she looked at him. Oh my, she breathed. He had matured into a man, broad shoulders, tall and strong. He was the man that she wanted in her bed.

That evening they celebrated Lydia's homecoming with cocktails and a dinner party at June and John's home. They talked mostly about Lydia's trip.

"What did you enjoy the most?" Jim asked.

"The people, mostly they were very kind to me. New York was fun, the west coast is beautiful and the east coast historic. I loved Palm Beach, The sun always shines and the sea is always warm. I have so much to tell you."

# *Chapter 34*

There were poignant memories of yesteryear as Jim sat in the church the following day. Dad's farewell, his confirmation into the faith, the days in the choir as a boy, and the last Christmas carol service when he had led the choir into the church singing, "Once in Royal David's City." Today, John Junior was entering into the faith. He and Lydia were to be his Godparents.

As was the custom, the proud parents stood at the entrance door of the village hall greeting their guests. Each of the guests presented a gift for the child, then signed their names in the christening book. Coach and June smiled as the sports team filed past the proud parents. Their present to John Junior was a silver cup. For once in his life, Coach was lost for words. He smiled, "Thank you gentlemen."

Following the traditional meal, Coach made the keynote speech as the proud father. He was in good form as he eloquently related June's, and his, past leading up to the birth of their first child, thanking everyone whom had attended the ceremony to celebrate his son joining the church. He smiled, "Life is good," and concluded, "thank you for coming to celebrate this special day."

Lydia, Louise Henning, lay in her bed naked, as was her custom, reminiscing on the day. She smiled thinking about the Christening. Young John had brought his parents much joy and happiness. Their marriage had been tough going over the years, and now they were reaping the joys of their union. She was proud that they had chosen her and Jim to be the Godparents to young John. He was a fine boy. She and Jim would guard him as if he were their own.

Her thoughts turned to her relationship with Jim, recalling that bloody awful night when the nightmare of her rape by the Gestapo had invaded her mind during their explosive amorous meeting. She had told him about the various sexual encounters during the war. He had been kind to her not quite, understanding the situation, and offering his friendship. She knew that the experience had scared the hell out of him and she had fled to the United States, devastated and ashamed of her past. Now, two years later, she must face him again. How would he react to her when they were alone? She was unsure. There was no lust, or love, in his eyes when they met yesterday, just one of the elation of two friends meeting after a long absence. Yes, she knew that he cared for her. Was the memory of their last night together still fresh in his mind? She didn't know. How should she deal with the situation? Should she tell him about her experiences with Peter? Should she attempt another seduction? She just didn't know. The only thing she knew was that she loved him and cared for him deeply, and she hoped that he loved her. Their upcoming time together would not be a one-night stand, or a two-week fling. She wanted him as her mate for the rest of her life. "Would he want her?" she asked herself. Yes, she was in love with him, 'hook line and sinker.' She always had been since the day she first met him, the day he winked his eye at her at the football game.

Lydia smiled remembering how she and Jim had met for the second time.

There was a grin on her face as she recalled the dance in the village hall, memories of her relationship with Jim, and "The Wings for Victory Parade," when he had approached her to ask if she would dance with him. She recalled his words as he held his hand out to introduce himself. He had fumbled the words, unsure of himself. His words "Oh hell, I have made a bloody mess of this, sorry!" She had smiled understanding his plight and she had been kind and understanding, in his predicament.

Their next meeting years later, when they met for the third time, she remembered how excited she was when she saw him. She blushed remembering the occasion. She could never understand, to this day, what made her act as she did. She had placed her hands on her hips, striking a somewhat seductive pose as she spoke, "Well are we go to stand here grinning like Cheshire cats all day, or are you going to ask me to dance?"

During the ensuing weeks, they had worked closely together to prepare him for his matric examination. It had been fun in many respects. She admired him for his diligence and his capacity for hard work. Slowly, she had grown fond of him; too fond of him, in many respects. The opportunity to join her mother and father on their trip was timely. Now, after an extended absence of nearly two years, she knew that he was the man that would open the box to her future. She smiled remembering their meeting yesterday on the cricket field. There was no tension in her body as she embraced him. She was willing to hold him close, wanting him to caress her. "Tomorrow, my Love," she whispered to herself as her fingers caressed her body. "I am yours, Jim Mitchell without reservation, or hesitation. Oh God," she prayed, "Please let him want me."

# Chapter 35

"It's good to be home, Jim!" she cried as they drove along country lanes leading to her home in north Wales.

"It's good to have you back, Lydia." There was a tension in his voice as he spoke.

"Are you okay?" she asked.

Jim smiled. "I guess I am a little scared about meeting your parents."

"Don't be, Jim. They are looking forward to meeting you. Over the last few months, I have talked to them about you."

"Do they know why we parted?"

"Yes, Jim, I have confided in them as I always will. You see Jim, they are not only my parents, they are also my best friends."

"Do they know how old I am?" he said.

"Yes," she replied emphatically. "I am five years older than you, Mitchell, and that's the last time I want to hear that number." She smiled, "Okay?"

"It's nice to meet you, Jim Mitchell," said Lydia's father as they shook hands. He was a tall, gray haired, imposing man with a soft southern United States accent. This is my wife Megan. Jim smiled, admiring the slim figure of Lydia's mother. "It is nice to meet you meet you Ma'am," as he shook her hand.

"Welcome to our home, Jim. Lydia has told us much about you," she said with a mischievous smile.

Jim was immediately struck by the sheer beauty of this grey-haired lady. As they shook hands, he felt her long fingers linger. There was a twinkle in her eye that made him feel comfortable in her presence.

Jim stood for a moment admiring the white walls and the slate roof of the cottage set against the backcloth of the Welsh mountains. It was a pretty garden with patches of flowers intertwining the deep green grass of the lawns, a pleasing sight reflecting the owners care and attention over the years.

"Come along in, Jim" said Megan, "Perhaps you would like to freshen up before dinner. Your bedroom is the first on the left. Make yourself at home."

Jim surveyed the room. There were several pictures of a tall, young man in uniform, one in a football strip, a large one showing a crowd of boys standing together, a football team photograph. So, this was Lydia's brother, the fighter pilot who was tragically killed in the Battle of Britain. Jim looked through the window admiring the view of Mount Snowdon in the distance. There was a knock at the door.

Lydia smiled radiantly. "They like you see silly, I knew they would."

During lunch, Lydia talked about their trip and the Christening.

"We love it here," said Ms Kendra in her soft Welsh accent. "Jack and I found this place shortly after we married. It's a bit isolated, but we like it," she said holding his hand. There was a smile on her face. "Its only five miles to the station, and we can still get to London easily."

"When do you graduate from college, James?" asked Jack.

Jim smiled, "I graduated two weeks ago, Sir."

"What's your discipline?"

"Electrical engineering, Sir."

"Lydia tells me that you have ambitions to become a chief engineer in the Mercantile Marine."

"Yes, I have an opportunity to join the Blue Star Shipping Company early next year."

"Your Granddad told me, when we had lunch a couple of weeks ago, that you have seagoing blood in the family."

"Yes," replied Jim. "It dates back many years, back to the days of Captain Cook, I believe."

"I wish you luck, it sounds like an interesting career. I am sure you're going to enjoy it."

"It's getting late, my dear. Time for me to get to my bed," murmured Megan.

"Sleep well. Welcome to our home, Jim, goodnight and sleep tight. We will see you in the morning!"

"It's a wonderful moonlight night. I feel like walking. Jimmy will you join me?" inquired Lydia.

"Only, if you call me Jim?"

"I am sorry. Okay Jim," she said mimicking his Cheshire accent.

The moon light was shimmering over the village houses as they walked to the seafront. "You are quiet tonight, Lydia," said Jim as he held her hand.

"I always am when Mum's around. In case you hadn't noticed, she's the talker in the family!"

He smiled, "Yes, I gathered that. You have great parents."

"You like them?" She asked somewhat anxiously.

"Yes I do, Lydia," said Jim enthusiastically. "Your dad is a very handsome man and your mother is a charmer. You look so much like her."

"Thank you. She's is a charmer all right." she said with a laugh. "She charmed daddy into staying in this country after World War I and he's never regretted it."

They walked silently for a while. "What's on your mind?" he asked.

"I was just thinking about tomorrow," she said somewhat nervously. "We will be staying at the cottage in Portmeirion. It is lovely, Jim. I'm sure you will like it. It's just on the edge of the village overlooking the sea."

"Would we be on our own?"

"Of course we will be, do you mind?" she asked anxiously.

Jim hesitated momentarily, unsure of how he would deal with the situation "No, why should I mind?" He said defensively.

"No reason," she replied. "Let's go home. It's getting a bit chilly. Will you join me in a nightcap?"

"Yes please," he laughed. "That's got my name written all over it, ma'am."

Lydia regarded the drinks Cabinet. "There's a good cognac! Would you like one?"

"Yes please," he replied.

They sat a while sipping their nightcaps, sharing one of her Havana cigars. "Are you okay?"

"Yes," he replied "I guess I'm nervous, this being our first time together for a while and meeting your parents."

"Don't be, Jim, its okay! I can understand how you feel." she stood, holding his face in the palms of her hands murmuring, "Kiss me good night, Jim Mitchell. I'm off to my bed, sleep tight."

# Chapter 36

The early morning mist was slowly lifting over the Valley as they made their way along the narrow roads to Portmeirion. His overnight anxiety of being alone with Lydia gave way to one of optimism as he felt a sense of the history of this ancient Celtic land, the years of feuding. He smiled remembering his history lessons: Boadicea, on her chariot leading the hordes of Celts into battle against the relentless onslaught of the bloody English. It had been many years since the last battle between these two great nations. The animosity still lingered to this day. This was the rugged borderland, wild, a beautiful a magic land with a rich history.

The Riley engine purred smoothly as it negotiated the curves of the road, the hood down, the wind in their faces, blowing their hair into horizontal streaks. Lydia remembered his birthday gift from his grandparents. He had a passion for driving his Riley. Yes, this was Jim Mitchell, the man she loved. He had a passion, for everything he did. That was his nature. Did he still have a passion for her she wondered?" She was unsure and nervous as she prayed, "please let it be so!"

"It's going to be a lovely day, Jim," she shouted above the noise as she nestled into the passenger seat, observing the beauty of her homeland set in this beautiful mountainous region of North Wales. It had been two years since she had last seen her home. She was excited. This was the day that she had looked forward to, her home and, hopefully, her man. "Oh God," she cried, "Please let it be so."

The road narrowed as the Riley climbed to the top of the hill overlooking the sea as they descended to Portmeirion.

"Wow, it's beautiful Lydia!" cried Jim. Lydia smiled in recognition. This was her home. The land she loved.

"We're nearly there, Jim!" she cried excitedly. "Around the next bend, then the road drops slowly to the cottage. It's the first cottage on the left-hand side." In the distance, Jim saw a white stone cottage with a slate roof.

"That's it!" she yelled. "We're home Jim! We're home!" she cried excitedly.

"It's beautiful Lydia!!" he exclaimed as he walked slowly into her home admiring a large living room, two fireplaces, a small kitchen with a wood burning stove, and two bedrooms. It was a quaint home, built to withstand the harshness of the coastal weather, small and snug.

"Hold me," she cried. "Hold me, Jim. I am scared out of my pants."

"Shush", he cried as he saw a tear in her eye. "Do you have whiskey?"

"Yes, we do," she whispered nervously.

"Then, pour two large ones," Jim commanded taking charge of the situation, "while I light the fires." Jim regarded her as she returned holding the drinks in her hand. "It's bloody chilly in here. Get to your bed, Madam," there was a faint appreciative smile on her face as she realized that Jim had taken control of the situation. "I will join you in a minute."

She was sitting in the middle of the bed, quietly sobbing, her body covered by a single sheet as Jim entered the room.

"Shush," he cried, "Its okay," he cried as he laid her head on the pillow. "Just let's hold each other for a moment," he whispered as she drank slowly from the glass. Lydia was silent for a while.

"Are you okay?"

"Yes, I think so Jim," she said shyly, "Thank you."

"Lydia," he murmured, "It's going to take a while. Don't let's rush it," Jim smiled affectionately holding her close. "We need to talk. Fetch the whisky bottle in here. I think we are going to need it." He smiled as she shyly climbed back into bed.

"I want to tell you a story," he paused. "When I was a little boy, I fell in love with a girl, and as we grew together, we became the best of friends. We were inseparable. We played together, we worked together and we had fun together. After my dad was killed in the war, she comforted me, and, as we grew, our love deepened. Those were the innocent days, when we thought that we would always be together. As we grew into puberty, our family told us that we could never marry, dashing our hopes of being together forever. We were blood cousins. At first, we rebelled, then later, we both realized the futility of our relationship. As the years went by, the bond between us remained. We stood on the edge of a precipice, neither of us knowing what to do. Then finally, her parents sent her away to her chosen profession. Later, while you were away, we met again for the last time, to say goodbye, and we bedded. Then we made a bond that could only be broken when either of us married. Months later, she married. I thought that it would hurt me, but it didn't." There were tears in Jim's eyes as he spoke looking into her eyes. "Her name was Maggie Bernadette O'Toole."

"I know Jim, I know," she murmured softly as her arm held him close. "I've always known about your relationship with Maggie. It is over, isn't it?"

"Yes it is, Lydia."

"I am sorry, Jim. I don't know whether to be happy, or sad," she whispered. "Much depends on your reaction to my story." She paused. "When we parted after that bloody awful night, I resolved to get rid of my fear of men. It didn't matter to me how I did it. I didn't care. I didn't even care what it cost me. I was determined that when, and if we made love again, that the bloody awful nightmare would never happen again, Jim. I know that it was terrible for you. It knocked the hell out of me, too. That's why I ran from you. I felt dirty, used, like a second-hand tart. During my visit to the United States, I consulted many psychiatrists; I thought I was going mad. None of them provided an answer until one day, I met with a young psychiatrist, and he suggested that the only way I could put my past behind me was to, in some way, recreate the situation." There were tears in her eyes as she whispered, "Jim I need to tell you the story. Hold me tight, please. It's not going to be easy, but if we are to be together, I need for you to know, and if we're not, what will it matter?"

Jim cradled her head on his breast as she slowly unfolded the story of her night with Peter Finch. She softly inquired, "Are you okay with that, Jim?" Her body was shaking and sweating in anxiety as the tears of remorse ran down ran down her cheeks onto his breast. "Oh, Jim!" she cried, "I'm not ashamed of what I did. I needed to get rid of my fear of men," she cried. "Please tell me that it was okay."

He was quiet for a moment. "You did that for me?"

"Yes, I did," she cried.

"Come here," he cried holding her tight. "I don't know whether to laugh, or to cry. You, Lydia Louise Henning, are a brave and wonderful lady. What the hell am I going to do with you?" he asked.

There was a coquettish smile on her face as she murmured softly, "Fuck me, Jim. Fuck me hard. I need to see you come over my belly." Her smile broadened as she murmured, "I guess we both need to know that it's okay."

The glow of the evening light shone through the small, pane window of the bedroom. She had fallen asleep on his shoulder. As he looked at her face, he moved the strands of her auburn hair covering her familiar high forehead and unveiling her high classical cheek bones, manicured full eyebrows tapering to their extremities, blue eyes, long, black eyelashes, and adorable perfect nose. Her full sensuous lips were slightly parted as she awoke. "Hullo, beauty," there was a tender look on her face. She smiled. "How do you feel?"

"Bloody marvelous!" he exclaimed, "it feels so bloody good. Hold me girl."

There was a warm glow in her body. She murmured softly to herself. "Thank you Peter, goodbye my friend. I'm hungry," she cried. "Pour me a Gin and tonic, and I will cook you a bloody good meal."

They lay on the sheepskin rug in front of the glimmering log fire slowly sipping their after dinner cognacs, listening to the record of Tchaikovsky's *Piano Concerto*. She looked into his eyes, instinctively knowing that he needed to talk.

"Penny for your thoughts," she murmured softly.

He looked at her in wonderment, "How the hell did you know that I want to talk?"

She laughed, "Mitchell, aren't you forgetting that I know you, I know how your mind works."

He laughed. "Yes, I guess you do, Lady."

"Well are you going to tell me, or should I guess?"

"Can we talk about sex?" he gulped nervously.

She laughed. "What do you want to know?"

"Don't laugh, Lydia, I am serious I really don't know a hell of a lot about sex. I guess what I want to know is how do I compare with your past lovers."

"Mitchell, there are three golden rules," she murmured. "Number one, you never tell me about your sex life with Maggie. Number two, I will never discuss my previous sex life and three, we never tell anybody about our sex life. Now to answer your question," she said holding his face in the palms of her hands with a coquettish smile on her face. "Sir, I am going to be crude. You have the biggest cock I've ever seen. Your sack is delicious and you have the finest pair of buttocks a lady could ask for. Now, does that answer your question?"

Jim looked at her. "Yes, I have two, Lady."

"Which way do you like it best?"

She smiled. "Anyway you like, your next question, Sir?"

"When you talk in bed, you use crude words."

She laughed. "My mother taught me to be a whore in bed, and a lady outside the bedroom." She walked across to the couch, placed her hands on the back, bending her knees slightly turning her head over her shoulders looking at him. Then with a coquettish smile on her face she murmured, "Can we continue where we left off?"

They lay on the sheepskin rug again. Their bodies entwined. She smiled as he kissed her lips.

"Mitchell, I don't want to talk about love. I don't want to talk about marriage. I just want to be your woman. Then one day, when we have achieved our bloody---- goals, I will find you." She smiled, "Then I will want to talk about children, about your children. Until then my beauty, we are going to have ourselves a ball." She laughed, "I have one request."

"And what would that be?" Jim asked.

She smiled, "I would like this whore of yours to get laid at least twice a day!"

# Chapter 37

It was a beautiful sunny morning as they walked hand in hand to the village. Lydia looked at him with a shy smile. "This will make them talk, Jim. It's the first time they've seen me with a man."

He laughed, "Are you worried?"

"Oh no," she replied, "quite the opposite. This is fun." She pointed out several landmarks of the village. "This is Jones the butcher, over there is Kevin the postmaster, next door is Owen's pub, which is closed on Sunday, and there, in front of us, is O'Brien the fishmonger."

"That's an Irish name."

"Yes it is," she replied. "O'Brien and his wife have been here forty years and he is still regarded as an outsider. His fish are excellent and people will forgive anything for good fish in this part of the world. That's where Mum was born," she said pointing to an old stone house at the end of the long row of houses. "She now owns the whole row, and a bit more, I think."

The shoreline was quiet as they walked along the seafront wall. The view of the harbor and lighthouse were fabulous. In the distance, they could see the fishing boats returning with the catch of the day. The sun shimmered over the lighthouse and the harbor. The sea was calm, disturbed only by the ripple of the bow of the returning fishing boats. They stood for a while, Jim's arms encircling her slim waist drawing her closer.

"Happy?"

"Yes," she replied, quietly touching his hand. "Let's take a walk to the pub. I feel a need for food and drink."

"Welcome back, Lydia," said Owen as they entered through the old oak door. Lydia greeted him in her native tongue, then introduced Jim. "This is my friend, James Mitchell. He's from Chester," she smiled knowingly, "just across the border."

"Welcome James," he said shaking his hand. "What can I get you to drink, Lydia?"

"Gin and tonic."

Jim paused, surveying draft beer the taps. "A pint of Newcastle Brown ale please, Sir."

There was an atmosphere about this old, historic, stone walled, village pub, a place where friends meet to enjoy themselves. A place where one could talk and discuss the happenings of the day, remember old times, eat a good meal and drink fine beer; it was the centre of village life in this remote part of North Wales.

"Are you hungry, Jim?"

"Yes, Lydia," he replied. "I could eat a horse."

She laughed. "Mitchell, despite rumors to the contrary, we are quite civilized in this part of the world. We don't eat horses. Try the fish and chips!"

Lydia felt his arm around her waist as they slowly walked back to her cottage.

"Would you like a nightcap?"

"Yes please, brandy."

She lay in his arms on the sheepskin carpet in the warmth of the flickering log fire. There was an atmosphere about this home, one that had always given her strength in the past, and in her hour of need. Tonight was such a night. They lay together in the glow of the flickering embers of the fire giving warmth to their bodies.

She purred like a kitten having tasted the milk, as Jim gently stroked her body.

"Are you happy, Jim, really happy?" She asked quietly.

"Yes, in a way I feel as though we have never been apart."

"Yes, I know my beauty, I feel the same way. Take me to bed. I just want to hold you and lay my head on your arms as I fall asleep."

Jim awoke to a noise of explosions and flashing lights. His first, early morning reaction, as his body began to sweat, was one of fear, bringing back memories of his wartime years. Then to his relief, he heard the sound of rain beating against the window panes.

"Are you okay?" said the voice lying by his side.

"Yes, I think so," Jim replied. "For a moment I thought it was a German bombing raid."

"No, my love, it is the sound of thunder clouds rolling across from the Atlantic Ocean towards the Welsh coastline."

"Thank God for that."

Lydia smiled as she touched his lips. "Let me make you some tea, my Love." She murmured softly, "This bloody war is still with you?"

"Yes, it is. I reckon it always will be."

Lydia smiled, somewhat relieved that her man had recovered from his initial reaction to the storm. She walked into the kitchen. Today would be a stormy day, it would a day of loving, just being with one another in the seclusion of their love nest.

She laid the breakfast tray in the kitchen and brewed the tea. Then with a second thought, toasted bread and placed it on the tray with butter and marmalade. For some reason that she couldn't explain, she felt hungry. "Must be the air," she said to herself. Her smile turned into a grin, more to the point, Jim's lovemaking was draining her body, and she needed sustenance.

There was a smile on his face as she returned to her bedroom carrying the breakfast tray. "One lump or two, Sir?" she asked solicitously.

"One please, Madam."

She sat in her bed drinking the tea. "Good morning, my darling," she murmured seductively. "Come sit with me."

The storm clouds moved nearer from the western approaches. Rain lashed against the windows of the cottage as they finished their frugal breakfast.

He turned and smiled. "Hello you," he said gently.

She smiled. "What would you like to do today?"

"Well there is one thing for sure, Lady, I ain't going out in this weather. Can we just stay in the cottage today?" He smiled. "I have a gift for you. While you were away, I put some words into verse."

Her face brightened, "Really, Jim, for me!"

"Yes for you, Lady," he said quietly. "I've called it 'An Ode to Lydia.'"

> She is a creature of delight
> Enchanting men upon their sight
> Her Gate beguiling as she strode
> Amongst the flowers of the field.
> Her charm, her smile pure, ecstasy.
> The flaming passion in her eyes.
> Her kindness and her winning ways
> As this a poor mortal learned the phrase.
> The lilt in her voice as she exclaimed
> I thought of you in foreign lands.
> Upon the sea I love.
> Then pensive in my bed I lay.
> Dreaming of the day, when you return
> To fill my life, with your warmth.
> To hold me close, for evermore.
> To kiss your sweet lips
> To run my fingers through your hair
> To see again, the smile upon your face

"Oh Jim, that was beautiful. No one has ever written such words for me," she cried.

Suddenly, she sat on his belly. She was excited as she placed the palms of her hands on his cheeks. She looked deep into his eyes, "You really do care for me?"

"Care for you? Care for you?" he cried. "Damn right I do, Lady."

There was a tear in her eye as she murmured, "Thank you, Jim, this means so much to me. Oh God, are we okay together now?"

"Yes, we are" he answered as he kissed her sweet lips.

"Thank you, Jim," she murmured through her tears, "Can I tell you a story. It is a good story, and I want you to know how I feel about you."

While I was away, there were many long hours to think about my life, and my future profession, as I spent the long days lying on the deck chairs on the *Queen Elizabeth*. The long evenings after the shows, when I was lying in my bed at night alone," she smiled, "I was thinking of you, your kindness in your letters. Jim, I'm not quite sure how to say this, you have made me a happy woman. I have cared for you since the day that you brought me that bunch of beautiful roses. Jim, I just need to be near you. The road ahead is not going to be easy for us. Last night made me free at last." She looked at him placing her hands on his cheeks. "I don't want talk about love. I don't want talk about marriage. I just want to be with you." She smiled. "Let's see where that takes us, my sweet." She paused. "Maybe one day," she said with a coquettish smile. "I will be your mistress, if you will have me? You changed my life, Jim Mitchell. You have turned me into a sexy, horny bitch again." She smiled, "Love me again, you sweet man." There was a smile on her face as she fell into a deep satisfying sleep.

Jim awoke in the late afternoon. Lydia was asleep, lying in his arms.

She stirred and smiled, "Hello you."

"Hello yourself, how do you feel?" he murmured.

"Bloody marvelous, Jim, boy I need a drink. Can I get you one?" Lydia asked.

"Gin and tonic, please."

"Coming right up, Sir," she said with a coquettish smile.

In the background, Jim could hear the sound of music, soft sensual music. The door opened as she carried the drinks tray dressed in one of Jim's white shirts and wearing red high-heeled shoes.

She laughed as she looked at him. "You know Mitchell I have always wanted to be a cocktail waitress."

"Madam," Jim replied. "Dressed like that you can serve me any day."

"Thank you, Sir, my pleasure," she murmured softly, "I feel like dressing up for dinner tonight. Have you ever been to a strip show?"

"No, not really, I've heard about them?"

She laughed. "Well here's the deal. You cook dinner, and I'll do a strip for you!!"

The evening light was passing. The storm that once raged over the village had passed, as they lay naked on the sheepskin rug in front of a roaring fire finishing the last drops of the South African Pinotage wine. It had been a fine meal of lamb chops and fresh raspberries with all the accoutrements. She smiled to herself as she watched the glimmering fire. For once in her life, she was truly happy; she had been loved by the only man she would ever care for.

The early morning sun shone brightly through the window as Jim awoke from a deep sleep to see a mass of shining auburn hair on the pillow next to him. She looked so calm, so happy. He didn't know that people could smile while they were sleeping. Slowly she stirred. "Good morning," she murmured as he kissed her sweet lips. "Will you make coffee?"

Jim looked at the bedside alarm clock; it was six forty-five a.m. "Would you like to walk today?" Jim asked as he nursed the good brew.

"Where? Snowdon?"

"That sounds good to me," he replied. "It's been years since I climbed to the top."

The sophisticated Lydia Louise Henning, dressed in her climbing boots, long wool socks, shorts and a wool sweater, her knapsack on her back, and her long hair flowing over her shoulders, looked delightful as they set off for the exciting day ahead.

Mount Snowdon, some thirty-five hundred feet above sea level, is the highest mountain in England and Wales; Jim remembered, some years ago, the gang had cycled to the foothills for a camping trip. He recalled Richard leading the way to the top of Snowdon. Derek, poor Derek complaining many times on the journey, realizing too late, that climbing was not his forte. He survived, bruised and battered, swearing that he would never do this again. "How do you feel?" asked Jim, as his climbing companion smiled a wry smile.

"Let's rest for a while. I'm not as fit as I used to be," she said as they sat admiring the spectacular views of the Cheshire plains.

Following a brief rest, they began to climb again. "That was hard work," she said as they made it to the top, the sun finally breaking the morning mist. "Oh Jimmy, isn't it so beautiful?" She said as they surveyed the spectacular views.

Jim could see the town of Llandudno, the town where Alice Liddell was born and raised. Conway Castle was to the north, Bangor, with its beautiful ancient cathedral, and the Isle of Anglesey to the north-west, then Cardigan Bay, in the southwest, then onto Harlech Castle the historic castle that inspired that beautiful old Welsh Regiment song, "Men of Harlech." Finally, as he completed his scan of the historic landscape, he saw Betws-y-coed nestling in the Vale of Conway.

"Isn't it just beautiful, Jimmy," she said gripping his hand. "I never want to leave this place" There was a sad smile on her face as she murmured, "I could live here forever and never more roam."

# Chapter 38

Jim awoke the next morning to the sound of rain hitting against the window. "Welsh summer," he said quizzically. He looked at her again, the mass of hair on the pillow. He decided he was hungry.

"What are you doing?" She asked as she entered the kitchen wearing Jim's shirt.

"Cooking breakfast," Jim replied. "I am starving. I need food. I am beat, and my legs hurt."

There was a knock at the door. "Blast!" she swore. "Can you get it, Jim," she said. "It's probably the postman."

"Lovely day for ducks, Sir," said the postman cheerfully when Jim opened the door. "Mail for Ms. Lydia," he said proffering a large envelope with American stamps on it and marked, registered airmail, private and confidential. "Would you sign here, Sir?"

They sat in the warm glow of the fire. Jim watched her opening the package. "Damn and blast!" she cried as she finished reading the letter. "I've got to go back to New York."

"When?" Jim asked in surprise.

"Next week," she replied. "Damn and blast, Jim, I am so sorry," she cried.

"Somehow I knew something would spoil our holiday. I need to get to the phone."

"Is it really important?"

"Yes, it is."

"What's the matter, Lydia?" he asked as she entered the cottage looking slightly worried.

"We need to talk, Jim," she said as they sat in front of the fire she held his hand looking into the fire. "There is something I must tell you." She paused. "Jim, be patient with me. I don't quite know how to tell you. I am on the board of my uncle's company. They are holding an extraordinary meeting to discuss a possible takeover and they need me. That's the reason I must go to New York.

I wasn't going to tell you, I didn't think that this meeting would happen so soon. I know that it's stupid. I felt that if I brought the whole of my baggage to you at once, you may not have wanted me."

Jim laughed. "Why, silly, are you so dammed insecure? Do you want to talk about it?" asked Jim.

"Yes," she replied, "if that's okay with you?"

"Of course it is, Lydia."

"It's a long story, Jim, bear with me. I met Uncle Henry a few times before the war. He was a kind and loving man. I guess that I was the daughter that he never had. Over the years, he never married. His first and only love was killed in a car accident," she paused. "We exchanged letters often and he loved the poems that I wrote for him. He enjoyed Shakespeare. For a little girl, he and I had so much in common.

As a boy, he worked in small railway company and eventually took over the business. As the company grew, he worked hard and it took a toll on his health. He survived the crash on Wall Street in 1929 and eventually took his company onto the market, retaining 45% of the shares. The company grew rapidly and he became quite rich. A few months before he died, he retired from the running of the business as it was becoming too much for its health," she paused; there was a tear in her eye. "Jimmy pour me a whiskey, this really hurts me."

"I am so glad that we did this trip. It was good for him, and I spent many long days with him. We talked about his life, his love of railroads, politics, and law. I used to read Shakespeare and poetry to him, long into the night. Sometimes we shared secrets," she smiled. "I told him about you. We talked about my hopes and fears, and my ambitions for the future. He was such a nice man. Jim, you would have loved him. I guess he was like your granddad in many ways.

"What ambitions?" Jim interjected.

"We talked about me qualifying in law, something I really want to do," she paused. "During my travels, I had many long hours to think, and you know my ambition is to become a lawyer one day. It's a profession where I can be someone, and do some good in the world." She laughed. "Jim, I will never make a good housewife. The practice of the law is in my blood. We talked about international law. His dear friend, Albert, whom I've met, lives in Switzerland. He also has a home in the United States. Both of them encouraged me to study that particular discipline. Albert even promised to get me a place in Stanford University when I obtain the necessary credentials. The last day I saw him, we talked for ages. The poor man was weak and he wanted me with him. I was so pleased that I could be there for him at the end. Jim we talked about life, about love, and about business. About love, he was brief. There was a smile on his face as he remembered the past secrets of his life. Then he talked about business, just a few thoughts. 'Beware of the airlines' he said."

She began to cry again. "On the last day," she sobbed, "he told me about his will. Hold me, Jim." She cried tears of despair running down her face. "It was so sad. He left me everything he had to me. When I asked him why, he smiled. 'You have been the love of my life young lady.'"

She sobbed, "Hold me Jim. That hurt me; I never knew how much he cared for me."

As Jim stroked her hair, she lay quietly on his shoulder, then murmured in a low voice, "Why do good men have to die?"

Jim didn't answer. "Why do you have to go, Lydia?"

There's an extraordinary board meeting to discuss a possible takeover bid, and I have been asked to attend."

"Why?" asked Jim.

She was quiet for a moment collecting her thoughts. "I must," she replied. "You see, I am the largest shareholder in the company. Alec, our company Chairman, has been trying to contact me for over a week now, and I know Mummy and Daddy have been away in London for a few days. They have sent telegrams. It is very important, and I owe it to the memory of my Uncle, Jim."

"Why beware of the airlines?" he asked. She smiled, "Are you really interested?"

"Yes, of course I am," he replied.

During Uncle Henry's last days, I spent many hours with him talking about his business. He was very knowledgeable and he talked about the future of transportation in the States, and in the world. The airplane, and the technology that the war brought, had changed his perspective of travel in the future. He forecast that the standard of living for the average American would improve over the years. More people would travel and airlines would provide faster and cheaper travel in the future. This would not only apply to the railways, but in time the Atlantic liners, such as the *Queen Elizabeth*, and the American liners, would be affected. The railways would need to review their infrastructure. Upgrade their propulsion units and rolling stock if they were ever to compete with airlines, and the cost of that would be enormous.

"How does this affect your inheritance?"

"That is why I'm going. The company has received a cash bid for its shares; it's a takeover bid. I want to be there. You see love I have the controlling interest."

"Will you sell?"

She paused, "The board has advised me to sell. It's a good offer."

"What would your uncle think?" Jim asked.

"From what he told me, and he was very specific, he would sell if the price was right."

"What will you do with the cash?"

She smiled, "I'll invest it in one of the larger merchant banks."

Suddenly Jim felt a little desolate. How would this affect the relationship? This talented lady, his friend, his mistress, his tutor who went to the United States for three months and stayed for two years, had returned aspiring to be an international lawyer and was a rich lady to boot. "I am being stupid acting the way," he said to himself.

Lydia smiled, placing the palm of her hand on Jim's cheek. "Oh Jim," she cried looking deep into his eyes, "please don't let this come between us."

"Don't be silly woman. Why should it?" replied Jim while appearing to be nonchalant.

Her hands caressed his hair as she murmured, "Thank you, Jim Mitchell. That was one hell of a test of our relationship. There will be others," said Lydia. "That's the nature of who we are. You and I are two very ambitious people with our own objectives, you to travel the world, me to become a lawyer. God willing, one day you and I will smooth out stupid egotistical ambitions."

"I hope so, Lydia. Are we okay now?"

"Yes, we are. Jim Mitchell, this is one hell of a romance."

Jim awoke the next morning to the touch of her loving fingers. "Jim, will you take me dancing tonight?"

"Where," he asked "on the top of Snowdon?"

"Don't be silly," she replied somewhat seriously. "There's a dinner dance at the Dorchester hotel in Chester and I would like to go dancing," she cried excitedly. "We can stay the night," she said attempting to 'gild the lily', "then we can go to the eleven o'clock service in the cathedral and have lunch at the Cheshire Cheese Inn. In the afternoon, the Liverpool Symphony Orchestra is performing Tchaikovsky's, *Symphony number two, Romeo, and Juliet.*

"That sounds good to me," said Jim, "it certainly will make a change Sunday afternoon cricket. Don't we have to book ahead?"

There was a coquettish smile on her face as she murmured, "I booked yesterday," she said.

"Why didn't you tell me?"

"I wanted it to be a surprise for you."

# Chapter 39

"Good afternoon Sir. Good afternoon Madam," said the tall immaculately dressed door attendant. "Welcome to the Dorchester Hotel. Will you be staying with us, Sir?" Jim nodded. "Thank you, I will see to your luggage. Shall I park the Riley?"

"Please," replied Jim. "I won't need it until tomorrow afternoon."

The décor of the Dorchester hotel lobby was stunning: the chandeliers, the artwork, the small restaurant on the left-hand side, and, as she walked through the double doors, the long mahogany reservation area. The front office manager smiled, greeting them as they neared the front desk. "Mr. Mitchell, welcome back, Sir. I have reserved Suite number 303 for you, and I see that you have made reservations for dinner this evening."

"Thank you, you are most kind," Jim replied.

"Will you be taking afternoon tea, Madam?" the Manager asked.

"Yes."

"Absolutely, Madam, it will take about fifteen minutes."

"It's enormous," she said as she entered the living room. The bath is big enough for both of us." There was a twinkle in her eye. "Do you think we could make it in there?"

Jim laughed, "Madam you have sex on the brain."

She laughed. "Yes isn't it wonderful and I enjoy getting screwed twice a day."

There was a knock on the door, "Room service!"

"Damn," she said, "a girl doesn't have a chance does she?"

The room service waiter served the afternoon tea. He laid out the salmon and cucumber sandwiches, scones, clotted cream, and raspberry jam in the suite dining room. "Shall I pour, Sir?"

"Please," replied Jim as he turned on the B. B. C. radio for the football scores.

"Liverpool 1 Arsenal 1; Derby County 1 Aston Villa 1; Manchester United 1 Everton 1;

"We have won!" yelled Jim referring to the weekly investment that he and the gang made on Littlewood's football pools. "There's eight draws," he yelled. "It's the jackpot!" he cried exuberantly.

"How much?" she asked.

"I don't know," he replied, "it all depends on how many people had the same fixtures; at a minimum, it could be a couple of hundred pounds."

Jim was excited as he dressed for the evening. The thought of winning two hundred pounds was exciting; he looked into the mirror. The skinny boy from Cheshire had grown into a blond haired, blue-eyed, tall, athletic, well-proportioned young man. He smiled looking much older than his age. He liked the cut of the dinner suit, the tightness of his cummerbund about his waist, the black cufflinks and shirt studs, and the bow tie, which took ages to position. "Is this real?" he asked himself. It didn't matter. He was having a great time with a wonderful lady. The days were taking care of themselves. Sad in a way he murmured. Soon they would part. Until then, they would have a ball. Until then, that's all that mattered.

"You like, Sir?"

"Wow!" he the exclaimed. "You look gorgeous. Are you sure that you would like to go dancing?"

"Zip me up," she said as she walked back into the living room wearing a white evening dress, cut in a V-neck, scalloped at the back accentuating her firm buttocks, and her jewelry, a simple pair of ruby earrings.

"You like?" she asked with a tantalizing smile.

"Lady," He said as he kissed her hand, "you really are beautiful."

She smiled, "and I am all yours. Take me to the ball, you gorgeous man."

"Good evening, Sir; good evening, Madam," said the maitre d' somewhat taken aback by the sheer beauty of the smiling lady standing before him.

"Table for two for Mitchell," said Jim.

"Ah, yes," he exclaimed. "Please follow me, Sir," he murmured as he led them to a secluded candlelit booth.

Jim held her hand tenderly as he saw tears of emotion slowly roll down her cheek. "Don't spoil it, love."

"No, I won't, Jim," she sobbed. "A girl can cry when she is happy, can't she?"

"Yes, I suppose so," he replied holding her hand, then changing the subject, he inquired, "What is your stance on the champagne, Madam?"

"I adore champagne!"

Jim regarded the Sommelier, "A bottle of Tattinger '46, then a bottle of your '38 Baume with the main course."

"Certainly, Sir."

"I would like to make a toast, Jim. Here's to the two of us. Two damn egotistical lovers determined to achieve their separate ambitions in life."

Jim raised his glass, "To us, Lydia."

"Oh, Jim," she cried, "Why don't we just forget it, the whole bloody thing, why don't we just forget it?" She cried the tears welling in her eyes.

"Are you serious, Lydia?"

"I don't really know, Jim," she cried. "I think that I would rather tell our kids that you and I did our thing, and not that you and I thought about doing our thing. No, I'm sorry, Jim. It's just that I have these feelings from time to time." Her face brightened, "Oh what the hell, let's toast my dear Uncle Henry. He is our host for this evening."

"To Uncle Henry," Jim replied then a fleeting thought passed his mind. "This man had changed their lives forever."

The superb meal and wine, the admiring glances across the table, glancing touch as their feet touched each other tenderly, the smiles, the magnificent ambience of the ballroom and the orchestra playing slow and sensuous music, heightened their senses.

She smiled, "Dance with me, darling."

They danced oblivious to all, their bodies close, exchanging glances, exchanging smiles, arousing their senses as their love and obsession for each other flowed between them.

"What a night," she said, as she sipped the '39 brandy while seated in the hotel lounge. "Will you smoke a cigar with me?"

"No thank you, Lydia, I think I will have a Dunhill." They sat for a while savoring the moment. "It's been a wonderful evening, Jim. I have waited so long to dance with you." She laughed. "Do you remember the night of the cricket club dance?"

"Yes I do. Wasn't that the night when you nearly seduced me?"

"No, my sweet," she murmured softly, "that was the night when you really turned me on in the middle of the dance floor."

The Sun was shining through the East window of their suite as she stirred herself. He was sleeping like a baby, his hair laid over his face. This was the man who had taken her into another world. He had loved her and taken her to new heights of ecstasy, to a world of happiness, a world of love, of tenderness, of caring, a world kindness and understanding. "Oh my love," she cried, "I love you with all my body with all my soul." She tousled his hair affectionately, kissing his eyes, kissing his lips, as he stirred, whispering softly, "Good morning lover, can we have breakfast in bed?"

Jim smiled. "What your position on pancakes?"

"I love pancakes."

Jim picked up the phone and ordered coffee, orange juice, and pancakes for two.

"Can we talk?"

"Sure." he replied, "what do you want talk about?"

"Well, I've changed my mind. I decided not to go to New York on the *Queen's.*

"Really?"

"It's going to take a long time that way, so I decided to fly with Trans World Airlines from London airport. That means that I will only be away from you for three days. Brilliant don't you think?"

"Bloody marvelous," Jim exclaimed. "You are a clever old thing."

"Less of the old, Mitchell," she said with a laugh, then added, "yes I think so."

"When do you leave?"

"Tuesday, I've also had some other thoughts."

"Do tell."

"Well, I've been thinking, when I get back from New York, I want to sell my house and rent a flat in Chester. Then we could live together until I have passed my finals and you join the Blue Star Line."

"All the time?" asked Jim.

"Well, not all the time. I thought you could live with your mum during the week, and we could live together on the weekend; then I could burn the midnight oil during the week and we could have fabulous weekends together."

"Huh, that will raise some eyebrows."

"Jim, I don't give a damn. I know my parents would not object, and I do not think your grandparents would mind; although, I would think that your mother would not be too pleased with the idea. I think we would need to talk to her."

He laughed. "That will be an interesting conversation Lydia, but I agree, and I love you for thinking about it."

They entered the cathedral to the strains of the first hymn:

> All things bright and beautiful
> All creatures Great and small
> All things at winds and wonderful
> The Lord God made them all.

As Jim knelt in his pew observing the traditions of the Anglican

Church, he had his usual conversation with his Dad, "I wish you were here to guide me." Somehow, he had the feeling that he was listening, and that his son was entering into a new world, a world where he would set his course, where he would make his own decisions led by the rules of life, respecting others as he respected himself.

They walked hand in hand to receive communion. Jim felt the warmth of her love. Somehow, this time it was special. Yes, in the eyes of the church, they were sinners. However, they were in love, and all things were bright and beautiful to them this bright Sunday morning.

"Good service," Jim said as they left the church.

"The sermon made me feel guilty," Lydia quietly said.

"Why?" Jim asked with a laugh.

"The sins of the flesh and all that," she replied.

"That is not what we have, my sweet," said Jim. "Our affair is an expression of love."

"Oh good," she said with a radiant smile. "I feel better with that explanation." She paused, "Why do you always make me feel so dammed well?"

"Because I do love you, silly."

"Thank you kind Sir," she replied.

Sunday lunch at the Cheshire Cheese Inn had always been a special occasion for Jim. There was so much history to this old hostelry, pictures on the wall of days gone by, and pictures of famous visitors from the past. "This," he said to himself, "has always been a welcome respite. What will you have, Lydia?"

"A pint of 'Greenall-Whitley' bitter beer."

"Make of that two," he said addressing the barman, "and two pork pies, please."

"Have you seen that," said Lydia as she pointed to a copy of the old rules of the hostelry.

No Thieves Fakirs Rogues or Tinkers<br>
No Skulking Loafers or Flee Bitten Tramps<br>
No slap or tickle o The Wenches<br>
No cock fighting

Bed for Night One Shilling
Stabling Horse 4 Pence
No Flintlocks, Daggers and Swords

The Gaumont Theatre was full as they sat awaiting the arrival of Thomas Beaching to direct the Liverpool Philharmonic Orchestra. Lydia studied the program Tchaikovsky's, *Symphony No. 2*, and *Romeo and Juliet*. Jim relaxed, leaning back in his seat closing his eyes. This was his usual posture for this occasion as he listened to the opening bars of the cello. He was in another world as he listened to the strains of the violins harmonizing with the brass, then the unknown variant of the Russian folk song. The second movement featured the "Wedding March" with an almost swaggering exuberance. The final movement was turbulent dominated by the Ukrainian folk song, "The Crane" finishing to a grandiose conclusion with a cheerful exuberant final spurt.

"Bravo!" applauded the audience as they all stood to applaud the orchestra's conductor, Thomas Beaching.

The fantasy overture of *Romeo and Juliet* depicted the story of the feud between two quarrelling noble families, the heartache representing the love between Romeo and his beloved Juliet, which kindly breaks down completely this with brutal fortissimo blows from the whole orchestra.

"Bravo!" applauded the music lovers, as orchestra, and conductor, took their third, and final, encore.

"What a superb performance," said Lydia as they left the auditorium. Jim smiled; he was still in another world.

The Riley RMC 2.5 litre snarled beautifully accepting the challenge as they drove along the A 55 to her home, passing Hawarden and Connors Quay. "You drive well, Jim," she observed.

"Thanks," he replied. "This is the second love of my life, young lady."

They lay in her bed at the cottage that night reminiscing of their two days in Chester together.

"Do you always talk to your dad in church?"

"Yes, most times. How did you know?"

"I heard your voice," she replied, "When you said, 'I wish you were here.' Do you still miss him?"

"Yes," Jim replied, "I always will. I often wonder what life would be like if he was here. You see, Lydia, I have never really had anybody that I can really turn to for advice. Yes, Granddad has been absolutely marvelous, and so was Mum, but it's not quite the same, and talking to him does help." She held his hand in her hand.

"I know from the little I knew of him that he would want you to be happy, Jim," she said then added, "Are you?"

"Yes, I am Lydia," Jim answered, as he put his arm around her, holding her close.

"You know something; these last few days have been absolutely marvelous. I feel as though I am in a different world, wondering if what is happening to me is real.

Pinch me. I feel as though I am riding on air, and I do not know what will happen when I stop. Can you understand what I'm saying?"

"Yes, I can," she replied. "I feel the same way. Jim, tell me it's real. Tell me this is real!" she cried. "I have been so happy these last few days, I wonder whether, like you, if it is real; but really it is, Jim, and so bloody wonderful that I to have to pinch myself at times to make me believe that I am here with you and you are with me, and there is a future for you and me." She moved and lay on his belly, clasping her hands on his head, looking into his eyes and murmured, "whatever this is Jimmy, it is bloody marvelous. Hang in with me, my Love; I know that one day we will reap the rewards that we deserve. You have made me so bloody happy, and the marvelous thing about it is that we are friends. You make me laugh and you make me happy Mitchell. Love me again sweet man. You have unleashed a tiger," she laughed lewdly and shouted, "Mitchell, I just can't get enough of you!"

# Chapter 40

The morning dew lay glistening in the fields against the backcloth of the Welsh mountains as Jim drove the Riley along the narrow roads leading to the Cheshire plains. Today, Lydia would fly to New York to conduct her business affairs.

"Are you excited?" Jim asked.

"Not really," she replied. It is the end of a family era. Actually, I feel sad in a way, yet happy knowing that Uncle Henry would approve. I keep thinking about him and all his hard work over the years building up the company. He loved me as he loved his railways. I guess that's life, that's business I suppose," she murmured.

"Yes I suppose so," replied Jim.

As they approached the terminal, the traffic was congested. "Would you like me to park and see you off?" asked Jim.

"No," she choked the words, the tears welling in her eyes. "I hate goodbyes, give me a kiss and I'll see you on Saturday, good-bye my sweet. Give my love to your Mum."

"Hullo, anybody at home?" he said as he entered his house.

"In the kitchen," she replied.

"Hello you," he cried affectionately hugging his mum.

"It's good to see you, my son, I've missed you."

"I've missed you too, Lady," he murmured softly.

She looked deep into his eyes. "Mitchell that is the first time you have called me lady" There was a tear of emotion in her eye and she murmured softly. "That's what your Dad used to call me. Come here and let me look at you. My, you look good, Jim Mitchell!"

He smiled. "Thanks Mum, you clean up nicely too!"

"Thanks, my Love. You always make me feel so good. Where is Lydia?"

"I have just dropped her off at the airport. She's gone to New York for couple of days on business."

There was a coquettish smile on her face, "Wow!" she cried. "I have you all to myself? Will you take your lady to dinner?"

There was an impish smile on his face as he murmured softly. "I would be delighted, Edith."

She smiled. He was the image of his dad, his loving ways and the ability to make her feel so good. They sat across from each other in the restaurant as Jim ordered the meal.

"Well, what have you been doing with yourself since I last saw you?" asked his Mum.

"Not a lot. We stayed at Lydia's home on our first night in Wales, and I met her parents. Then we stayed at their cottage in Portmeirion, and we did some walking. Saturday, we went to the Dorchester for a dinner and dance and stayed overnight. Sunday, we went to church, had lunch at the Cheshire Cheese pub. Then we went on to a concert at that the Gaumout. It was magic. The Liverpool Philharmonic performed Tchaikovsky's, *Piano Concerto Number Two*."

"Are you two sleeping together?"

Jim felt a flush in his cheeks. "Yes, we are Mum," he replied nervously. "I need to talk to you about our relationship."

"Leave it until we get home, my son. I have a feeling in my water that it's going to take some time."

"That depends on your reaction, Mum."

"That was a wonderful meal, Jim, thank you. Are you okay for money?" she asked anxiously as she reached for her pocketbook.

"Yes, I am Mum. Didn't Richard tell you? The gang won the pools last week. My share was three hundred pounds. So I'm not exactly broke, Mum."

"Well, I know who to come to if I want a loan, don't I?" she said jokingly. "I am pleased for you."

They sat on the same settee in front of the fireplace as they had done many times before over the years. He felt comfortable in what he was about to tell her. It was a good feeling. She wasn't just his Mum, the lady who he adored. She was also his best friend.

"Tell me about Lydia and you?" she asked anxiously.

"It's a long story, Mum. I guess it began way back on the night of the 'Wings for Victory Dance' in 1943 when I asked her to dance. Somehow, I guess, we were attracted to each other. Then, as you know, we didn't meet again until the night of 'Victory in Europe' dance."

"Yes, I remember you two caused quite a stir that night, and it started a hell of a lot of rumors in the village."

"Yes, I suppose it did. We didn't meet again for a while. Then I asked her to help me with my metric examinations. She knew that it involved both of us spending some time together; she talked to you."

"Yes, I remember it well," interjected Edith. "She was anxious to avoid rumors in the village, she being older than you and the fact that she was a divorcee. I told her that I trusted you both and that I didn't give a toss about rumors."

"Well," Jim continued. "We sort of made some rules which we kept until the night of the cricket club dance. By then, I had finished my last lesson, and the following week I sat my finals. I don't quite know what happened, but I guess we threw the rules out of the window and we kissed. I guess the growing affection we had for each other over the months surfaced, and we agreed to date. The following Saturday she invited me to her home to celebrate my exam results. It was a wonderful evening. We talked about her life, about Maggie, and our ambitions for the future. Then, after a while, we both realized that we were physically attracted to each and we slept together. Oh, hell!" Jim cried embarrassed by the situation unsure of how to continue.

Suddenly he felt his Mum's arm around his shoulders. "Are you okay, my son? I am listening."

"Oh Mum," he cried. "It was truly a wonderful experience. There were no inhibitions; it seemed so bloody natural," he murmured shyly. "I've always dreamed of how it might be. Oh Mum, it was truly beautiful," he sobbed as his Mum's arm tightened around his shoulders.

"Shush," whispered Edith. "It's okay, my Love, I understand."

"Thanks Mum," he murmured softly as he continued his story. "The following Monday, she left to accompany her parents on their holiday in the United States; then you know we exchanged the odd letter and we talked about our futures. When she returned, we decided to spend time together before she left for her studies in the United States and I joined Blue Star Line. Neither of us made promises to each other about our futures. However, we have agreed to meet again after we have qualified in our disciplines. It seems daft in a way, but we both want to be sure of our feelings. Can you understand that, Mum?"

"Yes, I can, and do, my Love. It's not going to be easy for you," replied Edith.

"I know Mum," he laughed. "Nothing that I do is easy, is it?"

"No it's not, my Love. You're a Mitchell." She smiled, "Mitchell's are worth it, my son, believing you me. So tell me where are you going to live?"

"We are going to rent a flat in Chester, away from the prying eyes of the villagers. Lydia's Mum and Dad think it's a good idea." Jim held his Mum's face in the palms of his hands. "Do we have your blessing?"

Edith looked at him affectionately. "Yes, my love. You have my blessing. Just hold me for a moment. I knew that one day I would lose you, but I never thought it would be so soon."

"Mum" he cried passionately. "Don't say that please, you haven't lost me. There's something special about you and I."

Edith smiled, "Yes, there is, my Love." She paused, "Have you told your Grandma yet?"

"No, I haven't. Lydia and I are having dinner with them the next week. I know that she will not like the idea. To be honest with you, Mum, I don't give a damn. She is not spoiling this for me. She was instrumental in breaking up my relationship with Maggie, and I can assure you she isn't going to ruin this one."

Jim parked the Riley in the airport car park the following Saturday morning before daylight, watching several flights take off and land in the distance. He saw her approaching, wearing a broad smile, the likes of which he hadn't seen since they first met. She stood for moment placing her luggage in the middle of the gangway her arms opened ready to greet her man. "Mitchell," she murmured. "Those were the longest three days I've ever experienced. Take me home, Lover. I need a large gin and tonic, an even larger steak, and a lot of loving."

"That you will, my darling. Give me your bags."

"Don't you want to know how the merger went?" she asked as the Riley sped along the A 4 roadway.

"I thought that you may tell me in the fullness of time."

"Now is a good time, Mitchell. It's all signed and sealed, and the proceeds are invested. Your mistress is now a rich bitch, who loves and adores you. It is mine, and it is ours to do with whatever we wish. I know your feelings, Jim, but I always want you to know, it's there if ever you need it." She put her hand on his knee. "Mitchell," she murmured, "that's the last I want to talk about it, okay?" she laughed. "Now all I have on my mind is the sex, sweet adorable sex. Oh by the way, what was your mother's reaction to you and me?"

"She was fine, and we have the blessing."

"Shake a leg, Mitchell, we have an appointment in forty-five minutes to see the estate agent. Hello," she said shaking him. "Anyone at home?"

"Huh," he mumbled. "I'll be ready in ten minutes. Let's eat on the road to Chester shall we?"

"Mr. Weaver, how nice to see you!" exclaimed Lydia as they entered the estate agents office.

"Thank you for seeing Jim and me so quickly. I really do appreciate it. What do have for me?"

The estate agent smiled. "Not a lot ma'am. I can find about three that will suit your needs. One, has been newly renovated and has an excellent view overlooking the River Dee, the builder is just finishing the final touches. It should be ready for occupancy next week; and two others in town which are fairly old properties."

"What do you think Jim?" asked Lydia.

"Location, location, location," he said.

"Yes, I agree. Let's take a look at the property overlooking the River Dee, Mr. Weaver, then we can take it from there."

The flat had superb views overlooking the river. Lydia looked at Jim and he replied with a wink. "Yes this will do Mr. Weaver, thank you. I'll pop into the office on Monday to sign the necessary paperwork."

"Thank you, I look forward to seeing you. You have made a good choice. Oh, by the way, the furniture is modern. Is that okay?"

"That it will be fine, Mr. Weaver."

# Chapter 41

The following week, they dined with Grandma and Granddad. Grandma Jenny served onion soup, roast leg of lamb, raspberry tart, red and white wine. Jim smiled. He felt sure if she had been the owner of a tiara, she would have worn it that night. She talked at length with Lydia about of the United States, about her mother and father, the cottage in North Wales, and her voyages on the Queen Elizabeth. Most of all about her future plans.

"Fascinating," remarked Grandma. "Lydia, how long are you are going to be away for?"

"Three years, maybe less, depending on how hard I work."

"Will you be coming home to see your parents?" she asked.

"No, Grandma," she replied. "They will be visiting me. I don't want to come home until I finish my studies. That, my dear, would put too much strain on both of us. Being away from Jim will be hard enough, and we could well break our resolve. That was a splendid meal Grandma, thank you."

"Well, I know you always enjoy a leg of lamb. Let's go into the living room shall we." She looked at her husband. I feel like a glass of port wine. Jim, Lydia, what will you have, my dears?"

"Hennessy brandy please, Grandma," replied Lydia.

She regarded Jim, "What would you like, my grandson?"

"I think I'll join you in a port, Grandma."

Now is the time, said Jim to himself. His grandparents had, had a good meal, they were relaxed and drinking their after dinner drinks. As usual, Granddad was smoking a cigar. Lydia had joined him, sitting next to him. Jim was sitting close to his Grandma. He smiled a little nervously; the moment was right as he murmured. "Grandma," he paused, "Granddad, Lydia and I have news."

Grandma smiled, she was hoping that they were going to announce their betrothal.

"Grandma, Lydia and I are going to live together until she goes to the States and I go to sea." For once in her life, Mary Mitchell was tongue struck. Her lips closed, unable to speak. She recovered slowly, from the news. It wasn't what she wanted. She looked at her husband.

There was a smile on his face as he remarked. "Well, that's a sensible idea. It is better than making love in a backseat of a car any day. Don't you think so Mary?"

"Yes I suppose so," she replied slowly recovering, regarding Lydia and Jim. "I still don't understand why you have to go to America to train as a lawyer, Lydia? And you Jim, why do you have to go to sea?"

"To be honest with you, Grandma I don't have too," replied Jim. "I don't. The alternative is to spend two years in the army, probably fighting in Korea. I am not a coward, Grandma. I will fight to the death to defend my country, but I'm bloody sure that I am not going to be bullet fodder for the politicians."

Granddad looked at her. "I agree with him Mary. I do not agree with what is going on in Korea; you have the communists in the North and the puppet government in the South. I do not know how this going to finish in the short-term, but I will tell you this, Communism is not going to last forever. North and South Korea will one-day will be re-united. Communism is not here to stay, Mary; and from what Jack has told me, Harvard is the best place for his daughter to obtain her degree."

Lydia smiled. "Thank you, Granddad. Grandma, no matter which way it goes, we are going to be parted, and both Jim and I believe that what we're doing is right for us." There was a tear in her eye as she murmured. "Anyway, we're not going to rush into marriage. We don't really know each other, Grandma; were' having fun trying."

The church clock rang the midnight hour. The choir, singing "Once in Royal David's City," entered the body of the church led by a young boy chorister. Suddenly, Jim was overcome with emotion; a tear dripped onto his cheek as memories of yesterday came flooding back. Lydia, sensing his emotion, held his hands as he slowly recovered.

"James, how are you? Haven't seen you for a while," said the Reverend James in a reproachful voice. "We are still praying for the team, you know."

Jim smiled. "We need it, Sir." The Reverend James had been his friend, and Granddad's friend, since Jim's early choir days. "Thank you," Jim replied.

Reverend James turned to regard Lydia. "Lydia, my dear, you look radiant."

"Thank you, Sir," she said with a curtsy, "Happy Christmas to both and your family."

"The same to you and your family," Reverend James replied.

Lydia was silent as they drove to their home. "What's on your mind, Lydia?"

"Well," she paused, "Will Maggie be at Granddad's party?"

"Yes of course she will."

"Oh," she said. "I hate it when she monopolizes you every time that we meet."

"She always will. We have been friends since we were kids together. I do not understand why you feel this way. The family loves you as much as they love her. She is special. She always has been and always will be. Do not upset yourself."

"I'm sorry, Love, it's just her bloody 'airs and graces' that bother me."

"Lydia, it's a fact of life in our family, she is special and the family loves her dearly."

"Do you still love her?"

"Of course I do, silly. We have grown up together and you can't stop loving a person just like that. Oh Lydia, let it be, my love. You know the story."

"Yes I do, Love. I remember you telling me about Maggie months ago, and I know it must have hurt both of you badly."

"Yes it did. Now can we leave the subject please?"

She slept in Jim's arms. The sweet fragrance of her well-loved body heightened his affection. He knew now that he cared deeply for this a wonderful woman. He smiled as he gently felt the tresses of her long, auburn hair on his chest. Slowly, her words of the evening flowed into his mind. "Do you still love Maggie?" His mind wrestled to find the truth. How could he ever say no, remembering his first meeting with her when she said, 'I think I like you?' The years that followed, growing up together were turbulent, wonderful days, the formative days of love. They lived in a world of their own, save when we met. Yes, she was my love. 'Do you still love her?' she had asked. Jim smiled. Yes, he did, and they were destined to love each other forever wandering on the sea of love, cursed like Van De Decken sailing forever on the *Flying Dutchman*. "Oh God," he prayed. "Take good care of them."

"Grandma's living room was crowded with family and guests as Jim and Lydia arrived. One by one they circulated the room greeting everyone, and wishing them the compliments the season. It was good to see his aunts, uncles and dearest friends again. Lydia was the center of attention. She was new to the family, young, charismatic, full of fun, and enjoying herself, knowing that she was Jim's girl. In the distance, he saw Maggie standing alone by the window overlooking the lower 10, her eyes pulling him towards her. There was a tingle of excitement as their fingers touched. They both wanted to hold the other in their arms. Jim desired to run his fingers through her black hair and kiss those adorable lips. He looked deeply into her eyes. He could feel her love. "Hello Jim," she murmured in a low voice. "How are you my love?"

"Fine Maggie, Happy Christmas," Jim smiled tenderly. "How are you?"

responded Maggie warmly.

"Hello Maggie, Happy Christmas," Lydia said as she appeared by Jim's side. The spell was broken. The moment had passed.

"Happy Christmas, Lydia. Jim's Mum tells me that you're home for a little while before you begin your studies at Harvard. I wish you well." She paused looking directly into her eyes and murmured. "I hope, my dear that you and I can be friends one day. We have a lot in common."

Jim joined his Uncle Will and Maggie's escort for the party, a young man that she had attended school with a few years ago. He remembered the story from their previous meeting!

"Hello," said Jim, "My name is Jim Mitchell."

"Yes, I know" smiled the tall, blond haired youth, "I am Maggie's friend."

"Are you talking about me, Jim?" asked Maggie as she joined them.

"Who else would we talk about, dearest cousin," he said jestingly.

"Robert gets me another drink!" she ordered.

"Maggie, that wasn't very nice. You really have upset me, that sort of behavior is below you. Madam, meet me in the dining room," he said. As she approached him, he murmured angrily, "Maggie what the hell are you doing? You don't treat people like that."

She looked astonished at Jim's rebuke. "Damn you, Jimmy Mitchell, what the hell has it got to do with you?" she whispered.

"Can't you see he adores you?"

"Yes, I suppose so," she pouted, "but it's nothing to do with you. You have Lydia. Mind your own damn business."

"Maggie, don't do this, my sweet."

He noticed a tear in her eye, "I'm sorry, Jim. Don't you see it's not easy seeing the man I love with another girl?"

"Dinner is ready," announced Grandma.

"You have done a wonderful job," said Jim as he escorted his Grandma to her seat.

The family sat in their traditional places. Granddad at the head of the table, his principal guest was Lydia, who sat on his left, and Maggie on his right. Granddad, as usual, stood offering the traditional prayers for the Christmas dinner. Granddad waxed liquid over the years. Granddad had found a spot on the upper ten, which was ideal for growing both red and white grapes and was now becoming somewhat of an expert in the wine making. This was obviously his subject of conversation for the meal.

"When do you join your ship, Jim?" asked his Uncle Will.

"I don't really know, Uncle Will," he replied. "Hopefully they will find me a berth sometime towards the end of February."

"Are you looking forward to it?"

"Yes, in a way, I have mixed feelings. Anyway," he said with a laugh, "it's better than doing two years in the army, particularly with this Korea thing."

Over the years, Jim had always been amazed as to how quickly the Christmas party passed. Granddad rose to give his usual speech. He felt Maggie's hand touch his as it had done many times in the past this year. It appeared that his speech was shorter than usual, and Jim noticed a smile on Grandma's face when he neared to the end. "We need to see the family grow, to carry on its traditions." Suddenly he felt her hand tighten its grip. There was a tear in her eye, "To the family and our guests!"

"To the family and guests!" everyone replied.

"That was a superb party, Jim," Lydia said as she drove the Riley down the Ridgeway to join the Chester Road. "Your Granddad was wonderful to me, Jim. I never thought that I would be his guest of honor."

"Well young lady, you were obviously his favorite tonight. You charmed the hell out of him."

"I didn't mean to do that. Everyone was so kind to me. I really did feel at home."

"Good," replied Jim. "They love you dearly Lydia, and they have accepted you into the family, so all your worries about the party, and Maggie, were for naught, young lady."

"I know," she replied. "I guess I was just being silly, but honestly, my Love, thanks for your support last night. You will never know how much I appreciate that."

"That's the way I feel about your parents, Lydia," said Jim.

"I know," she said ruefully. "Mum adores you."

"It's been a perfect Christmas Day, my Love," she smiled as she lay in his arms. "You have a wonderful family, Jim."

"Yes I know, my sweet," said Jim, "but they think we are a bit stupid; you to study, and me to travel the world."

"Yes I know," Lydia replied. "My Mum feels the same way."

"Really?" inquired Jim.

"Yes, she thinks that we should marry and have lots of children."

"So does Granddad and Grandma."

She laughed. "So that's what your Granddad was talking about in his speech."

"Yes," said Jim ruefully. "He would like nothing better than for me to run the farm." He paused, "Oh God, are we being stupid Lydia?" Jim thought for a while. "Maybe," he replied, "but I don't think you and I would work out until we have done our thing."

"No I suppose not, we are a pair of ambitious, egotistical so-and-so's, hoping that one day we can have it all."

"I hope so, my Love," said Jim as he drifted into a deep sleep.

It was a bright sunny morning, unusually warm, as they drove the winding roads to Lydia's parent's home to celebrate Boxing Day. Once again, he imagined the scenery, the old cottages, the local people kind and generous and even to the Englishman from across the border. There were many pleasant memories of the past. The days when he and the gang had their camping holidays in this part of the world. Jim smiled remembering trying to light a fire outside the tent during a rainstorm. That was a failure and their evening meal consisted of cold baked beans and bread. That day they were chased by a bull, which had the audacity to think that the field belonged to him. Their usual camping site was his domain, or was it the other way around. Jim never knew. His thoughts were broken as they arrived and greeted by Megan and Jack.

"Welcome, Jimmy," she said with a wonderful smile. Jim loved this grey-haired mother of his lady.

"Happy Boxing Day, Mum," Lydia cried as she kissed her.

"It's nice to be here, Megan," Jim said as he looked at the old stone cottage with the grey slate roof. The garden was beautiful in its winter setting, their home delightful with the backcloth of Mount Snowdon.

"Anyone for a walk?"" asked Jack.

"Not me," replied Megan.

"Or me," said Jim.

Jack smiled, "Well I guess that's just Lydia and I. We won't be too long."

"Would you like some tea, Jimmy?"

"Yes please, Megan."

"I have Garibaldi biscuits. Let's sit in the sun lounge; it's nice and warm."

"Lydia tells me that you're an author?"

"Yes, I suppose I am," replied Megan with a slight lilt in her voice.

"I haven't read any of your books."

"I write for children."

"Do tell," said Jim.

"It started some years ago; I was a little bored with life. The children were at boarding school and I needed something to do. So, I put pen to paper." She laughed, "Much to my surprise, they published it. Since then, I make notes in the winter and go to the cottage in the summer to write."

"Do you use a pen name?"

"Yes, Elizabeth Brag."

"I know all the works; they're wonderful reading." Jim saw a glow of pride in her face.

"Well, thank you, Sir." Megan paused. "Jim, I just want to say one thing while we're alone. You have worked miracles with our daughter. I never thought the day would come when she would be so happy again. Thank you. Jack and I are so grateful."

There was a tear in her eye.

"Shush," said Jim as he walked across the room to her. "Megan, you have a wonderful daughter. I feel so proud to know her, and that you and Jack understand what we're doing." He smiled, "In many ways we are very similar. Both of us are very ambitious and determined to reach our goals come hell or high water."

Megan laughed. "Quite a phrase, Jim," she murmured. "Yes I know where you're coming from. Jack and I have known for a long time about Lydia's ambitions. Little did we know that she would meet you, an equally ambitious man. You and Lydia are like two peas in a pod. What you're about to undertake, will not be easy for either of you. I hope that it all works out for you. You could have just one hell of the future together," she smiled, "giving me grandchildren." Her face lit brightly as she touched Jim's hand. "Let me get you some more tea, my dear," she said. "What makes Jim Mitchell tick?" Megan asked as she returned to the room.

"I don't really know, Megan, I guess it's a number of things, most of which are rolled in to a big ball. First, I love my family, and, someday, I want a family of my own. I enjoy music, poetry, reading, and most sports. I am sort of an average to good scholar, and last but not least, my friends. He smiled. In the future, one day I would like to marry your daughter, if she will have me. Apart from that, I do not really know now. I hope to qualify as the Chief Engineer in the Merchant Marines. That will open many opportunities for me in the future, and Granddad wants me to run the farm when he retires."

"But that's not enough is it?" Maggie asked as she quizzically viewed Jim.

"How do you know?" Jim asked.

"You and Lydia have the same characteristics. Neither of you will be satisfied until you achieve your goals in life. You know, Jimmy," she said in a soft voice. "She can be strong minded. Do not lose each other along the way. You are so good for her. One day I want her to give me grandchildren," she rose and kissed him on the forehead. "I hope they are yours, Jim."

"We are, home!" shouted Lydia. "What have you two been doing?" she said as she walked into the sunroom looking somewhat hot after a long walk with her father.

"Talking," Jim, replied.

"About what?"

"Never mind, young lady," said Megan. "It's been a Jim and Megan afternoon."

"Oh, okay," she said, "anyone for a sherry?"

That evening Jack cooked a splendid meal of Cock-a-leaky soup, a traditional Welsh soup, Welsh rack of lamb and Christmas pudding. It was a wonderful meal. Later they stood around the piano singing traditional Welsh songs, the songs of yesteryear, the finale being "Men of Harlech."

"Thank you for your hospitality Jack. It was a great party. I think I'm losing my voice," croaked Jim as they left the next morning. "See you at the New Year's Eve Ball."

The weather had changed dramatically. The trip to the cottage was hazardous. The overnight snow had made the winding roads slippery. Jim admired Lydia's skill at the wheel as she guided the Riley into the hills. The scenery, at the first pass into the valley, was exhilarating, the sheer beauty of a winter wonderland. David "the post" had cleared the drive leading up to the cottage, and the glow of the fires welcomed them back to her home in this beautiful part of Wales.

"We are home, Jim," she cried wrapping her arms around his neck kissing him fully on the lips.

"It's good to be back, my love, this is a wonderful place."

"Yes I know," she said, "this is our love nest, Jim."

The day turned into night, the snowstorm intensified to blizzard conditions. As the storm passed, it left an eerie silence over the hills and valleys. They took comfort in the knowledge that they had fuel and food for the many days isolated in the warmth of their love unfettered by the world around them. It was time to fill their souls with the emotions of music: Tchaikovsky, Mozart, Grieg, Chopin, Rachmaninov, Bach and Strauss. The music of love and romance, and, all is well that ends well, *Romeo and Juliet*. Above all, it was a time for love, sweet gentle love.

All too quickly, the Sun, and the rain, ended the isolation. They spent one last night at the pub drinking "Wrexham" ale, eating steak and kidney pie, and drinking a fine French Beaujolais. Tomorrow would be New Year's Eve, time to celebrate yet another year with the family, her friends, and "Yes" he smiled, "the gang."

"Oh! I've asked Daddy to invite the gang and their girlfriends to his suite before dinner. He's also invited a couple of his clients and they will be staying overnight at the Grosvenor."

"What?" Jim exclaimed.

She looked at him a little sheepish, "I'm sorry my sweet. I've been so absorbed by you the last four days, I forgot to tell you."

The suite was crowded when Lydia and Jim arrived and were greeted by Megan. "Jim Mitchell," she murmured softly, "you look so dammed handsome. Lydia you look radiant my darling, let me introduce you around."

One by one, they met Jack and Megan's guests. In the corner of the room, Jim saw his Granddad and Grandma. At first, he didn't recognize them. Grandma had long, silver hair falling over her shoulders. This is a first. She looked radiant wearing a long, black evening gown. Granddad, a tall, slim figure dressed in a black dinner suit looking too dammed handsome for his years. "Grandma, you look gorgeous," said Jim. She smiled and preened with pleasure. "Your hair looks wonderful!"

"Get away with you, Jimmy Mitchell!" she said, "You're a charmer just like your Granddad."

"Thanks for the compliment, Grandma. Will you save me a dance later?"

"Ask me when you're ready," she whispered proudly.

"Hello Granddad, Grandma," said Lydia as she greeted them.

"You look like a million dollars, young lady," said Granddad.

"Well thank you kindly, Sir," she said as she curtseyed to him. "May I have a dance with you later?"

"You may young lady," he replied, "I shall look forward to it."

Over in the corner, Jim saw the tall figure of an old school friend. "Megan come and meet Johnny Herbert. He's an old friend of mine, a school mate from years ago."

"Johnny, how nice to see you," said Jim has they shook hands. "You know Mrs. Davis?"

"No I don't. I am delighted to meet you ma'am," he paused. "This is my friend, Jenny," he turned and smiled. "Jenny, this is a fellow that broke my nose in the school boxing final. How's your eye, Mitchell?"

"Recovered nicely, thank you," Jim replied with a laugh.

"It was a good match, Jim. They are still talking about it today. I suppose, in a way, you in I made some history at the school."

"Yes, we did, old friend, we must catch up some time."

"James, how are you?" asked Richard

"Fine, Richard," he replied.

"Sorry were late. Linda was still mucking out the stables when I called for her."

Jim smiled as he heard the renowned horse owner swearing. "Let me introduce you to Mrs. Davis. "Megan this is the gang: Richard, Derek, and Brian."

"So you're the gang," she said with a smile. "It's good to meet you. Jim has told me all about you."

"All?" asked Brian jokingly. "Should we leave now, or should we wait until you throw us out?"

"You're okay, I'm the hostess," then Megan regarded their ladies. "And who are these fine ladies?"

"Sorry, please accept my apologies," exclaimed Richard, "this is Melinda, Vicki and Sylvia."

"Hello gang," said Lydia and she made her way towards them.

"Wow!" said Richard, "you look gorgeous." Lydia curtsied, "Thank you, kind Sir."

The newly decorated ballroom looked splendid as the party entered. The sheer white sculptured ceilings were enhanced by a rich, gold leaf Cove. The silk clad wall covering was enhanced by the beautifully, gold framed artwork and mirrors. The dimly lit, gold plated chandeliers cast seductive shadows onto the scene. The celebration garlands and balloons gave a beautiful luxurious setting for the ball. They dined on excellent traditional fare, French wines and danced the night away. Time passed quickly. Midnight was on the revelers, "Ten, nine, eight, seven, six, five, four, three, two, and one!" Then they sang the traditional New Year's Scottish song, "Should auld acquaintance be forgot and never brought to mind."

Lydia cupped Jim's face in the palms of her hands and murmured softly, "Happy New Year, my Darling."

# Chapter 42

It was a cold winter's night as she lay in his arms in a restless sleep. Tomorrow she would learn her fate in her final examination. The intervening months since she had returned from the United States had consumed the two lovers, along with the various points of law and the case histories quoted at breakfast, lunch and dinner and sometimes at 2:00 a.m. She loved her profession with a passion, determined to succeed in a world dominated by the opposite sex.

During the last months, Jim learned to admire this lady, her determination, and her intellect. This was a lady who had experienced the horrors of war, a lady who swore that she would never enter into a relationship again, and the lady who had tutored him in the classical readings, the arts, and language. They had a friendship based on kindness, understanding, and compassion for each other's needs out of which grew a platonic love; and the odd look of admiration had grown into a love affair so in inexplicable, so vibrant, so real, so wonderful. Despite all this, they would soon part in order to satisfy their egotistical ambitions, she to study international law at Harvard, he to travel the world and to secure his ambition to become a Chief Engineer in the Mercantile Marine.

How would the world treat them? Would they be faithful to each other, or would temptations drive them apart. It was a time of doubt and fear, that inexplicable time just before dawn. The dawn of a new and exciting era in their lives. There future was cast in stone. Jim's thoughts turned to himself. The last months had been a defining moment in his life, crowned yesterday at noon, when he learned that the Blue Star Shipping Company had found him a berth on a cargo passenger liner sailing to South Africa, Australia, and New Zealand. During the latter years, he had enjoyed his apprenticeship, the academic beauty, his college professors and the practical hands-on work with Griff, Ken and Jack, the installation of both steam and diesel plants driving electrical transmission. He had grown with this experience. He had enjoyed his success on both the football and cricket field, and was now captain of his team. He had received the accolades for the team's achievements in his final years. "The cups," he thought, "were in coach's trophy cabinet."

It was now the small hours of the morning: a time of fear, a time of doubt before the dawn, a dawn full of promise, a time for renewal to awake from the dreams of the night. "What time is it Jim?" she asked as she finally stirred from her restless sleep. "Is it light, my Love? Hold me close," she murmured.

His thoughts turned to the past, and to the new day before him. There was a driving force within him, the need to succeed. Where did it come from? What was he trying to prove? That he could succeed in the world without the guidance of his father. "God I miss him," he cried. There was a determination never to be poor again. Never to wear a patch over his frayed clothing, or tight shoes. Or was it just a need for love, admiration and affection? He was no longer known as Jim Mitchell's son. He was now his own man. He had proved it many times. During his training, he had set his goals with a promise to himself that he would succeed, and one day he would marry the girl of his dreams. "Life has its pitfalls," he said to himself as he remembered the love of his sweet cousin Maggie, their plight as young lovers, and a sweet loving memory of the past. The temptation to love her was still there. The memory of their last meeting at Christmas still lingered as he looked into her beautiful blue eyes, remembering her words, "Do you feel it Jimmy?" His answer, "Yes my love." It was then he realized that their love affair was over, and had been for sometime, but he had refused to recognize the fact. Now it was just a fantasy in his mind, or was it? Would he ever really know?

Jim looked at Lydia's tousled her hair as she lay on the pillow. He knew at last that she was the lady of his dreams, or was it deep infatuation, born out of kindness, born out of a deep sexual satisfying affair. He didn't know. Would they be faithful to each other during their years apart, or would the temptations of the world drive them apart? It was time for doubt, a time of fear for their future, that awful frightening time, before the birth of a new dawn, the dawn of a new career in their lives. Their careers were cast in stone, two egotistical ambitious creatures of God soon to part. He fell asleep in a restless sleep, and was awakened by a knock on the door. Slowly he raised his weary body to answer the call. His bleary eyes focused on the postman, the harbinger of good and bad tidings holding a brown envelope in his hand, "Good morning, Sir."

"Who is it darling?" she asked.

"The postman, for you," he replied.

"Open it please," she said nervously.

Jim read the single page and yelled, "You've passed! You've passed, Lydia."

She ran towards him, wrapping her legs and her arms around him. "Oh Jimmy, Oh Jim! Isn't it wonderful! Let me read it. I passed, Jim! I passed!" she cried. "Hold me close, lover." Slowly the tears of joy, of relief ran down her pale sleepless face. The sweet, wonderful sense of success had her body shaking with joy at her victory, the euphoria of achieving her goal.

"Congratulations my love," Jim said proudly.

"Tonight we celebrate," she murmured looking into his eyes. "Jim, take me to our cottage, please, my love. I want to spend our last few days together in Portmeirion."

The days that followed were enchanted, endless hours filled with a dreamlike quality as though time might have been suspended. The hours merged into nights; the nights drifted into dawn. Every single moment was spun out. Intertwined as though it would be their last hour together, neither wanting to leave each other. Each evening they lay in each other's arms in front of the fireplace. Lying on their beloved white sheepskin rug, they loved with a passion assuaged flaring again with a stronger, brighter flame, hoping that the tomorrow may not arrive. Their plight bound them inextricably together, deepening their love, deepening their understanding of each other.

The time had arrived. They lay in bed locked in each other's arms. She smiled. "These last days had been wonderful, my love. Now you have exposed my true feelings. Jim whatever happens to us, I will always be your mistress. One day I will find you. Jim, you have brought me into the world again, a world full of happiness. Thank you, my Love. Life for you and I will not to be easy," she murmured. "We are moving into a new world. Be happy, my Love," she cried, a tear falling from her blue eyes. "Love the one you're with, my darling."

The following morning, Jim drove her to her home. As they arrived, she opened the door of the Riley and murmured, "Go quickly, my Love, Godspeed."

Jim drove to the nearest lay-by. His head rested in his hand on the steering wheel. There were tears running down his face as he cried, "I love you, Lydia Louise Henning."

# Chapter 43

"Newcastle!" yelled the overnight train cabin steward. Jim opened the window blind in the compartment; it was barely light. He could see the outlines of other trains as they approached the final station of the journey. The air was dank and dusty, a dismal atmosphere, he noticed, much different from the world he knew. He dressed slowly, washing his hands and face, combing his hair. He was entering into another world and he was unsure of himself. His first thought was to turn around to go home. He smiled as he said to himself, "Mitchell, don't be so bloody silly." He walked onto the end of the platform to be greeted, by a cab driver.

"Where to, mate?"

"Middle docks South Shields, please."

"Okay," he said. The intonation of his voice confirmed that he was in 'Geordie –land.' He remembered one of his fellow apprentices recounting the history of this part of the world. This is the land of the River Tyne, the land of fun loving people with a rich history of coal mining and fine shipyards dating back to the middle of the nineteenth century. He was entering into a new world. His destination was one of England's major repair and dry docks, now being revived following the '30s depression and World War II, part of the growing British marine fleet.

"This is it," said of the cabbie. "That will be one pound, ten shillings, sir. You will probably find the ship you're looking for at the end of the Middle Docks, on the left about two hundred yards from here."

There was an air of expectancy in his gait as he carried his suitcase past storage sheds and gigantic cranes. The place was a hive of activity. There were trucks moving parts, and moving hull plates. There were a number of Blue Funnel ships around, a couple of Bibby line vessels, and a huge passenger ship owned by Cunard called the Mauritania. He was excited. He was now entering the world of shipping, the world of marine engineering. In the distance, he saw the 'Sydney Star.' "Oh," he said to himself as he scanned the length of her hull, forecastle, the cargo hatches, the bridge, officers and passenger accommodation and a funnel with a "Blue Star" logo, then another hatch and her stern accommodation for the crew. "Not a pleasant sight," he said to himself. It looked like a 'rust bucket' lying in the dry dock. There was a sanguine smile on his face. This hull of rusty iron, a ship built to carry cargo to and from Britain, the continents, and from places all around the world, barely fit the description, and photographs, that he had received from the Blue star shipping company. It had a refrigerated capacity to carry lamb, beef, and fruit from South America, New Zealand, Australia and South Africa, along with other British exports, at a speed of 22 knots. It had a wartime history of valiant work during World War II, carrying troops and munitions to the Allied troops stationed all around the world. The *Sydney Star* had an adventurous career in World War II when in 1941, on a convoy to Malta, she was attacked by German U-boat's and torpedoed on the port side of number three hatch. Cargo, some four hundred sixty troops and crew were transferred to a ship in the convoy, and then proceeded towards Malta. The following morning, dive-bombers heavily attacked her and fortunately, there were no direct hits. Thus, listing heavily and sinking by the head, she finally arrived in Malta that afternoon for urgent repairs. The Captain and Chief Engineer were awarded the OBE in recognition for their outstanding service.

Jim walked up the gangway and was greeted by a naval seaman who directed him to the Chief Engineer's quarters. He nervously knocked at the door, then heard a yell, "Come!"

Sitting at his desk in a large cabin, was his new boss. "Jim Mitchell, reporting for duty, Sir," said Jim in a firm voice. The tall frame of Larry Caldwell smiled, "Welcome aboard, Mitchell. I have been expecting you. Did you travel well?" he asked.

"Yes thank you, Sir." The brief ceremony over, he was now a junior engineer on the pride of the Blue Star Line, the *Sydney Star*.

"Anybody at home?" inquired a voice as the cabin door opened; a tall, redheaded man entered.

"Welcome aboard, John Thompson. How was your leave?"

"Marvelous, thank you, Sir," replied John.

"Let me introduce you. This is Jim Mitchell a new junior engineer who has joined us today."

"Welcome Jim Mitchell, it is good to meet you," greeted John Thompson.

"Thank you, Sir," Jim replied.

"I need a break, gentlemen. Let us go to lunch. I can then tell you about our plans for the next few days. It would appear that we are likely to get out of dry dock in about ten days. At that time, the office tells me that I will be getting another five engineering officers and two deck officers to take us around the coast. We should have our full complement of engineers and deck officers when we arrive in London. That is not quite what I would like, but those are the cards that we have been dealt. Now, let us talk about the next few days, shall we? John, you will take the evening shift, Mitchell will take the night shift, and I will take the day shift for a while until the other engineers arrive."

"Why don't you, and Jim Mitchell, get settled in? We are all staying at the Excelsior," he laughed. "It's improved tremendously since I stayed there last. I am sure they are going to make us comfortable until we start living on board. Let us meet at eight o'clock tomorrow morning. Then I can introduce you around to the shore gang."

During the next weeks, Jim learned the layout of the ship's engine room. The diesel electric power plant was similar to the plant that he had helped install and commission during his apprenticeship. The twin six-cylinder Burmmeister and Wain main propulsion engines were huge and impressive. The final inspection was of the hull, propellers, and sacrificial anodes. The ship's hull was underway. The hull painting was complete: a bright red color below the waterline and black above. The superstructure gleamed with fresh white paint. The red funnel was the background to the white circle encircling the Blue Star emblem designating the ships company. Jim smiled. The transformation from a rust bucket was remarkable. The *Sydney Star* was now a sleek, cargo passenger ship, 'The Pride of the Line.'

The vessel was now ready to leave the dry dock. Jim watched the water flooding the dry dock, flowing into the vessel from the blocks. Almost simultaneously, two tugboats arrived, attaching their ropes and expertly maneuvering the vessel out of the dry dock to the adjacent berth. It was altogether a fascinating experience.

The days before the vessel left Middle Docks were hectic. The engine room, which looked like a spare parts department, gradually fell into place. 'Ship shape and a Bristol fashion, a nautical term, pertaining to the readiness of the ship for sea duty; the preparations were complete. The ship was ready for sea, a voyage from Middle Docks South Shields to London Victoria Docks where she would load its cargo.

The ship came alive under its own electrical power. Jim moved his gear from the hotel to his spacious cabin for the trip. It was his home for the next several months and it felt good. A real bed, a day bed, a desk and a bathroom fitted with a real shower, toilet and sink. He could imagine his mother's thoughts, "That's really posh, Jim Mitchell." He had learned another maritime phrase for posh, an old Blue Funnel term for their first-class passengers sailing to the Far East: Port side out, starboard side home! The following Saturday morning was memorable insomuch that Jim missed a football game on Newcastle's home pitch. The visitors that day would be his old favorite team Everton. He complained heavily to himself, but there was nothing much that he could do except say goodbye to his home for the next few weeks. The *Sydney Star* was now on her way down the River Tyne heading for the North Sea, then to the English Channel and London Victoria and Albert Docks. It was a fascinating site. The vessel glided down the Tyne passing the numerous dockyards and the North East beaches. Gradually the coastline disappeared. As they left the lee of the land, a westerly wind started to blow on the port quarter. The color of the sea changed from a muddy brown to a blue green with white caps, causing a gentle rocking motion, which grew in intensity to a strong pitching motion as the *Sydney Star* bow started to rise and fall. This was Jim's initiation to life at sea. The ship's bell rang the change of watch. Jim moved slowly, unsteady on his feet to his quarters changing into his coveralls to begin his first 'watch' at sea as a junior engineering officer.

John Thompson smiled as he looked at his junior engineer. "Are you okay Jim?"

There was a languid smile on his face as he replied, "I think so, Sir, its bloody rough outside."

Jim Thompson laughed. "You haven't seen anything yet, Jim boy."

The four to eight watches passed quickly, and he was grateful when the following watch relieved him. He showered, changed, and walked to the wardroom for a pint before dinner.

"Well, Mitchell, what do you think of your duties so far?" said the Chief Engineer as he joined John Thompson and Jim for a beer before dinner.

"It's a bit different than I thought, Sir, but the electrical system is similar to what I have been used to in the past."

"I'm pleased to hear that Jim Mitchell. Should you have any questions, let me know. I'll be more than pleased to help you," the Chief Engineer offered.

The following morning, the *Sydney Star* arrived at the estuary to the River Thames and joined a number of cargo ships awaiting entry to the London docks facility. Slowly, the *Sydney Star* maneuvered into her position to transit the river. "So this is London," Jim said to himself as the ship glided on still water past the Bexley Heath Power Station, the factories and storage facilities along the shores of the River Thames. In the distance, he saw the tall cranes and barges plying their goods to the dock land. He was intrigued at the activity, the bustle, and the contrasting types of cargo ships awaiting their turn to move into the locks, a fascinating experience. Eventually it was their turn. The lock gates opened and the vessel was maneuvered by the attending tugboats. Then the lock gates shut, the ship gradually rose as the massive pumps increased the level. Within minutes, the gates opened and the ship slid slowly into its berth.

By tradition, the company representatives are the first to join the vessel. Their first duty was to bring the mail and letters aboard for the crew, the crew's only lifeline to their home and to their loved ones. For some, it would be months away from their loved ones. "Not a way to conduct a relationship," Jim observed silently.

"Would you like to come ashore with me tonight for a pint, Jim?" asked John Thompson following their afternoon watch.

"Yes please," Jim replied to his senior engineer. He remembered Griff Kitching telling him tails of the east end of London. Stories about the dock land, the men who made their living from servicing the ships, unloading and loading the cargoes, the travelers from many lands, and the old dockside village of Lime House and Rotherhithe. Many years ago, a number of Swedish chemist's immigrated to this area to purvey their skills. There were Norwegian churches and Chinese restaurants run by descendants of a mid-seventeenth century immigrants to this area.

John Thompson told Jim about the history and construction of the royal group of docks, which were constructed in the mid-nineteenth century, the largest dock system in the world.

Jim had entered into another world, a world of commerce like nothing he had seen before. A world of fanatical support for one of the world's greatest football team's "West Ham United," the team that had eliminated the mighty Liverpool football club from the Football Association cup. There were streets upon streets of row houses and small shops that sold every conceivable item that one would ever need, and John talked about the Dockers' way of life, the cockneys born within the sound of Bow Bells and the social life in the pubs.

That night, they walked along the narrow cobblestone streets lit by gas lamps, casting their shadows in an eerie manner, reminding him of some of the films that he had seen in the past, and Sexton Blake, the crime investigator who become famous over the years for his exploits. Also, this was the area that had suffered the German bombing. There were huge gaps between houses that had been occupied before the war, a grim reminder of those dark days. In the distance, he could hear one of the areas' popular songs:

'Any time you're Lambeth way,

Any evening any day

You will find us all doing the Lambeth walk.'

The sound of a taxi horn drowned out the rest of the words. Jim's expectations of a good night out were high as he entered the smoke-filled bar of the Silvertown Pub.

"Your back, John, I've missed you!" Jim smiled. John's description of the best-looking girl in town was accurate. She was, to use the colloquial term, a "knock-out."

"Nellie, this is my mate, Jim Mitchell."

"Hello Jim,"" she said, "you look good young fella."

"Well thank you, young lady."

"It's been a long time since I was called a lady, thank you, Sir."

"Where are you from, Jim?" she asked.

"Cheshire," he replied.

"You sound pretty 'posh.' Haven't heard anybody talk like you before."

"What would you like to drink, me darling?" Her smile was flirtatious and she knew it. "My name is Rosy, and I'm your waitress for the night. What can I do for you, love?" she murmured with an audacious smile.

"Two pints of Newcastle Brown ale, please." Jim looked at Nellie, "And you, love?"

"Gin and Orange, if you please."

"I think I'm going to like ya," she smiled.

At first, Jim found it was difficult to understand the dialect. "Cheers," said John, "the first tonight." After a while, a good-looking redhead walked to the table.

"Hello. How's John tonight?" she asked.

"Not too bad Gloria, this is my mate Jim."

Jim shook her hand and she said, "You're not bad looking, are ya?" Between songs, they talked mostly about her 'old man.' "He is away in the far east on a Blue Funnel ship. Don't see him often," she added.

She put her hand on Jim's knee. "You fancy a bit tonight, Jim?" she said with a smile. At first, Jim did not understand what she was saying. Then he remembered Griff description of 'pub ladies.' "I don't charge a lot. I could give you a really good time," she added.

"No thanks love," Jim replied. "But thank you for asking."

Last orders please, ladies and gentlemen." Jim finished his drink.

"Will you be okay?" asked John. "I'm going home with Sue. See you in the morning."

"Would you like another beer, love?" asked Rosy with a saucy smile.

"Just a half pint please, Rosy."

As she put his drink on the table, she looked at him. "Are you okay Jim?" she asked.

"A bit lonely, love," replied Jim.

"I know what you mean. You want to take me home? No hanky-panky, I'm a good girl."

"Yes, sure, thank you," replied Jim.

# *Chapter 44*

Life in port, on the *Sydney Star*, was somewhat different from the ordered, and regulated, life on board when the ship was at sea. Jim had enjoyed the short trip from South Shields to the Victoria and Albert Docks. Now, there was the noise of the winches loading the ship's cargo, and from the workers from South Shields while completing unfinished work from our extensive lay- up. Because of time constraints, most of the crew concentrated on their shore diversions. John Thomson disappeared into the arms of his girlfriend. Jim was lonely in a town that was busy in this vibrant, bustling world of the London Docklands. One evening after a shore meal, he decided to return to see if Rosy was still around. The pub, as usual, was busy, the patrons singing, and animated conversation in a smoke filled atmosphere. Out of the crowded bar, Rosy appeared carrying a tray of drinks held high. "Hello Jim," she smiled. "I'll be back in a few minutes. What can I do for you young man?" she asked in a provocative tone.

"One pint of Newcastle please." As she served Jim's drink, she lingered awhile. "Do you get any time off?" Jim asked.

She smiled, "Saturday."

"Can we have a day out?"

"Are you asking me for a date?" She laughed.

"Yes," he stuttered, "Yes, I suppose I am."

"Yes. What have you in mind?" asked Rosy coyly.

"West Ham football team's playing at home on Saturday. Will you come with me to the game? In addition, maybe we could have a meal afterwards. How near is the Prospect of Whitby?"

"Not far," she exclaimed. "That is a hell of a date, young man," she said and replied, "Yes, I would love to. Thanks, I am looking forward to it."

The football match on Saturday was West Ham versus Arsenal, a London 'derby' game. Nothing given, nothing gained; the intensity of these supporters created a fantastic atmosphere between elation and despair for both sets of supporters as the battle raged. Jim laughed. His date was excited using comments that strained the English language to its core, extending his knowledge of the local Cockney vocabulary considerably. Watching her, and listening to her, was great fun, a new experience for the lad from Cheshire. He was beginning to enjoy the atmosphere of the East End dockland. Yes, in many ways it was a fun atmosphere. As Rosy said many times, "they were a bit 'posh' in Cheshire," and he tended to agree with her. The match was over, two goals apiece, and his date's voice was husky from the stress and emotion of the game.

"The Prospect" as it was fondly referred to, was a fashionable pub at the time. It generated an upscale West End clientele and provided a good supper menu. Rosy and Jim were escorted to a table at the far end of the bar by the Maitre D. "Will this be all right, Sir?" he asked.

"Fine thank you," replied Jim.

"Core blimey," yelled Rosy, surprise at her new surroundings. "This is really posh, Jim. Have you seen this?" she exclaimed pointing to the prices of food on the menu. Jim laughed. "The price of a gin and tonic," she continued, "I can't believe it! It's nearly twice as much as my pub charges!" she exclaimed.

The food was delicious. "This is good!" she exclaimed as she made her way through a large steak and kidney pie. "How are your fish and chips, Jim?"

"They are good, love," he said. "They're the best I've had since I last ate at Hignets."

"What's that?" she asked

"It's a fish and chip shop in the city of Chester."

"That Chester place," she observed, "is supposed to be very nice."

"Yes it is, Rosy."

"Will you take me there one day?" she asked.

"Maybe," he replied. "If you're a good girl," he added with a laugh.

Jim's date summed up her first visit to this historical pub as posh. She made him laugh when she exclaimed. "The prices they charge are nearly twice as much as we pay, Jim."

"Don't worry, Rosy" Jim replied, "I think it's worth it for the experience! You know it's quite famous."

"Yes, okay, if you say so," she replied.

That night, on the way to her home, she told Jim her story. As a young girl, she had married a man who left her, as she put it, without a penny. "I had many chances to go on the game (prostitution), but I didn't want to. The thought of lying in bed with men of all sorts and sizes didn't turn me on. I earn my living the hard way. I work in a factory five days a week, and I tend tables at the pub five nights. Don't feel sorry for me!" she exclaimed, "I'm happy, and I have a boyfriend. He is home every six months. She sighed. "Yes. It gets a bit lonely, but that's life."

The following three days were hectic with the preparation for the voyage. The workers cleaned the bilges, the engine room pumps and the engine covers. The various liquid flow and return pipe work was freshly painted in designated colors. John Thompson, the Senior Second Engineer, smiled when they had completed their tasks. "This, Jim, is what an engine room should look like."

The Chief Engineer called his pre-voyage meeting at the end of the day. "We leave at 1600 hours tomorrow, and sea watches start at midday. Passengers embarked at 1300 hours. There were twelve passengers and a doctor, "she's a Kiwi, who has just finished her training, and going home to her boyfriend and family."

Our first port of call is Tenerife for bunkers, then on to the city of Cape Town, Perth, Sydney and Wellington. Loading for home has not been determined.

Jim was excited by the news. He was beginning his first trip to sea to fulfill his ambitions. That evening he sat at his desk writing to his family, and Lydia, telling them of his excitement of his experience; relating to John and June his experience at West Ham football club. His thoughts were interrupted by a knock on the door. "Enter," he called.

It was Morgan his steward, "Last post, Sir."

Jim opened the envelope. It was a letter from Lydia, posted in America two weeks previously. There was a tear in his eye as he finished reading her letter. Her parting words, "I love you, Jim Mitchell. Have a good trip, your loving mistress."

The main engines roared as the starting compressed air turned the huge pistons of the twin diesel engines. The Chief Engineer started the starboard engine, and John had the honor of starting the port side main engine. The noise, and vibration, abated as they finally settled to a slow turn of twenty revolutions per minute. "Dead slow ahead!" rang the bridge telegraph. Slowly and quietly, the *Sydney Star* slipped from her berth, through the locks and into the lower reaches of the River Thames. The ship, crew, and passengers were on their way to another land.

"Let's have a beer before dinner, Jim, to celebrate the start of your first trip to sea. I'm a buying," said John Thompson.

The wardroom bar looked splendid. It was new, with three beer dispensers, the mirror and back cocktail bar, and gain rails for glasses, a cooler and selection of red and white wines. Jim smiled as he saw the Newcastle Brown Ale logo. The wardroom was open for business, the only customer, a redheaded lady. "Hello," she said, "I am Elizabeth Black, I'm your doctor for the trip," she said nervously. "The Captain said I could use the wardroom. You must be part of the 4-8 watch?"

"Yes I am, ma'am. My name is Jim Mitchell. I am the junior

engineering officer of the watch," he said as he addressed the small redheaded Lady with long, red, curly hair, wearing a pair of dark-rimmed glasses and dress hanging loosely from her shoulders disguising whatever figure she may have had.

"Hello my name is Brian Barton. I am the ships mate, welcome."

She smiled thank you. "The captain said that I may eat at your table. I hope you don't mind?" she murmured nervously.

"May I get you a drink, ma'am?" asked Jim.

"Gin and tonic, if you please, Sir."

"As you're pouring, Mitchell, I think I would enjoy a pint of Newcastle."

"One for me," said John Thompson as he walked into the room. "You must be Elizabeth Black? Nice meet you, ma'am."

"Thank you, it's nice to meet you, John Thompson."

Over dinner, in the officer's mess, she talked about her internship at the Hammersmith Hospital and asked questions about the ship and what were their positions and responsibilities. She was a very interesting lady, Jim thought. He had never met a doctor. He smiled ruefully, except for the Doc that fixed his left foot after one of the rougher football matches.

Jim lay in bed that night looking at the photographs of his family. He was pleased finally; he had a letter from Lydia. Yes, he was missing her, her gentle touch, her loving ways and her gentle sweet talk. "Oh God!" he cried. "Had they made the right decision? What's done is done. You've made your bed and you must lie on it," he said softly remembering his mother's words.

He smiled optimistically. "This is not a bad life Jim," he said to himself. "You get paid for what you do, and you can see the world. The food is excellent and you like what you're doing: the morning four to eight watch, the afternoon four to eight watch, the occasional drink in the wardroom, and the camaraderie of his fellow officers. Slowly, the movement of the ship rocked him to sleep, as they sailed on to Tenerife in the Canary Islands at a speed of twenty knots.

One evening, over dinner, which had now turned in to be a regular foursome, Brian said, "Batten your gear down tonight. We are in for a 'blow' later. There's a storm coming in from the west, 'Force Seven.'"

Jim woke. It was 0300 hours. The *Sydney Star*'s bow was pitching into the oncoming waves and rolling, a sort of corkscrew action. He felt sick in his belly, a nauseous feeling, and his head hurt, a fuzzy feeling. Slowly, he raised himself from his bunk and managed to struggle into his boiler suit for his next watch.

"You will get used to it," said John commiserating with him as he entered the control room. The bridge phone rang and Jim answered it. "Reduce revs to eighty rpm's. We haven't seen the last of this storm yet."

During the watch, Jim was sick several times, and it was impossible for him to do the engine room log; recording instead, pressures, temperatures normal for conditions. Gradually, as the watch progressed, his body got used to the movement. His head cleared and he felt some relief from his malady.

At the end of the watch, Jim observed the storm from the safety of his cabin. From time to time, the sea slopped over his window. There was a musty smell in his cabin, damp and wet. The sea was green, without caps, the swells were huge. As the nausea returned, slowly he made his way to the doctor's surgery seeking some relief.

Elizabeth Black smiled, "You too, Jim?"

"Yes, I'm afraid so," he answered.

"Nothing much I can do," she said. "Eat some dry toast, drink some water and lie down. That's what I'm about to do, and, hopefully, we will meet tonight for dinner."

# Chapter 45

The next morning, the *Sydney Star* arrived in Tenerife. He was excited. In the distance, he could see the ruins of Capt. Morgan's Castle. This was his first sight of a foreign country. It was a country that had stood the test of time; its history dating back many decades, a history of war of occupation and the singular beauty of the island settled around about 1000 B.C. In recent history, Lancelot Malocella of Genoa accidentally rediscovered the islands. It was said that Christopher Columbus, on his way in an attempt to discover the Americas, made a 'stop over' at La Gomorra. Admiral Lord Nelson suffered his only defeat in his career while trying to conquer Santa Cruz. This was also, where he lost his arm. In 1927, the Canary Islands were divided into two provinces under Spanish influence, Santa Cruz de Tenerife and Los Palmas de Gran Canary.

In the background, Jim could see Mount Teide towering over the island, an impressive site as they walked slowly past the market square to the smooth sandy beach. The water was crystal clear, a sort of aqua color. There was an excitement in his body, as he walked ashore with Elizabeth. His first experience of a sandy beach, and it felt good. The sea was calm as they swam across to an outlying rock.

"How do you feel, Elizabeth?" Jim asked.

"Bloody marvelous! Isn't it wonderful?" she said as they dived to the depths of the bay, entering a world of beautiful coral, a fantastic scene of beauty. The fish were so many colors, so beautiful and so dramatic.

"How do you feel, Jim Mitchell?" she murmured as they surfaced.

"Great!" he replied. "This is what I came to sea for."

They lay on their towels on the sand watching the sea waves break on to the beach It was a lazy day for two friends to relax and enjoy the beauty of the stark silence.

She looked at him and smiled. "This is the first time that I've lain on the beach naked with a man who was also naked. Do you mind, Jim."

"No, not at all; although, I must say, this is the first time, but not the last time. You really have a beautiful body."

"Do you find me sexy?" She paused, "I guess what I'm asking shall we have sex?"

Jim looked at her. "You have a beautiful body, Elizabeth. Yes, it would satisfy our lust for a moment, then it would be awkward for of us both on the ship, and we would regret it. It's not just about the sex, because I really do fancy you. Neither of us are free, and I don't want a 'wham bam, thank you ma'am.'"

She laughed, "Stop talking, Jim, and hold me for a while."

The following evening they were invited to meet the passengers for drinks, the "old man" always included his off duty officers in the social evenings on the ship. Brian, the ships mate, summed up our hosts as a mixed bunch of travelers. There was a professor and his wife, taking a sabbatical to New Zealand; a New Zealand family who had been home to visit their family and friends; two older people with their grandchildren. There were a couple of fairly interesting young ladies who were apparently nurses finishing their training at the Children's Hospital in Kensington, and an elderly gentleman with his younger wife. They were an interesting couple. He had served as an army lieutenant in the World War I, and had been wounded several times. His wife, a nurse, by profession had escorted him on various trips all over the world. This trip was to Australia and New Zealand where he was going to stay with some of his fellow World War I comrades. From there he was going to go across the Pacific to Honolulu, then onto Canada, and then home again, a trip that would take them nearly six months.

The voyage to Cape Town was smooth and without incident as Jim settled down to a routine seafaring life. Daytime: breakfast, deck tennis, sunbathing and afternoon kip. In the evening, a beer, dinner, life in the wardroom and his colleagues. He started a regiment of studies for his second engineer's certificate using the experience and knowledge he had gained, which came mostly from his mentor John Thompson.

His body was turning into a dark brown color, and his blonde hair, now somewhat shorter, got even lighter by the day. Time passed quickly. He lifted weights, ran around the deck, followed by a series of press-ups. On the odd occasion, mostly after dinner, he spent time on deck with Elizabeth. He found her to be interesting, and despite the differences in age and professions, they had a lot in common. In many ways, they were soul mates. She was going home to a man she had not seen for four years, and he starting on a journey, which he hoped, would lead him to Lydia in time. They had exchanged stories and confidences about being apart from their loved ones, and the frustrations entailed as they resolved to stay true with their love. Jim smiled as she told him about their parting, some four years ago, when she had told him, "to love the one that they were with" They had talked about their relationships openly and occasionally with feelings. In many respects, it became a healing process for Elizabeth, they laughed and slowly, became close friends and had fun evenings.

The night before the ship arrived in Cape Town they talked together about this wonderful subcontinent. Jim recalled his geography lessons at school, and some of the tales Griff Kitchen had told him. The Republic of South Africa was a large massive country, equal to the size of France and Spain combined. There were huge resources of gold and diamonds. A prospector, named George Harrison, discovered the richest gold reef in the world. Within three years, the bleak, high Veldt had grown dramatically. Soon afterwards, Johannesburg had grown into the largest city south of Cairo. The speed in which it grew was due to the power of such men as Cecil Rhodes, who owned diamond mines in Kimberley. He provided capital to exploit the rich gold bearing reefs of Witwatersrand. Rhodes founded the 'Chamber of Mines,' which created common policies regarding recruitment wages, and working conditions, for the colored workers at the end of the nineteenth century.

It had institutionalized the color bar. This ensured that black men could aspire to nothing more than manual labor.

Cape Town, South Africa is one of the oldest ports in southern Africa. It is reputed to be one of the most beautiful cities in the world. The massive sandstone rock of Table Mountain, often draped in a tablecloth of clouds, formed an imposing backdrop to the city. The pristine beaches were the finest in southern Africa, set against the magnificent cliffs hugging the coastline.

During breakfast, Jim listened attentively as John outlined a shore excursion to climb the Table Mountain. "The best route," he said "is to start at the Kirtsenbozen Gardens. It's a bit of a climb," he continued as they walked through the forest and Shelton Gorge to the top of the back. When they reached the top, they sat for a while, somewhat exhausted, and admiring the Hely Hutchinson Dam, a wonderful feat of engineering. Then they slowly walked along the top. There were magnificent views towards the Hottentots' Holland Mountains, False Day and the peninsular to Cape Point. That evening they talked about their fantastic experience.

"One day I would like to return," said Elizabeth.

Brian smiled. "You could do that Elizabeth if you would like to become the full-time doctor on the ship. Personally, I have a feeling in my water that we will be back again next trip."

Jim walked on deck after his morning watch to see the preparations for unloading part of the cargo. In the distance, he could see the city with its unique minarets, the Tory buildings and churches. It was beautiful. In the background stood Table Mountain covered by layers of white cloud. The ruggedness of the mountain formed a backdrop to the city. In many ways, it was an impressive, yet awe-inspiring sight to behold.

During dinner that night, Brian informed the table that we would be in Cape Town for three days. "The 'old man' is not at all pleased with the unloading schedule. It is going to take longer than he anticipated."

The following morning at breakfast, Elizabeth inquired as to an escort for shopping. There was little enthusiasm. She smiled, tempting her three colleagues. "I'll buy lunch," she said hoping to tempt at least one of her companions to escort her. Finally, Jim relented. She smiled as they walked along the streets. "You're a poppet, Jim. Thank you, I really do appreciate this. First, I want to shop, then I'll buy you lunch, and then we can look at the sites."

"What are you looking for?"

"Oh, gifts for my folks and maybe something with diamonds. They are supposed to be a bargain here. The city was alive with business people, shoppers and people just staring in wonder at the whole thing. It was a sort of festive time. The women wore multicolored dresses with matching turbans, which were pretty. There were black people, brown people, and white people. This was a novel site for the lad from Cheshire. He stood aside to let a black woman with two children pass, until he realized that the whites have the right of way irrespective of gender. There was a little cafe in a cul-de-sac with a sign 'whites only,' which he did not quite understand. The accents of the waiter and the customers were difficult to understand, even stranger than the cockney dialect of the east end of London. They were shown to a table, offered the menu and a wine list.

"Have you tasted South African wine before?" Jim asked.

"Yes, a couple of times." she replied. "Jim," she smiled, "my dad reckons that South African wines are amongst the best in the world. Let us have a carafe of white wine. I am going to order a salad. What about you?"

"I'm," he murmured, "that sounds good, a glass of the house wine and salad will go down very nicely, thank you, Elizabeth. What do you think of the trip so far?"

Jim smiled as she answered, "Bloody marvelous, I think that I was really lucky to meet up with you. Its fun, don't you think?"

"Well that's kind of you, Elizabeth. I am even getting used to your accent and funny ways."

"Cheers Jim," she replied.

That was a good lunch, Elizabeth. Thanks," said Jim as they walked along the streets to the Castle of Good Hope, the oldest building in South Africa, then on to the Cape Malay district to see the oldest mosque in South Africa. They took their shoes off, laid them beside the porch, and slowly entered inside. The light was a fantastic, a mass of blue, gold, red and orange emanating from the dome. Jim said a prayer to his Dad and for Lydia and the family. It was altogether a magnificent sight, and a perfect way to end the day.

The following day, John was on duty. The Chief Engineer needed to do some shopping. Bryan, the mate, had organized with the agent to have a car ready for Elizabeth and Jim to go to the beach. As they walked down the gangway, the ship's notice board read: Ship sails at eight o'clock p.m., all aboard by seven o'clock p.m.

They walked along the sandy deserted beach listening to the roar of the South Atlantic rollers. It was a magnificent sight, the waves pounding on the shore

It was a beautiful gorgeous day. They lay on the beach for ages soaking up the rays, talking, taking the occasional dip into the waves, eating lunch with a somewhat cool beer from the hamper, and just relaxing, a sort of day to lounge around and enjoy fine conversation. They walked together to the waiting car. He felt her hand caress his fingers. He looked into her eyes. "Thank you, Sir. It's been a wonderful day." Jim smiled as he felt her arm around his waist. "Friends?" she murmured.

"Yes," Jim replied.

The engines were running and maneuvering speeds when he relieved his opposite number on the eight to twelve watch. The ship was on its way, leaving the quay, making its way through the breakwater. The sea looked, cold, and blue as Jim stood on the bridge pounded by massive huge rollers, whose violent affect caused the ship to shudder from bow to stern. Then for a moment, the ship held steady. The quality of the light, the smell and tone of the air, the denser flock of seabirds, the sea, it was indisputably the Cape. The ship was in the great South Atlantic. The swells, known as cape rollers, had gained their size and momentum from their long journey up from the seas of Antarctica. Nowhere else could the legend of the Flying Dutchman be quite as credible, or as inevitable, as Van Der Decken who cursed the ocean; his punishment for his blasphemy was that he was doomed to sail the waters of the Cape eternally. The ship heaved and rolled for a while until the early hours of the next morning. Then, the *Sydney Star* settled down to a cruising speed, and the ship returned to normal service.

Following his p.m. watch the next day, Jim showered, shaved and put on his newly pressed number ten uniform for dinner. Brian and Elizabeth greeted him as he entered the wardroom.

"I poured you a pint Jim," she said. "I'm having a gin and tonic. I was just telling Brian what a wonderful day you and I had in Cape Town.

"Anyone for a stretch on the deck?" inquired Elizabeth as they finished their after dinner coffee.

"Yes," replied Jim.

The ship was heading southeast, around the Cape of Good Hope, past Cape Aquillhas, into the Indian Ocean. It was a beautiful night as he gazed into the sky, viewing the wonders of the universe. Would humans, as we know them, ever visit the planets? Would Flash Gordon films ever materialize?

"Penny for your thoughts," said Elizabeth.

"Just thinking about the universe," said Jim quizzically.

"Quite the regular Zeus, aren't you?" He felt her hand touch his. "The wardroom's still open. Let me buy you a nightcap. Thank you again for our day in Cape Town."

"What's on your mind, Elizabeth?"

She smiled. "How did you know?"

"I don't really know," he said, "it's just something I picked up from you today."

"Okay," she said, "let me tell you. It's about my boyfriend. It's been four years since I've seen him. We made a pact that we would meet up again, and when we met, we would see how we felt. I have known him since we were at school together. It was a good relationship, fun, but I am not sure whether we were in love or not. He spent most of his time playing sports and did not care for sailing, yet somehow we stuck together. Now we are getting near to home; I am getting nervous. I have been faithful to him. I got laid a couple of times, and it was not very good. We did agree to love the one we were with. I can tell you from experience that is not very good. Now I don't know how the hell I feel towards him."

"I don't think you will know until you meet him, Elizabeth. I suppose I will have to face that one day, so I know how you feel. Thanks for the drink," said Jim. "See you tomorrow. Take it easy." As he rose from his chair, he kissed her on the forehead and murmured, "Don't worry it will all work out for the best."

*Chapter 46*

The days were long and the nights were cool during the voyage of the *Sydney Star* to Fremantle, Australia. The seas were a gentle swell, the only highlight were two ships passing going in the opposite direction. Life on board was a wonderful experience. Jim settled down to a routine: regular engineering watch, after-dinner conversations, the camaraderie of the wardroom and listening to his fellow officers tell tales of bygone years. His routine also included sunbathing, exercising the body, deck games, study, and the occasional meeting with Elizabeth on deck after dinner, sharing experiences, a surreal moment in his life. Jim was looking forward to Australia, the continent that he had studied in the geography classes at school.

"Tell me about New Zealand, Liz?" he asked.

"What do you want to know?"

"Well, I didn't learn much about the islands when I was at school. I was just wondering if you would educate me."

She smiled. "It's God's country, Jim, and is the most marvelous country in the world. I never appreciated this until I left. It is a greatly diversified land, with many opportunities and has quite a history. In many ways," she smiled. "It's a land where you can lie on the beach in the morning, and climb a mountain in the afternoon. It is a great place to go swimming, surfing, and sailing. It really is God is country, free of pollution. The air is fresh and invigorating. You know, sometimes when I was in London, I found it somewhat difficult to breathe freely.

In contrast, the wind, particularly on the North Island, always seems to be fresh and invigorating. Am I am boring you?"

"No, not at all," said Jim. "I am fascinated. Please go on."

We were one of the first countries in the world to have a national health plan. The longevity of the people on our islands is high mainly due to the laid-back, pervasive attitude of the Kiwis. The only thing that we take seriously is our downtime and sport. As you probably know, New Zealand men are very fond of their sports to the exclusion of many other things in their life, apart from beer," she laughed.

"Do you know that the majority of the pubs on our islands close at six o'clock p.m.? If you want to meet a lady for a cocktail, the only acceptable venue is the cocktail bar at the Occidental Hotel."

"What do you do with your spare time?" Jim asked.

"I never seemed to get much spare time. When I do, I like to go sailing, do a bit of fishing and watch cricket."

"What's the social life like?" he asked.

"It's good," she replied. "We have lots of cinemas and I love watching films. There are theatres mind you, and they compare with the West End Theatres. We have classical concerts and occasionally we have parties, mostly on the beach."

"Why do they call you Kiwis?" he asked.

"I knew somehow that you would get around to asking that question. The first settlers named our national emblem after the Kiwi bird because of its call: 'Kiwi, Kiwi, Kiwi.'" She smiled. "The bird is flightless, but delightful, quiet yet strong."

"Have you traveled much?" inquired Jim.

"Not a lot, Jim," she answered. "Most of my time has been taken up with education and sailing. One day I really would like to travel the island. You know I have never been to Auckland, although it is not very far. I would like to see a volcano and maybe go down south to visit the Southern Alps. A few years ago, we sailed down south and got as far as Christchurch. It's a very beautiful city with the same hustle and bustle that we experience in Wellington."

"It sounds fascinating, Elizabeth, I'm looking forward to my visit. Thanks, I appreciate your input."

The ship arrived alongside our berth in Fremantle early the following morning. Somewhere in the past, Jim had read a brief history of how the continent of Australia was originally settled as a penal colony. It was, by any standards, a huge continent, mostly undeveloped along its magnificent shorelines. To the north there was the desert and a Great Barrier Reef, and to the south, the Great Australian Bight.

The Australians fought with distinction in the first and second world wars, at Gallipoli, in the first war, alongside Jim's Uncle Will, and in the second war, with men from his village.

He had wonderful memories of the second cricket test match at Old Trafford, Don Brahman the captain of Australia and Cyril Washbrook for England. It is a rich country for sport, particularly cricket and rugby. The country that housed some of his fellow compatriots that immigrated to this great land three years ago, family history told Jim that there were a number of Mitchells now living in the country. He smiled, possibly some of the convicts. "How long do you think we will be here, Brian?" asked Jim at dinner.

"Possibly two days," he replied, "my estimation three days."

Elizabeth was delighted. She envisaged two days ashore at least. Beaches and shopping were at the top of her list. She looked at Jim with a broad smile and asked if he would accompany her, John Thomson having given him a couple of day watches off.

"Okay," said Jim. "Here's the deal, one-day cricket, one-day beach and one day shopping."

"Thank you kindly, Sir, I appreciate your time!"

Fremantle was the port for the city of Perth, a city that had many historical features. The history Museum, now housed in a convict built building, the Maritime Museum was reputed to have many interesting exhibits of shipwrecks, and the prison was supposed to be the most imposing structure in the town.

Later that morning, they hopped a bus to Perth and headed for the beaches. The scenery was magnificent, the beaches, wide and sandy, against crystal clear water breaking on the beach from the mild breeze offshore. Following a long swim, they laid on the beach near the Swan River.

Jim agreed with Elizabeth's enthusiasm for the area. Later, as they ate a fine lunch at a laid back, sidewalk café, she smiled triumphantly. "I told you it was good."

The country town atmosphere was much different from their experience in Cape Town. It was a sort of atmosphere that said, "Come back and see us sometime." Jim smiled. "Yes," one day he would.

The following day, they took a trip by boat to a deserted island, armed with the cook's special shore hamper lunch and a couple of cold beers. The weather and the sea were perfect. Jim was excited to be with his companion. She wasn't the best-looking lady in the world, but she had a way with her. She was kind and sweet.

That evening, after the Dockers closed the ships hatches for the last time, *Sydney Star* was ready for sea again. Jim stood on the deck watching the departure, vowing that one day he would return. The climate and the friendly people beckoned him back to this fair city.

The lights of the city were fading were over the horizon. The moon was in full bloom, a perfect setting. "It was a lovely day, Jim, thank you for taking me ashore."

He turned to face her and murmured, "No, thank you," he said. "I really enjoy your company."

It was midnight when he turned in for some sleep, only to be awakened shortly afterwards by banging noise. The general alarm bell sounded. "What's the problem?" he asked the Chief Engineer as he entered the engine room. "Number three unit on the starboard engine appears to have exhaust valve problems."

The cool calm voice of the Chief Engineer commanded the situation. "Stephen, carry on with watch. Jim, break out the crane. Alan, break out a spare valve." He looked at John. "You're in charge, John. I'm going to see the 'Old Man.'" Two hours later, and the loss of sweat, the engine was back in service. It was four o'clock a.m., the regular time for Jim's watch. The Chief smiled. "Take a break you two. Stephen and I will run your watch until 0500 hours."

"Thank you, Sir," said John as he and Jim disappeared up the ladder to get a shower.

"Are you okay?" Jim turned. It was Elizabeth. "I just wanted to know if you are okay."

"That was sweet of you, thank you. I am fine."

The next morning, Jim listened to John recounting their experience over breakfast with the mate. "'The Old Man' is pleased that we got underway so soon. He will probably send a case of beer to the wardroom" (a custom of old in the merchant marine). After breakfast, Jim looked at the notice board in bold letters:

OFFICERS AND CREW<br>
MEDICAL INSPECTION<br>
1000 HRS TO 1700 HRS<br>
PLACE: DOCTOR'S SURGERY

That day sleep came easily. He was awakened by a voice, "Mountain to Mohammed. Inspection time, Jim."

"You're joking!" he said. She laughed and belted his backside. "Mitchell if you want to go ashore in Sydney, you better come for inspection. There's a good boy."

During the following morning watch, they prepared for standby arrival in Sydney. The Chief Engineer, as usual, appeared in the Engine Room well ahead of time. As usual, the watch mechanic brought him coffee. Today he looked different than normal. Jim suddenly realized the reason. His wife, a New Zealand girl, would be joining the ship once we got alongside. Somehow, Jim had never thought of him as a married man. It seemed odd in a way, everyone else he knew was single except Brian, and he was divorced. He recalled an old song, "'I'm not the Marrying Kind." The bell for standby rang. He and John slowed the engines as the telegraph indicated 'slow ahead.' "Must be the pilot coming on board," said the Chief.

It was eight o'clock and the eight to twelve o'clock shift relieved the four to eight o'clock watch. Jim rushed up the engine room ladder and reached the deck just as the ship was passing under the Sydney Harbor Bridge, one of the highlights of his planned trip. He stared, watching for a while as the tugs maneuvered the *Sydney Star* into its berth.

Sydney was the home of the aboriginal people. Anthropologist believed that they had reached Sydney Harbor some forty thousand years before. James Cook landed in Botany Bay in 1768, and the British convicts, guards, officers arrived in 1788, to establish a penal colony, to build roads and construct buildings. Some of the officers became farmers. By the eighteenth century, the farms were producing crops, and supplies arrived on a regular basis. By the 1890's the country moved towards preparation and nationalization, the Australian identity began to take shape.

The ferry to Mandalay from Circular Quay was an interesting journey. It afforded a good view of the harbor and the Bridge, which was built in 1910. Jim was excited for the day. The prospect of surfing was exhilarating. Elizabeth smiled. "Now don't overdo it, young man," she said. "I don't want you to end up in hospital, exhausted and with broken limbs."

"Yes ma'am," he said jokingly.

"Not bad for your first run young man," said his instructor. Jim felt exhilarated by his success in his first lesson. His second ride was good, but he wanted more. Then he remembered Elizabeth's words. "Maybe next time," he said to himself.

John Thompson, Brian, and Doc had watched his progress and congratulated him on his success. "You're a natural," said Brian. "It's a pity we aren't staying here a bit longer. You young man, would really get the hang of it."

The next day, they watched part of the cricket match between New South Wales and Queensland, a fascinating game, exciting and enthralling. "It was different from cricket at home," he thought as Queensland mounted an attack on New South Wales bowling. His thoughts turned to last summer, the game where he and Richard had taken their side from the brink of defeat to a final victory, and regained the trophy. It was lunchtime. He sat alone in the stands eating a ham sandwich and drinking a beer. Suddenly, he felt alone, alone with the memories of yesterday. The games that he and Maggie had watched at Old Trafford, he smiled as he recollected the lunch in the members Pavilion. Maggie, it seemed like the light years since he was last with her. She was a surreal feeling in his young mind. The memory of her was slowly fading to the past. A notion that he tried to convince himself was natural, or was it? He did not really know. It seemed strange. He had taken on this new life. Somehow, things were different. It felt strange. He was eleven thousand miles away from her, and it was close to Christmas. Yes, he was missing her, as he always knew that he would. He also knew that she would miss him, but those were the cards they were dealt.

Later that evening, he stood on deck. In the distance, he could see the outline of the South Island of New Zealand. It was a dark night and the only lights were from the port, and starboard running lights of the *Sydney Star*. "Yes, we were nearly there," he said to himself. The journey was half way completed; he had learned much, met a few, and enjoyed, for the most part, his first trip away from his homeland. In a few days time it will be Christmas. That was the time that he would miss being home the most. That would be a time to say farewell to his new friend. "She was fun," Jim thought. "Elizabeth Black, you really are a very nice lady."

In the distance, he could hear familiar footsteps on the wooden deck, yes very familiar. It was the doctor from New Zealand. "Hello," he greeted her, "missed you at dinner tonight. Are you okay?"

"Jim, I had a letter from my boyfriend. It's ironic, after four years he found himself a girlfriend, and is engaged to be married." A half hearted laugh emanated from her voice, "at least he could have told me earlier."

"I'm sorry, Liz, that was a bloody awful thing to do. The timing is brutal." He looked into her eyes, there was a wan smile, and she murmured "his life a bitch."

"Yes," he concluded, "Let's look at the good side now. Shush," said Jim. "It's better that you know now than when you arrived home. Dry your eyes and I will buy you a beer. Have you eaten?"

"No, I haven't," she replied.

"Then I'll get you a sandwich from the cook."

She looked at Jim with a smile, "How come you make me feel better?" she asked.

"I don't really know Elizabeth."

Her mood changed as they walked to the wardroom. "A beer," Jim suggested.

"No, pour me whiskey, I'm not sure whether to celebrate, or mourn, my loss. I guess whiskey is good for either. Pour me another one please."

# Chapter 47

The ship was quiet as they lay along their unloading berth in Wellington N Z. He was awakened by the alarm clock. It was time for the a.m. watch. As he entered the engine room, the sound of one single generator greeted him. Somehow, it felt quiet compared with the noise of the main engines when they were at sea. There was a single respite. Bill, his watch mechanic, was early for his duties, the first of which was the ceremony of the morning, coffee and biscuits. John was sitting at his desk attending to the port watch, keeping schedules. "How do you feel about doing day work for the next two weeks?"

"That would be magic," Jim replied. "What are we doing?"

"Myself, the Senior Third Engineer, the Junior Third Engineer, and you will be opening up the crank case of the starboard engine for inspection by the Lloyd's Insurer's surveyor. We start early Monday morning."

Jim looked in amazement. "You're telling me that I've got a whole day off?"

"No," he replied. "Make that two and a half days off from the end this watch." He added, "I am off to Lower Hut to see one of my friends, and I'll be back at eight o'clock a.m. on Monday for an eight o'clock a.m. start."

The shops were decorated for the upcoming Christmas Holiday. It seemed odd to his mind. The temperatures were in the eighties, the sky was blue, and yet, it was the Christmas.

"Strange," he murmured. He walked along the streets looking into the shop windows. He was eleven thousand miles away from home, and it was Christmas. This would be the first Christmas that he hadn't attended Grandma's Christmas festivities. "They will manage without me," he said dismissing the subject. He walked to the bar of the Oriental Hotel and ordered a light ale.

"First time here?" asked the barman.

Jim nodded. Somehow, he found it easy to understand the dialect, having talked to Elizabeth over the last thirty days.

"Where are you from?"

"A small village in Cheshire, England, by the way," Jim continued. "My name is Jim Mitchell," he said shaking the bar attendant's hand. "Nice to meet you, Sir."

"Nice to meet you too, Jim Mitchell. My name is Adam Smith. What ship are you on?"

"The *Sydney Star*," Jim replied. "We're here for a couple of weeks."

The bar attendant smiled. "I dare say you'll be here a little longer. The long shore-men are intent on striking again. It's coming up to Christmas," he said with a laugh. "Somehow, at this time of the year, there is usually a dispute of one kind or another." Then he added critically, "They always want a longer holiday at this time of the year."

"Thanks for the beer," said Jim.

"That's okay, come back and see us sometime."

"I will," said Jim, "nice to meet you, Sir."

He stopped at the flower stand at the end of the quay. He looked at the array of flowers. There were roses, tulips, and magnolias; just like the flowers, he had often seen in his Mum's garden at home, Grandma's garden and the Chester market.

"Would you like some flowers, young man?"

"Yes, I would," he replied. "Can you wait until later tonight, then I will have a dozen yellow roses, if I may?"

She eyed him curiously, "New girlfriend, young man?"

Yes," he replied. "Well, not really, a friend, someone that I met a few weeks ago."

"Good luck, young man, I'll have them ready for you."

"Time for a catnap," said Jim to himself as he returned to his cabin. It could be a long night. He was excited to see Elizabeth in her home environment, and it would be good to get off the ship for a few hours to see the lights of the city of Wellington by night. He fell into a deep slumber.

The sound of the alarm clock awakened him. He showered and dressed in his civilian clothes, looking forward to having dinner with Elizabeth Black. During the trip, they had had fun. She was good to be with albeit that she was a few years older than he and a little dowdy, but a very interesting lady.

The taxi ride along the narrow, hilly road to Mt. Vernon afforded spectacular views of Wellington Harbor, reputed to be one of the most beautiful, natural harbors in the world. The houses were perched on the hillsides. He smiled to himself, "John, that was an understatement." The cargo ships in their berths, the yachts coming home from a day's sailing, placed all against the splendid backdrop of the hills; it was truly one of the most spectacular sights that he'd ever seen.

"Here we are, young man," said the taxi driver as he stopped at the entrance to a small white house perched on a hillside set in the background of green lawns and flowerbeds.

"Thank you, Sir," he replied.

He turned. In the distance, he saw a petite, red-haired woman walking down the path from her home dressed in a tight fitting cocktail dress. He hesitated. No, it cannot be. "This must be the wrong address," he said to himself, and was about to apologize, when he recognized her voice.

"Hello, Jim Mitchell. Welcome to my home," her eyes sparkled with pleasure as she saw Jim's gift. "For me?" she asked excitedly.

Jim smiled, "For you, my fellow traveler from the high seas."

"Oh, these are my favorite color. Thank you kindly, Sir," she said kissing him on his forehead. Then with a deep curtsy, she murmured, "Oh Jim, these are so beautiful, my dear." She then added, "You appeared to be a little hesitant when you arrived."

Jim felt a little embarrassed as he mumbled, "you look somewhat different Elizabeth!"

She laughed, "I thought perhaps you might like to see the real Elizabeth Black tonight. Let me pour you a drink and I'll tell you a story."

"How's your drink?" she asked as they sat watching the sun disappearing over the western approaches to the harbor.

"Great," Jim replied. "You have a beautiful home, Elizabeth."

"Well thank you, Sir. I like it. Daddy had it built for me some years ago. It is my pride and joy. I've missed it so much while I was away. Now, let me tell you the story of my dressing habit," she said with a laugh. "When I went for the interview for the doctor's job on the ship, I was dressed to the nines in Carnaby Street's finest; complete with heels. Well, I guess that the Personnel Officer was somewhat taken aback. He explained to me that I was traveling on a cargo boat with an all-male crew, and he was concerned that I could upset the morale. Well, I needed a passage and we came to an agreement that I would dress somewhat dowdily, to disguise my figure and I wouldn't wear makeup." She laughed. "It did the trick, and I got the job."

"Well it certainly worked, Elizabeth," replied Jim. There was a glint in his eye as he murmured, "Apart from a couple of times when we went swimming together. What makes Liz tick? Jim asked curiously.

"I don't really know," she answered. "All my life I have had one goal in mind, to become a doctor. After college, I went to medical school, graduated in general practice and then joined my Dad's practice. After a while, I guess I had the bug to specialize in gynecology so I applied to Guys Hospital in London. That was a marvelous experience, but it came with a price." There was an ironic smile on her face as she murmured, "I now realize that I have sacrificed most of my life to my profession." There was a tear in her eye as she murmured, "Sorry Jim, I get this way sometimes. You see I'm going to be thirty-five years of age on my next birthday. I was just thinking of what I've missed in life. Marriage, kids 'n all that stuff. Oh hell, I'm sorry, Jim. Let's have another drink shall we and I'll put some music on."

The night was hot and humid as they danced slowly to the haunting sound of a single saxophone backed by the slow sensual rhythm of a drumbeat. Slowly, as the minutes passed, Jim realized that the woman in his arms was changing from his friend to a soft, sensuous woman. She smiled as his arm wrapped around her waist. Leaning backwards, she removed his tie opening the buttons on his shirt, and placing her hands on his breasts. There was a seductive smile on her lips as she held his face. Looking deep into her eyes, he felt the thrust of her sex against his leg as their bodies swayed to the music.

She smiled seductively as their eyes met and whispered, "Will you stay for breakfast? What are you smiling at?" she asked in a soft whisper.

"You, just you," Jim replied

# *Chapter 48*

The days that followed were enchanting endless hours, filled with rapture. They existed only for themselves, wanting each other, rejoicing in each other. They were overwhelmed with their attraction for each other, with an intensity that neither had known before. Elizabeth was filled with incredulity, her feelings overpowered by the intensity of her emotions. For once in her life, she did not pause to analyze her feelings. She was ecstatic, overpowered by a compelling force, a miracle. She never knew that she was capable of such emotions. She smiled remembering his words, "There's a force within you."

Her love for him exposed her heart. His touch brought her to life. Her guard was down, and she was vulnerable. "Oh God," she cried, "Let this be real." A mere glance at him, as he lay asleep, excited her every being. Their ardent lovemaking, took her into another world, a world that existed beyond her wildest dreams. She smiled as she watched over him as he slept. He had awakened a sleeping tigress. A boy she had met only weeks before. She remembered the night as they stood together leaning over the ship's rail, watching the stars in the sky, and the days and nights sailing the sea on her yacht. It was now time for the *Sydney Star* to leave this wonderful, beautiful place called Wellington. In her heart, she cared for him. Now, the ship was sailing, the hatches were battened down. The ships whistle sounded slowly, very slowly, as it made its way out to sea. There were tears in her eyes as she murmured,

"Farewell, my Love," then prayed, "Oh, dear God, guard him well."
There were more tears in her eyes as she read his poem:

> Farewell my Lady of our days
> Farewell my Lady of our nights
> The beauty of your silken form
> The kindness of your heart
> Your love that is so true
> Will live in this my breast,
> Until the day when I return
> To see your smiling face
> To hold you in my arms again
> Forever from the sea
> By Jim Mitchell

*Chapter 49*

The rain clouds settled over Littleton Harbor as the *Sydney Star* arrived to load it is cargo of New Zealand lamb; next destination. London. England. The four to eight o'clock watch shutdown the main engines, and prepared the winches for loading. Jim was due for a spell of night duty, working between twelve p.m. and eight o'clock a.m. He smiled ruefully, "penance for the good days, and the good times, in Wellington."

That evening, he laid on his bed thinking about Elizabeth. It had been sixty-three days since they had first met in the ship's officer's wardroom. She, a little nervous, as she introduced herself, "Hello, my name is Elizabeth Black. I'm the ship's doctor for the voyage, and the Captain said I could use the officer's wardroom."

Jim had a regarded the long, auburn-haired, diminutive woman with a smile. There was something about her, something endearing. She was nervous and looked as though she needed to be taken care of. In many ways, she reminded him of a younger version of his Mum, a kind and loving creature.

During the days that followed, they became friends. She was a cultured woman, devoted to her profession. She was a woman who knew exactly what she wanted to do with her life. As the days passed, their friendship deepened. Her kindness, and loving ways, had touched his very soul.

The memories deepened as Jim recalled the first night together in her home overlooking Wellington Harbor. They had danced to the erotic sounds of South American music. Then after dinner, they had sat on her verandah in the warmth of the moonlight night when they had kissed for the first time. Jim smiled at the memory and her words as he held her close, "Will you stay for breakfast?"

They had loved with an unbelievable tenderness. Afterwards, they had lain in each other's arms in the moonlight bedroom and she murmured, "Jim, we are two ships that passing in the night. Let's celebrate our time together, my beauty."

Jim's first watch passed without incident. The routine of checking the ships electrical power, logging pressures and temperatures, ensured the safety of the vessel. Then he started the diesel electrical generators to service the ships loading operation of cargo.

His watch over, Jim showered and dressed for breakfast, a meal that he had looked forward to during his long overnight duty in the engine room. As he entered the officer's mess, the Chief Engineer greeted him.

"Good morning Jim, I would you like to join us? My wife Mary," and he paused, "Have you two met?"

"No, Sir, I haven't, had the pleasure." Jim replied as he shook her hand. "Welcome Ma'am. How was your trip?" he inquired.

"Fine thank you, Sir, it's nice to be on board again."

It was then he remembered John Thompson telling him that the Chief's wife was a Kiwi who lived in Auckland, and recalled, that during the ships stay in Wellington, the Chief had taken a few days leave to visit her and her mother.

"John tells me that you have the midnight to eight duties. What are your plans for you're off duty hours?" she asked.

"Hadn't thought about it too much, Ma'am," he replied, "although I would like to visit Christchurch."

"It's well worth the visit. It is without a doubt one of the most beautiful cities in New Zealand. I'm sure that you would enjoy it. I have a couple of books on the city, if you would like to borrow them."

The following Wednesday he caught a train to the city. It was a bright morning with a nip of frost in the air. He alighted at the Christchurch Central Station and walked to Victoria Square. He remembered the Chief Engineer's wife, Mary, saying that Christchurch was the most English city outside of England. He smiled. "That it was," he said to himself as he admired the gentle, flowing river and fine architectural buildings. During their conversation, she had outlined points of interest for him. One of the notes was a visit to the Cathedral Church of Christ, an imposing structure that dominated the downtown Christchurch.

The building, constructed in the nineteenth century, with a huge Gothic Tower, fascinated Jim. Later, after a brief stop for lunch, he walked along the river embankment. The college students had broken school for the day. He smiled remembering his school days in Chester.

Later he walked to the botanical gardens, then into Haley Park where he bought postcards for home and a selection of New Zealand stamps. There was something special about this city. It was a peaceful, very English city and he felt at home. The people were kind and friendly, recognizing that they had a young Brit in their midst. The highlight of the day was a visit to the Cathedral and Christ Church College. "One of the most memorable days in his travel," he said to himself as he sat for while on the bench overlooking the river, writing postcards to his loved ones eleven thousand miles away. "Yes," he said to himself, "this is a beautiful country, God's country, that had been kind and generous to him."

Chapter 50

"Mitchell," Jim answered the engine room phone. "Hello Jim, Brian here. We are nearly finished loading. I anticipate that we can have standby for departure at seven o'clock p.m. There is a bit of a blow outside the Harbor. Ask John to check around the engine room as we may have quite a bit of movement. The 'Old Man' is keen to leave on time. We are on our way home, Jim. Are you excited?"

The sleek hull of the *Sydney Star*, fully loaded, left its berth slowly moving into the Pacific Ocean. "It's a long trip," said John as he walked into the control room. "Are you excited 'Boyo?'"

"Yes, I am, John, it's been a fun."

"There's a bit more excitement to come," said John "We are calling in at Pitcairn Island before traversing the Panama Canal."

"Wow!"' thought Jim, as memories of the film *Mutiny on the Bounty* flooded back.

After his four to eight, watch-keeping duties, Jim stood alone on deck, surveying the coastline and the receding lights of Littleton Harbor on the port side of the ship. His thoughts were of Elizabeth. What was she doing? There was a pang of remorse in his breast, a feeling of sadness in his heart, and memories of this kind, loving woman. "Take care Liz, I will miss you lady."

After a long shower, Jim dressed. He entered the wardroom to join the 'mate' Brian, and his Second Engineer John.

Halfway through the main course Brian observed, with a wry smile, "Am I the only one that's missing her?"

"No," said Jim, "I have missed her since we left Wellington."

"In love are we?" asked John with a smile.

"No, I am just so lucky to have met a wonderful lady," answered Jim

"That you are," said Brian.

"A toast," said John, raising his glass, "To a wonderful, beautiful lady!"

"To Elizabeth," they replied in unison.

"Who's the new doctor?" asked John.

"He's a young one, straight out of med school," commented Brian. "From what I can see, he is still wet behind the ears," he said with a laugh then added, "He is bound for one of London's top hospitals, no doubt to make a name for himself."

"Excuse me, gentlemen," said Jim, "I'm off to my bed. This midnight to eight port watch may be good for the soul, but I feel quite whacked."

"Goodnight, see you in the morning."

Jim lay in his bed unable to sleep through the movement of the ship, a strange corkscrew movement rolling and pitching. His mind, as usual, was active, reminiscing about the good times that he had with Elizabeth in New Zealand. They were fond memories. He would not easily forget her kindness and the tender love that she had brought into his young life. Then his mind wondered to the journey ahead. He was excited for both the day and the voyage across the Pacific Ocean, 5,800 miles to Panama Canal. Yet another good reason that he had opted for the life of a Marine Engineer.

During his stint on the midnight to eight watch, he had studied the great oceans from the books in the ship's library. From his study, he had learned that the Latin name for this vast Pacific Ocean was Mare Pacifica or 'peaceful sea', the name bestowed upon it by the Portuguese explorer Ferdinand Magellan. It is the world's largest body of water and encompassed one third of the earth's surface. The Pacific Ocean contains approximately twenty-five thousand islands. The majority of them found south of the equator. The water temperature in the Pacific varied tremendously from freezing in the extreme north, and in the south to about 29° Celsius near the equator. "An interesting fact," he mused. The water near the equator is less salty than that found in the mid latitudes because of the abundant rain precipitation throughout the year.

The Pacific Ocean was first sighted by the Europeans, early in the sixteenth century, first by Vasco Nunez de Balboa, and then by a Ferdinand Magellan, who crossed the Pacific during his circumnavigation of the world. In 1564, the Conquistadors crossed the ocean from Mexico led by Miguel Lopez de Legazpi, who sailed to the Philippines and Marianna Islands during the remainder of the sixteenth century. Spanish influence was paramount with ships sailing from Spain to the Philippines, New Guinea and the Solomon Islands.

During the seventeenth century, the Dutch explorers sailing around Southern Africa dominated discovery and trade. Able Tasman discovered Tasmania and New Zealand in 1642.

The eighteenth century marked a burst of exploration by the Russians in Alaska and the Aleutian Islands, the French in Polynesia and the British in the three voyages by James Cook to the South Pacific and Australia, Hawaii, and the North American Pacific.

Growing imperialism during the nineteenth century, resulted in the occupation of much of Oceania by Great Britain and France, followed by the United States. A significant contribution to oceanographic knowledge was made by the voyages of the *HMS Beagle* in 1830, and Charles Darwin aboard the *HMS Challenger* during the 1870's.

There are seventeen independent states located in the Pacific, the most notable of which are Australia and New Zealand, the Philippines, China, the west coast of the United States, Chile, and Ecuador.

Life aboard the *Sydney Star* quickly settled into a seagoing routine of watch-keeping duties, the chef and his assistants preparing and cooking tasty dishes for passengers, ship's officers, and crew. The Engineering Department was busy repairing, and making good, to engineering spares, along with performance load tests on the main engines and electrical generators.

The days were long and languid. There was plenty of time for deck games, studying, sunbathing and writing notes for Jim's upcoming

Second Engineers examination. Each day at midday, the calendar was marked with great anticipation. Each day was nearer to home. One morning, three days out from Littleton, the ships public address system announced that a pair of albatross, which were flying astern following the ships wake, had joined us.

The history of the albatross, its' habits, its' abilities to fly on the wing, and sleep on the wing, was remarkable. Jim looked in awe at this fine bird flying over the stern following the wake. In his mind, it was the most beautiful bird he had ever seen, pure white feathers, with a wingspan of some twenty-four feet and a body length of four feet. Its' mission was to absorb as much fish and squid, then return to land to feed its' youngsters. Its' athleticism was a remarkable, enthralling sight. This monster of a bird had the ability to cover hundreds of miles on single journeys.

Jim stood next to the ships boatswain, Jack Headley, a sailor of many years. During the trip, he had talked to Jack many times. He was a wise experienced man who knew his seagoing abilities well. There was a sense of history about him. He was one of the few crewmembers that had remained on the ship during the war when the *Sydney Star* had been attacked, and nearly sunk, by a German U-boat in the Mediterranean Sea near Malta.

"This," he said referring to the albatross, "will bring us good luck during the voyage."

Two days later the albatross left during the night on their homeward journey.

This unique creature was part of the folklore of the world's sailors.

# Chapter 51

The *Sydney Star* was one day out of Pitcairn. Jim was leaning over the rail watching the sea go by, his thoughts on home remembering the time when Derek, Brian, Richard and himself decided to have a night out at the cinema. They had gone to the Gaumont Theatre, in Chester to see Charles Laughton in the film *Mutiny on the Bounty*. It had been for them, a riveting historical drama telling a tale of Britain's exploration of the world. He smiled wondering where the gang were, what they were doing, wishing that they were with him to share his experience.

A couple of days before, one of the ships passenger's had decided that he would give a lecture to those that were interested on the history of Pitcairn island. To his credit, the lecturer admitted that he had little direct knowledge of the island, but spent some considerable time reading its history.

"Pitcairn Island," he began, "is unique not because of its geography or its physical presence. It is a small volcanic island with approximately 1.75 miles of land area located halfway between New Zealand and South America. Its' history, you all probably know, having seen the film on the *Bounty* sometime in the past.

In 1989, Fletcher Christian, Master's Mate of the British ship, *HMS Bounty*, led a revolt against Captain William Bligh. The *Bounty* was returning from a mission of collecting breadfruit plants to be used as a potential food source on the new world plantation. There were many reasons for the mutiny. Many members of the crew had enjoyed their stay in Tahiti where they were treated like nobility, a far different situation than their life on board, under the harsh discipline of Captain Bligh, and living in cramped conditions with little food or fresh water.

During the mutiny, eighteen other crewmembers were set adrift in an open boat with one week's provisions and a few simple navigation instruments. Bligh, a Master Mariner, sailed the small crowded boat through three thousand five hundred miles of open sea to the Dutch colony of Timor in the East Indies.

Once Bligh and his loyalists departed, the First Mate, Fletcher Christian, assumed command of the *Bounty*. Under his command were twenty-four crewmembers, some of whom had no part in the mutiny, and fully expected to be absolved of all blame in the rebellion. The others were split between those who wanted to return to Tahiti and those who wanted to find a hiding place. Fletcher Christian was amongst the latter group

Following several unsuccessful attempts to settle on the South Sea Islands, the *Bounty* returned to Tahiti where the non-mutineers were allowed to remain on the island. The remaining crew, nine mutineers, six Polynesian men and twelve Polynesian women, left for their journey and final settling on Pitcairn Island."

"Pitcairn Island dead ahead, Sir," reported Brian to the Captain as he entered the bridge. The ship would lie off on the leeward side of the island to unload mail, various provisions and medical supplies. Estimated time at anchorage was four hours, in which time the islanders were allowed on board to display their native crafts, their only source of income. Jim purchased two items, one for Grandma and the other one for his Mum. The descendants of the mutineers were kind, happy people. They were pleased to see new faces, particularly those in uniform. They still preserved the remnants of some of the ships Officer's uniforms from the *HMS Bounty*. They were a 'touchy-feely' group of people, proud of their heritage, and enjoyed a visit from a British ship. They were content to live on this beautiful island under the protection of the United Kingdom.

# *Chapter 52*

Life on the *Sydney Star* quickly regained its seagoing mode. The long hot days and the beautiful starlight nights, punctuated the remaining days of Jim's journey and arrival in Panama, which he anxiously awaited. The next morning he met his friend, the Boatswain, on deck doing his morning rounds.

"What do you know about the Panama Canal," asked Jim hoping for some snippets of information, which may add to his fairly rudimentary knowledge on the subject.

"Not a lot, young Sir," he replied reminding Jim, as always, that he was the Junior Officer, and he, being the Senior Boatswain of the ship, was the highest rank, the Petty Officer, on any seagoing vessel. "Have you tried at the library?" he asked.

"Yes I have. I found something about the history of de Lesseps, but not a lot about the engineering side."

"Have you tried the Chief Engineer?" he asked.

The Boatswain's advice was, as usual, excellent. The Chief Engineer produced a book on the subject, which he eagerly borrowed to study.

The dream of constructing a water passage across the Isthmus of Panama uniting the Pacific and the Atlantic Oceans dates to the early sixteenth century, with the first crossing by Vasco Nunez de Balboa, who discovered the narrow strip of land separating the two oceans. During the intervening years, several surveys had been undertaken to establish the validity of constructing a canal passage. In 1875, Ferdinand de

Lesseps, the hero of the construction of the Suez Canal, stated his first public interest in the inter-oceanic canal, linking Colon, on the Atlantic side of Panama, to Balboa, on the Pacific side. In the year 1880, the first group of French engineers arrived to start the task of constructing the canal. During the years that followed, men and machinery poured into Panama to confront the enormous geographical obstacles of the Isthmus, the backbone of the Continental Divide, the Culebra Cut and the mighty Chagres River.

French engineering stood at its pinnacle in the nineteenth century. Their finest engineers and machinery were put to work. Eight years of valiant, and determined, effort was made on the Isthmus. The climate, torrential rain, incessant heat and fatal disease took its toll. Finely financial management, stock failure, and bad publicity, eventually forced the failure of the company. Eventually, the work of finishing construction passed to the United States of America. The work was completed by August 15, 1914, and the canal was officially opened by the transit passage of the steamship, *Ancon*.

The construction of the Panama Canal is recognized to be one of the engineering wonders of the world. The Atlantic approach was gained by three sets of two lane lock chambers. The ship enters, the lock gates close, water is pumped into the chamber and lifts the ship to the level of the Gatun Lake some eighty-five feet above sea level. The vessel then proceeds to the Gatun Lake, then onto the Pedro Miguel lock. From there, to the Miraflores Lake, proceeding to the Miraflores locks, where it is lowered to the sea level of the Pacific Ocean.

# Chapter 53

The *Sydney Star* arrived at Balboa in the early hours of the morning, anchoring prior to making passage through the canal on the south to north passage. The *Sydney Star* was slated to be number three in line, one hour before the end of Jim's 4- 8 watch-keeping duties. The engineering staff adopted a standby mode for the maneuver of the ship through the canal. The previous day the Chief Engineer outlined his roster to ensure that the engine room staff worked the maximum of one-hour spell of duty with two hours off, to combat the projected intensity of heat during the eight-hour passage through the canal.

Jim exited the engine room, excited for the day. "This," he said to himself, "would be the pinnacle of sightseeing," an experience that he really had looked forward to since he had left London months ago. He showered and changed into a clean pair of coveralls, and watched the passage of the ship through the first lock, the Miraflores. It was a fascinating experience as he watched the mules attach ropes to both fore and aft of the ship and slowly maneuver the *Sydney Star* into the first lock. There was an air of excitement as he watched the water flood the chamber, the ship's hull gradually rose to the level of the lake, then, as the exit gate opened, the mules assisted the *Sydney Star* on her way into the Miraflores Lake. It was a fascinating experience and he marveled at that the expertise shown in the progress of this eleven thousand ton ship through the lock. Slowly, the *Sydney Star* made its way under its own steam, guided by the canal pilot to the Pedro Miguel lock. Jim smiled as they started the journey. This was very different to the Manchester Ship Canal locks, the beginning of his childhood dreams that led him to start his quest to travel the world.

Later, Jim and the four to eight watch returned to the engine room for another stint of duty. The engine room was unusually hot, and they were advised by the ship's doctor to drink limejuice and a regular consumption of salt tablets, the order of the day to offset the effects of the heat during his next spell of duty.

On deck, the ship encountered a severe rainstorm, which entailed the stoppage of all ships in transit. There was one solitary advantage. It cooled the temperature of the engine room. Later that evening after his watch, Jim sat in the wardroom discussing the exciting and fascinating events of the day. At dinner that evening, the topic of conversation moved forward to the ships next stop, the upcoming fuel bunkering in Curacao.

"Do you feel like going ashore, Mitchell?" asked John Thompson.

"Yes, I would like to see old Captain Morgan's Castle."

"The last time I saw the Castle was about six years ago. It was in ruins."

"That's a pity," said Jim. "I was looking forward to a visit."

"Cheer up," replied John. "Bryan and I are going into Willemstad for a couple of beers and a bit of shopping. It is a great place to visit; you are welcome to join us. It will be your last trip ashore until we reach the Victoria and Albert Docks in London in eleven days time."

"Thank you," replied Jim, "that would be great."

*Chapter 54*

Curacao is the largest of five islands of the Netherlands Antilles and lies in the Caribbean Sea 60 km off the Venezuelan coast. For centuries, Curacao had earned its reputation in global trade as one of the foremost refineries of Venezuelan oil in the Caribbean.

The island's history dates back to around 2500 BC, when the first inhabitants migrated from Venezuela. Later, the Caiquetios and Sarawak speaking people arrived from Venezuelan around 500 AD. They were an agricultural people that farmed maze manioc, hunted rabbit and deer. Fish was a large part of their diet. They lived in pole huts and made ceramic vessels, as well as, ornaments and implements of shell, stone, and bone.

Some two thousand Caiquetios are estimated to have been living on the nearby islands of Aruba and Bonaire. When the Spaniards first landed on the islands, legend has it that they were impressed by the relatively large stature of the Caiquetios, and dubbed Curacao the island of giants.

The Spaniards transported most of them to Hispaniola to work in their prosperous mines. When the Dutch took the island in 1634, they deported most of the remaining Caiquetios, fearing that they would be spies for the Spaniards. By the beginning of the nineteenth century none of the original inhabitants remained.

Today, the Dutch have left their mark on Curacao, the most striking of which is their architecture. Nowhere else in the world are there so many exquisite seventeenth and eighteenth century Dutch colonial buildings. In time, the styles were modified to fit the realities of the tropical climate, incorporating Caribbean influences such as verandas and porches, fretwork and shutters.

The capital city of the island is called Willemstad, a city which is sited in the centre of the access by a man made canal, which links the city and the inland dock area to the Caribbean Sea. The hustle and bustle of the city gives an unmistakable festive air. The pavements are clean, the shops are inviting and most restaurants having seating inside and outside on the pavements. The waiters are friendly, the service is excellent and the Amsteel beer is a connoisseur's delight.

"It's hard to beat Willemstad shopping," Brian commented as they sat at a table of an outside café drinking a glass of beer and consuming a variety of fine Dutch cheeses with crispy crackers.

"What did you buy, Jim?" asked Brian.

"A gold cross for my Mum and an electric razor for myself," replied Jim.

The conversation revolved around the shopping expedition for a while, then John reminisced, telling the story about his six-week stay on the island during a refit of one of the ships that he had sailed in some years before.

Jim smiled listening to John's tales. During the voyage, he had related many tales of the sea, and it was intriguing to listen to his stories about the various voyages he had made around the world. In the months that he had known him, he had learned much from him apart from his engineering skills. He was, in Jim's mind, the young version of the ancient Mariner, and could capture an audience with his many stories. He was also a ladies' man who could "charm the birds out of the trees." He was also his best friend and mentor, who had answered numerous questions that Jim had asked about the design of engines and ships, safety procedures and emergency procedures that would help him to achieve his ambition of obtaining his Chief Engineers certificate.

# Chapter 55

It was a night full of stars, as the *Sydney Star* left its berth to begin the last leg of Jim's momentous journey around the world. Ahead were hours of final study for his upcoming examination for his Second Engineers' Marine Engineering Certificate, and the opportunity to be with his family and friends after many months away. As the *Sydney Star* approached Lands End, the most westerly part of England, the excitement of returning home steadily increased. Civilian clothes were cleaned and pressed, suitcases prepared for packing. The Engineering Department worked hard on their hands to make them presentable, fingernails were cut, filed, and polished, and homecoming gifts were wrapped. The whole ship's crew had the "Channels' duty-free items listed on the customs declaration. Shoes were brightly polished. Jim smiled in anticipation. He was ready to step down the gangplank, ready in his mind and body. There was still one day remaining before the ship docked in the Victoria docks. The final part of the ceremony would be signing off the ships articles, telegrams to Granddad and his Mum, discussing the voyage report with the Superintendent Engineer, and the next ship assignment.

The Assistant Superintendent Engineer Personnel Officer, Paddy Fitzsimons, was aware of Jim's plans. He needed to serve a further four months on board a ship to qualify his sea time prior to taking the Second Engineer's Certificate. Jim was also aware that there would be pressure on him to return to the *Sydney Star* for another long trip, which conflicted with the timing of his Second Engineers' examinations.

Paddy shook Jim's hand warmly as he entered the office. "Well, Jim, how was the trip?"

"It was hard work, but I enjoyed it," Jim replied. "I learned a lot from John Thomson, had a lot of fun and now I am ready for some shore leave."

"Are you ready for another trip on the *Sydney*?" asked Patrick.

"Yes, it's a great ship," replied Jim, "but I would prefer a voyage of three to four months so that I can take my examination for my Seconds Engineers Certificate at the earliest possible time."

Paddy smiled to himself. He was aware of Jim Mitchell's ambition, and he was torn between a rock and hard place. There was an opening on the *Brazil Star*. However, he was also aware that the Chief Engineer of the *Sydney Star* had requested him back on board as Senior Fourth Engineer. In addition, he was aware that the next trip on the *Sydney Star* would last seven to eight months. This young man's dream was to become a Chief Engineer before the age of twenty-five, and he was in sore need of top-notch engineers in the company. This young man had ambitions, and his report on his first trip was excellent.

Paddy Fitzsimons smiled. "Here's the deal, Jim. Join the *Brazil Star* a week tomorrow as Fourth Engineer. Yes, I am aware that this will cut down your leave by seven days, but that is the best I can do now. Jim it's a win, win situation for both of us."

"Thank you, Sir, it's a deal," Jim replied; he had won the day.

Later that day, suitcase in hand, he boarded the express train at Waterloo Station to Crewe. He had bought a novel at the bookshop to fill in the time, its' value was naught. The strong feeling of anticipation and excitement buried deep inside him was now coming to the forefront. Fond memories of his first trip to sea came flooding back to him, along with memories of his friends John, Brian, and, above all, Elizabeth Black.

"Home on leave?" inquired the little old woman sitting opposite him in the first-class compartment.

"Yes I am, Ma'am," he replied.

"How long has it been?" she asked.

"Ten months and twenty-seven days," he replied. "Give or take ten hours," he added with a smile.

Later, he slept a while only to be awakened by the train porter announcing that the train would arrive at Crewe station in fifteen minutes. Just enough time to freshen up from the trip.

There was a lump in his throat, a tear of happiness, as the train entered the station. There were tears in his eyes as he stepped off the train. Jim saw his Granddad and Grandma in the distance waiting for him.

"It's so bloody good to see you my son!" exclaimed Grandma as she looked into his eyes, then with a laugh she added, "I sent away a white boy, what happened?"

Jim laughed at her remark, "It's hot out there, Grandma," he replied.

That night, Jim slept at the farm. It was good to be home again. They talked late into the night reminiscing about the old days and events that happened while he was a way. There had always been something special about his relationship with his grandparents, a love garnered from his early days as a child.

The following morning, he rose early, excited about the day that would be a special day, spent alone with the love of his life, his mother Edith. The Riley purred as Jim opened the throttle of the engine. In a way, he could feel Lydia with him. The letter that he had received from her when he docked in London had worried him. She was working hard to achieve her ambition. He smiled as he remembered one of the lines from her letter, "Jim, my Love, being apart from you is so hard, and it hurts my love."

"Anyone at home?" said Jim as he entered the cottage. Her face smiled radiantly as they hugged each other. There were tears, as there always were with Mum.

"Let me a look at you," she said as they parted from their hug. "Have you grown, or have I got smaller?" she asked with a laugh.

"I don't know, Love," he replied. "You look good to me, lady."

"The minutes, the hours, the days had passed quickly," murmured Jim to himself as he sat on the train reminiscing over the last few days. They had been special days with his mother. He reflected on the long awaited reunion with the gang, his visits to Aunty Lucy, and Aunty Ethel, time spent on the farm with his Granddad and Grandma, the day spent with Lydia's parents and a bittersweet phone call to Lydia. He was now ready to begin his second trip to sea. This time he would visit South America aboard the flagship of the South American fleet, the *Brazil Star.* He was aware for the first time, that he was living in two worlds, the world of home, his childhood of his youth, and the world travel. There were times when he regretted his decision to become a Marine Engineer. There was an ironic smile on his face as he murmured to himself, "You have made your bed, and you must lie on it, for better or for worse." The ecstasy of the homecoming followed the regrets of leaving. Ahead of him was another adventure. He was ready and waiting.

# *Chapter 56*

The slim, white lines of the *Brazil Star* came into view as Jim's taxi made its way into the Victoria Dock complex. She was long and sleek with beautiful lines just as Paddy had described her: 478 feet long, 68 feet breadth and a draft of 30 feet. The flagship of the Blue Star's South American fleet comprised of the *Uruguay Star*, the *Argentinean Star*, and the *Paraguay Star*. She had the capacity of carrying fifty-one passengers, with six refrigerated cargo holds. The main propulsion units was powered by two Babcock and Wilcox sinuous header boilers, with double reduction gear to one shaft, giving a surface speed of twenty nautical miles per hour.

"Permission to come aboard, Sir" said Jim to the officer of the watch. "My name is Jim Mitchell. I am the ship's Senior Fourth Engineer."

"Welcome aboard, Sir. One moment, please, I will get your steward to show you to your quarters."

Jim mused as he opened the door to his cabin. "Huh," he said to himself, "much better than the *Sydney Star* did." Jim read a note on his desk from the Chief Engineer. "Welcome aboard, Jim, I am looking forward to meeting you. I will be dining in the mess shortly after noon; join me for lunch, sincerely, John Watson."

"Hello, Sir," said Jim as he approached the uniformed Chief Engineer. "Jim Mitchell."

"Welcome aboard, Jim, I have been looking forward to meeting you.

Take a pew, the Shepherds pie is particularly good today," he smiled holding the menu.

"Thank you, Sir," said Jim. "It's good to be on board. I am looking forward to the trip."

"John Thompson and Paddy Fitzsimons speak very highly of you. Both have recommended you to me. You will be taking the eight to twelve watch."

Jim was pleased. "Paddy has told me that the plant is very similar to the steam plant that I worked on during my apprenticeship with BICC. I am looking forward to the opportunity."

"Good!" he exclaimed. "I will show you around the engine room after lunch. The first sea watches start at midday tomorrow. We should be sailing at 1800 hours. That will give you an opportunity to familiarize yourself with the engine room. Your Junior Engineer will be Bob Frances, returning from leave later today."

Jim unpacked his gear and settled into his cabin, then wrote a few short notes to his loved ones. He lay on the day bed reminiscing about his brief shore leave, his meeting with the gang, and a great time with his mother. Now he was on his way into a new venture. He looked at Elizabeth Black's photograph. Her last letter had pleased him. She had met a young doctor from England who had joined her father's practice and they were now dating. He smiled again, "Dear Elizabeth, he is a lucky man. Take care, one day we will meet again," he said as he closed his eyes for an afternoon nap.

Jim stood on the wing of the bridge as the *Brazil Star* left its berth at the Royal Victoria and Albert Docks complex, making its way slowly down the River Thames, heading for Lisbon, Rio de Janeiro, Santos, Monte Video, and Buenos Aires. The lure of the sea was on him again, the sense of adventure that had first intrigued his mind many years ago when he and Richard had first watched the ships on the Manchester Ship Canal heading for foreign lands.

This would be an adventure. He could feel it in his bones, a challenge that he gladly accepted. The game was on, and his mind concentrated on the work ahead. He was aware of what he needed to do, and what he must do to survive. Failure was not an option. In four months, he would reach the halfway stage of his ambition and nothing, he repeated, nothing would stand in this way. Gone were the days, the fun days of the four to eight o'clock watch as a Junior Engineer. He was responsible for the engine room for eight hours each day on this trip, and the unglamorous, nonsocial life of the eight to twelve o'clock watch. There was an ironic smile on his face. The egoistic ambition was with him. Now was time for him to grasp the nettle and achieve the first half his ambition. He would be sitting for the Second Engineers' certificate on his return to London.

Jim stood on the bridge deck, fascinated by the beauty of the landscape as the *Brazil Star* entered the port of Lisbon. It would be a brief port of call to board the remaining passengers for the trip, and an opportunity for Jim to take a couple of hours of shore leave before the long trip across the Atlantic Ocean.

# Chapter 57

Portugal has a rich history as a seafaring nation during the fourteenth century and the fifteenth century. Portuguese explorers launched the great age of European exploration. Balomeu Diaz commanded the first European voyage around of the Cape of Good Hope, and Vasco de Gama sailed around the Cape and discovered a sea route to Asia, leading to the establishment of a vast Portuguese empire in Africa and South America.

It was a warm, sunny afternoon, and Jim went ashore to do a little sightseeing. His objective was to visit the Don Pedro IV square to see the monument of the first Emperor of Brazil, an amazing statue of the leader of a great country. On his way back to the ship, he stopped at one of the many curbside restaurants overlooking the harbor to sample the local beer. The scene of the harbor was perfect, he mused as he sat sipping the lager his thoughts broken by a tall elegant, older, gentleman dressed immaculately in a white suit and a straw hat.

""May I join you?" he asked.

"Certainly, Sir," replied Jim.

"Hello, my name is Nikolai Cavalantis."

"Delighted to meet with you, Sir," replied Jim greeting him with a handshake. "I am the Senior Fourth Engineer of the *Brazil Star*."

"Yes, I know, young man," he said politely, "I saw you on the wing of the bridge when we were coming into port. It's nice to meet you. My wife, my sister-in-law, and I are traveling to Brazil." He paused. "May I buy you another beer?"

"Thank you, Sir," replied Jim intrigued by his presence. In many ways, he reminded Jim of a younger version of his grandfather, the wrinkles on his forehead, his eyes, and his long, sinewy hands. "An interesting man," he said to himself.

"Did you enjoy your trip ashore, young man?" he asked.

"Yes, I did, Sir. Unfortunately, there was little time, but it is a fascinating city and I am looking forward to returning one day."

"Yes, I agree it's a fascinating city. My ancestors came from this part, and my wife simply adores it. We spent the last few days here sightseeing. Do you enjoy engineering?" he asked.

"Yes, I do, Sir. It is a fascinating subject, and one that I am completely enthralled with. It covers a whole spectrum of subjects including planning and man management. May I inquire as to what you do for a living?"

"To be honest with you, Sir, I am not altogether sure. I suppose that I do a little of this and a little of that. Never had a job as such, don't you know, although my father is an Hotelier and, no doubt, one day I will be forced to run his empire. We have just finished a European holiday and I'm looking forward to the polo season back home in Rio."

"Would you like another beer?" asked Jim.

"Yes, I would, thank you," Nikolai replied.

Their ensuing conversation covered many subjects from engineering, man management, and construction diplomacy to the art of navigation, holiday destinations in Europe, and life on board passenger cargo liners.

Jim smiled inwardly. This was an interesting man, very similar to his grandfather. He did most of the talking. He was an interesting character, knowledgeable on many subjects.

"Thanks for the conversation!" exclaimed Nikolai "I suppose we should be getting back. Most enjoyable, perhaps we can meet again. I would be interested in your views on English politics."

"That would be great," replied Jim. "I have enjoyed the conversation, thank you."

"I have just remembered that I am throwing a party on Sunday night for some friends. Would you like to join us?"

"I am sorry," replied Jim. "I have the eight to twelve watch."

"Then I am sure that you can make it. Our parties usually go on to the early hours of the morning."

"In that case I will accept, Sir."

The tropical sub-Atlantic ocean, at this time of the year, was known to be temperamental. The waters lived up to expectation as the vessel headed for a Rio at a somewhat reduced speed in order to maintain a degree of comfort for the passengers.

It was midnight. The ship was five days out of Lisbon. Jim had looked forward to the party, his first social event since the ship had left London. It was twelve forty-five a.m., he showered and he dressed into his messkit. That brought back memories of Elizabeth Black, the night of her welcome home party. He looked at her photograph on the wall. He dressed and sipped on his first gin and tonic of the day. "Cheers Liz, I miss you. Take a good care sweet lady."

"James, how nice to see you," said Nikolai. "Thank you for coming. Let me introduce you around, this is my wife Maria." Jim regarded the tall, broad- shouldered, elegant, olive skinned, Brazilian Lady dressed in a white evening dress. She extended her hand to greet him, her liquid, green eyes raking his body, the sensuous touch of her fingers lingering for a while. She smiled. Her lips pursed, tantalizing him with her seductive smile. "Hello, James," she murmured in the soft sultry voice. "Welcome to our gathering. Nikolai has told me much about you."

"It's nice to meet you, Ma'am. I have looked forward to this evening."

"James, I would like you to meet my younger sister, Melissa."

Jim regarded her as they shook hands. "Hello, James," she whispered. She was a fascinating smaller version of her sister, who obviously was enjoying herself at the party. "It's nice to meet you, Sir. Tell me, what do you do on the ship? And why haven't I seen you before?"

"I'm an engineer Ma'am; my duties extend between eight o'clock a.m. to midday, and eight o'clock p.m. to midnight, not the most hospitable hours for socializing."

"That's a pity. I was looking for someone to dance with me earlier this evening. Do you dance?"

"Yes I do, Ma'am," Jim replied

"Oh, well," she replied, "Maybe another time on the voyage."

"James, sorry I was delayed," said Nikolai, "your cocktail, Sir. By the way, will you join me at the lunch tomorrow? I'm looking forward to continuing our conversation."

"Yes, Sir," Jim replied, "I shall look forward to it."

Later, Jim excused himself and stood on deck watching the moon's reflection on the calmer sea, listening to strains of tango music emanating from the party; suddenly, Melissa interrupted his thoughts.

"Dance with me?" she asked invitingly.

Jim looked deep into her eyes stroking her hair as her arms encircled his body. He could feel her warmth; the smell of her perfume excited him as they slowly danced around the deck in the moonlight. He gazed momentarily at this singular South American beauty. She smiled seductively as her hand slowly moved to his buttocks, then slowly to his sack, exciting him, raising him, intoxicating him. Then, holding his hand, she gently guided him through the passenger accommodation to her suite, opening the door silently. With a coquettish smile, she unzipped her long evening gown. As it fell to the floor, she murmured softly, "You like?"

Jim was mesmerized by the sheer beauty of her olive skinned body, her full breasts and dark hard nipples standing proud amid the beauty of her areoles. "You are truly beautiful, Melissa."

She smiled a sensuous smile. "Thank you Jimmy," she murmured as she slowly, deftly removed his uniform laying him naked on the bed.

There was tenderness about her as their lips met for the first time; a coquettish smile as the tips of her fingers slowly, gently, with a sensuous touch, raked his body, a sensation that he had never known before driving his mind into a blue haze of sexual desire. She drew his head onto her breasts, her lips purring with abject pleasure as he suckled her proud, hard nipples, his tongue exciting the very core of her body. She held his head in the palm of her hands, smiling. Her lips caressing the lobes of his ears, and eyes whispering, "oh my beauty, love me slowly." There was a moment of tender sensation as she guided his hard cock into her waiting sex.

She smiled as they stroked together in perfect harmony, murmuring words of pleasure as the sexual fever reached a crescendo. "Now, my beauty Let it come, let it come," she shouted as she thrust her hips to meet him.

Their bodies covered in the sweat of love, exhausted by the intensity of passion, lingering as they lay together with a tender emotion, caressing, smiling, and glowing in the rapture of deep sexual adoration.

# Chapter 58

The hours of the days passed quickly, and the nights were full of unbelievable passion with the beautiful, beguiling Melissa. There were no regrets, or love, as they pleasured themselves night after night fulfilling their utmost desires, living in a world of sexual satisfaction, an unbelievable experience with a woman whose love knew no bounds. She smiled as they parted, murmuring softly, "We will meet again."

Jim stood on the bridge of the *Brazil Star* watching the arrival of his ship into Río de Janeoiro, one of the most beautiful harbors in the world. The imposing Sugarloaf Mountain, an impressive backdrop to the city, crowned by the impressive statue of Jesus Christ standing atop, added to the sheer beauty of the scene.

The *Brazil Star* received a huge welcome as she arrived in the port to the sound of the traditional samba music. The ladies, dancing in their colorful dresses, created ambiance to the scene. Soon it would be time to say goodbye to his newfound friends Nikolai, his wife Maria, and Melissa. She smiled as they parted, "We will meet again, lovely man. We will meet again one day soon I hope."

Hours later, the *Brazil Star* left port; her journey was to Santos, Montevideo and finally Buenos Aires.

# Chapter 59

It was early in the morning when Jim had completed his last watch on the ship. He lay in bed reminiscing about of the voyage, the nights of passionate love with the beguiling Melissa, the beautiful beaches of Copacabana, the tango club in Buenos Aires, his upcoming leave and days and hours of study for his examinations for his Second Engineer's certificate. Suddenly, there was an air of confidence within him. "Damn-it!" he shouted out loud. "You can do this." The fears, the doubts in his mind vanished. "Yes, Mitchell, you are ready for the fray and you will pass, failure is not an option." On arrival at the Victoria and Albert Docks, he received his long awaited mail from his loved ones, one from Grandma and one from his Mum, but no letter from Lydia. He felt disappointed. He was now ill at ease with their relationship. He received an intriguing a note from Maggie. He smiled as he read it. "Where the hell are you? You promised to watch one of my performances. We are running out of time Mitchell. The play will be closing next month. Damn you, Mitchell! Come and see me please!" Jim's smile broadened as he read the last line. "Jim Mitchell, I miss you. It's been too long and damn it, don't you know that I love you."

He had packed his seagoing kit into storage. It had been a good trip. He had made many friends, and now the time had come for him to leave the *Brazil Star*. "For what?" he asked himself. He did not know; he did not care. His mind was focused on one thing only, his Second Engineer's examination.

It was a dank, stormy morning as Jim sat in the examination room. The examination clerk regarded his watch, and then waited shortly before he presented the first morning's questions to the four candidates. He walked slowly around the room facing the upturned document on each of their tables, then stood in front and announced, "Gentlemen you may now start your examination."

Jim read the questions on the examination papers. He smiled as he reviewed the questions, most of which he had reviewed recently in his studies and answered them with a degree of confidence. During the following days, he was able to answer all of the searching questions. On the third day, he faced the Examiner of Engineers, the ultimate test, and an oral examination. The most dreaded part of the examinations, a period where the Examiner delved into your mind, gauged your reaction to his searching questions, searching for the answers. Finally, the trial was over. The Examiner smiled. There was silence; then the words he had longed to hear. "You have passed, Mr. Mitchell, congratulations."

Jim's mind was in a haze as he left the examination room. There was a sense of relief, and unbelievable excitement, in his body, the anticipation and nervousness had left. He was on shore leave for the next few weeks, a time to celebrate. He had no firm plans. Yes, he would see his family in the fullness of time, and meet up with the gang. I hope that Richard would be home.

As he walked along the road leading to the bus stop, he passed a newspaper stand. He read a headline on the Billboard 'Last performance- The Soldier Boy starring Maggie O'Toole.' Suddenly, his heart began to beat faster. He was excited, "Oh, Maggie," remembering her words from her letter and thoughts of yesteryear. "One day I will be famous, then you will have to pay to see me on the stage." "Why not," he said to himself. Over the years, he had avoided seeing her on his trips to London. Now, he was excited and proud of her. This was his Maggie. "Why not?" He repeated as he ran to the nearest telephone box and rang the number.

"Maggie O'Toole."

"Hello Maggie."

"Is that you, Jim?" she answered excitedly.

"Yes it is, my darling," he murmured emotionally.

"Where the hell of you been. I've written to you several times and you haven't answered Mitchell. Where are you?" she asked impatiently.

"In London," he replied. "It's your last night and I want to see you in the play."

She laughed, "Better late than never, Mitchell, I suppose. I will have a ticket waiting for you at the box office, and a pass to my dressing room afterwards. Don't be late!"

Jim was escorted to his seat in the centre, first row minutes before the play started. This would be the first time that he had seen Maggie perform on stage. He was struck with emotion as she entered stage left to tumultuous applause. "Oh my," he murmured excitedly. This was a different Maggie then he had known all his life. She was truly beautiful. Her stage presence was imposing, her elocution superb, absolutely fantastic. At the end of play, she bowed to each curtain call. The final call, she walked alone to the front of the stage, pointed to Jim, and with a deep curtsy, she blew him a kiss. Jim smiled. This was his Maggie. He stood applauding until the last of the patrons left the theatre.

"Are you Jim Mitchell?" asked the young usherette.

"Yes I am," he replied.

"I was told to escort you to Miss O'Toole's dressing-room."

Jim knocked at the star's dressing-room door. "Come," she murmured. As he entered, she regarded him, "It's about bloody time, Mitchell. Where the hell have you been?" she cried ecstatically, tears of joy welling in her eyes. She threw her wrap to the floor. Standing naked before him, she whispered, "Hold me, Jim, I've missed you so much."

Jim held her face with the palms of his hands; looking deep into her eyes, he kissed her waiting lips, holding her in a close embrace as only he knew how.

"Miss me?" he murmured.

"You know bloody well I have. Come and talk to me while I shower and change. I got so much to tell you. There is a stage reception for the cast and the media. This is our last hurrah. You, Sir, will be my guest of honor for the night. How do I look?" She murmured as she walked to her dressing table wearing a long, white gown, cut low in the front barely concealing the nipples of her beautiful breasts."

"Bloody marvelous," he replied.

"Thank you, Sir." Then with a coquettish smile she murmured, "Do you still fancy me?"

"You know damn well I do," he retorted.

"Oh good, take me to the reception cousin."

Maggie walked slowly to the stage holding Jim's arm. This was her night. There was something unbelievable about it. He was here holding her just like the old days when he escorted her to Grandma's dining room at the Christmas celebrations. Tonight he was her man, the only man that she had ever really loved. As they entered the stage, she paused to accept the applause of her fellow thespians. The cameras clicked. The flashes filled the stage with light. She smiled. For once in her life, she was nervous as her fingers tightened on his arms. Then there was a silence as she called, "Ladies and gentlemen I would like you to meet my long lost cousin, Jim Mitchell." Jim raised his hand acknowledging their greeting as they circled the stage. The noisy room was filled with people talking and laughing, and Maggie accepting the good wishes of her public. Finally, it was time to go to the next celebration, a dinner in her honor.

Jim smiled as they entered the restaurant. On his arm was his Maggie. The Star of the long-running play was greeted with warm applause as she walked slowly to her table, stopping occasionally to talk, and to embrace her well-wishers. It was a sight to behold. She was magnificent. This shaggy little cousin was now the star of stage, television, and films. She had worked her way to the top of her profession and she deserved the accolades. Jim was elated for her success. She sat at the head of the table next to the producer and director, smiling graciously during the meal. Finally, it was time for speeches. She rose from her seat. It was her time. With a smiling face, she regarded her audience. Jim smiled as he recognized the words. "I, Maggie O'Toole, stand before you tonight to humbly thank you all for the success in this, the longest running play for a number of years. Mr. Producer, Henry," she smiled regarding him, "without your foresight there would have been no play. Mr. Director, Alex," she said regarding him, "without your genius this would have been a second-rate play. To the cast of this fine production," she smiled as she regarded each one of them. "Without you there would have been no play. Without you I would still be," she smiled, "that vivacious bitch from Cheshire. Now, thanks to you, you have brought the success, and sincerely I thank you. It's never been easygoing." There was a chorus of "No!"

"Alas we come to the end, and I bid you farewell, and wish you well in the future. I hope that we will meet again. It's been fun thank you." She bowed gracefully as Jim stood watching her closely. She smiled whispering in his ear, "Take me home Mitchell."

Maggie awoke the following morning to the birds singing in Hyde Park. He was cuddling her head on his breast. The chill of excitement ran down her spine. She was in the arms of her man, the only man that she had ever really loved. Oh my love, she whispered as she recalled their lovemaking. He had caressed her body with his lips with his tongue, bringing her ecstatically into a world of passionate unbelievable sexual fulfillment. Her appetite had been insatiable, as she had raised his ardor wanting him, as there would be no 'morrow. She moved slowly caressing his hair, kissing his lips, as he lay exhausted. He smiled as his eyelids opened and murmured softly, "Good morning, my beauty, how are you?"

Bloody marvelous, thank you kindly, Sir. God we were magnificent together Jim."

"Yes we were, my Love," then murmured. "Where do we go from here?"

"Anywhere you want to go, my Love."

Jim placed his hands on the cheeks of her face and looked deep into her eyes, "Where do you want to go, Maggie?"

"Away from here for as long as we can, my Love," she murmured quietly.

"When we were kids, we often talked about taking a trip to the South of France."

"Oh Jim, that would be marvelous. Can we do that, my Love?" There were tears in her eyes. "Oh Jim, I can't believe it! Oh yes, my Love," she cried excitedly. "I want to go to Paris, Monte Carlo, Nice, Cannes, and St Tropez. I want to lie on the beach and get my arse and tits tanned. I want to get laid three times a day." She looked at him with a coquettish smile, "OK, maybe twice, Mitchell, Oh God, we will be glorious, just, you and me." She jumped from the bed and ran to the telephone. "Can we leave today? We can stay overnight in Calais, then the Ritz Carlton in Paris."

"Yes we can, my Love." His thoughts turned to the past. Nothing had changed. She was the young girl that he fell in love with so many years ago.

"Oh Jim, this is marvelous. Cook some breakfast while I organize the Jaguar and ring Mary Lou," she smiled, "and pack a few pairs of knickers. Then we need to talk, my Love."

She smiled as she entered the kitchen. "All done, two nights at the Ritz Carlton and we are staying at Mary Lou's Villa in Nice."

She sat on his belly. "Just like the old times," she announced. "We need to make some rules, my Love. I am no angel, I have a boyfriend and you have Lydia. I do not want to talk about them. I do not want talk about the family. I want it just to be you. I am whatever you want me to be. It is going to be hard when we part, so, my Love, it will just be you and me. We will be glorious together as we always have been." She cried ecstatically, "A deal?"

"A deal my beauty," he cried as his arms pulled her to him sealing their bargain with a long loving kiss.

It was three-thirty p.m. as they left her Hyde Park apartment heading to Dover. Maggie O'Toole sat on the passenger seat of her new X K Jaguar, her legs tucked underneath her buttock, excited like a schoolgirl. "Oh Jim," she said to herself as she looked at him, "I would give it all up just to be with you my love. Yes, I know we can't do that, but we can have each other for a while, just you and me, my darling." There was a tear in her eyes as she kissed him, smiling triumphantly. He would be hers for a while. She would be in the arms of the only man that she had ever loved.

The following morning, they headed for Paris, the city of light, the city of love, the city for lovers of all ages. She smiled as she touched his arm. "Oh Jim, it's glorious. I want to visit the artists on the left bank and buy some pictures, ride up the Eiffel Tower to see the beautiful views of Paris, then the Latin Quarter, the Arc De Triomphe, the Champs-Elysées, and the Louvre. Jim smiled as she murmured. "In the evening, I want to eat at small outdoor cafes to taste the gastronomic pleasures of French food, and if we have time I would like to see the show at the Follies. It will remind me of my time at the "Windmill Theatre," and I want to take lots of photographs." She laughed. ""Can I take one of you in the nude?"

"Yes my love," Jim replied, then laughing he added, "I can imagine you showing them to your kids in the years to come."

She laughed with a whimsical look on her face as she murmured, "This is my cousin Jim, isn't he beautiful?"

# Chapter 60

Maggie, Bernadette O'Toole sat on the balcony overlooking the Mediterranean Sea. This had been their home for the last days, reminiscing time together. Time had never been kind to them. The days had passed quickly as she tearfully reminisced about her time with her man: the perfect days in the city of lights, the Louvre, the Eiffel tower, the show at the Latin Quarter, the Arc De Triomphe and an evening at the Follies Bergère at La Tore Argent, a boat trip down the River Seine, and splendid luncheons of baguettes, salad and cheese. Their nights together were full of love, sweet, adorable sex, and wanting and wishing time to stand still in this wonderful city. Soon it was time to leave this wonderful city of light. Ahead of them was the beauty of Provence. An overnight stay in the city of Baume, then onto Vieux Lyon to explore the historic alleyways, and to savor the gastronomic delights in the outdoor cafes of this historical beautiful quaint city.

That evening, they dined on Foie Gras and Braised Duck in wine, washed down with a fine Cote du Rhone in one of the renowned alleyway outdoor cafes.

There had been an air of expectation as they left Lyon early the next morning to travel over the scenic beauty of Alps Maritimes via Grenoble. A memorable lunch at Castellane, under the awe-inspiring abbey, then onto their final destination, Mary Lou's villa overlooking the resort of Nice, where they were greeted by the housekeeper and cook, a young lady from Corsica who prepared a fine meal of lobster salad and braised duck in red wine sauce. The days that followed, were spent exploring the market place in Nice, the beauty of Cannes, lying on the beach in St. Tropez, walking along the seashore 'naked as the day they were born', the halcyon days by Mary Lou's villa, the pool, and early cocktails before a fine dinner prepared by the lady from Corsica. Maggie smiled. The second bottle of Beaune had made her giggle like a school kid as they danced naked under the moonlight. There never was a love like this. She mused to herself. It was so perfect. Yet it wasn't hers. It wasn't Jim's. She cried as they lay on the bed. She sobbed, "Oh Jim, let's give it all up my love, to hell with a world. You and I are beautiful together." The following day was spent in Monte Carlo, lunch and dinner at the Hermitage. "Oh Jim," she murmured, "I will never forget this moment, my darling."

They attended the salon Touzet in the beautiful casino. Jim sat at the blackjack table, his first real experience of gambling in a casino. Playing blackjack was very similar to the game that he had played on the ships, a game called pontoon. She has stood behind him and whispered, "Good luck, Mitchell." She had watched him closely, his chips stacked high. Then slowly over time, they went to a low, then his luck began to rise. He was riding on a high. The next hand the dealer dealt him an ace, then a second ace. He split the cards and the dealer smiled as he moved the whole of his winnings equally. It was a tense moment. He could feel Maggie's fingers squeezing his hands firmly as the dealer dealt. The next two cards, first a king, then another king, a double blackjack. Jim tossed a chip to the dealer with a smile, and retired, collecting his winnings. "Where to now, my Love?" she murmured. He smiled, holding her hand, leading her to the jewelers, a place where the high-rollers buy their gals diamonds. There was a tear in her eye as she remembered his words, "Maggie, my Love, you are my gal," as he slipped a ring on her finger. She murmured to herself, "I'm Jim Mitchell's gal, I suppose." There was the sadness in her eyes. The ring was on her right finger. It was then she felt his hands on her naked breasts as he kissed her forehead. "Good morning, my darling, how's my gal?"

# Chapter 61

The moon was casting its shimmering light over the calm waters of the English Channel. It was an early morning in mid-June. It had been two years and three months since he had passed his Second Engineers examination. In the distance, he could see the ragged coastline of the county of Cornwell and one solitary flashing light, the Lizard Lighthouse, guiding and welcoming home the seamen of the British Mercantile Marine. This coastline had a rich history of naval tradition, some memorable, such a Drake, who had dallied at his game of bowls prior to scuttling the Spanish Armada, the Dartmouth Naval College, Cowes, the Isle of Wight yachting centre of the world. Others were less memorable, the ship wreckers whose bonfires enticed rich cargo ships onto the rocks, the hanging judge Jeffrey's, and the highwaymen of note who had robbed and plundered.

The *Argentina Star* would travel past Portland, Bill Ventnor, and Beachy Head lighthouses, the white cliffs of Dover and finally The River Thames and the Royal London docks.

The air was cool and refreshing to Jim as he sat on a deckchair absorbing the atmosphere. Ahead, was a long passenger liner heading for the port of Southampton, astern an oil tanker heading for the Fawley Refinery.

He was excited. Ahead was his final examination where success would realize his ambition to become a Chief Engineer before he was twenty-five years of age. It had been a long voyage getting to his final.

There was an air of confidence about him as his mind addressed the subjects. The long hours study together with the years of practical experience would ensure his success. The time had passed quickly. He had sailed to South Africa, Australia, and Auckland, New Zealand. He had made passage through the Suez Canal to Bombay, revisited South America and had formed a deep relationship with his friend Nikolai. He dallied in the arms of the beautiful Melissa. His leave in the United Kingdom had been spent with his family and the gang. His relationship with Lydia had been a frustrating affair, neither knowing as to what the outcome of their separation, both aware of the risks to their relationship. Now, time was near for them to meet again, he felt a cold sweat in his body, there was fear in his heart.

"What will become of us?" he asked himself. There was no answer to his question. "Was it worth it?" he asked himself. Again, there was no answer.

The *Argentina Star* had arrived alongside its berth at the Victoria docks. The mail had been brought on board by the Pilot. There was one letter from Elizabeth Black telling him that she was to be married in the spring to her young doctor, who had joined her father's practice, and letters from his family. He also received a letter from Nikolai telling him that his father intended to retire, and had bought a chain of hotels in Europe, with headquarters in Switzerland; he would soon be responsible for their operation. His friend who had told him at their first meeting that he did a little of this and a little of that was due to head up his father's empire. There was a note from Paddy Fitzsimons to the effect that he had arranged for his final examination the following week. He had three days of rest to himself prior to starting his examinations. He was now stepping into a different world, a world that would search his soul, his body, and his mind again for the answers to his future.

Jim packed his gear into storage, said farewell to his shipmates, then checked into a dockside hotel. He had a hankering for a pint of Newcastle Brown Ale and a visit with Rosy.

"Hello, Love," she said with a smile "Back again?"

""Yes, Rosy, it's nice to see you."

"What will you have, Love?"

"A pint of Newcastle Brown Ale, if you please."

"Coming up, young sir," she replied.

""How long has it been since I last saw you?"

"Twelve months," she smiled. "Where are you staying?"

"At the Fox Hotel up the road," replied Jim.

"You don't want to stay there, Jim. It's got fleas, come and stay with me," she smiled. "No hanky-panky, young man."

It was at nine a.m. the following Monday, Jim read the first set of questions of the examination. He was ready for the fray. During the following four days, he labored over the examination questions. During the last two years he had studied hard, which had positioned him well for the fray. There was light at the end of the tunnel on the fifth day. He sat alone in the Chief Examiner's office, battered and bruised from a long and arduous examination, awaiting the final hurdle, the oral examination. The office door opened to reveal the Chief Examiner, ready to pose the most searching of questions.

"Mitchell," he said looking at Jim over his glasses.

"Yes, sir," replied Jim, anxious for the results.

"Didn't I have you for your Second Engineer's certificate?"

Jim smiled ruefully. "Yes, Sir," he replied.

"Huh," he replied. "You remembered?"

During the next forty-five minutes, Jim answered the questions posed to him with a quiet confidence.

The moment of truth was here, the most deafening silence that he'd ever heard, awaiting the results of his labors. The examiner referred to some papers on his desk, after a while the dreaded moment arrived, success or failure. He looked up and smiled.

"You have passed, Mr. Mitchell," he said with a smile. "Well done," he said as he shook Jim's hand.

Jim felt sick as he left the examiner's office. His legs felt like rubber.

His whole body was engulfed in the emotion of the hour. He wanted to yell out to let the whole world know his feelings. The words could not, or would not, come out. There was a sense of relief as he walked slowly to the nearest telephone box, lifted the receiver and dialed three numbers: the first, instinctively, to let Paddy Fitzsimons know that he had been successful, the next to his mother, then his granddad.

Later, Jim sat in the 'Brown Hen Pub', sipping a glass of chardonnay wine and eating a meat pie, contemplating his future. He smiled at first. Jim could not believe what Paddy had said, so much that he asked him to repeat his words.

"Jim, Congratulations, you are now the Chief Engineer of the *Imperial Star*. I want you to take her down to Cape Town where you will relieve John Thompson as Superintendent Engineer for a couple of months. He needs to get to Wellington as quickly as possible."

Jim clasped his hands in prayer. "Thank you, Lord. he prayed. "Thank you for all the success that you have given me." His thoughts turned to his father. "Thank you, Dad. Thank you for bringing me into this world, this wonderful and magic world." He concluded with simple words, "I wish you were here to help me celebrate my good fortune."

The long, sleek lines of the *Imperial Star* glistened following a fresh coat of paint in dry dock. Jim went aboard to be greeted by the First Mate.

"Welcome aboard, Sir," he said. "The Captain sends his compliments. Would you join him?"

"Thanks, Bill" he replied. "It's good to be back again."

"Jim, it's good to see you. Welcome. It's been a long time. Congratulations."

Jim smiled "Congratulations to you Brian, I am so pleased that you have your Captaincy."

"Thanks, old friend take a pew." He paused. "We have much to talk about, would you like to eat here, or shall we go down to the mess?"

"Here will be fine, Brian."

Later, Jim settled in his quarters. They were certainly far more spacious and opulent than he had had on the other vessels. There was a huge a day room and a separate bedroom with views over the foredeck.

He noted, with satisfaction, that the company had kept their word. They had supplied him with new uniforms. He smiled, even a couple of pairs of new shoes.

It was sailing day; the captain held his usual briefing, "I have ordered the tugs for a five-thirty departure. We will bunker in the Canary Islands. Our first port of call is Cape Town. We are expecting twenty-two passengers on board at four o'clock. There will be a cocktail party to welcome them aboard at eight o'clock and, I would like as many of you as possible to attend."

The bridge telephone rang. "Full away, Sir," said the Junior Engineer.

Jim climbed the engine room ladder, made his way to his quarters, removed his cover-all and showered. Then with a towel around his waist, he poured himself a beer. It had been a good day. There was a smile of satisfaction on his face, as he tasted the good brew. This was his first experience at taking his own ship to sea. He lay back on his day bed and said to himself, "a cat nap."

Jim was awakened by a knock on his office door. "Good evening, Sir," said Henry, Jim's Steward.

"The Chief Steward sends his compliments and asks if you would kind enough to sit at table five in the passenger dining room. I have pressed your mess kit for the evening. Will there be anything else, Sir?" he asked.

"Yes, top the ice bucket up, I am expecting some of my officers for cocktails."

Jim showered for the evening. He smiled, as he looked into the mirror his hair shorter in deference to his new position. He smiled at the reflection. It was what more of a grin of satisfaction if truth were known. He looked at his uniform epaulets. "Four years, eight months and three days," he murmured in elation as he poured his first gin and tonic of the day and smoked his second Dunhill. "There was no rush," he said to himself as he savored the moment.

The bell' rang four times denoting that it was 2000 hours on the ship. Jim made his way to the cocktail party in the passengers lounge. He smiled. The young officer's were attending upon the new ship's doctor. Huh, said to him, that is no plain Jane. In the distance, he saw the captain talking to one of the passengers a tall, lady with long, auburn hair wearing a white evening dress, scalloped below her waistline extenuating the curves of her body.

"Wow!" he breathed as he approached. She turned slightly. "Was it her?" he asked himself. His heart missed a beat, his legs felt weak with excitement. He stood for a moment regaining his composure. "Was it her?" he asked himself, offering a quite prayer.

"Good evening, Jim," said the Captain. "Ms Henning may I introduce our Chief Engineer, James Mitchell."

She turned. Their eyes met. He remembered the perfect sculptured, radiant face, the high cheekbones, deep-set liquid hazel eyes, manicured eyebrows, the long lashes, her angular nose, full red lips slightly parted, her long, deep, auburn hair cascading over her deep cut evening gown accentuating her perfect breasts. She was a rare beauty.

Jim stood captivated by the moment, "Was she his?"

She smiled drawing close to him, "Hello, James," she murmured as she kissed him gently on his lips.

"Lydia."

"You know each other?" asked Brian in surprise.

"Yes we do, Sir," she paused with a smile. "I am his mistress."

TO BE CONTINUED:

WHEN
WE WERE
Young
•THE FUTURE•